A KINGDOM OF FLAME AND FURY

Book One of 'The Four Kingdoms'

By: Whitney Dean

Author's Instagram: authorwhitneydean
Cover Design: Pavla Leitgebova (darkerstaredits)
Proofreading: Brittany Ann
Marketing: Peachy Keen Author Services

Ebook ISBN: 979-8-9860118-0-6
Paperback ISBN: 978-0-578-39102-1
Harback ISBN: 979-8-9860118-1-3

PLAYLIST

CH 1: you should see me in a crown - Billie Eilish
CH 2: Run - One Republic
CH 3: Twisted - Missio
CH 4: Close ft. Tove Lo - Nick Jonas
CH 5: Death of a Bachelor - Panic! At The Disco
CH 6: What A Time - Julia Michaels ft Niall Horan
CH 7: one night - Christina Perri
CH 8: Coming Back For You - Maroon 5
CH 9: Why Don't You Save Me? - Kan Wakan
CH 10: Teeth - 5 Seconds of Summer
CH 11: What's Up Danger: Blackway & Black Caviar
CH 12: Let Her Go - Passenger
CH 13: Power Over Me - Dermot Kennedy
CH 14: Way Down We Go - KALEO
CH 15: Feel Like Shit - Tate McRae
CH 16: Say Something - A Great Big World & Christina Aguilera
CH 17: Smile - Maisie Peters
CH 18: Ashes - Stellar
CH 19: White Flag - Bishop Briggs
CH 20: Lose You To Love Me - Selena Gomez
CH 21: Reckless - Jaxson Gamble
CH 22: Climb - ADONA
CH 23: Castle - Halsey
CH 24: Do I Wanna Know - Arctic Monkeys
CH 25: Smells Like Teen Spirit - Malia J
CH 26: Poor Marionette - Sarah Cothran
CH 27: Goddess - Xana
CH 28: Earned It - The Weekend
CH 29: Love Me Like You Do - Ellie Goulding
CH 30: Dangerous Woman - Rosenfeld
CH 31: Unsteady - X Ambassadors
CH 32: Hit Me With Your Best Shot - ADONA
CH 33: Traitor - Olivia Rodrigo

A KINGDOM OF FLAME AND FURY

For M - For opening the curtains to keep the darkness away.

And to the ones who felt like they could never be accepted for their own brand of darkness. You have a place here.

A KINGDOM OF FLAME AND FURY

AUTHOR'S NOTE

This is Book One of a Dark Fantasy series.
It contains sexually explicit scenes, graphic content and is
intended for mature readers.

Reader discretion is advised.

I was coming down from a high of burning the throats of two thieves when I looked to the sky and saw the sun starting to set. I needed to go if I was going to make the beginning of the festival. I would leave their charred remains for the crows, deep within the trees of the Black Forest.

CHAPTER ONE

Raven

Standing in front of my giant floor-length mirror, I unfastened the gold ties of my robe, and it fell in a pool of velvet at my feet. I lifted my arms over my head and tilted it back, my skin stretching taut across my throat. Clasping my hands together above my head, I intertwined my fingers and rolled it side to side. Small pops of bones sounded in my neck.

Despite loving my kingdom and its people, it wasn't often that I attended many of the events thrown to celebrate how much it had thrived since taking the throne. Attention didn't sit well when it was thrust upon me, and I didn't want to steal it away from the cause of my attendance. My people deserved to be celebrated — to drink all night and dance through the streets without worrying about their queen's thoughts.

But this evening was different.

It was the Festival of Dreams, the one event I loved to attend every year. No one ever recognized me because I was nothing, if not an excellent master of disguise. I never donned the same disguise twice and always dressed down and not in my day-to-day, way-too-extravagant dresses that came with being queen.

The Festival of Dreams was started just under one hundred years ago, when the war ended, and kingdoms were recovering from the loss of life. It signified the new beginnings of Seolia and to dream that we would never be subjected to something so devastating again: to dream of a world without malice, without the power hungry royals that caused the war in the first place, and to always stand together for the kingdoms in our realm and for others who felt without a voice.

Under my rule and our previous king, King Leonidas, and the king before him, we had managed to maintain the peace and keep the dream alive. And I would celebrate that with my subjects, only not as the queen they had come to know.

Like all royals, I held a secret.

Lowering my head, I focused on my naked body in the mirror and willed my magic to the surface, slowly lowering my arms. And with them, my change followed. Shifting into one of my other forms was as easy as breathing, and I was looking forward to letting one come out to play.

Instead of my usual long, ebony hair, icy-blonde locks skimmed my shoulders. "Mm…" I pondered aloud, reaching my fingers out and touching the glass of my mirror in front of me.

Frost was typically my most favored form for public outings and the easiest to wield. I looked downright angelic, contrasting to the demon I'd rather be.

Summoning ice to the tips of my fingers, I drew snowflakes on the mirror's glass and then melted them, my entire body coming to life as heat overtook it. My icy-blonde hair turned into a fiery-red bob that cut right at my jawline.

Blaze was brought out when I felt feistiest — and angriest — and my tongue would coat with the taste of blood. Blood I wanted to draw — which lately had been more often. But the festival was all about peace, so when I shook my head, I shifted once more into Terra. Mother Nature herself.

My fingertips drowned the fire with a mixture of icy water and wind, cleaning the charred marks off the glass.

I raised my fingers to my hair and flicked my pointer finger, winding my now-violet hair up to rest on top of my head in a braided bun. Wisps of hair framed my face, and I took one strand and twisted it around my finger, trying to decide next on what to wear.

I sidestepped around my mirror and meandered to my wardrobe, swinging open the heavy handcrafted cherry doors. Velvet dresses on hangers puffed out, the skirts spilling over. I sighed. So much fucking pouf. It was a miracle I didn't topple over every day.

I parted down the middle of the velvet dresses and reached for a hidden drawer that housed a plethora of leather fitted outfits crafted explicitly for nights when I needed to get away from my life of royalty.

I grabbed my slickest pair of leather tights and a matching black, puffed-sleeve bustier and shut the wardrobe doors, returning to my mirror to watch myself dress.

Most, if not all, other queens would have ladies who would help them bathe, dress, and fix hair… breathe, basically. But I preferred to be alone. It was the only time I could be. I had so many responsibilities to answer to, and it was hard to get my thoughts straight until I was locked away in my own quarters or roaming my kingdom in disguise at night.

After dressing, I stared at myself and blinked my eyelids in a quick flutter, transforming my irises from dark green to golden with violet specks, completing my shift to Terra.

I pulled a tube of lipstick from my vanity beside my mirror and painted the dark-red color on my lips, licking them until they glistened. Raising one hand, I brushed my lips with the tips of my fingers, drawing them slowly down my chin and neck and pausing to linger on the skin between my breasts, which were pushed higher because of my bustier.

It had been too long since someone touched me here. Being a queen without a king was fine with me, but having a warm body next to me to keep me satisfied all through the night was preferable to release on my own.

My own hand wasn't quite as sweet as a man's tongue.

I turned my head toward the open glass doors of my balcony and strolled onto the terrace, leaning my elbows on the rounded, waist-high clay wall that encased me. My eyes roved slowly over my kingdom. It was small in size and contained on a small island. My palace was situated on a tall mountainside, and sprinkled throughout the grassy knolls below was my village, comforting and quaint with the red rooftops of cottages and shops.

Surrounding us, as far as the eye could see, was water —
miles, and miles of pure blue aqua on every side. From my
balcony, I could see the ivory sails of ships docked in my harbor
and the white foam of the water as it splashed onto the sides of
the vessels.

Snug on the far side of my castle sat the Black Forest. It was
winter, which meant my mountainside was covered in snow, and
white patches were sprinkled on the roofs in my village. The trees
were bare, and even their trunks looked like they were welcoming
winter, borrowing the black and charcoal colors of the sky.
Everything looked grayer during winter. Darker. It soothed me.

After admiring my kingdom, I secured my coin pouch around
my wrist and grabbed the black boots next to my door, sliding
them on. They reached up to the middle of my thighs and were
sexy as fuck to wear. My hopes were high that I could find a
visiting patron and seduce him in a barn somewhere. The
unsuspecting men always finished and went on with their lives,
never knowing that they had fucked the Queen of Seolia. There
had been many, but never any that kept my attention for more
than just one night. Satisfying — and an excellent release — but
forgettable.

I couldn't leave through my chambers like I usually would to
attend the festival tonight. No one could see me leave the palace,
and only two people in my entire kingdom knew that I would be
doing so. My aunt, who was too old to attend, and one of my
royal advisers: Cade.

My aunt, Isla, was the one who introduced me to the Festival of Dreams back when I was just a villager and assumed no one in the castle knew who I was. The festival was always held at night when I felt I could hide in the shadows and practice my magic without anyone noticing.

I liked to form into Frost when the boys would chase the other young girls around the festival, stealing their candies or just being little shits. I would blind them temporarily with tiny flecks of ice and keep them away long enough for the girls to hide.

At the end of the night, when some of the villagers retired home or were passed out drunk in the streets, I'd beckon Blaze and light up hay bales to keep them warm, spinning dirt around them with Terra so the fire wouldn't spread.

Little did I know, as each year passed, I was being watched — by none other than the king himself.

That was why, when I turned ten, I was stunned when royal guards pounded on the door of Isla's cottage to move us to the castle. Isla knew of my abilities and helped me learn to control them, but she wasn't truly my aunt at all. My birth and entire backstory remained a complete mystery.

Dropped off on Isla's porch in a basket with a single blanket and my name and birthday scrawled on a ripped piece of parchment, I was crying in the dead of night when she opened her front door to see an olive-skinned baby with a full head of black hair.

It wasn't even a choice, Isla always said — she would love me as her own until her last breath. If anyone ever asked, Isla told them that my parents were two drunks from her side of the family who couldn't afford to raise a child. No one ever questioned it, and that was the story we had maintained for twenty-four years.

When I was brought to the castle, Isla never left my side and held my hand when the king's adviser, John, explained to us that the fallen king, Leonidas, willed me to be the heir to his throne. No reason was ever given, and there wasn't a connection in our bloodlines that anyone could find.

I wasn't sure I had a bloodline. I, by all accounts, had absolutely no right to the throne. But, the king had no queen and no heirs of his own. He ruled over the kingdom by himself and left it in the hands of a ten-year-old girl who held deep secrets of her own.

This turn of events was, of course, highly contested by the royal court and by the majority of the village. People knew of Isla and the orphan she took in, but we served no greater purpose besides supplying corn leading into the harsher winter months. We kept to ourselves in the corner, sharing a border with the Black Forest, and only socialized when we needed to sell our crops for coins. But, since the king had no nearby bloodline, I took the throne less than a year later and had a very small coronation, only attended by members of the royal court and Isla.

Cade, one of the most recently appointed royal advisers — and the youngest — took a liking to me rather quickly with my spitfire tongue and thirst for knowledge. I had a tutor in the village as a girl, but she'd tire of my need for more books, parchment, and knowledge. I wanted to know everything. I didn't understand why, but memorizing facts about the surrounding kingdoms just seemed necessary. It came in handy when Cade would quiz me about them while trying to teach me the art of negotiation.

Seolia was surrounded by three kingdoms: Reales, Thoya, and Perosan. Our island was situated in the middle of the three kingdoms. The three kingdoms depended on Seolia for passage through the channel to the other kingdoms and villages to trade crops and grains. At the same time, Seolia relied heavily on the domains for steel, fabrics, and furnishings. Each kingdom played a vital role in the survival of the others, and it had been nearly a century since the last war when Reales had tried to take control of Perosan and fought against Seolia and Thoya for it.

A treaty was established after thousands of lives were lost: each kingdom would be treated as equal and rely on Seolia to close passages if whispers of threats crossed any of the borders. When I was pushed onto the throne, the court feared Reales would awaken their thirst for power and attack, but it had been quiet for nearly two decades.

When the four kingdoms merged into one realm, people of every color escaped their villages and kingdoms from faraway countries to take refuge in one of the four kingdoms. The Circle of Peace was what villagers eventually named the kingdoms once memories of war started to fade, and I was determined to keep it that way for as long as I held the crown.

As the remembrance of wars fought crossed my mind, the warmth of Blaze burned my insides, and I willed it to calm with Frost, shaking the feeling of needing to destruct. The thought of anyone threatening my crown drove me to the brink of madness, and sometimes it took both Frost and Terra to calm the fire that brewed deep in my belly. I knew I was dangerous, and sometimes I feared the ferocity of my magic. It was deep-rooted and old. I wasn't sure how I knew that, but I could *feel* it.

My birth story and the mystery surrounding it continued to plague me and would sometimes keep me up at night, which was when I would steal off into the darkness to explore the Black Forest. The forest frightened the villagers because of the tales from long ago.

It was said that before my time, whispers of dark magic made their way through the four kingdoms, and King Leonidas had blocked it off until his soldiers investigated. When some returned, and the rest didn't, the king pulled them out and never sent anyone back in. The blockages were removed, but even without them, villagers never wandered past the border.

But, it called to me. Nothing about being in the forest frightened me. In fact, it felt more like home than any place I'd lived, even my own wing of the castle. I knew every inch of the castle from my late nights exploring with Cade, but it never truly felt like my own. To my knowledge, I hadn't done anything to earn it. It was a gigantic structure with golden stone walls so high that you couldn't see the tops of the two towers that defined it on cloudy days.

When Cade taught me the history of war, I accidentally revealed Blaze to him by charring the pages of the text in my hands out of anger. By then, his allegiance was pledged to me and my well-being; he'd kept my secret for almost fifteen years. Of course, as I became older, my stubbornness and need for exploration of my kingdom outside the palace walls only grew and despite him trying to keep me from going out at night alone, he knew I could take care of myself and wouldn't fuss too much as long as I was back before breakfast the next morning.

The Black Forest was always where I'd go, spending hours playing with my elements, pushing myself to master each one. I had never broken my promise to him, and he had remained loyal to me. Over the last nearly fifteen years, we'd become inseparable.

I was turning twenty-five soon, and Cade was turning thirty-three. Our birthdays fell within a week of one another's and always toward the end of the winter months. Instead of celebrations, we would always have picnics on his balcony and relished that our kingdom was thriving. We would laugh well into the night and, most of the time fell asleep in a heap of blankets and empty wine bottles. Our yearly celebration was only three months away, and I was almost as excited about that as I was about the festival.

Cade moved me into the king's corridor to avoid walking through the castle on nights when I would sneak off into the forest. Before, I had been staying with my aunt on the opposite side of the castle, not ready to leave her side yet. When I turned sixteen and had been the queen for six years, my aunt returned to her cottage because she trusted that I would be safe with Cade next to me. We spent the coming years together, learning every nook and cranny in the castle. Cade taught me all the hidden corridors in the king's room and how he'd also get through the castle unnoticed. He never bothered using them, at least to Cade's knowledge, because there had never been a threat against him or our kingdom.

I walked to the far side of my bedroom and placed my hand against the small notch protruding from the wall, pushing it in. A small door creaked open, and I lowered to my knees, crawling through the opening and standing vertically when the hallway stretched wide open.

I ran my fingertips along the wall where Cade and I had etched our names into it and smiled, shaking my head at the memories of our beginnings together in the castle.

I would see him at the festival somewhere, flirting with a visitor and offering to give her a tour of the castle. The women loved him, and he took advantage of that, flashing his perfect smile and melting them there on the spot. Cade was attractive, and as a young girl, I had a crush on him, but he was eight years older than me and an adult when we met. He was always with other girls when he wasn't with me, so I outgrew it. But, he was easy to love and entirely too charming for his own good with his dark blond hair and enticing blue eyes. We looked like complete opposites when we stood next to one another, with my tanned skin and black hair against his creamy complexion and sandy locks.

I made a mental note to install more lighting as I walked down the dim hallway. During the winter months, everything seemed darker in the castle, and the darkness made it even colder in my secret corridors with no windows. I often had to light my fingertips to provide a little more light and warmth.

Blaze could be controlled, but I remained cautious. Whenever I experienced any emotion lately, she was always the first to bubble up, and it took more willpower than usual to keep her sedated. When I was able to lure thieves or anyone who broke my laws into the forest, I did, just so I could keep her sated. Continuously shoving her down felt like choking.

I iced my fingertips to extinguish my flames, gnawing on the inside of my cheek at the thought of being out of control. There was no pull in me to harm any of my own people, but it felt like I needed to seek out trouble lately, which was hard to do when stuck on an island. My fire was an unquenchable thirst. Overall, I had always been a very peaceful and calm soul until the prior three months, which only made my need to inflict pain much more bewildering.

I paused my stroll and drew a deep breath through my nose, exhaling through my mouth. The door to exit the underground corridor was a body's length away, leading into an empty wooden barn that the king purchased long ago for this reason. I never knew him personally, but I remained grateful to him for seemingly thinking ahead to needing secret corridors in the castle. From my understanding, they weren't added to the castle until he became king, though no one was ever told the reason why he wanted them.

Nervousness and excitement rushed through me as I hopped up the steps that led to the door, bouncing back and forth on the balls of my feet. Only once a year was I granted front row access to join my people at the festival under disguise. They never would have excluded me from any that I wished to join and would welcome me joyfully, but having all the attention on me made me uncomfortable. Blending in at the Festival of Dreams remained the easiest. Villagers dressed up and put on wigs for this particular one, which was why my bright violet hair wouldn't stand out against the typical blonde, brown, and red hair of the villagers. For this, I was just Raven. Or, well, Terra.

Pushing the door open, I immediately heard the pop of the bonfires and smelled rum and wine being drunk in heaps outside. The door shut behind me as I walked quickly through the small, dark structure. "I'll kill Cade if he forgot to unlock this," I muttered, shoving slightly at the creaky door that led into the village. After another shove, the door swung open, and I grinned, stepping out onto the snow-covered ground.

"Take the long way?" A deep, familiar drawl asked from behind me.

I snorted and rolled my head to the left, seeing Cade appear from the side of the barn. "I like to keep you waiting," I replied, moving my gaze back to the crowd of villagers formed around a bonfire.

"I never get used to seeing you like this," he said.

I felt his intense stare on me.

"Decided on Terra tonight, I see. The hair will blend well with tonight's theme's colors." He dipped his chin toward the center of the village.

My eyes averted away from the crowd and moved over the cottages where I spotted purple, gold, and midnight-blue stars and moons hanging from the roofs of every shop and cottage, and scattered along the snow was matching confetti.

He laughed and nodded toward a group of children giggling while making snow angels on the ground. "The kids in the village had fun dyeing paper from the school to make these." He held a hand out to me with confetti in his palm. "For your dreams."

The corners of my mouth tilted up as I looked at his palm. I pinched the confetti between my fingers, admiring how they seemed to shimmer in the light of the moon rising above us, and slipped the confetti into the opening of the coin pouch hanging from my wrist. "Thank you, Cade." I gave him a small smile.

His stare lingered a second before his eyes pulled away from me, and he dipped his chin in a nod.

"Now, stop drooling and go away. You know you can't stay with me." I gave him a slight shove on his shoulder as we started toward a bonfire. He was quiet next to me, and I glanced at him, raising my eyebrows at the tension in his face. "Why do you look so pained? It's very unattractive. Like this." I scrunched my nose and crossed my eyes, sticking my tongue out.

A slight, amused grin appeared on his mouth as he looked at me, but he continued his silent retreat, falling a few steps back. I couldn't stop and talk to him. He was well known in the kingdom, and everyone in the village knew how close we were. If we looked enveloped in deep conversation, people would wonder about the violet-haired woman and why her skin tone matched so well with their queen's. The risk of too many questions had to keep us apart for the evening.

"Just be careful tonight. And you look beautiful," he said when he finally spoke up just loud enough for me to hear before he broke off in the opposite direction, holding his hand behind him in a small wave.

I stopped my slow pace and watched him walk away, cocking my head in confusion at his warning. He had never warned me to be careful in my own kingdom. There was never anything to fear. He cautioned me for a reason, and I could have strangled him for choosing this moment to walk away after dropping that on me.

I closed my eyes, willing my ice to chill the warmth creeping over my skin. Blaze was quick to ignite at any sign of a threat, and as far as I knew, there wasn't one — but I suddenly felt more guarded. For a second, I wondered if I should turn around and go back to the castle. "You look forward to this every year," I grumbled, resting my hands on my hips. "You're going to relax and focus on killing Cade later." I giggled while I thought of ways I could. He was my best friend, but like all men, he could be infuriating, and shoving him off a balcony didn't seem too bad of an idea.

I looked around from where I stood and spotted him already in conversation with a stunning blonde woman. That didn't take him long. He would bring her back to the castle, fuck her, and discard her before breakfast. I never had a chance to meet any of his conquests, but he seemed to only choose women with blonde hair. His punishment could be me bringing someone back to the castle and making him entertain him over a meal.

He never approved of the risk I took when it came to sleeping with strangers. Thinking about it, I had never actually fucked a man as myself. I was always careful not to drop whichever form I'd taken for the night. For all the villagers knew, I was a virgin and destined never to marry or bear children. It had never been a priority. My magic was a mystery, but I didn't think I could live forever, though I did heal at an alarmingly quick rate.

That was something Cade and I learned a few years ago when he was insistent on teaching me how to sword-fight. I protested heavily, but he wouldn't let it go. He told me that while my magic was strong, I may not be able to stop steel, and it was essential to have another option.

To prove him wrong, I had tried. He'd come at me with a sword in his hand, and while I could burn his exposed skin, he overpowered me quickly. I healed any piece of him I'd burned, and then he had another idea — to prevent me from burning him again, he donned steel around his body, blocking any sight of his bare skin. When he lunged for me again, I was helpless.

Blaze couldn't do enough harm to make him stop, and with Frost, I could only build ice blocks around myself like a protective dome, which he sliced through with little effort.

If we had been outside and not in a room, Terra may have been able to bring him down by shaking the earth underneath his feet, but could I stop more than one soldier that way? There was never any way of knowing.

He had also been training me in hand-to-hand combat for years, which I wasn't sure I would ever need since I had my own skill set. But it was fun, throwing punches and trying to take someone down as toned as he was.

Blocking had always been my biggest struggle when holding my own sword. I had no problems on the defense, but when it came to taking the first step, I experienced a mental block at the idea of hurting someone unjustifiably. It took months of training and gaining upper and lower body strength to wield a sword, and I still wasn't great at it. I once missed a block against Cade, and his sword's point punctured the skin right above my heart.

We both learned something else about me that day: I could freeze any internal organ, even my own heart. Though Cade's sword didn't cut deep enough to touch my heart, the adrenaline from the puncture had me quickly shifting into Frost to protect all of my internal organs. With the knowledge of being able to freeze internally, it stood to reason that I could set myself on fire, which was another reason Blaze had to be controlled. If my emotions ever reached a boiling point, I may be my own demise.

The wound in my chest from Cade's sword had me doubled over, but within minutes, the puncture had closed after I used a combination of Frost and Blaze to soothe. He had asked if I could always combine them like that, and I explained that while I could use pieces of my magic all at once, they were strongest when my entire being morphed into one of them.

If I were to morph into Frost, I could pull bits of Blaze out, but it was like getting drops of water while dying of thirst. I had never been able to fully wield all three at once, and trying tired me out quickly. Morphing into forms one after another didn't wear me out, but focusing on morphing and wielding was mentally exhausting. If I could somehow harness all three while remaining myself or in one form, I would be unstoppable. Not that any of it mattered because I had never been threatened.

————

Amid my thoughts, I wandered into the middle of the village, where booths lined the streets. Each booth had choices of food, wines, or crafts made by the local villagers. Not only was the Festival of Dreams an excellent way for our peaceful village to be celebrated, but the outside patrons from visiting kingdoms brought in money for my people to sell what they made, and I always brought enough coins to support them.

I stopped at a booth run by a small girl and her mother, beaming at the little girl who donned paper flowers in her light-blonde locks. "Look how pretty you are," I cooed to the young girl, grazing over the flowers on a small table with my fingertips. They resembled the ones in the girl's hair and were bright pinks and yellows made of airy tissue paper.

The little one curtsied to me and grabbed a handful of flowers from the table, extending her tiny hand to me. "These would look the most beautiful in your purple hair!" she exclaimed, pushing them into my open palm.

Her mother placed her hands on the shoulders of the girl and pulled her back, smiling at me and then her daughter. "I have a very enthusiastic peddler," she said, shaking her head. "Eva, you can't shove them at people. You need to wait for them to choose their own."

I held my empty hand and motioned to the mother that it was perfectly fine. "I think the colors she chose for me are perfect, and I was hoping she'd help me put them in my hair." I lowered to my knees in front of Eva and slowly handed her the flowers back one by one as she fastened them all over my messy bun with small bands.

"You remind me of a butterfly," she whispered as she fastened the last flower in my hair.

I glanced up and spotted Cade watching me from a distance, a bright smile on his face as he raised a mug of what I assumed to be rum at me. His choice of the night hung off of him, and I rolled my eyes, giving him a slight shake of my head. He winked.

When I felt Eva's tiny hands leave my hair, I wrapped my arms around her in a warm hug. "Thank you, sweet one. These flowers are so lovely." I dropped my arms around her and reached into my coin pouch, pulling out five golden coins. I put them into the small hand of my hairdresser. "I hope I see you again." Winking at her, I rose to extend my hand to her mother. "You have a darling girl," I told her, bidding farewell, and continued my tour of what other treasures the booths lined down our cobblestone road may hold.

I ended up with a knit scarf, some candies, and some scented vanilla candles. I tilted my head to beckon Cade to meet me around the corner. Once we were out of sight, I shoved the goods into his arms. "Take these back with you. I don't want to carry them around with me."

He looked at everything in his arms and then at me. "What the hell am I supposed to do with all of this?" He wrapped the scarf around his neck.

"Take it to your room, and I'll come to get it later. Don't give your... lady... any of my candies. Those are for me."

He made a face pretending to mock but then nodded. "Fine. We're about to head back. Are you leaving soon?"

My eyes narrowed at the suspicious concern in his voice. "I'm fine, Cade. I'm a big girl." I wiggled my fingertips at him, lighting them with flames. "I have a weapon, literally on me, at all times."

He loosened an annoyed sigh and shifted my things in his arms, reaching up to touch one of the flowers in my hair. "I like these. They make you look nicer than you are."

I shoved at his shoulder, and he stumbled, almost dropping my candles. "Go away," I teased.

He tilted his chin up in goodbye. I kicked some snow toward him with the toe of my boot as mine.

———

After what felt like hours of greeting villagers and definitely drinking too much, I took a breather against the wall of one of the cottages on the outskirts of the village. I'd kept my eyes wide open for any attractive patrons, but no one had caught my eye.

My lips pouted at the idea of not receiving the release I desperately craved, but the heavy amounts of wine I had inhaled from the various booths were working to numb the pain.

Closing my eyes, I inhaled the smells surrounding me, smiling at the sounds of villagers' laughter and loud chatter. While my beginning in life may have seemed unfair, it brought me to Seolia to be the ruler of this kingdom, and it would always be my greatest honor.

As the youngest queen in Seolia's history, I felt I related well to the needs of my people and understood their wants. I didn't tire of hearing requests and wanted to provide the best for all of them. There were bad seeds everywhere, but the crimes were few and far between, mainly once word spread that those who tried were met with a dark fate — which meant that Seolia was overall a lively place to live.

Opening my eyes and suddenly very sleepy from the wine and hours of walking, I pushed off the wall and began my trek to the small barn that housed my hidden door.

As I started toward the middle of town, I stopped abruptly at a pair of dark-gray eyes that were zeroed in on me. I felt zoned in, trapped, and shivers danced across my bones. My tongue skimmed across my bottom lip as the gray eyes prowled closer.

Everything went silent as I drank in the body accompanying them, and I was suddenly highly aware of my heartbeat.

A broad chest came into view first that seemed to inhale and exhale as rapidly as I was. My gaze stayed on the rise and fall of his chest until he was an arm's length away, towering over me. Standing still too far away was a tall, muscular man whose skin looked like it had been kissed by the sun, and he was the most delicious one I had ever laid eyes on.

If I believed in love at first sight, this would have been it.

I took him in. Unapologetically. My sexual desires had never made me ashamed, and he was definitely one of them.

He had to be a soldier of some sort because his heavy black shirt clung to him, and I could see the outline of his toned stomach underneath the fabric. His long legs were covered in black pants tucked into boots; boots that weren't from a village like my own — his were made from some canvas that must have come from a neighboring kingdom, which meant he was not from Seolia.

His hair was slicked back, as black as mine, and it curled under his ears. His jawline could cut steel, and his lips were full. I tracked the movement of his jaw clenching and loosening, making my insides feel like honey. My gaze traveled back up to his, and neither of us smiled. We just stared. Enamored. I had never seen gray eyes like his. "I've been looking for you all night." My voice was breathy as it escaped.

All inhibitions were lost as he grabbed my hand with his, which was big enough to wrap around mine completely. His skin was callused, and I wanted it all over me.

He tugged at me, and I obliged, letting him pull me in to walk behind him. Tall. He was so tall that I had to tilt my chin up to look at him as he guided us away from the crowd, weaving us through the booths and behind a row of brown-stone shops.

Everyone was so drunk that I doubted any of them would have noticed if we were to go at it in the middle of the festival, but being alone with him lit my body up, my stomach tightening at the thought of his body on mine.

We tucked into a corner behind the modest buildings, the light from the bonfires seeming far away. Since we were both in black, we became invisible in the shadows. He took advantage and dropped my hand, moving his hands to my shoulders and pushing me against the wall. I responded quickly and pulled at his shirt's fabric, leaning on my toes to crash my mouth against his.

His tongue shoved into my mouth, entwining with mine, causing me to moan softly into his mouth. He tasted so good, like rum, and I wanted to drink from him. He smelled like pine — all man and rugged — and I suddenly wanted to invent a pine-flavored rum and live off it for the rest of time.

He wrapped his hands around my waist, and his thumbs pushed the fabric of my shirt up enough to expose my belly button. Keeping one hand on my waist, the fingertips of his other hand grazed across my stomach. I drew in a sharp breath through my nose, the sensation from just his fingertips putting me in a daze.

I pulled my mouth from his, remaining close enough for the tips of our noses to touch. Both of our chests heaved, and I could feel his heartbeat against mine, thundering in the same rhythm — like one heart shared between two and all we'd done was kiss.

"Who are you?" I managed to get out, though I wasn't sure what I was asking. I put my hands on his muscular arms to try and get a better look at his face, but all I could see was the outline of a delicious jaw that I was sure could cut right through me, and I'd beg him to do it again.

He didn't answer me at first, pushing his hips against mine and pinning me to the wall. I felt how hard he was for me against my stomach. My core begged me to relent, but I wanted more of him. I wanted to hear his voice.

He removed his hands from my waist and placed them either side of my head, his palms resting against the wall to cage me in.

"Zeke."

It sounded like a low snarl and melted across my skin like warm chocolate. I waited for more, but it never came. I couldn't offer him my name, and I had never needed to. I had never cared about any randoms I fucked here every year enough to ask for their name or think of a fake one for myself.

But this man. *This man.* He was the devil; I just knew it.

"Zeke," I repeated slowly, enjoying how his name tasted on my tongue. I felt him pulse against my skin as I said his name. He was feeling everything I was. My hands left his arms to squeeze between our chests, resting my palms against his hard stomach. "I'll see you in my dreams, Zeke."

I bent and slid out from underneath his cage, sauntered slowly back into the crowd, swaying my hips, and felt his eyes on my back the entire time.

CHAPTER TWO

Raven

When I made it back inside the dark barn, I fell to my knees. I hadn't breathed since I left Zeke standing there. Hard to get was never a game I played, but something about him made me not want to leave, which meant he wouldn't be someone I could have fucked for release. As hard as walking away from him was, and despite the sensation I still felt from his body pressed against mine, the way his voice sounded, how desperately he seemed to want me... fuck, I had to stop. I couldn't risk getting attached to anyone and wondering where he came from or if he'd be back.

But damn, that man seemed almost too good to be true, and I wondered if I dreamt him up in my drunken stupor.

I rose to my feet and cursed under my breath. My hand would have to be the only pleasure I found. Again.

To be completely *un*fair, if I couldn't have physical pleasure from someone else, neither could Cade — which was why when I made my way back through the hidden corridors, I didn't linger in my chambers long and found myself banging on his door.

My fitted leathers were still on, but I shifted back into myself, my violet hair and golden eyes retired for the night. I shouldn't have been in my festival clothes, but I was willing to do anything to avoid a heavy dress. I arched my back just thinking about the weight of them on me. I was going to send for some new ones as soon as possible. I was too young for the aches I felt in my back from trying to remain upright in them for hours at a time, even as beautiful as they were.

While waiting for him to come to the door, I braided my long hair and let it hang down my back, resting my hands on my hips as I lingered impatiently. After a moment longer, he finally deigned to answer my knocking and crossed his arms over his bare chest.

I shoved at his crossed arms and pushed him back into his entryway. "You move fast. Tell her to leave," I demanded, nodding toward his bedroom.

"Whom?" He countered, smugly grinning at me.

My earlier thoughts of murdering him returned. My irritation for tall men tonight was high, and I shoved at him again. "You fucking know who. I need to talk to you."

He shook his head and sighed, disappearing back into his room. I meandered into his office and sat on his desk — waiting again. A ghost of envy tickled my shoulders, and I shook it off as the blonde from the festival scurried out of his bedroom, her hair mussed. My eyes rolled.

I called out to the young woman, and she jumped, turning her attention to look across the hall into his office, where I was perched. She curtsied to me, looking quite frantic to be caught in my royal adviser's bedroom. I didn't want her to feel embarrassed, so I hopped off the desk and walked to where she remained in a curtsy. "You're very beautiful," I said, lifting her chin with my finger to meet my eyes.

And she was. Her skin was delicate, pale. Her eyes were a light blue, like a Blue Star flower. She was taller than me, and there was strength in her small frame. Though it was soft, there was an intensity about how she stared at me. Like she knew me somehow.

I brushed it off. "You can do much better than our dear Cade here. Raise your standards."

I heard him chuckle behind me as I patted her elbow and ushered her toward the door, closing it once she was down the hallway. I turned to Cade as I flipped my braid, moving it to fall down my chest. "Why are they always blonde? Have a thing against brunettes?"

He ignored my question, and I followed him into his lounge, watching as he sat in a chair next to one of his grand windows that overlooked our village. He spread his legs out as he leaned back in the chair, perching his forearm across the back. "What do you want, Raven?"

"That's no way to speak to your queen." My eyes roamed over his body as he sat there. He was attractive, and my girlish crush didn't seem too embarrassing when I took the time to actually look at him. His chest and arms were well defined with muscles, but his stomach made warmth spread across my cheeks.

His abs were tight, and it looked like he had practiced sit-ups every day of his life. His father was an army general many years ago, so his physique was thanks to years of training with him. I'd seen him shirtless often, mostly when we'd sneak off to the water's edge along the docks and swim. But tonight, I was wound up tight, and he had suddenly become a man.

"You should be on your knees," I muttered, my eyes still thirsting across his stomach.

When my gaze lifted back to his, his eyebrow was cocked in curiosity as to why I was here and *staring*. I cleared my throat and diverted my attention away from his body. I needed to stop drinking so much. "Do you remember when we used to sneak off and go swim by the docks?" I asked, walking to the window adjacent to where he sat and staring down at the village I had left moments prior, still brimming with life. I wondered if Zeke was still there. If he found someone else.

From the corner of my eye, Cade nodded as he kept his gaze on me.

"I felt so safe. Like nothing would ever touch us."

A soft sigh from him.

"You're not telling me something." I touched my forehead against the window and watched my breath coat the cold glass.

His fingers wrapped around mine. "Raven, I can still take you swimming and keep you safe. I'll always keep you safe." His reply was a soft murmur.

I rolled my head against the glass just enough to look at him. The air between us felt heavy. My fingers left his grasp to rest my palm against his cheek. He leaned into it, and I brushed my thumb against his skin. "What aren't you telling me?"

Another sigh, more frustrated than before. He leaned forward, my hand dropping from his cheek as I watched his entire body tense. I gave him a moment to collect himself before he stood up from his chair and pulled me into his arms, wrapping me into a tight hug. My arms curled around his waist as his lips pressed against my hair.

Whispering against my hair, he finally said, "About a week ago, there was a note hammered to the castle's front gate." He released me and left his lounge to walk into his office.

His long strides had me practically skipping as I fought to catch up. He was already at his desk when I entered the office, pulling open a drawer. He brandished a note, flicking it a couple times with his wrist like touching it burned his skin.

I walked to his desk and ripped it from his hand, my eyebrows drawing together at the message written down in big, black letters. Ignorance clouded my eyes as I read the note aloud, "The orphan doesn't belong here."

Tears stung my eyes as the realization dawned on me. "Me. I don't belong here." I dropped the note back to his desk. Even after twenty-five years, being referred to as *the orphan* stung, pulling at something deep inside me. At the end of the day, I was still abandoned. I didn't belong anywhere, not truly. It was a harsh reminder to see it written down.

He grabbed me, pulling me into his arms again. "Listen to me, darling." His drawl was so soothing. "We're going to find out who did this. We have guards stationed at every gate entrance day and night, watching for anyone suspicious." He untied his arms around my body and placed his hands on my shoulders, pulling me back to where he could see my face and shaking me until I lifted my chin to meet his eyes. "You are our queen, Raven. This is your home."

But was it?

All I could do was nod in response, the lump that formed in my throat preventing me from speaking. I lifted up on my toes and pecked his cheek. He seemed reluctant to release me. I blew a bubble in my mouth and rubbed my eyes with the palms of my hands. "I need to sleep. We'll talk more about this tomorrow."

I turned to walk to the door, but he was hot on my heels, putting his hand against it before I could open it to leave. "Stay with me. We'll drink. Talk." There was concern in his voice again. "Swimming? I'll even let you drag me into the forest."

"Swimming? In winter?" I gave him a reassuring nod and patted his arm. "I really just want to sleep."

He didn't move, pushing out his bottom lip. "Stay with me, Raven. We'll sleep on the balcony." He was being persistent. His fingers circled my wrist, and he started to swing it, tugging at my arm until I finally nodded. Staying with him would be better than the mental anguish I would put me through on my own.

"Fine, you heathen."

He smiled as he pulled me into his bedroom, grabbed the pillows and blankets off his bed, and threw them onto the terrace.

"Give me a shirt," I demanded.

He walked to his wardrobe and pulled open a drawer, tossing a shirt at me, laughing as it smacked me in the face.

"You're such a jackass." I giggled, grabbing the hem of my shirt and pulling it over my head until I was in just a bralette and my pants.

He looked down at the floor and rubbed the back of his neck with his hand as I pulled his shirt over my head.

"Am I that bad?"

He snorted, making me roll my eyes as I padded onto the terrace. "Do you have any more of that confetti?"

He disappeared into the lounge, and I laid down on the ground, shimmying out of my pants and throwing them behind my head. I rested my head against his pillow and pulled the blanket over me, staring at the stars above us. I hadn't felt like an orphan in over two decades. My aunt and Cade wrapped me in so much love and adoration that I stopped seeing the black clouds hanging over my head.

Isla took me in, treated me like her own daughter, taught me to read and how to properly socialize with other kids, giving me a chance to be part of something, part of a family. Cade took me under his wing and taught me to be a ruler. He was patient with me, always protecting me against any doubt that rose against me in the formative years of being the new queen.

I had formed my own family, and as the years passed, the pain of being abandoned in a basket was buried deep inside me, and the pain subsided.

I coughed as the sobs hit me all at once, curling my knees to my chest under the blanket. I felt small — smaller than I had in a long time. Even with so much magic in my veins, words written by a stranger could bring me to my knees.

Cade heard my sobs and rushed to me, shushing me as he sat beside me. "Raven…" he murmured, rubbing the back of my head. "Darling, it's okay. We're going to figure this out." After sliding under the blanket, he tugged me to him and pressed his cheek against my temple.

Tears continued to fall down my cheeks, but my sobs quieted. It was only the silence surrounding us, and how could silence be so loud?

He extended his palm out in front of me and wiggled his fingers. I sniffled and reached for it, pinching the confetti between my fingers. Lifting my arm behind our heads, I sprinkled the pieces onto our pillows. I felt him smile against my skin, and I sniffled again, squeezing my eyes shut.

"Sometimes I wish I could erase it - my history. Everything. Sometimes, I don't want to be me. I tire of having so many questions every day and so much doubt about who I am and if I should be here."

He shifted behind me and put his hand gently on my shoulder, pushing me down to my back. "Look at me, Raven."

I opened one eye, and he chuckled, waiting until I opened both before speaking, "I never once doubted you and your love for this kingdom. I never want to hear you say again that you wish to erase our history." The tip of his nose touched mine. "I don't want to imagine a life without you. You were meant to be here, Raven. You will realize that one day."

He pulled one of my candies from behind his back and pushed it against my lips until I giggled through my sniffles and took a bite of the oozy caramel treat. He popped the rest of it in his mouth. "Now sleep, darling. I have you." He pulled at my waist until I was on my side again, his arm enveloping me from behind and tugging me closer to him.

Tomorrow, we'd talk about who could've left the horrid note. He'd gather the rest of the advisers, and we'd go over every detail. Tomorrow, I'd be the queen. But tonight, I was just the orphan who was given a palace — a palace I hadn't earned in a castle that didn't feel like mine.

And I was going to let myself feel it.

Much to my disappointment, I didn't dream.

———————

The sun was high before I woke up. Rays of sunlight pooled across my body, warming my skin and seemingly trying to comfort me from the night before. I slowly sat up and stretched my arms above my head.

My head was pounding from a massive hangover, but there was work to be done, and feeling sorry for myself wouldn't accomplish anything. I looked to my left, and Cade was still peacefully sleeping next to me. Smiling, I gently moved a piece of his hair falling over his eyes to behind his ear.

I needed to bathe. Get ready for the long day ahead. I rolled my neck side to side and crawled silently out from underneath the blanket, careful not to disturb him. I picked up my discarded clothes and tiptoed out of his room, clicking the door behind me before I padded down the hallway. I felt like I was performing the walk of shame, leaving a man's room in his shirt — but my servants had seen me do it many times. Sleepovers happened at least twice a week, and we almost always woke up with hangovers.

I entered my chambers and walked to the bathroom, turning the water on in my bathtub. Taking a deep inhale of the steam rising from the hot water, I stepped in, drawing in a sharp breath as the scolding water cradled my body and sank down until I could relax against the cool marble.

A good scrubbing of last night's activities would feel like a fresh start and bring my confidence to the forefront. I didn't enjoy feeling feeble, and without trying most of the time, I intimidated those who didn't know me well. Despite the love that surrounded me during my upbringing, trust was not something I typically gave freely.

That was why when it came to matters of the kingdom, I listened to my court but then would have private meetings with Cade to review every option before making a decision. It was the only way I had ruled my entire reign, and everyone in our kingdom, and the ones surrounding us, knew that without Cade by my side, expecting a decision from me would not happen quickly.

I was still a young queen and valued Cade's experience. Cade was only eighteen when I became queen, but ever since he was a child, he was taught the ways of the kingdom by his mother and father. He learned how to fight, intimidate, and exude self-control in any situation from his father and learned from his mother about negotiating with other kingdoms, who had served as a royal secretary to the former king. He grew up in the palace and around the people who still served on my court.

His parents retired early into my reign and still lived in the village but spent most of their days in their garden, living a happy retired life. We'd spend hours at his parent's cottage some nights, asking for opinions and listening to stories from the early days of King Leonidas's reign.

From what I could gather from those who served him, he was a just and fair king but mysterious and kept to himself — much like me. When he traveled, he'd only take a select few with him, and no one was ever allowed to talk about what they witnessed or encountered along the way. If I didn't know any better, I'd say the king had some secrets, which only added to my frustration of never knowing why he'd chosen me as his successor.

Sighing, I closed my eyes and let my head fall against the tub, drawing in a slow breath. Upon release, a pair of gray eyes flashed across my mind. I was taken back to the night before, stumbling upon Zeke. It didn't feel like it was just last night that I was pressed against his muscular body, his tongue moving with mine. My hand traveled across my breasts, my nipples hardening at the graze of my fingertips.

I remembered how his hands gripped my waist, pushing his hips against mine, and that thought pushed my hand down my stomach and to my throbbing core that had been begging for attention. I rubbed my clit teasingly with my middle finger, slightly arching my back off the tub at the intensity of pleasure from the slightest touch.

As I was about to pick up the pace, a loud knock on my bedroom door had me freezing and growling in frustration. An orgasm would have been the cherry on top of a relaxing morning, but now I would have to face the day with no release. Again.

Standing and wrapping myself in a plush robe, I padded to the door as water sloshed behind me. I swung it open to find Cade staring at me. "Didn't I *just* see you?"

"Busy?" he asked, the corner of his mouth tilted up at the flushed coloring of my face and the way I was still soaked from not drying off.

"Your timing is impeccable, Cade. What do you want?" I held the door open for him but left him in the doorway as I walked to my wardrobe to pull out a dress for the day.

"Breakfast."

My mind immediately flashed to Zeke's tongue. I wished he could devour me for breakfast instead. Again, my body flushed at the thought of him, and I kept myself turned away from Cade.

"You seem chipper this morning."

"I had a wonderful night with a friend." I didn't glance at him, but a smile pulled up on my cheeks. "Now go." I flicked my hand, motioning for him to leave so I could dress.

"Always happy to lend a hand, you know."

I shot him a glare.

He snickered. "I must run downstairs, but then I'll be back to get you in ten minutes." He closed the door, and I heard his boots thumping as he walked away. This was payback for interrupting his quickie. I would take my time getting dressed. He could fucking starve.

I'd chosen a formfitting dress for the day, resolving to stop wearing ones that made me want to fall over. This dress was a deep purple and made of velvet that clung to my body and accentuated my curves. The sleeves were long and formed a deep V at my wrists, exposing the delicate skin behind them. It was floor-length, so I decided to wear the same pair of boots that hit my thighs. They would give me a boost of confidence, and I needed that. It wasn't something I typically struggled with, but last night had me bewildered.

My lips still showed faded red lipstick from the night before, and my hair was messy from the bath, but both were quick fixes. I cleaned off the red, replaced it with a light pink shade, left my hair down, now combed, and placed a jeweled diadem on top of my head. It was one of my favorites of all the jewels I was given when I became queen. It was made of gold with purple and green round diamonds that made up the center row. The purple matched my dress, and the green favored my irises.

Since King Leonidas never married, the jewels and crowns in my possession were from the last queen who ruled the kingdom. I loved the idea of wearing things from an earlier period. It felt as if I was part of the history of Seolia.

Throwing open my door, I rolled my eyes at Cade's perfect timing. "You're less poofy today," he remarked, taking his place at my side as we began our walk to the dining hall.

I giggled and weaved my arm through his, batting my eyelashes at him. "You're so good with your words, Cade. It's a wonder how you're still single."

He shoved his elbow into my ribs at my retort. "I'm single because you're such a helpless doe without me and because you kick women out of my room."

I wouldn't give him the satisfaction of agreeing with him, even though we both knew it was true. I had no doubt that if I needed to, I could figure out how to rule on my own, but having him by my side was so much more fun.

A twinge of jealousy pulled at my gut at the idea of him moving his attention to someone else. I'd never given it much thought before, but it was on my mind that he could fall in love one day and not be there whenever I needed him.

He noticed the smile leave my face, nudging my side again gently. I frowned and kept my eyes on the floor before us. "I apologize for ruining your evening."

He kept his eyes on me. I could see him studying me from the corner of my eye. "I wouldn't have had it any other way."

My body relaxed.

"But there's something else I didn't tell you last night."

I dropped my arm from his and stopped, putting my hands around my waist as I turned to face him. Sighing, he mirrored me and rocked on his heels. "Lately, there's been reports of someone spreading rumors about you. Only those rumors are true."

It felt like my blood was draining.

"Whoever it is has been informing villagers of your... abilities," he finished in a whisper.

Suddenly the note made sense. Dark magic returning to the kingdoms had always been feared, and though we both knew I'd never harm anyone who didn't deserve it, I was not prepared for anyone to know what I possessed.

I stared at him, my mouth agape at the information he spilled on me. I'd been queen for nearly fifteen years without a whisper of my magic anywhere, and now I was getting threatening notes hammered to my very own gates.

My chest rose and fell quickly the more I thought about it, the heat of my fire pooling in my belly, wanting to spill over at the new threat looming outside my castle walls.

I sidestepped around Cade and rested my palms against the cool stone wall, trying to calm myself, but the heat from my hands began to bleed through, leaving singed marks on the rock.

"Raven," he warned, placing his hand on my back. "Take a breath. Look at me."

But I couldn't. Another thought formed in my mind as I sifted through emotions. How long had he known about this? Why hadn't he told me? He said he found the note a week ago, and he'd been sitting on all of this without giving me any information.

I turned to face him quickly, my green eyes turning bright red as Blaze ached to be let free. "Why haven't you told me about any of this? It's been a week, and I'm just now learning that people may want me gone now that they've learned of my magic. And you just let me play at the festival last night like everything was fine? Normal?"

Tears brimmed behind my eyelids at my anger toward my best friend. It wasn't like him to withhold information from me, and even more disturbing that he could hide possible life-threatening news.

He took a step toward me, risking himself against my fire, and put the palms of his hands against my cheeks. "I didn't tell you because I wanted to have a solution before I shared it. It drives me insane not knowing who's doing this. I want to protect you against this. That's always been my sole goal as your adviser. As your best friend. I've always feared this may happen, but it's been quiet for so long that I was unprepared."

He dropped his hands from my face. I could see that he was also struggling with irritation. Not only did I want to protect myself, but I wanted to protect him.

I palmed my eyes with my hands and took a few deep breaths. My body shook with fiery fury. Magic was at the edges of my very being, desperate to be freed. I had to control it, or it would overtake me. I willed Frost to fight through Blaze's heat, torn inside at the anger and the need to soothe it all at once. It wore me out, trying to push the cold air through my body over the insatiable warmth.

I dropped my hands from my eyes once some of the darkness inside me subsided and my eyes returned to their natural green. He reached a hand out to me, but I took a step back and shook my head. I didn't want to risk hurting him if my emotions bubbled up again.

The hurt on his face at my rejection made me want to take it back, but I couldn't. "I'm still heated. I don't want to hurt you." I needed to get out of this dark hallway. "I want more lights in these hallways. Winter makes the castle too fucking dark."

I spun and began my stroll again to the dining hall. I heard him walking behind me, but we made no further efforts to sync up again.

———————

As we passed through the open foyer of the dining room, my table of advisers stood and bowed. I dipped my chin and smiled, urging them to take their seats and continue eating.

I had a large table, but only three advisers, including Cade. John and Luisa made up the other seats at my table. Besides Cade, I was closest to Luisa. She was an older woman, tall and thin with kind brown eyes and white hair.

The dining room was large and one of the most frequented areas in the castle. The walls were ivory in color but covered in portraits of past royals and a commissioned landscape painting of Seolia that hung on the central wall. Two tall windows looked out to one of our snow-capped mountains and brought in the perfect amount of natural light. It was where we held all of our meetings, most frequently over breakfast.

Taking our seats, me at the head of the table and Cade beside me, I reached for an apple from a bowl. I took a bite, savoring the sweet juice on my tongue, and ran the tip of it along my lips to catch any juice that tried to escape my bite. My cheeks heated as I noticed Cade watching me, but I ignored him and looked at John and Luisa.

The eyes that stared back at me were assembled by King Leonidas. We had expected some turnover after I took the throne, but each adviser stayed, their trust in the king deep-rooted. They still seemed to remain curious about me and why the king had chosen me to rule over his kingdom… a kingdom he had fiercely protected.

Aside from Cade, the advisers were older and may decide to retire soon. I wasn't sure I would replace them. I wasn't close to many other people. Or any people, really. Cade had spent years being extremely picky over who I interacted with, wanting to protect me.

"Cade has caught me up on what we've long feared would happen. As you all know, I am just as confused by the king's wish to have me as his successor, but I feel as if we've had a tranquil fifteen years, and our kingdom is flourishing."

A small smile formed on my face at the murmurs of agreement from my advisers. I continued, "Does anyone have any thoughts on why this is happening? Or thoughts on who could be spreading these rumors about me?"

The first one to speak was Luisa. "My queen, we've had our guards in the village for a week to listen for any piece of information we can use. All they've come back with is that this person isn't just telling those in our kingdom, but also the ones surrounding."

I was incredulous. "Other kingdoms? What purpose would that possibly serve?"

Someone cleared their throat, and my eyes moved to John, the man who had sworn me in as queen and one of the men who had traveled with King Leonidas when he'd take those mystery excursions. "I fear for you, Your Majesty."

My brows crinkled, and I waited for him to continue with bated breath. Cade's jaw was clenched.

"War is coming, my queen."

It was evident by the sudden eruption of voices at my table that the threat of war had not been discussed before this.

I held up a hand, and the room fell silent. "John, is there something in particular that makes you believe that?"

He stood from the table and rested his knuckles on it, leaning over slightly to look directly at me. "King Leonidas worried about this, you know. Or do you? I supposed I've never mentioned it before."

My eyes narrowed at his sarcasm.

"But when he presented his will to me many years ago as he lay on his deathbed, he made me swear to protect you against all doubters."

I suddenly felt a chill run down my spine as I anticipated the words he'd say next. I could sense something was coming.

"And then," John continued, his eyes never leaving mine — "He muttered his final word to me, and I kept it to myself all these years, not wanting to break my promise to him. And do you know what that word was?"

I didn't want him to continue. The room was dead silent except for the heavy breathing of Cade next to me and my own heart pounding in my ears. I implored John with my eyes to stay silent, to keep my secret. He only leaned farther over the table, and I drew back, pressing my back into the chair, even though he remained feet away.

"Magic."

CHAPTER THREE

Zeke

Seolia. I'd been in this place for a week and was about to lose my mind. The entire kingdom was secluded on an island, and I'd been banished here for weeks to seduce their queen, whom I hadn't met yet. I barely knew anything about her, not caring enough to learn her name.

I looked out over the vast blue waters from my deck. I'd stayed on this ship most of the time, except when I nearly died from boredom and roamed around the forest cluttered with trees that looked like death.

I scoffed when Mira pulled me aside to tell me of her master plan. I had to trick a queen into falling in love with me and bring her back to Reales as my fiancée. My fiancée. I had to make this woman my wife. I was thirty years old and nowhere near ready to settle down.

When I argued, trying to convince Mira that my services were needed in Reales, she promised that they weren't and then promptly reminded me that she'd keep my mother and brother locked away until I returned with her prize.

Not that she was ever going to let them free.

When I had asked why this was so important, I was given the bare minimum of details, only leaving with the information that I must succeed.

I exhaled a long breath as I recalled how I became part of her court in the first place. All thanks to dear old dad, informing Mira of my abilities long before our king became ill.

Rudolf was a decent man, a fair ruler, who didn't use people for his own personal gain like his daughter. He was still breathing when she took over, anointing herself as queen two years ago. Since then, I've been at her side every day, torturing prisoners and pulling memories from the recesses of their minds to threaten them, using what they love against them to do Mira's bidding.

Our once bountiful town was now quiet and gray, our people afraid of being snatched up at random. When I didn't want to play her twisted games, she sent soldiers in the dead of night to rip my mother and brother from their beds and imprisoned them in the castle where I slept.

Rudolf didn't take his last breath until three months ago when she set this plan into motion.

The worst part of this, although not surprising, was that my father was part of this plan, and I had to wait in the forest until he came to tell me it was time. He was Rudolf's brother but had lived in Seolia since I was a boy, playing nice with the royals and pledging allegiance to their king instead of Rudolf.

Of course, being the king's nephew, I took advantage of my status, even though it wasn't rightfully mine. It was as easy as breathing, hating my father since he wasn't indeed my father at all. He was my brother's, but he adopted me as a young boy after falling in love with my mother.

He was good to us for a while until he became bored and left for Seolia, revealing to Mira before she took the throne that she could use me and my abilities in his absence. I was only five years old when he left for Seolia to join court here, though I remained unsure why the sudden change.

He'd visit, but I refused to see him as I aged. I was relieved to see him gone. I cared for my mom and brother alone, working once old enough until Mira became queen. I was summoned to my newly appointed position as commander, training her soldiers during the day and doing her dirty work at night. More often than not, whoever we brought in to negotiate with wouldn't give in, and I'd have to kill them. It had become a sport, and I enjoyed it more than I did when they surrendered.

Mira had bred something in me — something twisted.

I looked forward to nighttime when I knew she would call me in to torture someone. I only enjoyed killing the ones who truly deserved it, like rapists and other pieces of shit who started trickling in since Mira's reign began.

They knew they would have a second chance with Mira if they agreed to whatever she asked for, so there was no fear of coming to our kingdom. What they didn't know, though, was that before Mira could find them, I did. In the middle of the night, when I could truly be alone, I hunted them and savored hearing their pleas for their lives to be spared. I never did, piercing their hearts instead.

Arms circled my waist, and my body tensed as I looked down at them. Mira really decided to torture me on this excursion by sending Jeanine with me to inform kingdoms about the magic Seolia's queen possesses. I hadn't been home in weeks, first stopping in Perosan and Thoya before we came here. Seolia was so secluded from the other three kingdoms in our so-called Circle of Peace that no one had yet heard that dark magic was making its way back, slowly trickling into every land.

"We have time if you want to…." Jeanine trailed off.

I peeled her arms off from around my waist, dropping them as I turned to face her. We'd been here for a week, and she was an easy fuck and decent to look at and had been good for curing boredom, but the only positive thing about this trip was getting away from her. I only started fucking her because she belonged to Mira, and I wanted more information about why I needed to come here. How could I seduce another woman if she followed me around?

I tucked a loose strand of blonde hair behind her ear. She looked at me like I hung the fucking moon. I resisted rolling my eyes and put on my charming smile, baring my teeth. "Jeanine, we can't fuck anymore."

It was blunt, but nothing else seemed to work with her. I had tried to end it multiple times, but she somehow always ended up at my door, and I'd give in to the pleasure. But, I needed a clear mind going into this. My focus needed to remain on the queen.

Jeanine's face fell as a frown formed on her mouth.

I sidestepped around her, descending the small ramp onto the dock below. It was small, and we were tucked deep within the forest, having taken a hidden route that Mira told me about. Seolia kept the channels open for all kingdoms, but the courses were all mapped and heavily guarded. Apparently, King Leonidas had his own route to get in and out of Seolia undetected. Another mystery I wasn't privy to.

Jeanine sulked off, disappearing into the hull below. My eyes rolled. She would be fine. She knew when we started this that it wasn't anything serious.

I heard a male voice from a distance, my lip curling as my father appeared through the trees. "You made it."

I didn't want to see him while here, but it was inevitable. "A week ago," I replied, crossing my arms over my chest.

"A week ago?" he asked me, turning his head toward the sound of Jeanine reappearing on deck. "Why is Jeanine here?"

I shrugged.

"Hello, John," Jeanine said, walking down the ramp to stand beside me.

"Jeanine," he replied but looked at me. Confusion clouded his eyes.

"I don't know," I said. "Mira wanted her here. She's been telling the village of some sort of magic your queen possesses. I figured you knew."

"You're the one who's been going around the village," John said aloud, but it didn't sound like he was talking to us. His voice seemed far away.

"When can I meet your queen? What's her name?"

"Raven," Jeanine and John replied in unison.

Raven. Her name sounded like an answer to a riddle — a riddle that was buried deep somewhere in my mind.

"Tomorrow. We have a festival tonight," John answered, looking back and forth between Jeanine and me.

I sensed bewilderment in him. He really didn't know she'd be here. "Jeanine, can you grab my jacket for me?" I asked her, my eyes not leaving John's face as she muttered something under her breath and left us. "What?"

"She wasn't part of the plan," he said, watching as she disappeared below deck.

"What *plan*? What is this all about?"

He didn't answer. Time hadn't been kind to him. He looked much older than he was. Maybe that was what happened when you abandoned your family and swore allegiance to a kingdom that wasn't your own.

"You weren't supposed to arrive until today. Why haven't you come to see me?"

"Because Mira told me you'd find me when it's time. What is going on?" I was becoming frustrated by his lack of answers.

"I need to get back to the palace. Raven will be returning—" He trailed off, clearing his throat. "Come to the castle tomorrow morning. We have a meeting, but she'll see you after."

I didn't say anything else as he turned to walk back into the forest. If Jeanine wasn't part of the plan, then why was she here? Why was I actually here? And why did Mira want Raven so bad?

I stretched my arms over my head and ran my fingers through my black hair, smoothing it back. Glad I dressed warmly. It was fucking cold here. It was winter, but a bite in the air made it seem even chillier.

A heavy piece of fabric hit my head, and I grunted, yanking it off to see Jeanine glaring at me. I pulled on the jacket she so kindly brought me and fastened the buttons until they reached my throat, throwing on my hood. "I'm going to explore the forest again. I'll meet you in the village for the festival. I need a drink."

I didn't listen for an answer before I left her, shoving my hands into my jacket pockets and starting toward the line of trees. I heard the small waterfall to my left and stopped at the spring I'd discovered earlier this week near our dock.

Surrounded by tall rocks laid a spring made of what looked like black water. I untucked my hands and crouched, holding them over the steaming water.

We needed to secure another lodging. I couldn't stay on the boat any longer, sharing a bed with a woman who was hell-bent on seducing me. If I did my job correctly, we'd need to find an inn or hopefully wrangle an invite to the castle.

I stood and slapped the tree trunk that appeared deadened from the harsh bite of the air. "Same," I muttered, tucking my hands back into my pockets. I should have brought heavier clothes, but winters in Reales were always predictable. We had a heavy snowfall in the beginning, which would level out and remain bearable until spring.

I looked around as I walked. We had to be miles from any other life forms. This was a vast forest, and I wasn't sure what I was looking for, but something drove me deeper.

An hour in, I heard gurgled screams of what sounded like men ahead. I jogged toward the noise and froze, nearly stumbling backward, when I noticed a fiery little redhead with her hands around the throats of two men. They thrashed as they tried to claw her off until their movements ceased. She removed her hands, and their bodies fell to the ground.

Her head rolled back, and she visibly relaxed, like killing them felt... good. My lips parted slightly at her, and their throats looked... burned. She burned through them. Her attention focused on the sky above her, and she muttered a curse word before quickly turning, leaving the corpses behind.

Well, that wasn't something you saw every day.

My dick was hard as I watched her walk away. I should have been more afraid, but I wasn't. I wanted her hands on me. I had felt her heat from here. There was nothing but anger brimming off her, and it felt good. Maybe this trip didn't have to be wasted on only the queen. Perhaps I could squeeze in a fiery fuck with that little demon.

She was delicious to look at as I watched her disappear back into the forest. How a tiny little thing like that could take down two grown men was impressive. I wanted to follow her, but I had to meet Jeanine in the village, and I couldn't focus on another woman yet. I would seek her out after I met the queen. There was nothing more fun for me than the chase.

I looked up and saw the sun setting, and I still had no idea where I was. I glanced once more at the corpses before turning north, hoping to find the castle along the way.

It was evening when I saw two tall towers break over the tree line. They were ivory and had to be twice as tall as the castle in Reales. My eyes roved over the balconies peeking through the branches, and I spotted someone leaning over one, looking in the opposite direction. Was that... purple hair? I squinted to get a better view, and then my eyes widened. Her jawline.

That was the same girl.

She lived in the castle. That was going to make it really easy. Did she have wigs she wore around? I lightly jogged, wanting a closer look, but she disappeared back inside.

When I looked ahead toward the village, Jeanine was staring at me with a look of disgust. I returned it with a bored expression on my face. She could sulk all she wanted to. My eyes were on something new — a tasty little treat that would hopefully burn my tongue with anger as she fucked it.

I heard laughter and looked toward the sound, spotting the village ahead. People were hanging things from the roofs of cottages and throwing some glittery shit on the ground.

I lifted a hand to some guards lined along the castle wall in a wave, and they watched me walk past without acknowledgment. Friendly. I walked onto a cobblestone road and looked down to the ground to see what was being thrown everywhere — paper confetti in the shapes of stars and moons.

An older woman stepped in front of me and handed me a freshly cut rose from her basketful of them. "Welcome to the Festival of Dreams!"

I dipped my chin toward the woman as I accepted her rose. Her pupils dilated as she stared at me. I didn't know why I had that effect on people. I was a raging assassin with a drinking problem. I looked like my mother with her black hair and smile, but I inherited my height from my actual father. Luca, my brother, favored John but had my height.

I looked again at Jeanine; her eyes were glued to a blond guy up ahead, quickly making a beeline for him. I chuckled to myself and watched as they immersed in a short conversation before the man excused himself from her and headed back toward the castle. Poor girl. The night was young.

I meandered farther into town and into a pub that sat on a corner with *Duck's* painted on the sign. A small bell rang above my head as I pushed open the door, welcoming me in. A few patrons were spread throughout the small pub, along with a handful of tables littered throughout the center of the room, with two smaller ones pressed against the back wall. Faded painted portraits of the channel, the castle, and the village was scattered on the walls. It was dark; the only light coming in was from the long window behind the bar. It stretched horizontal and was as long as the bar top, which an older gentleman was beckoning me to.

He tapped the counter to indicate that the seat was open, and I squatted on the barstool, stretching my long legs underneath it. He asked, "What'll you have?"

I looked behind him at the surprisingly large selection. Impressive. Not what I would have expected in a kingdom as small as this one. I pointed to a bottle right behind him. "That's the best rum I've ever had. We can't ever get it back home."

He turned and started to laugh at the bottle I thirsted after. He grabbed it and a glass, pouring it fully. "Queen Raven makes sure we have everything we need."

Raven. That name again. It made my entire body tighten every time I heard it. I shook my head a little, wanting to clear the feeling. I cupped the glass with my hand and threw the bitter liquid back, groaning as it burned down my throat.

Setting the empty glass down, I nodded for another. He poured me one and watched as I downed it just as quickly. It was the best thing I'd ever tasted, and Mira hadn't been able to secure a bottle since she took over. Vendors from other kingdoms weren't as willing to work with her as my uncle.

"The name is Arthur. Where do you come from?"

I clenched my teeth, sucking in cold air to chase the taste lingering on my tongue. "Zeke. Reales." I extended a hand, and he grabbed it, giving it a shake.

"Reales, eh? I used to travel there as a boy. Haven't been in ages. How's it holding up?"

I tapped the glass, and he poured me another.

It wasn't holding up well. It was a hellhole. Rapists and murderers ran amuck. I killed at least five people a day. Our queen was the devil's sister, but I didn't say any of that.

"It's still there," I muttered, throwing back my third glass. "I'll be staying for a while. Do you have plenty of this in stock?"

Arthur laughed again. It made me long for that sound back home, when it used to echo through town instead of the silence there now. "I'll make sure Queen Raven orders more. She comes through often."

"To drink?"

Arthur's coy grin was the only answer I needed. So, the queen had a little bit of rebellion in her veins. Interesting. Mira would never coexist with her 'peasants' as she called them, and Raven dabbled with them in pubs.

I reached into my pants pocket and pulled out a handful of gold coins, dropping them on the counter. "I'll frequent here often." I stood from the stool and dipped my chin to Arthur in a goodbye. "Thanks for the drink. You made this man's dream come true." Festival of Dreams, indeed.

He laughed again as I exited the pub.

My walk was a little heavier, rum making its way into my bloodstream. I looked around, and Jeanine was again talking to the blond. Good for her. I took a step off the curb and nearly stumbled, but I didn't. Taking a moment, I inhaled a deep breath and collected myself.

Walking past a row of booths, I stopped at one with basketfuls of candy on her table. "Caramel?"

She nodded enthusiastically, shoving a handful into my hand. "I baked them myself. They're chocolate with a caramel filling."

I unwrapped one and popped it into my mouth. It mixed well with the taste of rum still lingering. I put the rest in my coat pocket and asked for another handful. She obliged and dropped more of the candies into my hand. "They're delicious. Thank you." I handed her too many gold coins. She tried to object, but I waved my hand. "Worth it."

———

I peddled along, stopping by a few more booths, the alcohol beginning to wean off. I wanted to return to Duck's before calling it a night — if he hadn't been bled dry by all the other drunks stumbling around.

I stood by a bonfire, warming my hands, and ignored the looks of the women surrounding me.

I thought about Raven. Her name.

Something about it made my dark heart seem a little lighter. I hadn't met her, but we felt acquainted. I'd met a lot of royals but never any that hung out at local pubs. Maybe the next few weeks wouldn't be so bad.

I was about to take a step toward Duck's when movement caught at the corner of my eye. And I froze. Purple hair... violet. She was walking out from behind a cottage. I glanced around her for only a second and realized she was alone.

And then, her eyes met mine.

Flashes flit through my eyes, skating in the depths of my mind. I could see them like they were right in front of me. Me, in lives I'd never lived, with her. Laughing, crying, kissing. Together.

I knew her.

My lungs tried to draw in breaths, but I couldn't. I was trapped in her gaze. She wasn't moving either, just staring at me. Did she see it, too? And then her name was on my tongue.

Raven.

The redhead. This one. This was Raven. You, I knew you before. My feet started to move, and I was walking to her, needing to be in her presence. The crowd seemed to part for me, making a straight path to her.

Her eyes were golden, dancing with violet specks. Her cheeks were rosy. Her lips were full. And she was staring at me, drinking me in. While she was distracted, I pushed into her mind and couldn't find any memory of me besides the one sketching. She hadn't seen what I had.

My heart hammered as I stared at this exquisite beauty in front of me. Small, delicate. Fragile. But deep down, I somehow knew the world had hurt her. There was a darkness to her. I felt a sudden need to protect her. To keep her safe.

Fuck, was this what love felt like?

I felt overwhelmed, like the world around us no longer existed. All I wanted to do was stare at her.

"I've been looking for you all night," she said.

Her voice was the only thing I wanted to hear for the rest of time. It was soft and airy. Until this moment, this second, I hadn't realized that I had been looking for her my entire life.

I extended my hand, and she looked at it, but I sensed no doubt in her. I felt her body heat, her intrigue. She wanted this as much as I did. She placed her hand in mine; her skin was so soft. I pulled her, with no idea where to take her, but I needed to be alone with her.

I stole a glance back at her, and my mouth was wet at the sight of her in leather tights and boots that hugged her thighs. Her breasts were pushed up, and I was upset with the idea of any other man seeing her, suddenly furious that she'd show so much of herself.

I tugged her into a dark alley and dropped her hand, wrapping my fingers around her shoulders and pressing her back against a wall. She crawled up with her hands and pressed her mouth against mine. And I was in a frenzy. The familiarity of her tongue dancing with mine nearly took me down.

I had loved this woman before.

My hands circled around her waist, wanting to touch more of her, make her mine in this lifetime. My fingertips grazed across her belly button, and I heard her draw in a sharp breath before she broke from me.

Come back, I begged her silently. I need more of you.

Her lips lingered near mine, and I sucked in the breaths that left her. She searched my face with her eyes. She could feel the pull, but she couldn't understand why. Find me, I wanted to tell her. My eyes closed briefly, wanting to kiss her again, but she asked who I was.

I pushed my hips against hers, not wanting an inch spared between us. When I lifted my arms to trap her, I pulled a flower from her hair, but she didn't seem to notice. Her heat surrounded us, and I knew I would never be cold again if she was with me.

"Zeke."

A brief flash of recognition crossed her eyes before it was gone again. "Zeke," she repeated.

That was when I knew I needed to possess this creature.

Her lips were close to my ear, and I wanted to be buried deep inside her. "I'll see you in my dreams, Zeke."

And then she was gone, and I craved her warmth again. Her hips swayed as she walked away, and it took every ounce of self-control not to chase her, lock her away so no one could ever lay eyes on her again.

I leaned against the wall, unable to breathe or think of anything but what had just played in my mind when we locked eyes. Everything in my life before five minutes ago seemed trivial now.

You would be mine again, Raven.

I spent a sleepless night on my ship. Alone, thankfully. Jeanine must have found another place to stay. All I thought about was Raven. Her mouth on mine, our tongues greedy for each other, how she tasted like wine. How delicate her skin felt. I wondered how she would taste on my tongue if I went to my knees for her. Would she scream my name?

I reached into my briefs, starting to pump my shaft slowly while I thought of how she'd look riding me. That fiery little demon in the forest. My hand pumped faster. The feeling of her tongue again was in the front of my mind, imagining how it would feel if it circled my cock. My stomach tightened, and I groaned her name as I found my release, continuing to pump until the images of her became blurred in my mind.

I rolled onto my stomach, my chest heaving from how hard and quick I came from only the thought of her. I pulled my memories forward, the ones I experienced when I locked eyes with her. They were mere frames, never fully forming, but all I saw was her.

In worlds that had never existed, wearing things I had never seen, odd fabrics and cuts, but she was beautiful in all of them. I had no context to them, but I knew my sole purpose in every life was to love her. I regretted spending thirty years of my life never knowing her, finding relief in other women. I couldn't imagine ever touching someone else again. I wanted all of her, inside and out, only her.

I buried my face into my pillow. I had a mission. I was sent here to bring her back with me to Reales. That didn't sound bad, except for the reasoning involved Mira, and nothing good could ever involve Mira. I couldn't let Raven fall into any trap. I needed to keep her safe. I could complete my mission and keep her to myself. I could keep her safe. I would.

Streams of sunlight pushed through the cracks in the latched door, and I rolled over again, throwing the blanket off me. I needed to clear my mind before I saw her again. I pulled on a loose pair of pants and a short sleeve shirt, stepping into my canvas boots that I laced up quickly. It would be cold as fuck, but I would quickly work myself into a sweat.

I pushed open the door and stepped onto the deck, extending my arms above my head. The bones in my back popped and tugged. I grabbed my ankles one at a time, bending my knee behind me to stretch my legs. The cold air bit into my skin, and I jumped a little before I began a light jog off the dock and onto the snowy ground.

I circled around the spring caves and ran along the water's edge, listening to the sound of snow crunching under my boots. I ran until I could see more caves farther ahead but larger. Something small and black stepped out from one of them, and I slowed my run back to a jog, squinting my eyes at the tiny creature.

It stared at me, its eyes green. I slowed down to a walk, approaching the small cat. It trotted to me and rubbed its back along my legs. I leaned down and scooped it up, its head falling against my chest as I petted it. It purred at me, and I smiled, setting it gently back on the ground. Seeing a cat living on an island was odd, but I wasn't expecting to find Raven, either.

"I'll see you tomorrow," I told the animal, though I hoped it wouldn't be because I was back on my ship. I wanted to be in the castle near Raven.

I turned and jogged back toward the spring. I was sweating and pulled off my shirt as I approached it, throwing it to the ground. Stopping, I kneeled to remove my boots and shoved my pants off as I stood. I walked into the cave, seeking out the waterfall, and ducked under it, letting the cold water cool my skin and wash off the sweat.

I placed my palms on the cold stone and hung my head, inhaling slow breaths. My heart was beating wildly inside my chest — not from the jog, but from seeing Raven soon. I rubbed my hands over my hair and stepped out of the water, shaking my head free of the cold droplets, and then I crouched, lowering myself down into the hot spring.

The temperature change made my jaw clench, and I drew in cold air through my clenched teeth as my body adjusted. After a moment, I settled and relaxed into the water, leaning back against the stone wall behind me.

As much as I may want to, I couldn't tell her who I was — what we were to one another. I definitely couldn't tell her why I was truly here. She would have to fall in love with me naturally. I wasn't going to try and force it. I would get her back to Reales, but it would need to be on her terms. She would have to want it.

I put my hands on the edge of the wall and lifted myself out, standing to gather my discarded clothes and boots. I ran to the ship, the cold air biting my skin again. Never once had I ever wanted to impress a girl or needed to. They usually flocked to me, but I actually stood in my cabin, staring at the clothes I brought with me, and felt the need to look suitable for my girl.

I pulled on a long-sleeve black shirt and a heavy leather jacket with a hood to pull over my ears, so I didn't lose them to fucking frostbite. I tugged on a pair of black pants and tucked them into my canvas boots, one of the only two pairs of shoes I brought along on the trip.

I trembled with a mixture of excitement and sleeplessness. I left the hull and stepped back onto the wooden dock, adjusting the hood of my jacket and shoving my hands into my pockets. Maybe I could get an invite to the castle today, so I wouldn't have to continue staying miles away from her.

———————

The castle came into view, and I nodded to the guards as I approached the gate. "I'm here to have an audience with Queen Raven. I am from the kingdom of Reales with horrible news."

The guards looked at one another. One of them nodded while the other disappeared through the gate. I waited, ignoring my urge to pace. Or just rush in. Being chased through the castle would not be a great first impression.

The door to the steel gate opened, and the guard came back, along with a blond guy. I recognized him from the festival. Jeanine's fuck.

He tilted his chin up in greeting. "You're here to see Raven?"

Raven. They were familiar. The way he said her name was dominating. Intimate. It annoyed me.

I clenched my jaw as I nodded. "I'm here from Reales. I have to share some news with her."

He waited for me to say more, but I didn't. I kept my mouth shut, appearing indifferent. I wasn't going to tell him in case he offered to deliver the news instead. "Queen Mira is insistent that Queen Raven is the first one I tell."

My blond nuisance stood there, cocking an eyebrow. He was protective of her. I pushed into his recent memories and clenched the fabric of my coat pockets between my fingers. He hadn't spent the night with Jeanine. He spent it with Raven, sleeping beside her, his arms wrapped around her. I glimpsed her in his shirt and pulled out, unable to stomach it anymore.

Were they together? They couldn't be. Not with how she was with me last night. All over me. Desperate for more.

My new enemy motioned for me to follow him. I pushed the thought of killing him down and followed him inside, sensing his hesitation with me. I inhaled and smelled her on him. Pears and jasmine. Fuck, I hated whoever this was.

I needed to keep my composure.

He ushered me inside and led me down dimly lit hallways until guards pulled open large red doors that led into a throne room. It was much brighter than ours back home and warmer, even with the chilliness outside.

"She's getting dressed for breakfast, and then I'll bring her in."

He nodded toward a bench against the wall, but I didn't move to sit. Instead, I straightened. I was at least two inches taller than him. I didn't feel threatened by him. But why was her scent all over him?

"It may be a couple hours. We're meeting with advisers over breakfast."

We. He referred to them as one. He was staking claim of her.

"I'll be here," was all I could reply because if I had to hear him talk about her like she was his one more time, I would lose it.

Blondie didn't say another word as he left me alone. I would have to wait a couple hours to see her. I couldn't explore the castle in case I missed her. Instead, I paced, finally alone.

I sifted through the memories I pulled from his mind again, how he watched her as she slept beside him, rubbing her hair — which was black, not purple. Or red. How they laughed, how her cheeks were stained with tears. How his nose touched hers.

But there was never anything more. Their touching ended with her wrapped in his arms, fast asleep. They seemed comfortable together. Close. Maybe that was all it was. Friends.

I had to hold on to that, stopping my pacing. I inhaled an impatient breath as I sat on the bench and waited.

CHAPTER FOUR

Raven

Luisa's gasp filled the dining room. I looked to Cade, who stared back at me. Magic had become a curse word around the kingdom. I kept a cool exterior, even though my fire was once again pooled in my stomach, itching to protect me against the mental daggers being shot at me by my court.

"And?" It was my only response as my gaze traveled to John, pressing him to rechallenge me. This was the worst way he could have gone about this.

"And," John began, looking at Cade. "Word has gotten out. They know she possesses darkness. If other kingdoms learn of this… I am not sure what that could mean."

Cade straightened in his chair, a low growl erupting from his throat. "There is no darkness in her. She's never harmed anyone with her abilities, nor has she wished to."

I winced, biting my bottom lip as I averted my gaze from John and looked back to Cade. That wasn't entirely true. While the thought of harming any of my people made me feel ill, there had been times when I would become so angry at someone that the idea of burning or blinding them made me ache for their ashes at my feet. But that wasn't something I had ever shared with Cade. John was correct. There was a darkness inside of me, and it had become harder to shove down.

"You knew about this," John said.

It sounded like an accusation, but there was something else behind it that I didn't have time to digest before Cade growled. "Of course, I fucking knew," Cade responded, his voice like ice.

I had to agree with that. Of course, he fucking knew. He'd known since I was ten years old. I stood with a sudden need to protect him, taking a step closer to him, and he wrapped his hand around mine.

"It is still something that people around every kingdom have long feared. The return of witches. And if word starts to spread that one may be the very leader of this kingdom..." John trailed off, standing upright. He stepped around the table, crossing his hands behind his back. He knew he was getting to Cade, and he was egging it on.

At his words, Cade stood quickly, his chair nearly toppling over behind him as his fists balled at his sides. "She is no witch, and it would do you well to remember your place as a member of this court that serves our queen."

I supposed I could be a witch. We weren't really sure.

But, this was getting out of hand, and I needed to take control before something was said between my advisers that couldn't ever be taken back. Luisa was either in fear or shock, her eyes moving back and forth between Cade and John. This was certainly not how I wanted my morning to go. I wanted solutions, not more problems, and certainly not to be outed during breakfast at my own table.

I slowly took a step away from Cade, clasping my fingers together and resting my hands against my waist. I contemplated what to say next and how to explain why I had kept this secret.

"I do possess dark magic. I had a feeling it was something King Leonidas knew about because I've never been able to figure out why he gave me his throne and kingdom." I addressed all three, my gaze never staying on one face long. "And while I do apologize for not being forthcoming about this, it's never been something I've wanted to advertise about myself. I've read the texts in our libraries. I've heard the rumors about the Black Forest. I, too, understand that dark magic may have lived there once upon a time."

"But I can assure you that I am no more of a danger to you than a knife you use to cut your steak." My movements were heavily tracked as I moved around the table. "I love this kingdom, our people, and I am grateful to all of you here at this table who have taken me as your queen and never questioned my judgment."

I turned and stood directly in front of John, my exterior remaining relaxed while inside, I felt choked. "You served our king loyally and knew of his secrets. I would never ask that you share those with anyone else. But, I do ask that from now on, if you learn something about me, you talk to me directly instead of announcing it at my breakfast table. I have, after all, earned the same respect as your queen."

He flinched.

I stopped myself from smiling at his discomfort. "You made a promise to protect me, and before we proceed any further, I need to know if you intend on keeping that promise." It wasn't a threat, but it was a warning. Since John knew of my abilities, he was an enemy until he proved otherwise. He picked an odd time to reveal this to everyone, and with the new threat looming outside the palace, I didn't need this seeping into my home.

I saw the contemplation behind his eyes as he weighed my words, but I didn't back down and remained still as I waited for his answer. Cade's presence crept up behind me as he, too, waited. "I will always protect my queen," John muttered, barely loud enough for me to hear, as he took a small step back and bowed.

I cocked my head at his words, watching as he turned to his chair. I turned to Cade and locked eyes with him, silently asking where to go from here. He gave me a slight shrug. We had held this secret between us for so long that it seemed like an invasion of privacy for others to know. I swallowed and drew a deep breath, trying to steady my nerves.

I turned back to face my advisers. "I guess… you should all know what I can do. What I'm about to show you cannot leave this room. Now, more than ever, we must protect this secret. If John is correct and we could possibly face a war, what I possess could end up being our greatest weapon."

Nods of agreement followed my words. I had no choice but to trust them, as they had never given me a reason to doubt before.

I looked around the table for something I could use and grabbed the apple I had taken a bite out of earlier. Using my free hand, I reached up, removed the diadem from my head, and set it on the table. I inhaled deeply, extended my palm flat, and balanced the apple on my hand. "Frost," I whispered, closing my eyes.

The change on my skull happened first, my shoulders tingling as the tips of my shortened white hair skimmed across them. My eyes opened, changing from dark green to a light blue that seemed to sparkle with snowflakes that fell down my irises. In my hand, the apple on my palm was covered in dusty snow before it grew a thick dome of ice around it, encasing the apple inside.

Audible murmurs filled the room at my changed form and the magic that was just witnessed.

"She's not done," Cade muttered before nodding to me.

I closed my eyes again, hesitating as I double-checked that all my emotions were in control. "Blaze."

The feeling that washed over me was like coming home as my entire body lit up at the command. My white hair turned fiery red and shortened to my chin, cutting right at my jawline. I rolled my head back as the feeling of fury overtook me. It was like awakening a dormant beast after years of being locked up. My eyes revealed red flames behind my irises, burning, flickering. Free.

I blew a hot breath on the apple, the dome of ice immediately melting around the fruit. I glanced at Cade, whose lips parted slightly, taking all of me in. Seeing Blaze in full form was a rarity since I was always hesitant to bring her to the forefront. This was where I felt most threatening, most deadly. How good it felt to become this dark part of me made me panicky, and there was a part of me, and I didn't know how dominant that part was, that itched to stay like this.

I rolled my head to the side and bit down on my bottom lip as heat began to build in my stomach and coursed through my veins. Cade sensed the change in me and nudged my leg with the toe of his boot. My eyes snapped to him, his assertive stare being the only beckoning force in the room that could bring me back to reality. My tongue skated across my lips as I rolled my head slowly back to the apple, fire forming in my fingers as I turned it to ashes in my palm.

Not giving anyone a chance to speak, I closed my eyes again, and tears pooled in them at the demand to push Blaze back down. "Terra," I growled through gritted teeth, my fire hesitating and screaming inside me as it was overtaken by the force of earth.

I transformed into Terra, my violet hair copying the style from the festival in a braided bun at the top of my head. My eyes changed from red back to gold, which gave me a goddess-like glow.

With my free hand, I made a spinning motion with my fingers, and the ashes of the apple began to dance in the air before they landed on the table to form a tiny tornado that spun across the table, weaving in and out of plates laid in front of my advisers. When I snapped, the ash disappeared, only tiny particles of dust remnants left to float and fall still.

While everyone's eyes were focused on the dust, I closed my eyes and shifted out of my form, my long black hair and green eyes returning.

They all lifted their gaze to me, mouths hanging open. Luisa looked a little whitewashed at what she had just witnessed. I looked at Cade and watched as he scrutinized the others, looking for any sign of a threat.

"So… you inhabit the elements?" Luisa's voice was soft as she wrapped her fingers around mine, giving me a small smile.

Relief washed over me. "I possess earth, fire, and ice. The very wind that gives you chills on a blustery day is the same one that runs through my veins. I *am* the elements."

I was not ashamed. It was a head-scratcher, but the universe entrusted these to me. "My abilities are harmless toward the people we serve and protect. They only come out when they need to." I didn't give any more details than that. They'd heard the rumors of why our crime was so low, though they had never asked. "Cade has known about it since I was ten years old. He's kept my secret as a favor to me."

John looked to Cade, a grin tugging at the corner of his mouth. Cade's brow furrowed at it, seemingly lost in thought.

"I promise to continue protecting this kingdom with my life. That's all I've ever wanted to do. Please continue to do the same for me," I pleaded, feeling more exposed now than I had ever been.

All at once, my table of three advisers stood and bowed to me. I gave them all a broad smile and clasped my hands together under my chin, curtsying back.

"I will not let any of you down. Now, let's try and figure out who this mysterious stranger could be before they spin things out of control."

We spent the next two hours discussing what could be done. More guards would be sent into the village undercover to try and uncover any information they could. I didn't share with them that I snuck out sometimes at night to wander into the Black Forest, but I decided on my own that I would tonight to see if there was anything to be found. Cade suggested sending a group to the three neighboring kingdoms to see if any information could be found there.

When we decided it was a good place to start, we agreed to break and reconvene in a few days or sooner if anyone heard of anything else. When John and Luisa left, Cade and I remained in the dining hall alone.

I exhaled a jittery breath and sank into my chair, perching an elbow on the arm of my chair and resting my head in my hand. This was unexpected. So, King Leonidas was aware of my magic and had chosen me to take his place. It made me wonder how he knew and why he never tried to meet me. But, John had always known or suspected, and he never said a word.

"I didn't know this was going to happen," Cade said.

I nodded. My body felt tired like I had just run circles around my village.

"We have one more meeting, and then you can take a break." His voice was tired, too.

I raised my head to look at him, shooting him a confused glance. "What other meeting? Why are you being so secretive lately?" I was irritated by the events of the day and night before, and I was taking it out on him, but it still didn't make sense why he was suddenly not telling me things until right before they happened.

He ignored my questions and stood. I did the same but didn't move, waiting to hear who I had to meet after an exhaustive morning.

"He's from Reales. He has news that he insists he can only share with you."

From Reales. Wonderful. The one kingdom I had yet to visit during my reign. I rolled my eyes, gesturing to the door. "Lead the way then."

His eyes narrowed on me.

I returned his glare. "What? More secrets to share?"

"Why don't we start by losing the attitude?" He spat back.

I was really not in the mood to argue with him. He'd held back on me for a week and expected me to be okay with it. "Why don't we start by keeping your queen informed on what the fuck is happening in her own kingdom?" I shoved past him.

Withholding information from me was not a choice he had the freedom to make. I was his queen and deserved the respect that came with the position, even from him.

I felt his hard stare on my back as we walked to the throne room in silence. We were laughing on the balcony just last night and now we were pissed at each other. This back-and-forth shit was grating on my last nerve.

The guards standing at the throne room doors peeled them back once they saw me coming and bowed their heads. I gave them a subtle dip of my chin as I breezed past, stomping up the stairs to my throne and sitting.

"You're a fucking piece of work," he grumbled as he passed by to stand by my side, farther back than he usually would.

I sighed heavily. He was going to pout. I crossed my legs, the hem of my dress rising at the movement and exposing my thigh and boots. If he insisted on staring all day and being a dick, I would torture him the best way I knew how. He may have been my best friend, but even he couldn't resist lusting after bare skin. His stare remained on me as I leaned back on the throne, grinning smugly as the dress glided an inch higher.

While playing my cruel game, my focus had been solely on annoying him and not on who had been waiting on a bench to the side of the room. When he came into view as he sauntered to the center, I choked on absolutely nothing and broke into a coughing fit.

Zeke was standing there, looking even more devastating than he was the night before. He was in all black again, and I was almost positive that the shade had been invented just for him. He had a hood on, and pieces of his black hair were poking out, resting against his forehead. He pulled the hood back and ran a hand through his hair, the pieces following. I watched with parted lips. Never in my life had I been jealous of a hand, but I wanted to be the one doing that.

"You," I said aloud before realizing he had no idea who I was. I was Terra at the festival, and now I was myself, but I swear I saw the corners of his mouth tug up at my nervous greeting. "You. You're here. Hello." What a fucking lame recovery, but it was all I could manage.

He bowed to me, and my entire body warmed at the sight of him lowering himself to me. I bet he looked delicious on his knees.

"Your Majesty, I'm here from the kingdom of Reales. I came with the unfortunate task of telling you that our king has passed." He straightened after he shared the news and met my eyes, his ghost of a smile disappearing as we stared at one another a beat too long.

I untwined my fingers and rose from my throne, walking down the small steps of my station and stood in front of him, placing my hand on his elbow. My heart skipped a beat. "I am so sorry to hear that. I never had the chance to meet him, but I've heard wonderful things about his peacefulness. What happened to him?"

Zeke licked his lips, and I mentally cursed myself for where my thoughts went. His tongue had just been in my mouth. "In his sleep. He was ill for a very long time, but we are grateful that he felt no pain in the end. Of course, his daughter is devastated and is now responsible for taking his throne."

I gave him a sympathetic smile, dropping my hand from his arm. "What does she need from me? We're here to help in any way we can."

"I'm here to formally invite you to Reales in three months. It's an accurate amount of time for her to grieve and try to get a handle on becoming Queen of Reales."

I nodded in response, patting his arm again. Why couldn't I stop touching him? He didn't seem to mind. Never flinching. "Of course. I'd happily visit her and become acquainted with your new queen. Mira is her name, correct?"

He nodded. I should have dismissed him. "And what do they call you?" My mouth clearly didn't listen to my brain.

At my question, his quick smile returned before it was gone. His eyes burned into mine like we shared a secret, but he couldn't possibly know who I was. "Ezekiel, but I answer to Zeke."

Of course, I already knew his name because he was pressed against me hours prior. I just wanted an opportunity to say his name aloud again. "Zeke," I repeated. Why did it feel so familiar to me? "Please feel free to stay as long as you need. We have rooms available to you, and you can explore the palace and village as you wish."

He bowed to me, and my body flushed. I could be so annoying. I really needed to fuck someone soon to release the pressure building up every second.

"I would love a tour of your palace, Raven." My name on his tongue sounded delicious. "Would you be willing to honor me with your presence?" His voice was lowered like he wanted only me to hear him.

My hands were shaking. Something about him made me so nervous. Being alone with him was exactly what I wanted, but it also seemed like such a bad idea. Luckily for the illogical part of my brain, I enjoyed throwing caution to the wind. "I would love to. Tomorrow morning?"

He grabbed my shaky hand and pulled me a step closer to him, drawing it to his mouth and pressing his lips to my knuckles before murmuring against my skin, "I look forward to it."

Quite the balls on this one. And I liked it.

I licked my lips at the feeling of his mouth on my hand and he tracked the movement of my tongue. I dropped my eyes from his piercing gaze and watched him walk away in awe.

"You're drooling."

I jumped at the sound of Cade's voice beside me.

"Don't you have a blonde to bed?" I retorted, leaving him to stand there as I waltzed out of the throne room. We would make up. We'd had spats before, although this one felt a little tenser. We were just tired. We hadn't had a chance to talk about what happened this morning.

Usually, we would meet in his office and go over the ramifications of what revealing myself would be since it was a huge fucking deal. But for right now, I wanted nothing more than to visit my aunt for a little bit. I could discuss it with her instead. I wasn't sure how much longer I had with Isla. She wasn't moving around as quickly as she used to. Cade would be all I had left if she were to pass.

I promised myself to make up with him tomorrow.

———

There was still enough light in the day that I didn't need to disguise myself for the walk between my palace and Isla's cottage. I wasn't fearful for my safety, just more alert. It would take a lot more than one person to keep me locked away in my ivory tower.

I walked onto the palace grounds and through one of the gates on the far side of my castle. It was the gate closest to the Black Forest, where my former cottage was situated.

I kicked through the snow and listened to it crunch under my boots as my mind wandered back to Zeke. I couldn't stop picturing him bowing before me, the feeling of his lips on my hand. It tingled just thinking about it. His presence kept me on edge like he was a cliff that I desperately wanted to jump off. Nothing had ever made my heart beat faster than being so close to him, and I didn't even know him.

It couldn't be more than superficial attraction. He was magnificent to look at, how he towered over me. How he looked like he was cut from the same cloth as me. Only much taller and built like a god. I hadn't even seen him with clothes off, but his muscles bulged and dipped in all the right places each time I'd touched him. When did my mouth start to water?

I smacked my lips. It couldn't go any further. We'd need to keep it cordial. We could be friends. I couldn't think of any negative ramifications about having allies in neighboring kingdoms, especially ones like Reales. They did spur a war once, after all.

It sounded like a long time — a century. But, in the scheme of running kingdoms, the thirst for power didn't just evaporate. It was bred. I felt guilty that I had never made the trip to meet King Rudolf. He was always too ill to travel here, plagued with something that spanned years. I had heard rumors that it was from a broken heart, losing his queen at such a young age.

Queen Celestina was her name, and she was the true heir of Reales. She married Rudolf under her father's orders because of his peaceful attitude toward the rest of the kingdoms. The king wasn't too old, so Mira had to be in her late thirties, and now she'd lost both of her parents.

It must be difficult, not that I could understand. I never knew my parents or if I even had any. Sometimes I wondered if I was bred from demons. I snorted at the thought, knowing Cade would agree to that notion, especially after how I acted today.

———————

I heard an excited greeting as I approached Isla's cottage, and it pulled me from my thoughts. I looked up from the ground and smiled, waving at Isla sitting in a rocking chair on her porch. My walk turned into a sprint as I bounded up the steps that led to her porch and straight into her arms.

"My sweet girl is home!" she cried happily.

My eyes filled with tears at her voice. It had been too long since I'd seen her and her familiar scent made me ache for simpler times when it was just the two of us.

Isla kept her arm around me and led me into our quaint cottage. She hadn't changed a thing since I lived here with her. I plopped down in front of the lit fireplace, though I wasn't cold since I had my own heat, and watched her move around the kitchen as she began to brew tea for us. We looked absolutely nothing alike, not that we should've. Her whitened hair still showed hints of blonde, but she always kept it braided and out of her way. Just like I did with mine most of the time.

When she returned with my tea, I inhaled and smiled at the smell wafting into my nose. Jasmine. My favorite. I took a small sip, my forehead creasing as the weight of the day hit me all at once.

Isla leaned forward and grabbed my face in her hands, kissing my forehead. "Tell me all about it."

The words poured out of me in a hurry. I started with meeting Zeke at the festival as Terra and walking away from him, even though I felt such a strong pull to him whenever we shared space and how unnerving it was.

I told her about the note Cade showed me and how he promised to always protect me, but how betrayed I still felt that he had kept secrets from me for a week.

And all the while, my arms flailed wildly, my tea splashing around as I went into detail about how John outed me at breakfast to everyone and revealed my abilities to them.

I finished with the mysterious person telling everyone in my village about my dark magic and wondered aloud how they even knew about it since we had kept it a secret for so long.

Isla did nothing but listen, reaching out to grab my hand or my cup of tea and rubbing my cheek when I would start to cry.

"It just seems so unfair sometimes. I wasn't raised to rule a kingdom. I wasn't bred for it. I don't even know who I am. I'm going on fifteen years of ruling Seolia, and I feel like such an ass for being ungrateful. But it's so overwhelming. And I've always been able to express that to Cade, but lately… he's looking at me differently. He's being cautious around me. He's always been protective, but this is different. I don't know how to act around him anymore. I'm turning twenty-five soon and feel like such a child." I let out a big breath like I'd been holding it all day. It felt so sweet to release.

Isla was quiet for a few moments, letting all the information I just vomited onto her sink in. "It's okay that your court knows of your magic. We've protected it for so long that maybe it's time we let it out. It's a gift, whether you realize it yet or not. Right now, it may be your kingdom's salvation."

I raised an inquisitive eyebrow. "What do you mean?"

"You could be the very thing to save them if John is correct and war is possible. I may have done you a disservice, asking you to hide this part of yourself."

I shook my head, a quiet sob escaping me.

Isla joined me on the floor and grabbed both of my hands. "You are a treasure to me, Raven, and beloved by your people. We may not know why you were given to me, but King Leonidas saw something in you, and he protected this kingdom fiercely. He wouldn't have handed it to you unless he saw the same thing in you that he saw in himself. Perseverance. Justice. You've always protected those who couldn't protect themselves, and you will continue to do so, no matter who knows about your true self."

She tapped on my diadem with her finger. "Straighten your crown, dear girl. Face those who don't believe in you with pride in who you are."

The problem was, I wasn't sure who I was.

"And, well, as for being overwhelmed. Let yourself feel those feelings. You are under tremendous responsibility, and you are still a young queen. Don't bottle up, and don't feel guilty for feeling any of it," Isla finished, running her hand through my hair.

I asked, "And what about Cade? And Zeke?"

Isla patted my heart, beating full of sorrow in my chest. "Listen to this."

As night fell, I bid Isla goodnight and promised to return soon. When I came here, a small part wanted to stay and not deal with it anymore. After her pep talk with me, I left a little more positive.

Revealing my abilities wasn't a path I was prepared to take yet, but maybe it was time to not be so guarded about them all the time. They were a part of me, a big part, and I couldn't spend all of my energy trying to keep those pieces of me hidden. With this new threat of war, I needed to spend more time wielding my elements and continue trying to control all three of them at once.

I could practice with Cade. I had planned on going into the Black Forest tonight, but I was exhausted and didn't want to drag him out. Irritation still swelled every time I remembered that he kept things from me. "He's not your equal," I repeated over and over on the walk back to my palace. It was dark, and I contemplated shifting, but it wasn't much farther to the castle.

Right before I reached the gate, I heard twigs snapping, and I froze, snapping my head toward the sound. It was too dark to see anyone. I squinted, seeing only the guards in front of my gate. "Hello?" I called out, taking more tentative steps toward the castle.

The guards heard my voice and looked at me, taking a step forward. One of them shouted, "Are you all right, Queen Raven?"

I nodded, stopping. Someone was there, and I wasn't going to show unease. I looked to my left and saw a tall silhouette approaching. My fire came to life under my skin, itching to be let out. "They say only crazy people talk to themselves."

That oozy voice calmed me, and my body relaxed, the tension rolling off my shoulders. "I never claimed to be sane, Zeke." As he came into clearer view, I took a step toward him, placing my hands on my hips. "Why are you out so late?"

He stopped within a foot of me and looked around. "Your kingdom comes alive at night. I was in the village having a few drinks at a place called Duck's."

I laughed and nodded, looking past him into the village. "Duck's is definitely the place you'd go for a good time."

A slow smile spread on his mouth. "Would you know that personally? I've never known a queen to keep company at village pubs."

"Queens have a lot of secrets, Zeke," I replied with a coy grin.

"Like how they disguise themselves to attend village festivals?"

I froze at his question. "Excuse me?"

He grinned and tapped my boot with his. "I recognized the boots."

That wasn't embarrassing at all. I ran my hand through my hair and sighed, looking down at my boots. "Ah. I wouldn't have worn these if I had known you'd show up in my throne room."

"You sound disappointed."

I was quick to reply, "On the contrary."

He smiled brightly. It was charming to see. "Want a drink?" He nodded back toward the village.

I frowned. "Was it busy? I don't typically go out." At least, not when people were around while I was undisguised.

He shook his head at my question. "Only a couple stragglers. It's closing soon, but we have time for a couple drinks."

I wished I could shift, give myself some anonymity. We smiled at one another, and he held out his hand, again asking to lead me somewhere. I should go back to my room. Go to sleep. Wake up with a fresh head before our palace tour. But he was intoxicating. And absolutely devastating lit up by the moonlight. And I was curious as to why I felt such a magnetic pull to him.

So I took his hand.

CHAPTER FIVE

Zeke

I couldn't wipe the smile from my face as I left the throne room. Her heat encased her, and her attempt at pretending like we had never met was endearing. She was toying with blondie, but I hadn't sensed lust in her. It was all agitation. From him, though… my fingers curled into fists at my sides. He wanted her. He was envious of how we talked to one another, his eyes never leaving us, and how she kept touching me.

I didn't want to wait until tomorrow to see her, but I couldn't push her. I needed to go about this the right way. If I were to come on too strong, she might ask that I return to Reales. I could tell by how she interacted with people around her that she may not be close to many. There was something reserved about her but a fierceness, too. I could practically taste it on her.

I walked out of the castle back into the courtyard and nearly stumbled into John. "Fuck," I spat out. I'd seen him twice already. "What?" I asked him, crossing my arms over my chest. I wanted to go to Duck's and drink myself into a stupor until tomorrow.

"You met Raven then," he said.

I lifted a bored eyebrow.

"What do you think?"

"I think she's a spitfire." And she was. I wasn't lying. I just wasn't telling him everything.

John laughed softly at my words, looking back into the castle like he could see her.

"Why does Mira want me to marry her? Why does she want her in Reales?"

John didn't look at me, contemplating something. "Make sure she doesn't get suspicious about anything."

I still hadn't earned the right to know why I was here, apparently, only that Mira's intentions for Raven weren't pure. I didn't say anything else and left him standing there. I would have to figure it out on my own. I refused to hurt her if that was the endgame. I wouldn't play along with that.

I needed a drink. I walked briskly to Duck's, wanting my rum. When I entered the pub, it was busier than it had been at the festival. Arthur motioned me over with a towel in his hand. I slid onto a stool, grinning like a cat when he filled my glass full of exactly why I came here.

"I requested more bottles," he said to me.

I tipped my glass to him before I threw it back.

———————

I was quiet for a while. Five drinks in, and the thick liquid was replacing my blood. "I think I'm in love." My words were slurred as they tumbled out. "She has purple hair." Her hair was black, but I saw it when it was purple, and it looked so real.

Arthur chuckled as he cleaned out a glass left by another patron.

"Are soul mates real?" I had never believed in them, having spent at least fifteen years fucking my way through the female population of three of the four kingdoms. Nothing I felt ever resembled love. Or like. More like tolerance.

"Soul mates and twin flames are rare; they're both destined to be together." He leaned his forearms down against the bar top and looked at me. "I think my wife was mine. I never looked at another woman like I saw her. It was something else."

"What's the difference between soul mates and twin flames?"

Arthur smiled at me, probably because he couldn't understand what I said as I tipped back my sixth glass of rum. "Soul mates can be anyone. A friend, a lover, someone you met briefly."

Raven wasn't anyone.

"Twin flames are two halves of one soul. There's an intense connection that can't be replicated. There's pain associated with flames, both people mirroring one another. When you find your twin, you can't be apart from them without going a little mad."

Mad, as in getting drunk in a pub midafternoon because I couldn't be with her? If so, I was mad.

"How do you know so much about them?" He didn't seem like the type who would believe in things like this. I didn't think I could ever be one, either. Yet, here I was, getting wasted in a pub because I was wholly convinced that purple-haired demon was meant to be in my life.

"My wife did," he answered. "She read often. A lot about how magic used to live in our realm. Mates and flames are a rarity, and they used to be treasured. When they existed, there would be celebrations for days. At least, that's what her books used to tell her. I haven't met any, nor have there been any pairings in a very long time. It always intrigued her, so she'd sit on one of these stools every night and tell me about them or anything else she read." There was a sadness in his voice as he recalled time spent with his wife, whom I assumed he had lost. "Do you think your girl with purple hair may be one of those to you?"

I swished the rum around in my glass as I thought about his question through my unfocused mind, laden with alcohol. "Twin flame," I said. "I think she's my twin flame."

And if they were such a rarity, I was determined to do nothing but treasure her.

I didn't have to wait until tomorrow to see her again. Her hand was in mine, trusting me to guide her back into the village. I had been walking back from Duck's when I saw her stomping toward the castle, more irritation seeping out of her.

She always seemed conflicted about something, unable to process all the emotions that raged through her. I could practically hear her heart beating through her chest when I approached her, but my presence calmed her. And she looked absolutely radiant in the moonlight. It suited her.

She seemed relaxed, but she was chewing on her bottom lip. She was worried about a lot of people seeing her. According to Arthur, she frequented his pub, but I wondered how or when. Or with whom? I pushed that thought back.

She stopped and dropped her hand from mine. I immediately wanted to grab it again, but she was removing the diadem from her hair and handing it to me. I looked around the village. It was dark and empty. No one was going to see her.

She bent over and threw all her wild mane over, gathering it in her hands. Swinging up, she put the messy blob on her head. I couldn't help but grin, shaking my head a little. She was trying to blend in, but she didn't realize that she looked like no one I had ever seen. Her green eyes alone could bring a man to his knees, and I would readily fall to mine for her.

I pulled open my jacket and placed her diadem in one of my more oversized pockets before looking back at her. "I am not sure what you're hoping to accomplish with that."

She gave me a slight shrug, self-doubt creeping across her skin. How this alluring creature could ever doubt herself was beyond me. "It makes me uncomfortable when people feel they have to treat me differently because of my title."

I wanted to scoop her up. She was so pure.

"But you are their queen." I extended my hand out to her, and she took it.

As I led her in, she muttered, "It's just a title." She was so desperate to be part of something, to feel welcomed.

She looked around the room, and all I could do was watch her. That was all I *wanted* to do. I was perfectly content to just be in her presence. When she noticed Arthur, I followed her gaze. He stopped wiping down the bar, and a smile erupted across his face. Her attempt at a cover was already blown.

"If it isn't the queen walking into my pub." He came out from behind the bar and bowed to her, grabbing the hand I wasn't holding and kissing it.

I flinched as I stopped myself from pulling her away, not wanting to see anyone's mouth on her but mine, even if I did like Arthur.

"Hello, Arthur." She beamed at him like they were familiar, then tilted her head to me. "I want to introduce you to my friend, Zeke."

We were way more than just friends.

Arthur laughed and whipped my arm with his towel. "I have gotten to know Zeke well. He visits my pub daily lately. I've had to send out for more rum because he's cleaning me out. He was in here earlier, talking about some girl with purple hair."

I pinched the bridge of my nose as he ratted me out.

"Purple hair, Queen Raven. I don't think I believe him."

She stared at me as my cheeks heated. "Just call me Raven, Arthur. And no, I wouldn't believe him."

What a wicked woman. She dropped her hand from mine, and I watched her climb onto the barstool. Her feet couldn't fully touch the floor, and I grinned, sitting down on mine and stretching my legs out. I rested my elbows on the bar and shook my head at Arthur, who started to laugh at me, whipping my arm again with his towel. "What can I get you two? My treat."

Like hell, his treat. He'd had to restock already because of me.

"Rum for him, obviously," Raven said.

I chuckled at her.

"I'll take an ale or two. As long as you promise to keep my secret." She winked at Arthur.

He gave her a subtle nod. "You wouldn't believe how many secrets I have, Raven."

I glanced at him. He said her name like they were old friends. He did hold some of her secrets. She *had* visited here.

He turned from us, grabbed my glass, set it down in front of me, and poured my favorite rum. "Last bottle," he warned me.

I grabbed my glass, circling it around in my hand. I'd had way too many of these, but a couple more couldn't hurt.

He set a frozen glass in front of her, full of a golden ale. She nudged me, and I put my glass down, knowing what was coming. "It's a little too soon for you to start telling people about me."

She laughed as I hung my head between my hands, my cheeks reddening again. "This is why I don't talk to people."

That made her laugh harder. It was giggly and wonderful to hear. She held up her glass and turned slightly toward me. "Cheers me."

I grabbed my glass and knocked it to hers. "To girls with purple hair." I threw my drink back while she and Arthur both laughed again. I watched her drink her ale, sensing the tranquility settling her shoulders as she took another draw.

Arthur refilled my glass before leaving us alone to wipe down his tables.

"Tell me about Reales," she said.

I stared down at the rum in my glass, swirling it around before taking another sip. What could I tell her that wouldn't turn her off from visiting? "It's big."

She snorted. "Descriptive. Thanks."

A slight grin tugged at the corner of my mouth. I needed to give her something. "Ah, let's see." I thought of the things I loved about the Reales I used to know. "It spans out for miles, stretching so far back that it would take weeks, maybe months, to see all of it. There's a forest, like yours, full of pine trees."

I heard her inhale through her nose.

"It's always dark, even in the warm months." Or had been lately. The sun didn't want to witness the horrific crimes happening in my town.

Her knee knocked against my thigh, and the slightest touch had me itching to pull her to me. She took another sip and nodded at my words. I assumed she was trying to picture it. "I like dark," she said as she put her glass down. She started on the second one that Arthur came over to pour. "I can't imagine anything bigger than here. I've been to Perosan and Thoya, but I was young. I don't remember much of it."

She deserved to see the world.

"Not much of a traveler?" I asked her, unable to peel my eyes away from her as she inhaled her drink quickly.

So many questions I wanted to ask her. What was hurting you, Raven? Why were you always so deep in thought?

"Not much time." Her voice was low, and there was a sorrow to it. She was young, but there was such an old soul within her. How could she have already lived so much life?

I wanted to take her sorrow and let it rest in my bones instead.

"Do you want to see more?"

She nodded slowly, circling the rim of her glass with the tip of her finger. "I want to see it all. I've never been to Reales. It's the one kingdom in our realm I haven't visited."

I knew that — only because I would have noticed her if she had visited. "I can show you around when we get there." She wouldn't be leaving my sight, anyway. Not with the kind of people who walked around there.

She smiled at my offer, pulling the corner of her bottom lip between her teeth. I grinned at her blushing and then finished the last of my rum and pushed the glass to the edge of the bar, signaling that I was done.

Arthur came back to us, nodding toward our empty glasses. "Do you two want another?"

She looked at me. I didn't want this night to end.

I didn't want any of them to end with her.

I shook my head at Arthur but kept my eyes on her. "We have another excursion planned after this."

She tilted her head at me, confusion skating across her face. But it was quickly replaced with curiosity. She hopped down from her barstool. Giddiness was not an emotion I was used to, but that was what I felt when I realized that she didn't want to be done with me yet, either.

I dropped some gold coins on the bar as Arthur came around. My eyes narrowed slightly as he pulled her into his arms for a hug. "We love our queen, young man." He released her but kept his arm around her shoulders.

My jaw ticked.

"Bring her back in one piece."

She started to giggle, and I needed her in my arms. I reached over and grabbed her hand, pulling her away from Arthur and back to me. "I promise to bring her back as good as new." I dipped my chin to Arthur, and he waved goodbye as I led her out of the pub and back onto the crunchy snow. I pulled her close and wrapped my arm around her shoulders, peering down at those green eyes. "I have one more place to show you."

She nodded. Good girl.

I walked the familiar path toward the forest, and she was quiet beside me, lost somewhere in her mind again. I wanted to

search her memories to try and figure out why she was so
mangled and drawn into herself.

"Where are you taking me?" As we neared the border that led
to the forest, she glanced at a cottage that shared it.

I followed her gaze. Who was there? "I saw a place when I
docked here a couple days ago. I planned to come back here at
night to see it lit up only by the moonlight."

She stopped when twigs snapped under her feet, and I
glanced over my shoulder. She looked a little dazed. I worried she
downed her drinks too fast and wondered if I needed to escort
her back to her room and let her sleep it off. "Need a break?"

She looked at me like I asked her if we needed to return and
get her a cane. She snorted, and that sound again made me
smile. "No, I don't need a *break*. Do you know what this is?"

I raised my eyebrow at her question and looked back toward
the forest. "A forest?"

Her eyes rolled, and I had to hold back a laugh. "The Black
Forest."

Ah, it had a name. Made sense with how dark the trees were.

"Do you not like this place?" Please say you do, I pleaded
silently.

"I love it. But, no one ever goes in here."

That explained the lack of disturbances I had when we first
docked here — except for my friend: the black cat.

I threaded our fingers and pulled her flush against me. Fuck, I
wanted her. "And why's that?"

She sighed softly, and I loved how nervous I made her.

"Magic."

I stared down at her, my fingers loosening around hers. Magic. Right. The whole reason I was sent here. She possessed magic. The men she burned. "And do you believe there is?"

She contemplated something before she answered. "I know there is." Not a confession.

I dipped my chin to her and leaned closer, our mouths only inches apart. I could taste her breath. No one ever came in here; I could take her here. My dick hardened at the thought. But I wanted to show her the spring, make it our own. "Let's go make some magic then." My voice was low, only for her ears.

I took a step backward, tugging her over the border, and she smiled. I turned begrudgingly because all I wanted to do was stare at her and weaved through the trees.

"You said you saw something when you docked? The docks are pretty far away from here." She didn't know about mine then.

I shook my head. "Not the dock I found."

She looked around as she tried to figure out where I could be taking her, but I didn't sense fear in her. Only curiosity. She had the same taste for adventure as I did.

"We're almost there."

I smiled as her fingers wrapped around my wrist, pulling herself closer to me. She trusted me. And then I frowned. She shouldn't. I was here for reasons I couldn't tell her — for reasons I didn't want to tell her.

The castle had faded from view, but she looked more at home here than I had seen since I met her. She looked more… alive.

I led her through the last of the trees as the clearing opened up in front of us, revealing the spring that looked more like black sand in the moonlight. The only thing that gave it away was the steam rising from the water.

"You found a thermal spring." Her mouth was slack as she took it in. All I wanted to do was kiss her. "But how…" she whispered as I kept tugging her, bringing her along the side of the small cave until my dock came into view. My ship was still against the small dock, the sails barely moving. "This must be yours."

"It is. I took a different route here than what's laid out on our maps. This is where I ended up. I took a day to explore where I was and was surprised to see Seolia through the other side of the forest." I hated that I needed to lie to her.

"I'm just as astonished as you are. I've explored this forest many times but have never gone far enough to find this. It's breathtaking."

She was breathtaking, but I nodded as I pulled my hand from her grip. She frowned. I wanted to tell her not to worry because I would always find a way to touch her.

My hand found the small of her back, and I gently led her toward the makeshift cave surrounding the spring. "There's a small waterfall back here." I dipped my chin to the back of the cave.

She closed her eyes, listening to the soft sound of the falling water. I welcomed the memory sketching into my mind, knowing I'd recall how she looked in the moonlight frequently.

I took a step, using my hand on her back to guide her along the wall of the tall rocks. As we approached the waterfall, she stuck her hand out to the falling water that appeared white as it blended into the black spring underneath it. She laughed, using both hands to form a cup, the water filling them. She turned back to me and showed me what she did with her hands. "Thank you for bringing me here."

I wanted to take her everywhere.

I bowed my head to her gratitude and cupped my hands under hers, catching the water spilling on them. She stared at my face, and I searched her eyes. There was so much I wanted to tell her that I couldn't. She wanted to make sense of our connection. She could feel it.

She took a small step closer as our hands dropped until her body barely touched mine. I tensed, ignoring my need to touch her. I wanted everything to be her choice.

"Swim with me," she breathed, her voice soft as she wrapped her hands around mine and pulled me out of the cave.

I didn't think I was breathing, watching her as she dropped my hands and took a step away from me. She began to pull her dress up, and I stared, mesmerized by how her body moved.

She slowly slid the boots off of her thighs. My erection was painfully pushing against the fabric of my briefs. I could have

A KINGDOM OF FLAME AND FURY

come undone just from the slightest glance of her skin. She dropped the boots beside her and looked at me, waiting.

I wanted to defile her, make her scream, but she was too precious to me. I wanted to savor her. But she wanted me, and I could never turn her down. Her eyes were full of lust, and it was the first time she seemed wholly relaxed all night.

I toed the back of my boot and slid it off my foot, repeating the same with the other and kicking them carelessly to the side. I waited for her next move.

A seductive game of chess.

I sensed her nervousness return and wanted to wrap my arms around her. I didn't want her to be fearful of showing herself to me. She was perfect. The mere thought of her made me sweat. I couldn't begin to imagine the frenzy I would be in when I saw her body.

Her fingers trembled as she reached for the bottom hem of her dress, slowly raising it over her body. It pooled at her feet as she dropped it to the ground. All that was left were a pair of silky black panties and a matching bralette, and I couldn't take my eyes off of her body.

She was like a dream.

She was much shorter than me, but the thinness of her legs made them appear longer and connected to lusciously curvy hips that I wanted to wrap my hands around while she rode me. My tongue slowly licked my lips as I moved up to her stomach and across her still-covered breasts, her nipples hardened against the fabric. I wanted to take them between my teeth.

She was exquisite. Fragile. I wanted to worship her.

My mouth watered at the idea of tasting her. I bet she would taste so delicious on my tongue. She kneeled, and I pictured her on her knees before me, claiming her mouth. The fabric started to cling to her skin as she lowered herself into the water, and precum coated my tip. I didn't even have to touch her to come apart.

I couldn't stop staring at her, unmoving. And then I could practically smell her self-doubt return. How could she think I didn't want this as much as her?

I unfastened my jacket and tossed it over my boots, pulling my shirt over my head and discarding it the same way. I stopped breathing as she drank me in. All hers. I would always be just for her. I worked the buckle of my pants, pushing them down and stepping out of them. Her gaze moved to my hard erection pressing against my briefs. Her chest rose and fell quickly.

All for you, Raven. Only for you.

Her hand lifted from under the water and beckoned me with her finger. I gave her a sly grin at how sexy she was and lowered myself into the water. I leaned against the cool stone wall, not making a move to be closer to her. I wanted her permission.

There was still a body's length between us, and she looked at me curiously. I could tell that no one had ever let her make the first move. She was used to men taking her. She was going to have to come to me. It had to be her choice.

I still sensed her doubt, and I leered at her lasciviously.

I want you. Just come here.

She drew in a deep breath, trying to settle her nerves. "So you've been thinking about me," she said.

That was a severe understatement. I'd done nothing but think of her. I crossed my arms over my chest. Not touching her was extremely difficult. I nodded to her question.

She grinned. "Tell me about it."

"Do you want honesty?" My voice was hoarse as I asked her.

She visibly shivered and pulled in her bottom lip. Fuck, I needed her. She took another step toward me. She rewarded me for speaking. I'd read an entire goddamn book aloud for her if she would just come a little closer. "I wondered how you taste. If you scream when you come."

"Did you get off while thinking of me?"

I gave her another nod, clenching my fists as she took another step toward me. She was waiting for me to relent. She was only a handbreadth away. She looked at me from underneath her lashes, and I nearly did.

Say the words, I begged silently. Let me have you.

"Do you want to find out?"

Yes. I uncrossed my arms and found her waist, pulling her to me. She threw her arms around my neck and I lifted her out of the water, her legs circling around my middle. I answered her question with my mouth, crashing it against hers, picking up where we had left off the night before.

My tongue collided with hers, and I moved it slowly, wanting to take my time with her. She was a gift that I didn't want to unwrap just yet. The anticipation was euphoric.

My fingers kneaded roughly into her ass, and she moaned into my mouth, responding by biting into the soft flesh of my bottom lip. I groaned as I yanked back, lust awakening deep within me. She wanted pain. I lunged for her again, cupping one of my hands behind her head as her body balanced on my arm tucked underneath her.

I pushed my tongue greedily into her mouth again, and she tilted her head, allowing me to take as much as I wanted from her. My shaft was stiff against her, and she ground her ass down against it, moving her hips until she could feel the friction against her clit.

Fuck, she was riding me like this. I looked down between our bodies and started to pant while I watched how delicious she looked moving on me. I wanted to come but wasn't even close to finishing with her.

I pushed off the wall and spun us, sitting her on the edge. She pouted until I pressed my thumb against her clit, reveling in how soaked her panties were. I moved my thumb in circles on her, and she threw her head back, pushing harder against my finger, begging for more.

I obliged, pushed aside the fabric, and shoved two fingers into her wetness while working her clit with my thumb. She moaned softly, and I wanted to be the only one able to make that sound come from her. Her lungs were exhaling but not drawing in breaths, and I knew she was about to come when her walls tightened around my fingers.

I growled, removing my fingers. "Don't come for me yet."

She whimpered in my absence.

I grinned smugly at her trembling body. "Miss me?" I was a cocky bastard, but I knew how to make a girl beg.

I pushed down on her chest, lowering her down to her back. Her skin prickled from the cold stone underneath her. I would warm her up quickly. I unraveled my arm around her waist and put my hands on her knees, slowly pulling her legs apart to reveal more of her to me. My fingers slid teasingly along her inner thighs, circling slowly to the waistband of her panties hanging off her hip bones.

She covered her eyes with her arm, frustrated by my lack of touch with her. I slid her panties off her hips and down her thighs, stopping once they hit her knees. Blowing a hot breath on her thighs, she shivered and tried to close her knees from the sensation. I didn't let her, continuing my removal of her panties until they were off and tossing them behind me somewhere in the water. I spread her knees farther apart until I could see all of her and groaned at the sight.

She was the only thing I would ever want again.

"I can see how wet you are, even just illuminated by moonlight."

She bucked her hips.

I chuckled darkly. "Such an impatient queen."

She huffed, irritated at me, and lifted to rest on her elbows with narrowed eyes. I loved her anger. "I've thought of nothing but your tongue since last night. Do something with it," she demanded through gritted teeth.

She had thought about me, even as she slept beside another man. I wanted to dominate her. I wanted to be the only one she thought about for the rest of time.

I slid my hands up her thighs and pressed my fingers into her skin, dipping my nose to run it up her clit. My inhales were greedy as I took in my new favorite scent. My dick was throbbing, wanting to bury itself inside her, but I wanted a taste. "Your smell is intoxicating."

She stared at me, her green eyes appearing black. I grinned at her before I plunged into her core with my tongue. Fuck me; she was the sweetest thing I had ever tasted. My very own kind of fruit, and I would never have enough. Fuck the rum; Raven was officially the best thing I would ever have in my mouth.

Her fingers tangled in my hair as she watched me devour her, my lips sealing around her clit and sucking. She moaned, thrusting her hips against my mouth. I took it hungrily. I released her clit and kept my tongue's rhythm inside her, keeping a quick but steady pace.

"Don't stop," she begged me.

I was never going to stop. If I could spend the rest of my days with her fucking my tongue, it would be a life well lived. I groaned against her flesh, and the vibration from my deep grumble sent her over, her walls tightening around my tongue as she poured onto me. She fell back against the ground as her back arched. I didn't stop yet, wanting more of her taste. I sucked her clit again as she rode her wave, her fingers still pulling at my hair as she cried for me.

Fuck, she came hard. And quick. Her taste was coated across my lips. "So, so sweet," I murmured against her, licking up her thigh to catch any of her release that escaped me.

She rose back up to her elbows, and her mouth fell slack as she stared at my mouth, soaked with her release. She sat up quickly and leaned down to catch my mouth with hers, sucking her taste off of me. I opened for her, letting her tongue tangle with mine, and she moaned at how I was covered in her.

My hands found around her ass again, and I pulled her off the edge, lowering her back into the water with me. She wrapped her legs around my waist as I waded us backward into the warm water. "I'm not done with you yet, queen," I snarled against her mouth. I was going to make her come for me again.

I moved us to the other side of the spring, gliding into the small cave and leaning back against the wall. My hands moved to grip her waist, and I thrust up against her. I was so painfully hard for her. She uncoiled her legs from around my waist and lowered herself into the water, hurriedly finding the waistband of my briefs and shoving them down before she tried to climb me again. My sweet girl. I lifted her high enough to bite at her nipple through the fabric of her bralette.

She clicked her tongue at me. "Naughty."

She had no idea. She pushed it against my mouth again, and I brought a hand up, easily shredding through the fabric, chuckling slightly at her gasp. I opened my mouth, sucking her nipple between my lips, and tugged. She cried out softly from the pain before reaching a hand down between our bodies. I lowered her enough for her fingers to wrap around my shaft, and fuck, I almost came from it.

She aligned my tip with her entrance and rolled her hips, slowly taking me in. She was so tight, and I groaned, unable to stop myself from thrusting into her, wanting to claim her. Mine, mine, I needed her to be only mine. She wiggled her hips, trying to adjust to how swollen I was for her, and balanced herself on the rock behind my head with her hand.

"I don't know if I can take all of you," she said, continuously rolling her hips to take more, inch by inch.

She would because if there was one thing I was certain about in this life, it was that her body was made to be on mine. "You can," I promised her. "You will. You and your perfect little body will take it all."

Her head rolled back as I bucked into her, fully sheathing myself to the hilt. Her eyes were in a daze as they met mine, my thrusts into her slow, torturous. She was like coming home. Our bodies were meant to be writhing together, coming undone. I would always want to replicate this feeling and feel her body trembling on mine, wrought with pleasure.

She was close again as her arms wrapped around my neck, her chest heaving.

"Take it, Raven. Show me what you can do."

My command was all she needed to unleash, grinding her hips roughly against mine, her tits bouncing as she rocked back and forth on my dick. I grunted, returning her thrusts with my own, my eyes moving from her face to watch how her pussy moved against me. "Fuck, Raven. Come with me," I pleaded with her. I couldn't hold back any longer. I wanted my cum dripping from her.

Our hips moved perfectly synchronously, and she whimpered, her legs shaking as I pulsed, filling her with my hot release. That triggered her own, and she came, mixing with mine. She screamed my name as I continued pounding into her, wanting to lengthen her orgasm. I bit down on her collarbone, the pain sending her further over, and another wave of wetness coated my cock. This was the only way I ever wanted to hurt her.

Nothing in my life had ever been this good, this right.

She paused her movements against me, her brain trying to grapple for air. I watched her, my thunderous heart beating wildly in my chest. Her forehead fell against my throat as she tried to catch her breath, my pulse beating against it. I moved one of my hands to her chest and felt for her heart, its pounding matching the rhythm of mine. Everything about us was fated, even the beats of our blood pumping.

I laughed softly, and she raised her beautiful face to look at me. "For the record," I stated, tucking some hair behind her ear, "This is not why I brought you here."

She laughed, giving me a slight shrug. "That's so strange because that's exactly why I came. Multiple times."

I pinched her waist, and she giggled, moving to lift off of me, but I only wrapped my arms tighter around her waist, stopping her. This couldn't already be over. I peppered kisses along her jawline, and goose bumps trailed my lips.

She dipped her chin and pressed her mouth to mine. I cupped the back of her head, gripping her hair in my fingers. I wanted to stay like this. Do it all again. My cock was already hardening again, wanting my claim to seep out of her pores.

"There's something about you," I muttered against her mouth, searching her eyes. "I was under a spell when I saw you last night."

Her fingers played with the hair that clung to my neck as she stared at me, surprised by my sudden admission. I wanted her to recognize myself in her. It was so obvious. Her eyes had blurry recognition as her brain tried to catch up with what her heart was feeling, but I couldn't rush her.

"I should get you back," I whispered.

Her gaze moved to my mouth, seemingly in a trance. And then her eyes shifted to the light beginning to break across the rocks as dawn awakened. She lifted off of me quickly, her head knocking against the low wall of the cave.

I straightened with her, rubbing the spot she just smacked on her head. "In a hurry?"

She shook her head as she waded to the edge, lifting herself out. "No. Well, yes. I mean, no. I wish I didn't have to go back so soon. But you're right, it's almost daylight, and I made this stupid promise to Cade that I would never miss breakfast."

Cade. Mira mentioned Cade before, but only that he was close to the queen — that they were inseparable, long rumored to be more than just queen and adviser. The blond guy. Cade.

"Cade?" I repeated with a bite in my tone. I lifted myself out of the spring and grabbed my pants, pulling them on. My briefs were gone, drowned somewhere in the water with her panties. Jealousy was running rampant through me, my fists clenching and unclenching as I reached for my shirt. "Don't let me keep you from running to Cade."

"It's more complicated than that."

More complicated than sleeping in his arms two nights ago and then fucking me? She looked around for her panties that I knew she wouldn't find. I pulled on my jacket, and she watched me, biting her lip. I was pissed, and she knew it.

She pulled her dress over her head, covering her perfect body that was just on mine. I stepped into my boots and tightened their laces while she slid hers on. I took a step toward her, pulling the diadem from my pocket and extending it to her. She took it hesitantly and fastened it to her moistened hair. "I still want to see you today, though. Give you the tour I promised."

Of course, I wanted to see her again, but I also wanted to murder her boyfriend, and I had to decide which was more important. She was giving me a pleading look, and I sighed softly. "I'll find you this afternoon." I didn't want to disappoint her. I held out my hand, and she grabbed it, threading our fingers together as we began our walk back to the castle. Why did I have to share her? She fit perfectly every time we touched.

We were quiet for a long time, my envy refusing to settle. She looked nervous, probably doubting that I had forgiven her. I wasn't upset with her. I was extremely jealous. I didn't understand the situation between her and Cade. He wanted her, and she was desperate to get back to him. Did she want him, too? The thought made me sick. If Mira knew they were close, what would sending me here accomplish? Unless she was confident I could steal her away.

I needed to figure out why Mira desperately wanted her in Reales, but John refused to tell me anything. I needed to find time to search her memories, and see if there was anything there that could indicate what their connection was.

I cleared my throat. "The Black Forest does seem to have a certain air around it."

She perked up at my remark and looked around while nodding in agreement. "It's my favorite at night, but it's beautiful during the day, too."

I turned my head to look at her with a wicked grin over my shoulder. "It's my favorite at night, too." I was satisfied by the blush that reddened her cheeks.

She squeezed my hand in response.

"He looks unhappy," I grumbled, jerking my chin toward Cade pacing outside the gate. And here we were, performing the walk of shame from the forest's depths. I sensed nothing but anger coming from him and then jealousy as he looked at us, his eyes narrowed on me. She tried to pull her hand from mine, but I didn't let her, tightening my grip.

"Ah," I heard him say as his eyes rolled. What a prick.

"Cade..." she began to say as we stopped before him.

"She was safe," I spoke up.

They both stared at me in surprise.

"I don't fucking know you, man," Cade snapped.

He would get to know me real fucking quick.

She finally pulled her hand from mine and took a step toward Cade. My body went rigid.

"Can we talk about this inside? There's... people." She nodded toward the guards at the gate and villagers walking past.

He didn't respond and turned, stalking back off into the castle. She took a half-step to follow him but stopped and turned to me. She gave me an apologetic grin.

Don't do it, Raven. Don't apologize for him.

"I'm sorry about him. He's really protective, and we have some things going on that's made him more tense than usual."

That wasn't protectiveness. That was insecurity.

I didn't say anything and wrapped my arms around her waist, bending to softly press my lips to hers. Her body stiffened, and I sensed her fear. Fear of what? Being seen with me? I pulled back just enough to lock eyes with her and ignored her tension, leaning in again. I pushed my tongue through her lips until it collided with hers.

She sighed softly, her body relaxing into mine as she opened her mouth farther for me to take her, which I did. The world around us quieted again like everything moved in slow motion. Matching heartbeats again pounded in our connected chests. So right. It was all so right.

She pulled back suddenly, our embrace making her chest rise and fall quickly. I understood her confusion and nodded as if we shared a secret. I pressed my lips to her forehead and straightened, towering over her again.

"I'll see you this afternoon," I promised her, releasing her from my grasp and walking away. I felt her eyes on my back and grinned.

CHAPTER SIX

Raven

I watched him walk away, my fogged mind clearing, but my body remained warm from the heat of him pressed against me. I missed him, and I just had him. I didn't even know him. We were supposed to be just friends, but seeing him last night broke my resolution. "The fuck is happening to me," I groaned aloud before turning on my heel to walk into the castle.

The long walk to Cade's chambers was performed in hesitancy, even more so as I knocked on his door. I was exhausted. I hadn't slept in over a day. My energy was drained, and I absolutely did not want to face him yet. I leaned my forehead against the door as my knocking ceased.

When he finally opened, I stumbled, falling into him. He caught me by the elbow, narrowing his eyes as I met his gaze.

"Cade," I tried to begin, but he released me and walked away. I followed, but my irritation at him already rebuilding. "You can't keep walking away from me. I am still your queen, you ass."

He scoffed and laughed condescendingly. "You are not acting like *my* queen."

I was taken aback by his remark and crossed my arms over my chest. "Excuse me?"

"Disappearing into the night was fine when we knew you were safe, Raven, but you don't have that luxury anymore."

"I can do as I damn well please, Cade. It's my goddamn kingdom." And I was safe. Zeke kept me safe.

"For now," he retorted.

I glared. "What the fuck is that supposed to mean?"

"It means that if you don't stop letting your guard down around strangers, you will regret it."

"If this is about Zeke…" I held up my hand to stop him from continuing.

He did anyway. "We know nothing about him. He just shows up from Reales with no fucking warning, no letter from their queen to say he's coming. There's not even a record of him having a ship here."

I threw my arms up. "He showed me his ship. It's off a dock in the Black Forest."

He remained quiet, waiting for me to continue.

"I didn't know about it, but it's there next to a spring. He said he took a different route to get here, and that's how he found it."

Still nothing.

"I can take you there if you don't believe me." Though I didn't want to. I didn't want to take him somewhere I had just fucked someone else. My handprints were probably still embedded in steam on the rocks. I waited for a response, feeling like I was standing in a room with a stranger. "Cade, please."

He looked at me then, desperation clouding his eyes. "I still don't think you should get close to him."

"You sound jealous," I replied quietly.

He turned his back to me and walked to the window, staring at our village below. Tears filled my eyes, knowing that this moment was changing something in our friendship we had spent so many years protecting. He was jealous, and it wasn't something he had ever shown before. I had felt it for a while, slowly, but the changes were becoming more prominent day by day.

The older we became, the more the lines blurred around our friendship. Our touches were more flirty. We were noticing one another's bodies. He was staring at me more often. I knew that with him turning thirty-three soon, he was outgrowing the phase of his life where he could just fuck around. It seemed like a part of him needed more from someone. Sometimes I wondered if he wanted that someone to be me with how he looked at me.

But that couldn't be true. He had known me since I was a girl. He'd had seven years to say something if he wanted something more.

I couldn't stay here, and he didn't chase me when I walked out without another word. I wasn't sure if I wanted him to.

I waited until I was in my bedroom with the door closed, waited until I felt completely alone, and then I screamed.

Out of frustration, confusion.

I pulled my dress off and climbed into my sheets, covering my body with the quilt until even my head was covered — until I felt nothing but hot air surrounding me. I would feel better after I slept, even if it was just for a little bit.

Rolling to my side, I reached above my head and grabbed a pillow, bringing it down to cradle between my legs.

I suddenly craved Zeke.

He was my last thought before my eyes fluttered shut.

———————

I dreamed of being in a forest, but it wasn't my own. This one seemed to have fewer trees, allowing me to clearly see the water on the outskirts of whatever land I was on. This wasn't my island. I smelled metal, heavy air sticking to my body.

Crunchy leaves sounded behind me, and I whirled, face to face with a beautiful black horse. The brown of his eyes appeared golden, and his mane was long, silky.

It took a step toward me, and I stepped back. But then, it kneeled to me. I reached out and brushed my hand over its forehead. It neighed softly in response. "I know you," I whispered. When my gaze slowly rose to the tree line, I saw him standing there. Watching me.

Zeke.

———————

My eyes snapped open, and I felt around, scrunching the sheets between my fingers. Whatever I just experienced felt so real. But as I tried to recall it, images broke and scattered.

Grumbling, I buried my face into the pillow next to me. My lack of sleep over the last two days gave me a constant headache. I was about to try again when I heard a knock on the door. I threw my blankets off quickly, telling whoever was out there to give me a moment while I grabbed my dress and pulled it on, smoothing it over my body as I walked to the door.

Pulling it open, I was surprised to see Luisa standing on the other side. It wasn't often that anyone from my court, besides Cade, visited me directly. "Luisa, come in."

I pulled the door open wider and stepped to the side so she could walk through. She gave me a small curtsy and grabbed the door from my grasp, shutting it. "I have news," she muttered and nodded toward my office.

My eyes widened at the urgency in her voice, and I led her into the office I rarely used. Most of my business meetings took place in the dining room over breakfast or in Cade's office. It was only a little embarrassing that dust was piled on my desk. I quickly moved to it and wiped it off with my sleeve.

"I worry about John's allegiance," she said.

I wiped my dusty sleeve off with my hand. "What have you heard?"

"Not what I've heard, my queen. What I saw."

I blew out a breath. "And what did you see?"

"I left the palace to go into the village this morning to see a friend and pick up some fabrics that she had brought in from Perosan. I saw John standing behind a row of shops and talking quietly with someone wearing a hood. I couldn't tell who it was, and they weren't speaking loudly enough to pick up on anything, but he saw me watching him, and they split apart. I didn't want to follow either one of them alone."

"No, of course. I wouldn't have wanted you to. I appreciate you coming to me with this. Have you told anyone else?"

"No, m'lady. I came directly to you."

I nodded. I would need to tell Cade and decide together what to do about John. I had the sinking suspicion at our meeting yesterday that something was off with him, but I did not want to be correct.

"I'll leave you alone to prepare for the evening banquet."

"Banquet?" Confusion set in. "What banquet?"

"The annual Feast Day banquet; the one we host every year for the village after the Festival of Dreams."

Right. I felt sheepish for forgetting. The festival had only been three days ago, and I had been quite busy since then. My cheeks burned from embarrassment. "Of course. Excuse my forgetful mind."

Luisa extended her hand, wiggling her fingers. I gave her a small smile and placed my own in hers. "I've served a king, and I've served you. I've been honored to be part of both."

I squeezed her hand in gratitude and told her goodbye, watching her depart as I sunk onto my desk. The tour of my palace with Zeke would have to be delayed another day. I needed to find him, apologize, and then rush back to get dressed for the feast. But first, informing Cade about what Luisa shared with me seemed more pressing.

After our awkward conversation hours prior, I drew in a deep breath and braced myself to face Cade again. I didn't have long to prepare because he was standing there as I opened my door to leave. The silence drew out between us for a moment as we stared at each other, neither of us wanting to say the first word.

I gave in. "Luisa was just here." I took a step back and waved him inside, letting the door fall shut behind him.

He followed me into my sitting room and sat in one of my chairs, looking uncomfortable. I felt the same.

"She had a strange encounter with John today in the village. He was speaking to some hooded figure. Luisa didn't know who it could be and never saw their face. They saw her and parted. She didn't want to follow them alone."

His forehead creased as he took in the information, his body tense. He stayed silent.

"Could he be a part of all of this? If he knows of my magic, he could be the one telling people. Our traitor could be right here, under our roof."

He sighed and raised his hand to rub the crease on his forehead. "We have two choices: watch him and where he goes, or release him from his position on the court and run the risk of him sharing our — I mean your — secret."

The phrase change wasn't lost on me, but I ignored it. "Risk versus reward. Though I don't see a reward either way."

"If he stays or goes, we risk him exposing you either way. I'll stay close to him tonight and see who he converses with. If I notice anything suspicious, I'll tell you, and we'll go from there. We can talk about it again tomorrow."

I nodded and opened my mouth to say more, but he stood abruptly and bowed his head toward me, going to the door. All I did was watch him go, but before he shut the door, I remembered that he had come to see me. "Cade, wait."

He held his hand on the door before it closed but didn't reopen it to look at me.

"Why did you come here?"

A beat of silence. "It doesn't matter," he replied, closing the door.

I groaned at his response, at our tension. Of course, it mattered. I needed to follow him and try to work this out between the two of us, demanding that some normalcy remain. Living like this daily, never resolving anything, would be hell.

I left my room, resolved to find him again, and wandered into the courtyard, looking around to see if he was there. I had already checked his room, and he wasn't there. I was about to go back inside when I felt a different presence approach from behind me.

Without looking, I knew who it was. Goose bumps pimpled up on my arms, despite the heat flowing through my veins.

"There you are."

Zeke's voice was like honey in my ears. My head rolled to the side as his arms encased me from behind, pulling me back flush against his chest. I tried to turn my head to look at him but couldn't entirely turn while pressed to him, so I leaned my cheek against his chest. Lifting my chin up, I smiled at him, my hands lifting to rub against his arms around me.

"Here I am," I uttered back. I hated how breathy I sounded. Something about him threw me off-guard, and I never had time to fully form a thought before he put me in another daze.

"I dreamed of you," I whispered and immediately regretted it, my cheeks flushing. Fuck, I was going to scare him off.

His eyebrow cocked, a tiny grin tugging upward. "I want to take you somewhere." His lips brushed against my ear.

My heart fluttered at his breath against my skin. "Somewhere where?"

"Somewhere else I found."

"You're quite the huntsman."

A dark laugh. "I've already hunted for what I want. And devoured it."

My entire body heated at his words, the memory of his tongue lapping me up springing to the forefront of my mind.

"Come with me." His phrasing sounded like a question, but it was a demand.

And I wanted to, so much so that it made me bonkers. I turned in his arms, still tightly within his grasp, and gazed at him. "I actually came to deliver bad news. I have to delay our tour until tomorrow. I was reminded that we have a banquet tonight for the village."

Instead of answering, he leaned down to me again and nipped at my earlobe. "Come with me," he demanded again, his voice a low growl.

My body responded to his attention, my nipples hardening against my dress. The same dress I was in when we departed from one another earlier.

"I still smell me on you." He tightened his hold on me, my breasts pushing into his chest. He nipped at my earlobe again, taking it in his mouth and sucking.

"I've been busy." I giggled at his nibble and felt his smile against my skin. "I have to get ready for the banquet. And I need to find Cade."

His body stiffened against mine.

Fuck, I did it again. Tried to leave him for Cade. The following words fell out of my mouth in a rush. "I want you to come to the banquet tonight, though. You can have me after."

He pulled back from my ear to look into my eyes. I itched for him. I felt his heartbeat against my chest, slow and steady.

"I want to have you now." This man oozed brassy confidence. His mischievous grin returned at the blush on my cheeks. "But, I understand. You have an entire kingdom waiting to see you. I'm envious of all the eyes that will be on you."

I was learning that he was quite possessive, and we had only just met. "Then I will make sure to wear something incredibly devastating." I lifted on the tips of my toes to kiss the corner of his mouth, the tension in his body releasing at my touch. He wanted me as much as I wanted him. "I still smell me on you, too." My tongue ran over his bottom lip, and I felt him harden against my stomach.

His snarl was raspy. "You're the one teasing now."

"Find me tonight," I whispered against his mouth and shook myself out of his grip, not sparing another glance as I left him standing there, suddenly forgetting all about Cade.

———

Devastating, I was. I admired my outfit in the mirror and turned sideways to study my profile, my long hair cascading down my back. My dress was a floor-length gown made of deep blue velvet that molded to my body. A slit cut up my thigh and showed off my leg any time I swayed. The bodice crisscrossed over my chest and formed a deep-V that was met with a matching velvet belt tied into a bow on my hip.

The sleeves were short, and my wrists were adorned with delicate gold bracelets. I chose a white-gold diadem for this evening, admiring its simplicity. My shoe choice was a pair of silver, strappy heels that would give me more of a height advantage against the tower Zeke chose to be.

Typically, I would wait for Cade to pick me up, and we would walk to the banquet together, but since our friendship was currently fucked up, I knew I didn't have to wait for him.

Checking myself in my floor-length mirror, I smiled widely, giddy about seeing Zeke again. He had probably attended banquets and events at his kingdom, but there was nothing I was more proud of than my own people — even if maybe some of them wanted me gone. I pushed that thought to the back of my mind. Since my night at the Festival of Dreams had ended so upsettingly, I was determined to not let this one end the same.

I stood at the entrance to one of the ballrooms, trying to contain my mixture of excitement and anxiety. It was making me jittery. When two guards pulled the doors back, I put on my biggest smile and glided into the room. Gasps and murmurs from guests greeted me as they smiled and curtsied to me.

I beamed at them, meeting the eyes of ones brave enough to look at me as I passed by. Traditions were loosely followed in my kingdom, but I still commanded respect and was always quick to give it back. Even though I felt the furthest thing from it on a daily basis, I was still royalty.

My gaze fell to Zeke, and I gasped quietly at the sight of him.

He was in a bow at the back of the room. He smiled at me, his eyes moving down my body and back up to meet mine. I was held captive by his stare. As he straightened, I felt a tug somewhere deep in my bones. I placed my palm against my stomach, the air seeming to lessen around me. He watched me intently, his eyes narrowing — but from curiosity. He seemed to understand what I was experiencing.

Suddenly, I heard a ghost of a whisper from the recesses of my mind. It sounded like his voice.

Breathe.

It was only one word, but it nearly took me down. The sounds of the room became too loud like I had been standing all alone with him until that word. Until I took a breath. The tug disappeared as I averted my eyes from his. Only seconds had passed, but it seemed like time had stood still.

Gods almighty, what was happening to me?

I suddenly turned on the heel of my shoe and waved my hands until the voices surrounding me died down and all eyes returned to me. I fidgeted at the attention.

"Thank you all so much for being here and letting our palace serve you. It is an honor to be your queen and a responsibility I do not take lightly." I looked around the room, meeting the eyes of my people as I spoke. "Please enjoy this evening, and I hope some of you will be brave enough to ask me to dance."

Laughs from the crowd warmed me. I motioned for the musicians in the room to begin playing.

The room looked beautiful. I turned in a slow circle in adoration at the hard work my servants put into setting this banquet up. Tables lined the wall, full of meats, cheeses and fruits. The same paper confetti from the Festival of Dreams was scattered along the tablecloths and floor. Larger cutouts of moons and stars hung from the windows and ceiling of the grand room. I looked up, spinning around to take all of them in.

Arthur approached me first, snapping me out of my daze. He bowed, and I dipped my chin in a nod, my smile radiating. "May I have this dance, *Raven?*"

I nodded enthusiastically. "It'd be my honor."

He gently placed a hand on my waist and grabbed one of my hands, straightening our arms. I responded by putting my hand on his shoulder and motioning with my head for him to take the lead. I had learned a great deal about my kingdom, but some of the dances still hadn't been memorized.

Arthur, despite his age, moved quickly, and I giggled as he twirled me around the room. "I'm glad to see he kept his word and brought you back in one piece," he shouted over the song.

I laughed, squeezing his shoulder. "Did you stock up on rum? I think he may have a problem."

He laughed in his deep rumbly one that made everything seem lighter, happier. Arthur had seen me enter his pub often at night, always donning a different shift, never two in a row. I couldn't be sure, but now that rumors were circulating about me, he may be putting together that it was me the entire time. But, I trusted him to keep my secret. The thought of having a friend of my own outside of the castle made me hopeful that maybe others would accept me, too.

Another man soon interrupted us, asking if he could cut in and steal me away. Arthur's eyes rolled playfully as he handed me off. I parted from Arthur with a quick curtsy of gratitude and linked with the next man, who was younger.

"You look radiant tonight, Queen Raven."

I smiled at the compliment and asked his name.

"My name is Theodore, m'lady. I'm one of the loaders down at the docks."

"Thank you for your service, Theodore. I am sure that is no easy job."

"Happy to do it. I'm the third generation of men to do it in my family. And I'm sure my son after me will, too."

"How old is your son?"

"Teddy is seven. I have a girl, too. Eva. She's five."

I remembered meeting Eva at the festival and letting her adorn my hair with the flowers she made. "I know your little girl. She told me I looked like a butterfly." I smiled at the memory and glanced around, looking for Theodore's wife. "Is your wife here tonight? I'd love to see her again."

"She's not, m'lady. She's home with Eva and her brother. Eva has talked nonstop about the butterfly from the festival."

Shit. I had given myself away.

Theodore gave me a small grin. "It's true then. I hear things at the docks. Things I don't always believe. But I have to tell ya, the rumor of you having some sort of magic didn't seem far-fetched. She said her butterfly had eyes of gold. Yours are green."

"I…" I began, but I wasn't sure what to say. I wouldn't lie.

"Your secret is safe with me. I won't say anything, but someone is telling everyone about it. I don't know their reason, m'lady, but you would be surprised how many folks are on your side, even with the rumors. I've been here my entire life and have never seen so many happy with being here. So many are moving here so quickly that we've had to take on more workers at the dock. That's a testament to you, Queen Raven."

Hot tears pushed at my eyelids. "Thank you."

Theodore stopped our dance when the song ended and bowed to me, taking my hand and kissing it lightly as a sign of respect. When he straightened, he looked directly into my eyes and leaned forward slightly. "But, watch yourself. Some still believe that magic can't be used for anything other than bad." He spoke quietly to me as if he didn't want anyone to hear him with the sudden lack of song around us.

My mouth went dry. I didn't watch him walk away before I turned to find Cade, stopping short when I saw him deeply immersed in conversation with the same stunning blonde from the other night. He threw his head back in a laugh, and envy pooled in my gut. He hadn't laughed like that with me in days.

He looked good, too, in a black jacket and pants, his chest peeking out under his white shirt that was unbuttoned at the top. He must have felt my eyes on him because he was suddenly staring at me. I felt my ears heat from being caught staring at him. Again.

He took a half-step toward me but stopped abruptly, his face hardening. His change of demeanor baffled me, but then I knew why. I could feel him. Zeke came up behind me and wrapped his arms around my waist. My gaze remained on Cade's, pleading with him silently to stay with me. But he didn't and fixed his attention on the blonde again. I needed to talk to him, and his constant rejection annoyed me.

"You kept your promise," Zeke whispered against my ear.

I ignored the sudden drop in my stomach from Cade's snub and spun to face Zeke, putting the palms of my hands against his chest. "And which promise was that?"

He leaned down to me, which wasn't as far as he usually needed with my added height for the evening. "You look *incredibly* devastating."

My skin tightened at his compliment. This gorgeous man believed I was beautiful. I took a small step back and looked him up and down, exhaling softly. Like Cade, he was also in a black jacket and pants, but his shirt was black and matched his hair perfectly. A tailored suit. His top two buttons were undone, and I raised my hand to touch his exposed skin, tracing his collarbone with my fingertips. "Don't let anyone but me touch you tonight."

The corners of his mouth turned upward into a smirk, and he palmed the small of my back, spreading his fingers. "And I'm just supposed to watch men dance with you all night?" He brushed his lips against mine. "Touch you where I have?"

I nodded, still moving my fingertips across every inch of his exposed skin. "I want your eyes on me all night. I want to feel your jealousy." Something about him made me want to push boundaries. I didn't want his attention anywhere else but on me.

I could be possessive, too.

"Do I at least get to dance with you?" he asked, seemingly accepting my rules.

I moved my arms to wrap around his neck and nodded, swishing my hips in his arms to get him to move. His small grin turned into a full-blown smile as he tightened his arms around my waist and began to spin us to the fast-paced song.

I threw my head back in a laugh when he dipped me down, kicking my foot out, the slit from my dress exposing my thigh. He noticed and grazed his hand across the inside of it, goose bumps trailing in his wake.

He raised me until I stood on both feet again, moving his hands to my waist. "I love hearing you laugh," he called out.

I smiled and tugged at some of the hair on the back of his neck. "I would love to hear it from you more. You're so serious. Unless there's rum involved."

A shadow seemed to settle on him.

My smile faltered a little, sensing his mind had gone somewhere else. I gently tugged his hair again. "Come back to me."

He tipped his head at that, his lips parting slightly in surprise. "What do you mean?"

I gave him a slight shrug. "I can tell when your mind goes somewhere else. I can feel your absence."

He had no response. He stared at me for a moment before leaning forward to rest his forehead against mine.

It felt intimate. It felt right.

One of my hands moved from his neck to rest lightly against his cheek, the tip of my nose rubbing against his. "Let your guard down a little. I promise I won't bite."

At that, he laughed softly. The sound made me feel alive like I'd heard it before. "But what if I want you to bite?"

I mock-gasped, clicking my tongue. "Excuse me, sir, is that how you talk to a queen?"

He dropped his hands around my waist and fell to one knee, propping his other up and dipping his chin to me in a dramatic bow. "I apologize, Your Majesty. What can I do to earn your forgiveness?"

I placed my hands on my hips and walked in a circle around him, moving one hand to my chin like I was deep in thought. I was smiling, though, enjoying his playfulness. "I don't know. Are you good at anything?"

He stood at my question and yanked me to him by my wrist, holding my hand against his chest. "I think you already know the answer to that." He moved his mouth to my ear and whispered, "Would you like a reminder?" And nipped at my earlobe again.

Warmth spread across me, lighting up everything inside me until I felt sweat bead along my temple. He awakened something so deep inside of me that trying to control it was like trying to hold my breath underwater. It hurt my chest. "Yes," I murmured.

He put his hands on either side of my neck and tilted my head ever so slightly, pressing his mouth gently to mine. I didn't care that we were surrounded by people. It was like every nerve in my body was firing at once, and I didn't want it to end.

And then I felt the presence of someone beside us. My body went rigid at the voice saying my name. Zeke noticed as he broke our kiss, holding me tighter. He stared into my eyes, even as John spoke. "A dance, Your Majesty?"

Slowly, Zeke turned his attention to John, and the look between them piqued my interest. Zeke dropped my hand and stepped back, bending into a small bow as permission. I gave Zeke a small smile, and he winked at me before walking to one of the tables covered in food.

I released an annoyed breath and took John's extended hands. He led me into the pack of dancers, but I felt hesitant to follow him. He knew who I was and what I could do. Surely he wouldn't be bold enough to try anything in front of most of our village.

"You look lovely tonight. Though, I am sure I am not the only one to tell you that," he said, a curt smile plastered on his face.

I studied him for a moment. He was bald, and the wrinkles on his forehead seemed to start at his eyebrows and stretch across his skull. He was tall, though, taller than me. But most everyone was. To my knowledge, he had never been married or had any children. Kind of reclusive. Much like the king he served for so many years. And now me. He obviously had a type.

"Thank you, John. The real beauty is how well our servants decorated this room tonight." I wanted to keep the conversation light.

"What do you think of our traveler?"

"Zeke? I think he's excellent company." I tried to keep my face from flushing at the thought of him. Tried and failed.

"Doesn't say much. Do we really know anything about him?"

I glanced around the room at his question, spotting Zeke near a table. He was watching us, popping grapes into his mouth. Next to him, a woman gawked. My eyes narrowed.

A grin spread across his mouth, and he said something to the woman without even looking at her. She looked at me before dropping her eyes to the floor as she stepped away from Zeke. I couldn't help but smile as his gaze never left me. I didn't know what he said, but he played by my rules.

I turned my focus back to John. "Do we need to? He's from Reales. Do we know everything about everyone in other kingdoms?"

"Fair question, Your Majesty. But just the timing of it, is all."

I didn't say anything, imploring him to continue.

"With the news of someone leaking your secret, we should be cautious about all of our visitors."

My eyes rolled at the not-so-subtle accusation. "You're starting to sound like Cade."

"I am just looking out for my queen like I promised."

"A promise you'll keep. Right, John?"

As the song ended, John dropped his arms and bowed to me, his stare never wavering from mine. "Of course, Queen Raven." And then he was gone, and I had a hard time believing that.

I spent the next few songs dancing with more guests, making my rounds, and talking to as many as possible. I asked questions about their families and what they did in the village. I knew a good lot of them, always making it a priority to go into the village every month to meet anyone who had moved in from other countries. I wanted everyone to always feel welcome and at home in Seolia, especially when they were in my palace.

I felt a light touch on my hand and turned my head to see who it was. My heart dropped at the sight of Cade.

He was timid as he asked, "Dance with me?"

I took his hand and followed him back to the dance floor. My feet hurt from the standing and twirling I had subjected myself to tonight. Instead of the traditional stance I took with others, I coiled my arms around his neck and rested my head on his shoulder. We may have been standing too close for a queen and an adviser, but I didn't care. I had missed him and wanted to savor the feel of his body against mine, comforted by his presence.

"You look beautiful," he whispered against my temple.

Tears formed behind my eyelids. I couldn't speak. Being at odds with him physically hurt me. "Where's the pretty blonde?" was all I cared to ask, the earlier feeling of envy bubbling up again in my stomach.

I felt his grin against my skin, and it irritated me. What I felt wasn't at all amusing. It was downright perplexing, and it made me feel off-balance. He must have felt my body tense because he lowered his head in an attempt to get me to look at him, but I didn't. He would have seen my tears welling up.

His voice was soft as he answered, "I don't know. Somewhere, I guess."

"I won't interrupt you tonight."

"I'm not going to fuck her, Raven."

"I don't care what you do." I was being immature and lying.

"Yeah, I can tell." Sarcasm dripped from his voice.

"Do you think this is easy for me, Cade? I don't know what's going on."

"Then tell me about it."

"I can't because I don't know. All I know is that you're being weird around me, like I'm made of glass. And I'm not. You know I'm not."

"I know you're not. But I am trying to protect you. And myself."

I lifted my head. "Protect yourself from what? Me?"

He didn't say anything but held my gaze. The heavy air returned to encase us.

"Cade, I'd never hurt you. How could you think that?"

He nodded as he ran his tongue along his lips contemplatively. "That's not what I meant."

I shut my eyes and leaned my forehead against his shoulder, quivering in his hold even though I wasn't cold. Our arguments had never gone this far. This tension was something new, something unfamiliar. I turned my head against his chest just enough to look up at his face, my eyes rolling over his jawline and high cheekbones. The way his lashes curled up.

His chin dipped down to meet my eyes, and then he glanced at my mouth. For a second, I wondered if he was going to kiss me, and right as I was about to lean away, movement caught in the corner of my eye. I turned my head to see Zeke moving closer, his eyes burning into us.

Cade followed my gaze and his body went taut, tightening his hold on me. It was challenging to breathe. If there were any inches left between us before, there definitely weren't anymore.

"Cade," I whispered with some difficulty.

His eyes remained on Zeke, mine leaving to look back at Cade.

"Cade, look at me." At that, he did, and I gave him a small smile. "Meet me tomorrow, okay? We can talk then."

His face fell as he realized he would have to let me go. "Raven," he pleaded, shaking his head.

"Cade, please. I can't do this. Not tonight."

Zeke was slowly pacing toward us. I could see the internal struggle behind Cade's eyes.

"Cade, please." Tears pooled in my eyes again.

He kissed my forehead, breaking it against my skin just enough to whisper, "I'll be seeing you." And then he released me and backed away, breaking my gaze only to turn and leave me standing alone.

That felt more like a goodbye. I watched him go and wanted to chase after him. I reached up and touched where he had kissed my forehead, my eyes closing. When I moved to take a step toward the door to follow him, I was caught by fingers that wrapped around my wrist.

Zeke pulled on my arm and spun me back to him, my chest pushing against his as he caught me. My forehead immediately fell against his chest. I was utterly spent from the roller coaster of emotions I had just gone through in the span of a few hours. Again.

"Come back to me," he whispered, repeating my earlier plea. "I can only be jealous for so long, Raven."

My head lifted to peer up at him. "You don't even know me."

He pressed his lips gently against mine. "I've had to watch men touch you all night, make you laugh, while I've been clamoring for your attention all day." Another soft kiss. "And I do know you, Raven."

I was entranced as I listened to him, our bodies slowly swaying to the music. It did feel like we had known one another for longer than a few days. And he wanted to be selfish with me, and since he would only be here for a short time, I could let him be. I wanted him to be. "What did you say to her?"

A hesitant smile. "That I belonged to you."

That was all I needed to hear. "Take me somewhere."

He didn't respond but broke our bodies apart and kept his fingers wrapped around my wrist as he led us out of the ballroom that was still full of people dancing and laughing.

I threw it one last glance before the doors closed behind us, feeling a small ounce of joy that despite everything I was going through, my subjects were full of glee.

CHAPTER SEVEN

Raven

Maybe it was the lack of sleep, or how I didn't eat anything during the banquet, or perhaps I had let my guard down with Zeke, but I wasn't paying much attention to where he was taking me. I did know that my feet were killing me.

I tugged on his hand to stop, allowing me to kick off my shoes. I bent over to pick them up, but he scooped me up quickly and cradled me in his arms.

I giggled as I rested my head against his chest. "Another thing you're good at."

He smiled but didn't say anything as he walked us out of the castle and onto the palace grounds.

I looked up once we were past the gate. "Did you find another hidden spring somewhere?"

His flirtatious grin garnered one from me in response. He set me down on my feet and pointed off into the distance toward the village. "I found an abandoned barn and wanted to explore it. Though, it may be more difficult without any light."

The only abandoned barn I knew about was the one that housed the underground tunnel that led me in and out of the palace undetected. "How do you know it's abandoned?"

"I looked through a crack in the wood and assumed it was. No people, no animals."

This was risky. And I wasn't sure I had the energy to test more boundaries tonight. "It may be locked."

"It wasn't today."

That meant Cade hadn't checked it after I returned from the festival that night. Not that I could blame him. A lot happened that night, and we were a bit busy. That also meant that if there wasn't a lock, there wasn't a reason for me to argue about exploring it. I didn't want him growing suspicious. There wasn't much to explore. It was small and only had a loft other than my hidden door, which was hard to find if you weren't looking for it.

"Lead the way."

He would grow bored quickly. Nothing sounded better than a hot bath, and I could easily talk him into joining me.

He took my hand and laced our fingers, staying at my side as we meandered through the snow toward the barn. I couldn't help but smile at the intimate gesture, looking down at our locked fingers. I had to keep reminding myself that I barely knew him. John's accusation of Zeke's reason for being here was still fresh, though I paid it little mind. His king had just died, and I wasn't about to accuse him of being here for any other reason.

Then, I noticed my feet. I realized that we were walking in the snow, and I was barefoot. That would bother anyone else, but I remained warm all the time because of Blaze. Being in the cold didn't bother me, but he didn't know that.

I bounced on my toes, attempting to appear cold. "I guess I should have kept my shoes on."

He looked down at my feet and winced. "Oh, fuck, Raven. I'm sorry. I forgot." He stopped and dropped my hand, turning his back to me and crouching down. "Here, climb up."

I stared at him. "Excuse me?"

He turned to face me. "You've never done this?"

I lifted an eyebrow. "Done what?"

"Just... here." He turned and crouched again. "Jump on my back."

When I didn't make a move and remained standing in place, he gave me a sideways glance. "Put your hands on my shoulders and hop up. I'll do the rest."

I hesitated again, but he urged me again with his chin. I relented and leaned on the tips of my toes, reaching for his shoulders. Even with him in a crouch, I still felt minuscule next to him. I wrapped the tips of my fingers around his shoulders and bent my knees just enough to hop on his back, my chest lying level against him.

He wrapped his hands around my legs and lifted them up until they were wrapped around his middle. My velvet dress fit snug around my thighs, my arms encircling his shoulders. I rested my cheek against his head, feeling like I had grown two feet taller. "So... this is what it feels like to be you."

He laughed, his head rolling back.

My whole body shook, making me erupt into giggles. "Do you often transport people like this?"

He nodded against my head, his cheek pulling up in a smile. "All the time."

"We'll add it to your growing list of talents."

"That's turning out to be quite the list. Ever ridden a horse?"

"Don't," I warned, but he didn't listen and took off into a trot, his fingers gripping tightly on my thighs. I tightened my arms around his shoulders and squealed, closing my eyes as the cold air hit my face. "Zeke!" I shrieked, trying to blow the hair out of my face.

He laughed again, slowing his pace back to a steady walk. "Oh wait, that's right. You already know what it's like to ride me."

I guffawed at that and slapped his shoulder. "I don't remember it being quite that bumpy."

His laugh deepened, doubling over. I fell forward with him, squealing in his ear. He straightened back up, apologizing in between trying to catch his breath. Hearing him laugh released some of the tightness in my body that I had been holding. I was a little light-headed with glee.

When his breathing calmed, he squeezed my legs and released them, helping guide me slowly to the ground. I let go of him and lowered to the ground, taking one of his hands between mine, letting him lead me to the barn.

Upon approach, I saw that he was right. The lock was missing, which meant we could easily wander in. Zeke pulled at the handle on the door, and the traitorous thing opened right up.

I followed him in. "I'll look for something to light," he said, leaving me to stand in the dark.

He wasn't going to find anything. We kept it dark here on purpose. When his footsteps were far away, I silently bent down and felt for pieces of hay left over from the bales we removed. I gathered a small bunch and beckoned fire to my fingertips, the hay coming to life in my hand.

"I found a match on the ground," I lied when his head snapped toward the sudden burst of light.

He made his way to me and grinned. "Remind me to take you on all of my adventures." He untucked his shirt from his pants and tore a strip of it from the bottom.

My eyes widened in sheer awe of his ability to rip through fabric so easily. My flimsy bralette was one thing, but his shirt was thick material.

He grabbed the wad of hay from my hand and wrapped the strip of fabric around the bottom. "Tie it," he demanded.

I took the two ends and knotted them around the hay.

"This will burn out quickly, but it doesn't look like we'll need it. This is much smaller than I thought it'd be." He motioned around the barn while holding our makeshift light up.

No shit. I knew this already, but I nodded in agreement. "Not much to it."

"Not much, except that."

I followed his eyes up to the loft and exhaled. I had hoped he would overlook that. "Lift me up." There was nothing up there, either. Cade and I used to hide up there sometimes when we were younger. The dark space was the perfect place to practice lighting my palms.

Zeke put the light on the ground before he folded his hands over my waist. I braced myself as he bent his knees and hoisted me up. I grabbed the edge of the landing. "Higher. I'm not a giant like you."

He lowered his hands from my waist to cup my ass and gave me a big shove. "Is that enough, smart-ass?"

I snorted and moved my elbows farther on the loft, using it to anchor myself. "This isn't easy to do in a dress, you know." Swinging my legs, I raised my knee to join my arms on the ledge and used the leverage to pull myself up. I dusted off my hands, quite proud of my maneuvering. Sitting on the wooden deck, I dangled my feet off the side and looked at him below. "Nothing up here but me."

"Enough for me." He jumped, grabbed the edge of the landing, and was quick to hoist himself up, grinning smugly at how my jaw dropped.

"All you had to do was jump up here. I wasn't needed at all!"

"You're always needed. Plus, you offered," he replied, wrapping his arm around my shoulders and pulling me to him.

I rested my chin on his shoulder as I looked up at him, raising my hand to brush against his cheek. "I like you like this."

He turned to look at me, the gray in his eyes sharper, more inquisitive. "Like what?"

"Free," I replied in a whisper. "Why do I feel like I've known you longer than I have?" I wasn't actually asking him — I was asking myself. It was something I couldn't understand.

He didn't respond with words, and I didn't need him to. He gave me exactly what I wanted: his mouth on mine. His tongue pushed against my lips, and I opened for him, tangling mine with his. He exhaled into my mouth, and I took it, wanting to taste any part of him that he could give me. I deepened our kiss, and his arm currently wrapped around my shoulders moved to my waist, tugging at me.

I smiled through our kiss and moved my hand from his cheek to his chest, guiding him down onto his back. It didn't take much effort for him to oblige. As I turned to straddle him, our makeshift light burned out. Only light from the moon gleamed through the cracks in the barn.

The lack of light seemed to ignite something in him because his hands immediately cupped my ass and began moving me against him. My core heated at the new friction between us, and I whimpered against his mouth.

"I love the sounds you make." His voice was hoarse, like sand grating against my skin. He moved a hand to wrap around the back of my head, pushing my forehead down against his. "Why can't I stop thinking about you, Raven?" He thrust up again. "How can I be so addicted to you already?"

I fumbled with the buttons on his shirt, wondering if he would notice if I burned through the threads to make it quicker.

"I want you," was all I replied, pushing my tongue back into his mouth.

He waited for me to finish unbuttoning his shirt before he sat up on his elbows, allowing me to remove it off his body. I moved to the buckle of his pants next, unfastening it quickly, and pushed them down his hips. I licked my lips at the sight of him.

When I felt his hands on my waist, I yanked them off. He growled and tried again, but I searched for his discarded shirt and took one of his hands, wrapping the fabric around one of his wrists before I repeated it with the other. I tied a knot, keeping his hands bound. "Don't touch me," I commanded. I wanted the ability to explore the glory which was him on my own.

He snarled, bucking his hips against me. I moved down his body before grabbing the hem of my dress and slowly raising it over my body. He could only see my silhouette in the moonlit shadows, but it was enough to make him groan.

"Miss me?" I asked, repeating his question from when he teased me in the spring.

His chuckle was raspy in response.

I leaned down, my breasts rubbing against his swollen cock. He pushed up against me again. I shoved my tits together, letting him thrust between them, biting on my bottom lip as he began to pant. "I could come like this," he rasped as he throbbed between my flesh.

I was soaking wet but wanted to taste him before he could have me again. "Don't," I bit out. Sitting up on my knees, I scooted down just enough to align my mouth with his shaft. I reached between his legs and took his balls in my hand, gently massaging them as my tongue licked his length.

He let out an audible "Goddamn, "which had me drawing back in laughter. He gently knocked the top of my head with his hands, wanting to touch me. I reached up with my free hand and untied the fabric around his wrists. One of his hands immediately tangled in my hair, and it spurred me to open my mouth, taking his tip between my lips. I slowly circled my tongue around him, moaning at the taste of his precum.

"Fuck, baby," he groaned.

I froze at the nickname. It was familiar somehow. And it surprised me how much I wanted to hear it again.

"Call me that again," I demanded before sucking on his tip teasingly.

"Baby," he panted.

I whimpered, taking more of him in my mouth. His body shuddered beneath me. Both of my hands moved to grip his hips, needing to brace myself if I was going to try and take all of him in my mouth. I relaxed the back of my throat and drew more of him in, gagging as his tip hit the back of my throat.

"You can handle it, baby," he muttered in between his heavy breaths, slowly thrusting into my mouth.

I pinched his hips, and he did it again, tightening his grip on my hair. He guided my head on him, pushing me farther down with each thrust. I took him, my eyes watering as I continued to suck him off, my jaw sore from his size.

"Fuck, Raven. I'm going to come."

A moan escaped my throat as I wrapped my fingers around his base and squeezed, urging him to release into my mouth. He pulsed against my tongue as he exploded in my mouth, whispering my name repeatedly.

My sucking slowed, milking every last drop out of him. His grip on my hair loosened, his breathing heavy. Strained. I sat up slowly, buzzed by how his seed tasted sliding down my throat. This man was my own form of alcohol, and I was addicted.

He grabbed my waist and flipped me to my back. Sitting on his elbow, he leaned over me and thrust his tongue into my mouth. I felt his rapid heartbeat against my ribs and threw my head back when two of his fingers pushed into my core. It was so fucking dark that I couldn't see any of his movements and it kept me on edge.

He moved his fingers rhythmically in and out, muttering against my mouth, "You're so wet. Is that just from sucking me off?"

I bucked against his fingers. "I could've come just from tasting you."

A low, guttural growl came from deep in his throat. He pulled his fingers out of me but barely gave me a chance to miss him before I felt him between my legs, pulling them over his shoulders. His tongue dipped into me, and I cried out, moving my arms to my sides to find something to hold on to, but found nothing.

"I haven't thought of anything but how you taste." His voice was scratchy against me.

I threaded my fingers through his hair and pushed him back against me. His laugh was breathy before his tongue was back inside me, circling until he licked up my clit and started over, building me up until he could push me a step back.

"What are you trying to do to me?" I groaned, my mind hazy from how long he dragged this out. I wanted to come, but he felt *so wonderful* that I didn't want him to stop.

His mouth left me, and I cursed under my breath.

He laughed softly, kissing my hip bone. "I can't stop, Raven." And then kissed the other. "I don't ever want to stop." Then my belly button, leaving a trail of kisses as he traveled up until he could nip at the skin of my breasts. "You're my heaven." He found my collarbone. I had chills on every inch of my body. "You're my hell. And I want to burn in you." And then he found my lips, pressing his gently against mine.

I drew in a sharp breath as he filled me with one thrust.

"Come on me, baby."

He bucked into me roughly. I cupped my hands around his neck, pulling his mouth to mine again as I matched his thrusts with mine. We were panting together as we built. I screamed for him, cried for him, toppling over my peak as he came with me. It was an explosion of colors as our bodies moved together, riding the wave of our orgasms.

He claimed my mouth again with his tongue, moving it hungrily. I felt the sweat from his forehead against mine. I had fucked many men, but nothing ever came close to this. He made it seem like all the others had done it completely wrong. I had no idea pleasure like this could ever exist.

When he broke our kiss, it was only to whisper against my mouth, "We taste so fucking good together."

And he was right. We were our own flavor of candy.

Exhaustion suddenly washed over me, and I responded with a sleepy grin. My bed was just through that door beneath us; if I wanted to, I could show him. But he was rolling to his side and pulling me with him until I was safely tucked against his chest, his strong arm curling around my body.

"The moon has nothing on you, baby," he muttered against my ear and gently kissed my temple.

The softness of his voice and warmth from his body against mine made my eyelids droop heavily with sleep. "Baby, baby, baby," I whispered sleepily to him, a little delirious from the unfamiliar feeling of desire. More than desire.

The raspiness of his chuckle was the last thing I heard before the world around us faded.

CHAPTER EIGHT

Zeke

Raven slept beside me, her small frame slicked with sweat from our activities. I expelled a soft breath from my nose, a grin lifting a corner of my mouth as I replayed the memory in my mind. My fingertips brushed gently up and down her arm, hearing her sigh in her sleep. My sweet girl, who always had so many conflicting emotions filtering through her, was in a deep, peaceful sleep.

We had moved fast, but there wasn't another choice once I saw her. I needed her. I needed her now, even while she slept in my arms. But, I had the chance to sift through her memories and needed to take it. I wanted to try and find the answer as to why Mira wanted her in Reales so much.

I pushed into the depths of her mind, slowly filtering through year by year. There was so much angst. I stopped on a particular memory of her curled into a ball against what I assumed was her door, knees up to her chest, tears streaking down her face.

She looked young, maybe sixteen, and she was overcome with agony, looking toward a small door hidden in the wall. I cocked my head, trying to push deeper in. I tensed as Cade pushed through the door, coming to her and sliding down to sit beside her. He wrapped my very small love in his arms, trying to calm her tears. '*Let me show you something,*' he told her.

She looked up at him, so doe-eyed.

I moved ahead in the memory to see them exiting through a door… in here. A hidden door here led her in and out of the castle. The trips to Arthur's made sense. She had a way of sneaking in and out.

In the memory, Cade took her by the hand, and they ran in pitch black through the village and to the harbor, where he encouraged her to swim. She laughed, breathy noises coming from her as the tears continued to fall down her face. He picked her up and ran to the water, jumping off the dock with her in his arms.

They had been friends for a long time then. That was why they were so comfortable together. That would explain why he seemed so possessive over her.

I left the memory and continued pushing backward in time. I stopped at another, where she looked to be around ten, hiding under a bed in a small room. There was a knocking on a door, and the sound of men's voices echoed against her walls.

I wrapped my hand around her wrist as I felt her fear as an older woman came into her room, leaning down and wiping tears from her face. This woman loved her, but I still sensed Raven's hesitancy to move. Sadness had clung to her skin for her entire life. I could taste its thickness on my tongue. The woman encouraged Raven to stand, and my heart warmed at the sight of her as a child. Those big green eyes seemed too large for her face.

Another familiar pair of green eyes flashed through my own mind, and I blinked once, twice. I had seen eyes like hers before.

The men who stood at her cottage door were royal guards. They were beckoning her forward to follow them.

'*Come with us,*' one man said to her, coaxing her out of the cottage. '*Your life is about to change.*'

I was thrown out of the memory, falling back even farther. I was unwelcome there; her pain didn't want me to see it.

I followed her as a child while she walked alone at night. Why was she alone? She ducked in and out of buildings, pointing her finger at boys who ran past while chasing other little girls. The boys grabbed their faces and rubbed their eyes, blinking furiously while Raven giggled.

I smiled. She still sounded the same.

We were at the festival. She shooed the little girls being chased as they watched their chasers struggle to regain their vision. What had she done to them? I knew she could burn, but they weren't burnt.

I peered farther back into the darkness behind her. A male form watched her. She was alone, but he never advanced. When he stepped toward the light, I realized it was the king. Raven started skipping away, and he just smiled, following her until she was safely in her cottage.

Why did he have such an interest in her?

I dove deeper, trying to find how she was tied to Mira. What Mira could possibly want with this kind creature asleep in my arms?

She moaned softly in her sleep, and I froze, not wanting to disrupt her. She could feel my presence in her mind. Give me a little more time, I begged silently.

I waited for another moment. She sank lower against me. I was hard against her lower back, but I had to push through. And she needed sleep.

I gently pressed on, filtering until I saw her as a baby. My hair stood on end. I had seen her before. She was embedded in my own memories. That black hair, those green eyes. John brought us to the castle when I was a boy to show me the new princess. The Princess of Reales. It was Raven.

Raven was Mira's sister.

I tried to draw in breaths, but I couldn't. I didn't want to wake her, but a weight settled against my chest. I squeezed my eyes shut, plowing through her mind until I saw Mira clapping her hands joyfully as Queen Celestina handed a baby to her.

Baby Raven cooed as she tried to touch her sister's face, and Mira giggled. I had never seen Mira happy. Did she want Raven back because of their bloodline? Why had she waited so long?

I looked through more memories, needing more of Mira. I settled on one that was blurry, but Mira was hiding under a bed. Raven was screaming, and tears wet my eyes at her pain. Her mother was crying, holding Raven tightly to her chest.

'*Please let me have her,*' I heard a man say.

I blinked my eyes, trying to focus on who it was. My forehead creased as his face came into view. King Leonidas.

'*Celestina, please. She can reign over Seolia.*' There was anguish in his words as they tumbled out of his mouth.

Celestina shook her head, stepping away from Leonidas. '*She is the key, Leonidas. Don't you see?*' Celestina spoke through her sobs. '*We can control all four kingdoms with her. Rudolf has a nephew. They can marry. He's a prince.*'

Me. She was talking about me. She wanted us to marry and incite a war over the kingdoms.

'She's *my heir, Celestina. Not Rudolf's. You have another daughter.*' Leonidas tried to reason with her, but I felt her anger brewing, and she raised her palm toward Leonidas. Something black began to trickle from her fingers and then pain. I felt so much pain from Raven as her mother crumpled with her still cradled. Leonidas reached for Raven, trying to shush her tears. Mira remained still under the bed, covering her mouth in silent sobs. She had witnessed her mother murdered by Leonidas and saw him steal Raven away.

Golden strands began to escape Celestina's body and wrapped around Raven, pushing into her skin. The golden strands slowly turned gray and then black. Leonidas tried to pull Raven away, but they followed her, sinking deep into her chest. She was gasping, screaming, her green eyes widening. She inherited her mother's magic… and her sadness. All her darkness, her fury, it lived within Raven. That was why her anger was so loud.

Mira wanted that. She wanted Raven to continue with Celestina's plan. She wanted me to propose and bring her back madly in love with me, to where she couldn't stand the thought of us parting.

Mira wanted a war. She wanted to avenge her mother and control Seolia. She wanted all four kingdoms under her control, just like Celestina did.

I forged a few days ahead in her memories, watching as Leonidas handed a baby Raven to another man, begging him to keep her safe.

'*She can't come to the castle yet,*' he said, kissing her forehead over and over. 'They'll *know it was me. Find someone for her, someone who will take care of her until I can safely move her home.*'

He handed Raven to this man, who returned to his own cottage, yelling to his wife about a baby and needing to find a home for her. Somewhere that no one would ask questions, never seek her out. Hidden deep within the cottage, I saw a little blond boy with blue eyes, watching intently and staring at the baby in his mother's arms. Cade. He saw everything. Was that why they were so close?

I gasped as I pulled out of the deepest depths of her mind, panting as all the new information coursed through my brain.

Mira wanted to use Raven. She was going to use the connection in their blood to manipulate Raven into agreeing to marry me and invade Perosan and Thoya. She would bind our kingdoms for all eternity, showing the power we hold as one. Any children we bore would be heirs to both thrones.

No one would ever rise against us because our army in Reales was too great, too vast. That was why Mira made me commander. She wanted me to train them for this plan. She waited until Rudolf died to throw her plan into action, sending me to Raven as soon as possible.

But she couldn't anticipate that I would fall in love with her and find my flame that burned through every universe. And now I was a complacent piece in a war that was brewing.

This was why John wouldn't tell me what was going on. Jeanine wasn't part of the original plan to bind the kingdoms. Another reason Mira wanted her in Seolia was to tell everyone about Raven's magic, but why? I needed to talk to John. He needed to see that my allegiance was to Raven and not Mira. None of this explained why he chose to come here all those years ago.

A tear fell down my cheek. I couldn't keep going with this. I would have to end it with her, but how? She was on my mind every second. Any time we were apart, I felt like I may slip away. How could I leave her?

I looked down at her, peacefully sleeping against my chest, and another tear fell. I couldn't hurt her. I couldn't make her believe that I didn't want her. It would make her hate me. Maybe she needed to if it kept her kingdom safe.

I needed a plan.

Returning with her as my fiancée needed to remain the goal. Otherwise, Mira would make my mother and Luca suffer for it. Luca would love Raven. They both laughed like the world wasn't dark. I couldn't risk them now, or all the torturing I did would have been for nothing. Selling my soul wouldn't have been necessary.

I would sell it for Raven. But, leaving her seemed like my only option. I leaned down to press my lips gently to her temple. I had just found her. I waited a lifetime for her, and she was in my arms, falling in love with me. I could sense it on her. She could feel our connection.

What could I do? How could I help her?

The answer was very obvious, prickling my skin. Cade.

Their dance at the banquet crushed me. She was leaning into him, and he was desperate for her. I had to push them together. She would have to choose him. They had been friends for a long time, and I hadn't been with her long enough for her to choose me over him.

My heart broke at the idea of another man touching her, loving her, feeling her delicate skin. I shook my head. I couldn't.

She exhaled softly, and I pressed another kiss to her temple. But I had to. For her, I had to. I couldn't let her fall so deep in love with me that she would contemplate agreeing to Mira's plan.

Mira wanted to use her. I needed to find out how much Raven knew about her past. It hadn't seemed like she was aware of where she came from or that she had any family left. Mira was going to prey on her weakness, and I couldn't let her. I had to make Raven hate me.

"I have to become your villain, baby," I whispered as my voice broke. But I would stay. I would continue to watch her. I wasn't

162

expected home for at least three months, and I couldn't leave her yet. I would invade her dreams and pull at her memories so she could begin to connect the dots herself. I would plant doubt in her mind about Mira's intentions, so when they met, she would already be on edge. She'd suspect something before she had all of the information.

My anguished love. I would have to break your heart.

I would need to take my time. She wouldn't run to Cade if I abandoned her right away. I would find Jeanine tomorrow and have her meet me somewhere with Cade. I'd bring Raven and let the envy she experienced at seeing him with someone else free itself.

But she didn't want him. I knew she didn't. I felt no lust from her when they were together. He was her comfort, where she felt safe. And so much had been taken from her that she didn't want to lose him, too.

I could be her comfort. I hoped to be one day.

But, I knew Cade wanted her desperately. With me out of the picture, he could finally make his move.

I cringed at the image of them together, her body moving on his like it moved on mine. Could I do this? I peered down at her again, running my fingers through her hair and wrapping my arm tighter around her waist.

Her envy. It was one of the first emotions to bubble over. I'd have to use that to my advantage, make her believe there was someone else for me. It was only days ago that I fucked Jeanine for information. That did leave it open for interpretation.

I needed to break her slowly. It needed to hurt.

I was determined to keep her safe. I would do anything to keep her out of Mira's clutches. I'd stay away for a few weeks, and give her a chance to move on before I began to plant doubt.

Please don't fall in love with him, I pleaded with her. Please forgive me for the hell I would unleash on your soul.

I kissed her temple and closed my eyes, pushing into her mind again. I pulled from a memory that was deep within and cast it forward, letting it become her dream.

I needed to start while I had her because soon, I'd have to sneak around to see her.

Dream with me, my love.

I held her hand and led her through the dark forest of Reales. I glanced back at her, my gaze heavy with adoration and lust. If I couldn't show her that I loved her in reality, I could show her in our dreams. She opened her mouth to speak, but I pushed my finger against her mouth, urging her to stay silent.

I led her into a clearing where there was a small pond. She took a step forward but stopped when she heard a voice. An angelic voice. Soothing. She sought out the sound, wanting to know where it was coming from.

She stopped again, her head tilting at a woman far away from us with wavy black hair like hers. She was holding something in her arms as she swayed and sang. A coo. A cry and a shush. Her mother turned to us, holding a baby Raven in her arms.

I came up behind her, wrapping my hands around her waist as we watched together. Raven hummed the melody, and I smiled. Celestina's eyes rose to meet hers. "I knew you'd find me one day," she said.

My eyes widened. I scattered the memory, pulling us from it. I hadn't expected Celestina to find us. If I kept Raven in a dream too long, she'd want to stay, and I couldn't lose her in the realm of her memories. No matter what I felt or how much I wanted to stay in there with her, I would have to pull us out.

I didn't know how deep Celestina's magic was and if she could somehow keep Raven there, even as a ghost. I felt how much she wanted to touch Raven. I would need to keep dreams with Celestina few and far between. The love between a mother and a daughter was deep. Even with my abilities, I wasn't sure I could overcome it if I had to.

I lowered my head, resting it against the fluff of her hair and breathing her in. My favorite scent was now jasmine and pears. Her hand wrapped around my fingers that were on her waist. Even in her sleep, she wanted me. She trusted me.

Self-loathing settled on my skin. Some villains were born, but I would be made. I would be her devil to keep her protected.

"I love you," I whispered against her hair.

She hummed that melody in her sleep.

I would be her hell. But until then, she was snug in my arms.

I exhaled softly, pulling her closer to me.

Until then, she was mine.

I fell asleep to the memories of us in lifetimes before.

CHAPTER NINE

Raven

I was awakened by the sounds of voices far off in the distance. My eyes fluttered open slowly at the sound, squinting at the broken rays of sunlight trying to push through the cracks in the wood. Scattered images flitted through my brain from a dream. I arched my back to stretch and froze when I felt a body behind mine. Lifting my head, I turned slightly, and the memory came rushing back to me. Sleep. I'd slept soundly, for the first time in days, and with a warm body next to me.

Zeke was breathing deeply. I hadn't disturbed him yet with my wiggling. Moving cautiously, I rolled over until we were face to face. All our nights had been spent in the dark, and I hadn't had a chance to study him in the sunlight.

And what I saw was soul-shattering.

I propped up on my elbow and lightly traced the edge of his jawline with my fingertips. His black hair had fallen over his eyes, but I could still make out the tips of his eyelashes fluttering as he slept. Underneath those eyelashes were a pair of hypnotizing gray eyes. There were lines etched in his face, creases from a life lived. Misery clung to him, even as he dozed peacefully.

You beguiling, broken man, where had you come from?

My gaze traveled down his body, admiring the lines and grooves of his muscles and the way his veins were thick in his hands. As I had at the banquet, my fingers moved to lightly graze down his throat and collarbone.

He really was the most beautiful man. And he felt like mine.

He was like the moon fighting against the sun. Shadows stuck to him — shadows I wanted to cloak myself in.

His tanned arm tightened around me and shifted me closer to him, pushing our chests together, like even in his sleep he didn't think we were close enough. I sighed into him, leaning down to brush my lips against his. He stirred slightly, a low groan erupting from his throat. Smiling, I touched his lips again with mine. His eyes blinked open as he took me in, kissing me again, our mouths parting for our tongues to link.

Softly. Slowly. Like we'd been doing it for years.

He shifted his body weight against me until I was on my back and carefully rolled on top of me. He used his knee to push apart my legs, never breaking our kiss. I indulged him, curling my legs around his lower back.

He lowered himself as the tip of his length pressed against my entrance. Breaking our kiss, he pulled back just enough to watch my face while he pushed into my core. My head rolled back, but he quickly grabbed my chin between his fingers and shook his head. "I want to see you," he murmured sleepily, starting slow, torturous thrusts into me.

My mouth fell open as I took him, raising my hips against his to match his rhythm. His eyes never left mine as we moved together. Sweat beaded on his forehead, and I raised my head, pressing my lips to it. His head dipped down to rest against my shoulder.

"Who are you?" I breathed as I wrapped my arms around his neck. I held him tightly against me, putting my mouth beside his ear, and panted heavily against his skin.

At my sounds, he pushed deeper. We were nothing but tangled limbs, completely wrapped up in each other. My breathing hitched as I climbed closer to my release. He lifted his head from my shoulder to find my eyes. I closed them, but he pressed his lips against mine. "Stay with me," he begged, his voice a broken whisper.

My eyes fluttered open to meet his, and our breaths synced as he stayed buried inside me. Our sweat mixed together, our bodies slicked, even while moving steadily. This was soft. Gentle. And I felt my heart reaching for his.

When my walls tightened around him, he groaned. I tugged at the hair sticking to the back of his neck, wanting him to follow me over. He rolled his hips through my climax, finding his seconds later. He released into me, muttering my name like it was praise as he came.

His warmth mixed with mine, and he stayed on me, relaxing into me. I remained wrapped around him, not wanting it to end. I didn't want to let him go. It felt much more intimate than our previous nights together, like making love.

But how could that be when we only just met?

He kissed the tip of my nose once before moving to his side again, tugging at my waist to do the same until we were face to face, staring at one another. He held secrets behind those gray irises that I desperately wanted whispered against my skin.

"I want to take you out today," he finally said, breaking our silencing stares.

My nose crinkled up. "Like... in public?"

"As embarrassing as it may be for me to be seen with you...."

I dropped my mouth open and shoved at his shoulder but then frowned. "It won't be like the other night. I can't go out without drawing a lot of attention."

"Well, that won't do. I want you for myself." He was quiet while he contemplated something. "Can you wear another disguise? Maybe not one with purple hair?"

"But you like my purple hair. It's *all* you talk about."

He smiled, dragging one finger down the length of my spine. "Never listen to a drunk man's rambles."

Frost. I'd shift into Frost, and my hair would be blonde. "I have another disguise. I need to go to my room first. Bathe."

He leaned down to take a big whiff of me before nodding. "Definitely bathe."

I shoved at his shoulder harder than before, but it did nothing to him. "I smell like you, jerk. It's my new favorite scent."

He grinned. "And what scent is that?"

I kissed him softly. "Pine. And rum."

He laughed loudly. "And that's your new favorite?"

"I want to bathe in it." I giggled as he pinched my side, tickling me. "I'll just bottle you up. Keep you with me."

The corner of his mouth tugged up, but shadows clouded his eyes. I stared at them. It was like black clouded over the gray -- like a dark thunderstorm. I wanted to ask how, but he said my name, drawing me from my thoughts. "I'll pick you up this afternoon. Is that enough time?"

"More than enough."

I sat up and looked around the small loft for my dress. He did the same, finding our clothes in a pile behind him. He separated them, handed me my dress, and pulled his shirt over his shoulders, pushing the buttons to fasten over his chest.

I stood and pulled my dress over my body until it fell straight, smoothing it with my hands as I peeked through one of the cracks in the barn to gauge the time of day. I could feel his eyes on me as he continued to dress, only turning to him when I heard the clasp of the buckle on his pants. I had learned rather quickly that I couldn't stare at him naked without wanting to jump his bones.

"You going to be in trouble?"

I ignored his question and took a step to glance over the edge of the loft. I wasn't going to talk about Cade anymore when with him. "How do you plan on getting me down from here?" Cade and I used to have hay bales for an easy descent, but we removed them once Blaze began to show herself more often.

Zeke sat on the loft's edge and hopped off, landing squarely on his feet. He turned and held his arms up to me. "Jump, baby."

I shook my head, partially in awe at him again but also in disbelief at his suggestion. "You're fucking insane if you think I'm going to jump off of here. It's like fifty feet up."

He rolled his eyes. "You and your mouth. It's more like fifteen, but okay. Just sit down and slide off. I'll catch you."

I had to get down somehow, which seemed like the safest answer. I sat and scooted to the edge, gripping tightly as I hesitated.

"Raven, I'll catch you," he repeated softly.

I pushed myself off the ledge and dropped right into his arms. He cradled me as the flood of adrenaline from my fall rushed through me. But he caught me, just like he promised.

"Catching. Add it to my list."

I giggled as he set me down on my feet, smoothing my dress out again. Shit, still no shoes. Maybe he'd forget. I'd be fine. I stepped to the door that led out of the barn, but he grabbed my elbow and halted me.

"Not so fast," he muttered.

His glance had moved from me to the wall that housed my hideaway. For a second, a rush of fire spread through me, the hairs on my neck tingling as John's warning was brought to the forefront of my mind. If Zeke were here to ruin me, it would have helped his cause to know the ins and outs of the castle.

But then he looked back to me and down at my feet. "You're not wearing any shoes."

I loosened a sigh of relief. "That's right."

He turned and crouched.

I jumped on his back again. "I think this is how I want to be carried everywhere from now on."

A smile pulled up on his cheeks. "As long as you keep waking me up like you did today, we'll have a deal."

I blushed and rested my warm cheek against the side of his head as he carried me out of the barn. He stayed close to the stone wall that surrounded the castle. I felt the eyes of a passerby on us, but that was bothering me less the more I was with him. I could do much worse than Zeke, and it was about time they saw their queen socialize outside her inner circle, which only consisted of Cade.

Another intrusive thought seeped into my brain. Did he have someone back in Reales? I couldn't imagine a man who looked like him not having someone to warm *his* bed at night. And during the day. All hours, really. The thought made my tension return. Before I could stop myself, the words tumbled out of my mouth, "You don't have someone waiting for you back home, right?"

His body went rigid under mine. Shit. A few seconds ticked past, and I regretted asking him. Finally, he responded, but it didn't help. "No one I love."

That was a half-assed answer. Jealousy surged through me at the idea of someone else touching him, which was fucking insane. He didn't belong to me; I wasn't his, either. He was only in Seolia for a few days, and then he'd be leaving to return to Reales. His allegiance was sworn to another kingdom.

It was what all members of royal courts did in the four kingdoms. If you swore an oath to the ruler of one of them, it was a bond that was nearly impossible to break. Doing so could result in banishment or, worse, execution. That was why I hoped John planned on keeping his promise to me. As much as I would have loved to give in to the darkness growing inside of me, I didn't want it to be toward someone of my own court. I doubted I'd execute him, but banishing him didn't sound too bad.

So very luckily for me, the rest of my time with Zeke would now be spent wondering about who he'd be with once he left. I told myself not to get involved with him. I knew it would end up nowhere good. I should have listened. Here we were, only days later, and I didn't want him to go.

––––––––––

We remained quiet for the rest of the walk. When we reached the gate to enter the courtyard, I wasn't surprised to see Cade not waiting for me.

Zeke stopped and let me slide down before he turned to me and put my face between his hands. He tilted it to him, but I couldn't look at him. I was embarrassed that I cared so much already when he probably didn't.

When my eyes didn't meet his, he noticed and expelled a hot sigh that made my eyelids flutter, pressing a light kiss to my forehead. "I'll see you later, baby." He released me and left me standing alone in the courtyard.

I felt a heavy absence.

Like every time he left, he took a piece of me with him.

————

I had time alone to decompress for the first time in days.

I strolled into one of my libraries, sighing at the amount of dust on the shelves. In recent years, I hadn't had time to devour books like I used to. It was once an obsession of mine, pouring over pages, trying to inhale all the history of Seolia, and looking for books on dark magic. The history of that was not documented, or if it was, it was hidden or destroyed.

Most of what I'd heard about the Black Forest was by word of mouth, especially when I was a village kid. Isla would let me sit at the border, but even she was hesitant to allow me to escape past the trees. Living next to it for ten years, I never saw a single person dwell within. It wasn't until I became queen that I finally took my first steps into the forest and something in me awakened.

Before, I knew I had magic and could will it forward, but after crossing the border, I could feel it. It was like it suddenly inhabited my soul, my very being.

I had searched for books on the history of the forest, but nothing ever came of it. It'd always been the landscape of the island. The rumored history was that when Seolia was built upon the mountainside and grassy knolls, witches who lived in caves along the water's edge, deep within the trees, were angered by the disturbance. They tried to stop the process, casting spells upon the royals or enchantments that would turn them into beasts during full moons, leaving them to wander through the kingdom, thirsting for blood.

One hundred and fifty years ago, the king finally had enough and sent a legion of soldiers into the forest to murder the witches. But, ever since that time, people wandering into the forest would not come back out. The caves where the witches dwelled brought in brave travelers, banking on the idea that they'd finally reach them, but no one ever did.

When King Leonidas sent his soldiers decades ago after a small group of villagers disappeared, the ones who didn't return stopped anyone else from trying to seek out the caves.

I, however, found them. I'd walked around them, fallen asleep in them. They were quiet. The sounds of water splashing against their backs were the only noise I'd ever heard while wandering through them, desperate to find answers about where my magic came from and why I'd never felt at peace within the kingdom.

It hadn't been until recently that I became angrier, wanting to draw blood the second something threw me off-balance. It made me wonder if something deep inside of my skeleton was awakening. If the old magic that coursed through my veins was trying to warn me of something, protect what was mine. But the kingdom that the witches didn't want was what I was trying to protect. My magic was ironic.

I skimmed the titles on some of the spines of the books, blowing the dust off as I went. I really needed to get someone to organize all of them. I had one central library, which was closest to my chambers, and two others like the one I was in — smaller, more intimate. I smiled to myself as I recognized some of the titles that Cade had read with me when I first came to the castle.

Despair pricked my skin. I needed to make up with him.

But first, it was time to greet my people and hold an audience for them, ensuring they had everything they needed from me.

Almost exactly two hours later, I stood in my bedroom, cursing myself for cutting it so close. I'd been in the throne hall since I left the library, conversing with Luisa about requests we heard, who had noticeably been there in Cade's absence. He rarely missed an audience and was always there to help me. Luisa said he'd asked for time off when I inquired about where he was. I had asked her how much time off, but she had no answer for me.

I loved when I was ill-informed.

When I returned to my room, I looked everywhere for a note that Cade may have left for me with an explanation, but I found nothing. I hadn't seen him anywhere since the banquet, and not popping up to annoy me just wasn't like him. The panic of him being gone hadn't left me.

I never wanted him to leave, no matter how strange it was between us. He could pout and brood, but he needed to stay put. Luisa was wonderful, but she was no Cade. He knew what I thought before I thought it. We had a silent language, where we didn't have to say a word and still understood one another.

Losing that strong connection with someone would cause chaos in my daily life. He was my voice of reason. Without him, I would be a voice of unfinished decisions. And that was no way to live. How could I have been so naive to think that Cade would just remain by my side until we were both in the ground? He wasn't getting any younger. I'd always relied on him, and not knowing where he was at drove me crazy.

I didn't have time to stew about it. I needed to meet Zeke in the courtyard for our mysterious public outing.

I bathed and washed his scent off of me, which I didn't want to do, and willed Frost forward to shift. My icy blonde hair took the place of my long, black hair.

I pulled on my leather pants but decided to wear a black wool sweater instead of my usual bustier. By taking me out in public, I believed he wanted to get to know me instead of us finding a dark corner and fucking. Neither of us could keep our hands off each other, which was fine, but I had questions.

Since I was trying to appear a little less appealing to him, I pulled on a pair of black boots that sat right at my ankle instead of the thigh-hugging ones he seemed to enjoy.

Blinking my eyes, I checked the mirror. My green eyes morphed into the blue. At least as Frost, I felt calmer. It was a breath of fresh air to not have Blaze fighting for all of my attention. Frost seemed to help me keep a clear mind. And that was what Zeke deserved from me — not split attention on him and wondering where the fuck Cade was.

Standing in the courtyard, I spun slowly on my heel, looking for any sign of Zeke. Or Cade, for that matter, but found neither of them. I ran my fingers through my hair, the blonde bright against my tanned skin.

I'd been here for a few moments and didn't see either of my men. Typically, I could sense Zeke if he was close by. Somehow, and I wasn't sure how, I always knew when he was nearby. It wasn't just his scent that drew me to him; it was something else. A feeling.

I realized we never agreed to meet in the courtyard, though I hadn't brought him to my chambers, so I wasn't sure where else that would leave. Surely he wasn't waiting for me in my throne room.

I was about to go back inside when I heard voices. Two male voices. One of them was Zeke's, and the other was... John's? I looked around and ducked into a doorway as the voices drew closer. They were too quiet for me to grab entire sentences. I leaned forward and closed my eyes, concentrating on their words.

"Time."

"Mira."

"Impatient."

"Raven."

My nose wrinkled at the mention of my name. Why were they discussing me? I stepped out of the doorway to face the two men as they approached. They both clamped their mouths shut. It took a second for John to recognize me, only having seen me once as Frost, but recognition crossed over his face at my narrowed eyes.

Another second ticked by, and I put my hands on my hips, waiting for their acknowledgment. Maybe I'd loosened traditions *too* much. They finally took the hint and bowed to me. My eyes rolled. When they straightened, I kept my face still. Unreadable.

"Your Majesty," John began, taking a small step toward me.

My belly knotted. Everything about him set me on edge.

"Zeke was telling me about the loss in their kingdom. I wasn't aware."

I didn't buy that bullshit. My eyes cut to Zeke, asking him for confirmation. He just watched me, his jaw clenched. I wondered if maybe him randomly showing up was something to be more aware of.

He finally took a step toward me, and I remained motionless; even my eyes as they stayed locked on his. He made me thirsty. Saliva pooled in my mouth just from his proximity to me.

When we were an arm's length apart, I tilted my head back just enough to look up at him. If he tried to intimidate me, it wouldn't work. I was small but fierce. My arms crossed over my chest, and he tracked my movement, softening his gaze.

"Hey, baby," he whispered.

He warmed me to my core. He brushed his thumb over my cheekbone, and I leaned slightly into his touch. Damn him. He knew exactly what he was doing, and I was letting him. It was like he controlled my emotions and knew how to calm them. Behind us, John watched intently, and I fought off the urge to flip him off. My eyes snapped to him instead. Anger bubbled up under my skin, trying to push past my ice. Zeke sighed and dropped his hand from my face as I sidestepped around him.

"It is extremely unfortunate. I've been trying to show Zeke as much support as possible while he deals with losing his beloved king."

"That's exactly what he told me. You are such a gracious queen."

Zeke grabbed for my arm, but I moved out of his reach. I kept my stare on John, my irises glistening with the ice that danced behind them. "Even gracious queens can only be pushed so far, John. Only fools forget that."

No more warnings. That was a threat. The look he gave me could cut ice as his mouth thinned in a straight line. He didn't say another word before he disappeared through a doorway.

I turned on my toes to face Zeke, willing my fire to calm. "Don't talk about me with him."

He only stared at me, seemingly perplexed. I could see his curiosity, but I wasn't going to give him anything else. He came to me when I didn't try to close our distance. He hesitated before he leaned down to me, kissing me softly.

I resisted at first, still uncomfortable from seeing the two of them together, talking about me. He wanted to soothe me, and when he wrapped his arms around my waist and dipped his nose to mine, some of the tension left my body.

"I missed you," he purred.

I couldn't help the smile that formed. "You just saw me."

"I'm addicted." He took a step back, unashamedly drinking me in. "You're not exactly making it easy for me to take you out tonight. I don't want anyone seeing this."

I looked down and pulled at my oversized wool sweater, giggling. "I could fit two of me in here, and you *still* don't want to share me?"

"Raven, you could wear a burlap sack, and I'd still want to bury myself in you."

His mouth found mine again. My body lit up at his touch.

"Let's stay in," he mumbled against my lips.

I considered it, but my questions wouldn't find answers if we walked back through those doors. I wanted to know his mind, no matter how good his body felt. "Come on, this was your idea." I reached for his hand and walked backward, tugging him with me. This man was a beast, and it took a lot of effort to get him to move his feet. "It'll make it more fun to want me knowing you can't touch me."

"Baby, being in public would not stop me from touching you." He pulled on my hand until I was flush against him. "I'll fuck you wherever I want."

I bit down on my bottom lip, and he leaned in, taking it from me with his teeth. He gently sucked on it, and I sighed into his mouth, falling back into the daze he always had me in. Something had gotten into him. He was always hungry for me, but this was a need. He released my lip and walked backward again toward the castle.

I laughed as I shook my head. "What has gotten into you?" I wiggled out of his grip and took a step away from him, beckoning him forward with my finger. "Come on. You can share me for a little bit."

He lunged at me and wrapped his arms around my waist, pulling me up until my legs were curled around his middle. "I don't want to share you, Raven." He kissed me while he finally walked through the gate and on the pathway to the village.

I broke our kiss to look down at the ground. "Are you absolutely insistent on carrying me everywhere? If you're looking for a new position, I can think of much better things you're suited for."

His arms moved from around my waist to cup my ass, shifting me higher on him. He kissed along my jawline and neck, sending me into a frenzy. When he stopped, he had a smug smirk on his face. "Like what?"

"Possessing," I responded.

He laughed but then huffed. "I think you're not as obsessed with me as I am with you."

I couldn't help but laugh at the ire of his tone. "You're not hideous to look at, either. I'm not throwing a fit about it."

He playfully scowled at me. "It's my personality that brings them in."

I snorted, my eyes rolling. "The girls back in Reales love the brooding type?"

"It's not brooding; it's mysterious." He lowered me down to my feet. "It pulled you in."

"Happy to be one of the many," I replied sarcastically.

He glanced down at me with a frown.

I sighed softly. That sounded snippier than I meant it to. "Where are you taking me?"

He didn't answer at first, proving my earlier statement of how he liked to brood. Finally, he replied, though his tone wasn't as chipper as before, "There's a quieter pub I found. I figured we could eat, talk, and stare at each other. You can ask me all those questions sloshing around in that brain of yours."

"How do you know I have questions *sloshing*?"

"Your entire demeanor changes when you drown in your thoughts."

It was impressive that he had already picked up on that. "We have that in common, I guess."

A small grin.

"I do have questions. A few."

"I know. Let me get a couple drinks in before you start."

The rest of the walk to the pub was in silence, but it was comfortable. There was still some daylight left, and I enjoyed looking around the village without crowds forming around me. I saw Eva running through the streets with a few other little girls. Another woman adjusted flowers in the window of the flower shop. I made a mental note to stop and pick some up for Isla.

I inhaled deeply as we passed the bakery, drool pooling in my mouth. I stopped and stared through the window, trying to find the source of the heavenly smell. Pastries were being loaded on shelves behind the counter. "Yum," I said aloud. I was practically pressing my nose against the window as I watched.

Zeke tugged at my hand, and I pouted as he pulled me away, falling back into step with him. I really needed to get out more often in the daytime. There were so many wonderful shops. I could breathe freely when I wasn't in the stuffy castle.

Poor little queen. I rolled my eyes at myself.

Zeke pointed up ahead at the pub on the corner. People were filtering in and out of it, but it looked big enough to hold the number of bodies. I looked at the sign above the door and laughed. 'The Stag Shack' was painted sloppily on the wooden board. Men. As we entered, we were met with a bustling crowd, tables full of people laughing and drinking.

I had always been a little envious when I saw groups of friends. Even as a young girl, friends were hard for me to come by. It was like everyone could tell that I was different from them. When I became queen, I never had time to try and connect with anyone, except Cade.

Zeke pulled me through the mass of bodies and found two stools for us to sit at the bar. He handed me a long sheet of paper with a list of everything offered. I wasn't hungry. Again. I had grabbed a small breakfast before my meetings, but then Cade happened. Or the lack thereof.

"Surprise me," I said. "I'm not hungry, but I'll take a drink."

He leaned over the bar to the guy behind it, presumably the owner of the shack of stags. He ordered himself an ale and ordered me some sort of mixed drink. When I asked him what was in it, he said it would taste like fizzy apple juice.

And whatever the fuck it was, it was strong. There was barely any apple juice and all rum, but I relished how it felt going down.

"Another, please," I called out to the bartender at the opposite end of the bar, shaking my empty glass.

Zeke chuckled at me and threw the rest of his ale back, ordering another. "You're going to run another pub out of their rum stash."

When I felt a little more liquid confidence pushing through me, I turned on my stool to face Zeke. He sucked in air quickly through his teeth and braced himself for my line of questioning.

"How old are you?" It was embarrassing I didn't already know the answer to that one.

"Thirty."

"When is your birthday?"

"Just passed. Right before winter hit."

"Brothers? Sisters?"

He seemed to retreat into himself. I cocked my head. Did everything offend this man?

"One brother."

Great. I loved details. "Close to your parents?"

Again, he was quiet. He really didn't enjoy talking about himself. But it was only fair that I knew something about him. Everyone already knew my life story.

"I'm close to my mom."

Okay, not quite an answer. "So, you take care of her? And your brother?"

He nodded, not offering anything else.

I needed to steer the conversation away from family. It was hard for me to talk about, too. "You said you don't have anyone you love back home." It wasn't a question. I waited for confirmation.

He inhaled a breath and held it, diverting his gaze. Fuck. When he looked back at me, he nodded once.

"You have to give me something, Zeke. Should we not be doing what we're doing?"

The bartender put my fresh drink in front of me. I picked it up and threw it back, setting the glass down as I asked for another refill.

He sighed, rubbing his temple. "We're not going to stop doing what we're doing."

"That's not what I asked."

"Fuck, Raven. What do you want me to say? It's a gray area," he bit out.

He was snapping at *me.*

"A gray area? What the fuck does that mean?"

"It means that it's not wrong, but it's not right, either."

I narrowed my eyes. I was bitter, and it wasn't because I had just downed the third drink.

"Baby, come on." He nudged my knee with his.

I didn't meet his eyes. "You make such a big fucking deal about not sharing me, but you're fucking someone else, *baby.*"

"It's more fucking complicated than that, Raven."

For days, I'd told myself that we didn't belong to one another, but we'd done nothing but fuck and spend every available moment together. And earlier, our fucking shared a really close border with something deeper. But I didn't say any of that because I was infuriating. Instead, I left him with this zinger, "You're fucking unbelievable." And turned away from him, facing the crowd. I didn't want to talk about it anymore.

He groaned in frustration as he handed me another drink. I swirled it around in my hand, ice forming on the outside of my glass from my fingers. Frost was the most composed, but I felt all sorts of unfamiliar emotions. They were all coming to the surface, irritating even my calmest shift.

"I'll be right back," he muttered.

I didn't respond. Instead, I raised the glass to my lips and threw back my fourth drink., tasting less and less apple in each pour. When I brought the glass down, I saw a familiar face staring at me over the rim of my glass.

The glass cracked in my hand at the surprise. I cursed under my breath and returned it to the bar top behind me, but I kept my eyes on that face. That fucking face that just up and abandoned me. Cade.

And, of course, he wasn't alone. My gaze moved to the same blonde he'd been with lately, sitting next to him and leaning entirely too close to his ear to be having an actual conversation.

But, he kept his eyes on me. He sank lower into his seat, lifting his arm to rest on the back of the blonde's chair, and widened his legs — the same way he had in his room the other night when I couldn't stop staring at him. My eyes cut into tiny slits as she slid her hand up his thigh. I seethed, moving my focus back to Cade, whose eyes still hadn't left me.

What kind of sick game was he trying to play with me?

Instead of helping me today, he was here, trying to find someone to fuck. A mixture of envy and fury spread through me. My fire pushed against my ice, wanting to be let out to unleash what I felt right back onto him. He wanted this. He wanted to get a rise out of me. That was why he wasn't breaking eye contact, which was really unfair.

He'd had years of freely getting to fuck whomever he wanted. Years of *me* having to wait for *him* at breakfast and then rolling my eyes every time I had to see his freshly sexed smug waltz into my dining room. Years of wondering why he needed release with someone else when I was right there. If he wanted someone, why was I never what he wanted?

Realization fell on my shoulders, stealing my breath.

All those years of watching him, all the mornings I spent mocking him for whoever he had just discarded, were because I wanted it to be me. Not the being discarded part, but the wanting my company to be what he craved. Not necessarily to fuck, but to be beside. To cure loneliness.

I didn't want to share him.

My mouth fell open at the recognition. And then I was enraged. It'd been seven years. He could have made his move long ago, but he decided to wait until someone else paid attention to me before making it known how he felt about me.

He could sense me growing angrier as I sifted through my internal comprehension because his body tensed. He knew he had pushed me too far. I crossed my legs as I leaned coolly against the bar. I was falling for someone else, even if he wasn't truly mine. Nothing about this was fair.

Cade wanted a rise out of me, a reaction. He could fucking have one. I closed my eyes. I was tired of pushing down how I felt, ignoring every instinct. Why not show him? Why not burn the fucking pedestal he had me on right out from underneath us?

Why not show him my darkness?

I snapped my eyes open. But this time, they weren't blue.

They were bloodred.

CHAPTER TEN

Raven

Cade immediately sat up, and the blonde slid off of him as he stared at me, slightly shaking his head. Too fucking late, Cade. With a flick of my finger, I lit the table he was at ablaze. His date screamed and stood. He jumped up with her as the sizzling pop of the wood in front of them sent the rest of the crowd into a frenzy. Through the flames, his eyes met mine again. We stared at one another, even as bodies ran out of the pub. His blonde cowered behind him as if he could somehow fend off the dark magic burning their table.

I hopped off the barstool and grabbed an empty bucket beside the bar. Blinking, I shifted back into Frost and pointed down into the bucket, filling it with icy cold water. I could have easily extinguished my flame with a snap of my fingers, but this would be much more fun.

I sauntered over to the flaming table and threw the bucket of water onto it, extinguishing the fire. I filled the pail to the top again until water sloshed off the rim and threw it again, soaking Cade and splashing the girl behind him.

"You looked a little singed," I said, my voice flat.

Behind me, Zeke returned and wrapped his hand around my hip bone, pulling me back against him. Cade's eyes narrowed as he tracked our movement, the intimacy between us.

Zeke asked with amusement in his tone, "What happened?"

I shrugged and broke my stare with Cade to face Zeke. I put my hand on his chest, patting it lightly. "Give me a second, and we can go." Instead of returning to Cade, I walked around Zeke and dropped my coin pouch full of gold coins on the bar top. "Sorry for the mess," I said to the bartender with an apologetic grin. That much was true. I didn't enjoy taking business away from him, but it was still early enough in the day that patrons would return for the evening. The amount of money in my pouch was triple what he would have earned in the lost hour, so at least something positive was coming from this.

I grabbed Zeke's hand and pulled him behind me, satisfied with how Cade was trying to wring water out of his shirt. I stopped and turned to him as he glared at me. "I expect you to be at work tomorrow." He wanted me to show him that I cared, and he was probably regretting what he asked for.

I didn't say another word as I walked out.

So much of everything was raging inside of me. I was pissed at Cade for testing my boundaries — for waiting too long to reveal how he felt about me. I was indignant that Zeke had someone else back home that he'd be returning to soon.

And I'd still be dealing with the ramifications of my actions over the last few days, and still without answers as to who was telling people of my magic. It was bewildering why anyone would ever try and test me in attempting to incite a war, especially if they knew I possessed dark magic. I was absolutely exhausted, pushing down how I felt at every turn. I was the queen, but I wasn't allowed to show anyone who I truly was or what I could do. I thirsted for darkness, for blood, and that guilt overtook me, draining me every day.

"Raven," Zeke's voice broke through my thoughts. "Where are we going?"

I didn't answer and continued to pull him toward the barn. When we reached it, I yanked open the door and walked in, leaving him to stand in the doorframe. There was enough light left to see the hidden door outlined in the wall. I pushed the knob, and the door that led into the castle creaked open. Holding it open, I looked back to Zeke, whose mouth was in a hard line as he stared at me. I beckoned for him to follow me as I stepped into the hallway.

At first, it didn't seem like he would, but then I heard the sound of his boots coming up behind me. The door closed behind him, and it was just us in the dimly little hallway. I didn't care if he had someone else. I wanted to taint the memories of Cade and me from these corridors.

I put my hands on his shoulders and jumped, wrapping my legs around his waist. Before I was sure he had caught me, I shoved my tongue into his mouth. He cupped my ass, and the force from my jump had him backed against the wall.

He broke my assault on his mouth to try and find my eyes. "Raven," he whispered.

I shook my head. "Please," I pleaded. "Just choose me tonight."

I just needed someone to choose me.

I pushed my tongue into his mouth again, this time being met with his. We stayed like that, pressed against each other, trying to sort through our feelings with a kiss. He suddenly slid down the wall until I sat on his lap, my legs straddling his waist.

I reached down between us and fumbled with his pants, trying to push them down. He moved his hips enough to let me. He did the same to me next, pushing down on the waistband of my pants until they rested around my thighs.

I slid down on him. There was nothing gentle about this one, and I welcomed the pain. I took him in, all at once, drawing in a sharp breath as my walls expanded quickly to accommodate him.

"Say my name," I demanded, rolling my hips against him.

He looked into my eyes, cupping the back of my neck with his hand and pressing his lips to my throat. He kissed down my neck, nipping at the skin as I continued to grind on him.

"Raven," he growled against my throat.

I threw my head back as he thrust up, driving deeper.

"Again," I cried.

He moved from my throat to my mouth and bit down hard on my bottom lip. I yelped at the burst of pain, and he did it again, breaking my skin. The taste of my blood seeped into our kiss. "Raven," he whispered again, running his tongue over my bottom lip to catch the blood.

He was greedy, taking whatever I gave him, which was just anger. I rolled my hips over and over until our foreheads came together, slick with sweat. "Baby," he growled again and released, filling me with his warmth.

That spurred my own release, my cum cascading down his shaft as we rode through our climaxes together. Panting. The lust I felt for him was heady, constantly pulling me under.

And I wanted that to help. I wanted that to calm me, but I still felt something deep inside me that wanted to be let out.

My head fell to his chest as we stopped moving, a tear slipping down my cheek. It mixed with my blood, and I could taste the bitter saltiness of it.

He lifted my head from his chest to look at me, frowning at the sight of my single tear. The lines of his face hardened as he watched it drip down.

I was breaking. And he couldn't fix me.

I sighed and licked my lips, slowly rising off of him. I pulled my pants over my hips and took a step back so he could do the same. We were quiet as we looked at one another. So many unspoken words lingered between us. Finally, I shrugged and cocked my head toward the open hallway. "Want a tour?"

He looked back to the door that led out of the secret corridor. I couldn't blame him. There was a new heaviness between us, and he looked like he was fighting some conflict within himself, but then he tilted his head toward where I stood and gestured for me to continue.

Neither of us spoke as we moved down the hall, only occasionally stealing glances at each other. As the tunnels split, I pointed down one hall. "My chambers." And continued down the opposite one.

He remained silent behind me, only the sound of shoes scuffling surrounding us. I wished I could stop feeling so furious. I wanted to calm down, but I also didn't. Too much had changed over a few days. My head was spinning. I had been fucking someone who had someone waiting for him. He never told me. And I never asked. Now I wish I had never had. I wanted to remain ignorant.

I wanted to stop feeling like I was never enough for anyone. We felt so connected, but it was all just surface if he could be with someone else and tell me it was a *gray area*.

He sighed behind me. I wondered if he could somehow hear my thoughts, so I stopped thinking and silenced my brain as we approached the door. I twisted the creaky handle and pushed it open, waiting until he was inside before I closed it behind us.

He took a couple steps in and looked around before glancing back at me. "Locking me up?"

I kicked my shoes against the ground as I walked through the dimly lit dungeon beneath the castle. "Only if you're good," I mumbled, dragging my fingers across the iron bars of a holding cell.

The dungeon was large, and once upon a time, it was used frequently. There were eight hollowed-out cells, each wall surrounded by stone and gates made of heavy iron rods with strong steel padlocks. There were no guards that stood on watch because I rarely held anyone. No, I never held anyone.

There was some weaponry on the wall at the opposite end of the dungeon, with handcuffs and the key to the locks, but other than that, it was empty, except for the scuffling noise heading toward me. My eyebrow lifted as I looked down at the black cat rubbing against my legs, meowing at me.

He asked, "Pet?"

I crouched down, rubbing its soft fur. "I had no idea it was here. No one ever comes down here." The cat looked at me with large green eyes, and I stared back at it. I felt as if it was trying to tell me something. I was really losing it if I thought animals were trying to communicate with me.

I stood back up, and the cat walked away, disappearing up the stairs that led out of the dungeon.

"No one comes down here? You don't negotiate down here?"

My eyebrows squished together. "Negotiate?"

"When you want them to do something for you."

I tilted my head to the side. "That's not how I rule."

"There are no prisoners," he said. "Ever?"

I shook my head as I shrugged. "Crime is rare here. We never keep prisoners long enough to hold them."

"You let them go."

I hesitated. "Not quite." I stopped in front of an unlocked cell and stared into it. "I take care of them before they get here."

That was an admission I hadn't planned on.

"You…" He trailed off. "You kill." He didn't sound surprised.

I nodded. "Have you? Killed someone?"

His jaw contracted at my question, but he nodded.

That didn't surprise me in the least. I wondered if that was why he had shadows. I wrapped my fingers around one of the bars and hung off of it, biting my bottom lip. He watched me, his gaze intense. The taste of blood started to coat my tongue, drawing me back into my dark thoughts.

"Does it feel good when their flesh splits apart?" I leaned back against one of the iron rods.

He didn't move, except for his hands that were clenching and unclenching at his side. I dipped my head down as I watched the veins in his hands constrict. Blood.

"When you feel the blood coat your hands…." I swallowed as I dove deep into the black mist of my thoughts. "The thickness like honey on your fingers." I stared at my hand, holding it out in front of me. My own demented rage settled into my skeleton. My voice was scratchy as my eyes glazed over. "When you feel their loss of life cling to yours… does it make you feel alive?"

He advanced toward me, closing the space between us step by step. He grabbed my waist and pulled me to him. "Yes," he breathed. His response was like a snake slithering across my skin.

He pushed my pants down, and I leaned back against the bars again, watching as he lowered to his knees in front of me.

He grabbed my thigh and rested it over his shoulder before thrusting his tongue into my core. I wrapped my hands around two iron bars as I started to ride his tongue, rocking my hips against him.

He wanted to drink my darkness. I wanted to drown in his.

He pulled out suddenly and stood, backing away slowly to the far wall and grabbing a pair of handcuffs hanging from a hook, dangling them from his finger as he returned to me. I bit my lip as he grabbed my wrist and clamped it around the bar, repeating it with the other until I was chained to the iron. He wanted all the control, and he could have it.

"Whatever you're going to do... make it hurt."

His chuckle was dark enough to burn out the sun. He fisted my blonde hair in his hand, pulling roughly until my throat was exposed to him. His teeth clamped down on the skin between my shoulder and neck, his other hand kneading one of my breasts through my sweater.

My cuffs clattered against the bars as I tried to pull my arms down. I wanted to touch him, but I couldn't. I growled from frustration. His teeth sank lower into my skin, and I cried out as my flesh split, lightheaded as my blood pooled against his lips.

"My sweet baby," he snarled, licking over my wound. He pressed his mouth to mine. I tasted my blood mixed with our release from earlier. Our own brand of eclipse.

"I'm not yours," I bit out.

His smile was vicious as he bared his teeth to me. I leaned forward and pulled his bottom lip between my teeth, biting down until I drew blood of my own. He groaned into my mouth. I sucked his bite, drinking from him, wanting his blood to run through my veins. Become an imperishable part of me.

He cupped the back of my thighs and lifted me up, wrapping my legs around him. His eyes were on mine, but they were black and full of shadows. "You love me best in the dark," I whispered to him, running my tongue over my bottom lip, tasting remnants of his life lingering.

He fumbled with his pants, and they fell to the ground. And then he filled me vigorously like he couldn't claim me fast enough. He thrust up into me, his fingertips piercing into the skin of my hips. He tried to kiss me, but I didn't let him. Instead, I ducked my head to sink my teeth in his ear. He growled, bucking into me harder until the pain overcame my every sense.

I bent my elbows, using the leverage of my locked arms to match his thrusts with my own. His gaze was on my face, but mine was on how well our bodies fused together.

"Do not come yet," he snapped, stopping his thrusts and remaining buried inside me.

"Are you fucking joking," I shouted, trying to buck against him.

He kept me still and stepped forward, pinning me entirely against the bars. "You wanted it to hurt," he reminded me before he kissed along my jawline.

My arms were shaking, even though he kept my body weight balanced against him. "Beg," he murmured against my skin, licking over the shell of my ear.

"No," I gritted out.

His mouth made its way across my throat until he kissed me passionately. One of his hands slid underneath my sweater until it was pressed flat against my back, drawing me closer to him, stretching my arms. I groaned through our kiss from the pain and confusion of how much pleasure it was bringing me.

"Beg me, Raven," he repeated against my mouth. "Tell me how much you want me."

I had to weigh my options very quickly on whether I wanted to come or show him how stubborn I could be. The shit-eating grin on his face told me he already knew what I was going to choose, and to cement my choice, he rewarded me with one bone-breaking thrust.

Swallowing my pride, I whispered, "I want you."

He cocked an eyebrow, waiting for more. I glared at him, but I whimpered when he slowly started to pull out. "Please," I begged, missing the fullness of his cock. "I want you, only you."

"Say my name," he said, repeating my earlier plea.

Easiest request he could've given me. "Zeke."

He rewarded me again with a thrust. "Again, Raven."

So, I did. I said his name over and over until it came out in breathless rasps as he pounded into me, my entire body feeling like my bones were shattering into pieces.

I started to build, climbing on my hands and knees to my peak, screaming his name as I tumbled down into our murky oblivion. He groaned my name as he followed me over.

My heart thundered in my ears, and I felt his heartbeat in his chest like a duplicate of mine. He continued to hold me, waiting until our breathing calmed. The blood still dripped from the bite in my neck, making me dizzy, but I wanted it. I wanted the distress. He made me feel like it was okay. Like I was safe to swim in our shared obscurity.

He slowly let me down until my feet were on the ground, leaning in and licking the drops of blood from my neck. I moaned softly and tilted my head until he was gone. I slowly raised my head, the bite already beginning to close on its own as he returned to the wall, grabbing the key from a hook.

He returned and pulled my arms higher, and my muscles extended painfully. He was having trouble pushing down his own fury, wanting to let it overtake me again. He unlocked my wrists and returned the cuffs and key to the wall.

I brought my arms down and bent, reaching for my pants and bouncing on my toes as they glided over my hips. He stared at me like he recognized himself in me. We both had secrets. Pasts. An unquenchable thirst for stealing life that wasn't ours to take.

He towered over me, pressing me against the bars again. He grazed over the bite on my neck with his fingers, his brow furrowing at the healing break. And then his lips were on mine, gingerly, the shadows clearing from his eyes.

They lived within me now.

I grabbed his fingers from my neck and led him through the dark dungeon back into the hidden corridor. We were silent again because how could we recover from something like what had just transpired between us? We'd unlocked something in each other. Something sinister.

Instead of leading him back out to the barn, I led him into the tunnel that exited into my room. I pointed up ahead toward what looked like only a wall. "The door is on the ground. I know you're old, but do you think you could crawl through there?" I asked like he hadn't just held my entire body weight against iron bars while he fucked me.

He snorted at my dig and shrugged. "I guess we'll find out."

I dropped into a crouch and crawled the last foot toward the door, pressing against the knob to open the door. I waved him to follow me and crawled through the small space, straightening up quickly so I could turn around to watch him. I held back a smile as he grunted, barely squeezing through the small square. "I never met him, but I assume King Leonidas was a small guy if he designed that door."

When Zeke stood up in front of me, his head cocked. "You never met him?"

I shook my head, arching a brow. "You didn't know that?"

"Believe it or not, Raven, I don't know much about you."

I snorted and then dropped my jaw open at the seriousness on his face. "What do you want to know?"

He looked around my bedroom, choosing a chair across from my bed to sit in. He spread his knees and leaned down on them with his elbows, interlocking his fingers. "A lot. Like how someone who never met the king became queen."

"That's an answer I can't give you."

It was his turn to raise an eyebrow in curiosity.

I exhaled softly. "Because I don't know. I was just named in his will as the one to inherit his throne. He never married or had children, at least to our knowledge, so no one could contest it. Bloodlines have become so obscured since the merging of our kingdoms, and we've let so many people in along the way, someone just lost track. No one thought ahead and, I guess, assumed he'd wed at some point in his life."

"And where did you come from?"

These were much deeper than the questions I asked him. "I don't know." Another shitty answer. And one that I wish I had.

He eyed me, twisting his fingers. He seemed nervous.

"I really don't. I have no idea who I am. Just my name. My story has been spread throughout the realm for fifteen years. I'm really shocked that you haven't heard any of this."

"I didn't even know your name before I came here," he said.

That was hard to believe. I was at a loss for words.

"What's the deal with you and Cade?"

It was ironic to me how jealous he sounded. I winced at the mention of his name and rocked on my heels. "You keep asking me questions I don't know how to answer."

He looked annoyed. "Raven, you asked if I had someone. It's only fair that you answer."

I rubbed at my temples. The headache I thought I had beaten was threatening to return. "Cade has been my best friend since I took the throne."

A beat of silence. "He looks at you like he's in love with you."

I gave him a slight shrug as I sat on the edge of my bed. He was quiet as we continued to stare at each other. How was it possible to know someone's body so well and still feel like they were nothing more than a stranger? And why did I want to tell him that there was nothing for him to worry about? Whatever was happening between us wasn't permanent. I needed to not be attached to him.

And then he asked me a question that looked like it physically pained him, and I wondered if, maybe, he was attached to me, too. "Do you love him?"

That question had a lot of answers. He seemed to be simmering, bordering completely spilling over from jealousy the longer I stayed silent. "I love him, but I'm not in love with him. If that makes sense. It doesn't make sense to me most of the time."

He cracked his knuckles like he was pushing down an instinct to hit something.

I asked him quietly, "Do you love her?" Even though I knew he didn't. I wanted to hear it again.

He shook his head, his eyes falling from me to the floor. "I already told you I don't. It's not like that."

I didn't want to know anymore. I really needed to stop prying into his love life. He didn't owe me anything.

He stood from the chair and came to sit next to me on the bed, nudging me with his shoulder. I turned my head to meet his stare. "One more question?"

I braced, nodding once.

"Do you know anything about your family?"

I coughed out a laugh and shook my head. "I was bred from demons."

He grinned at that.

"I have no idea if I have a family. This kingdom is my family."

He was quiet again, seemingly contemplating something. He placed a hand on my knee and squeezed. "I should go. I need to go back into the village for something."

I slumped down lower into the mattress. "Do you have to?" I liked our falling asleep together, but I didn't say that.

He leaned over and pressed his lips to my temple, twirling strands of my blonde hair around his fingers. "I felt like I was with a stranger tonight. I didn't like it."

What he didn't know was that this was me. One part of me, anyway. I wasn't sure anyone would ever be able to accept that. Accept me. All of me.

I nodded and gave him a small smile. He stood from my bed, and I followed, walking him to my actual door, through the bedroom, and into the entryway of my chambers. "I hope you enjoyed your tour."

He laughed softly. He leaned down and quickly pecked my forehead. "I'll see you soon."

Not yet. I didn't want him to go yet.

I threw my arms around his neck and kissed him, trying to keep life pumping through this ticking time bomb of a relationship. I ran my tongue over the mark from my bite on his lip, and he sighed into me, pulling me closer to him.

Our bodies wanted to be together. Why couldn't that ever be enough? We called to one another deep within the framework of our skeletons. I could have stayed with him just like this, and we wouldn't have needed to worry about other lovers or beginnings or endings.

His hands grappled for my shirt, bunching the fabric tightly in his fingers. He didn't want to leave. He was making himself. He broke our kiss, breathless as he kissed the tip of my nose. "*My* Raven," he muttered before releasing me, not looking at me again as he walked through the open door.

I leaned against it and watched him leave. I had a sinking feeling that it would be one of the last times I ever did.

I sat back on my bed and stared at myself in the mirror. I looked tired, even as Frost. I ran my hand through my hair, not wanting to shift back just yet. It'd become darker outside, and I wanted to see Isla again. Her warm cottage sounded extremely welcoming. Maybe I could stay there, at least for the night.

I left my room, not bothering with the corridor. Walking through the courtyard and gate of the palace, I hopped on the familiar pathway that led to Isla's cottage.

How could so much have changed so quickly? It was giving me severe whiplash. I had royally fucked up things with Cade. But he also had it coming. He couldn't wait until I was unavailable to him to suddenly become interested in me. If that's even what it was. He practically had foreplay with the blonde at the pub. He didn't know I was going to be there with Zeke. He only decided to fuck with me once he saw me, effectively ruining my afternoon. This wasn't all on me. It was on him, too.

I needed to start mentally preparing to say goodbye to Zeke. He didn't belong here, and we couldn't be together. He was on the court of another kingdom, and I wouldn't allow him to risk that repercussion by trying to stay with me. Not that he even would. He seemed torn between me and whoever he had at home. And I would never try to take someone away from Queen Mira after losing her father. She needed to be surrounded by everyone close to her as she grieved.

I would make a point of visiting her right after my birthday. Not that I felt like celebrating, given the current state of my friendship with Cade.

And this mysterious person was still making their way through my village, trying to spook people. We still had no news about who this person was. I asked Luisa about it this morning, and she said that the guards undercover in the village still hadn't heard anything. How had this person snuck into my kingdom from a neighboring kingdom? Everyone who unloaded a ship had to go through our customs with a reason for being in Seolia. Unless merchant ships were hiding people, they would have had no way of getting in without a legitimate reason.

I needed to call a meeting tomorrow to discuss having soldiers stationed at the docks to ensure no one was finding another way in. The docks were littered with ships. Trying to swim up would have been suicide. There had to be something we weren't seeing.

So many issues, and I didn't have a solution for any of them.

I kicked at the snow on the path with my boots, watching as it scattered to the sides. I still hadn't told Cade yet about Theodore from the banquet knowing about my magic. Or about the clandestine meeting between John and Zeke, though I wondered if I was reading too far into that. Although, it was strange to find John being so chummy with someone he had accused of being here to cause trouble.

I groaned and palmed my eyes, rubbing them until I saw colors.

As I approached Isla's cottage, I noticed it was dark inside. It was too early to be asleep, so she had to be in the village, probably picking up pastries for her breakfast in the morning. I looked toward the village, sighing as I resigned to walk back that way. I wondered if I could talk her into joining me for dinner. I was still disguised, and we hadn't dined in public for fifteen years.

The guards watched me as I walked back by the gates. I waved, and they dipped their chins to me. I was almost positive they knew who I was. I'd snuck out enough.

Maybe my secret hadn't been kept as well as we thought.

As I walked back into the village, I headed first toward the bakery. Eyes were on me, but I hoped it was only because my hair was so blonde that it looked white, which was strange to see on someone my age. I didn't hold anyone's gaze longer than a couple seconds.

I approached the bakery and peered into the window, my heart stopping. Zeke was standing inside with the blonde woman that Cade was just with. They were talking together, and her arm was wrapped around his bicep. He shook it free but didn't move from her side. Had he seen her at the pub, and his interest was piqued? My fire pooled in my belly as envy stretched across my skin.

And then, so slowly, so hesitantly, he turned his head. Guilt was written all over his face. He took a half-step toward me, but I backed away and shook my head. He had just fucked me, and now he was with someone else. He tried to say something to me, but I didn't care. I turned from him and quickly weaved through the crowd, breaking into a jog, and didn't stop until I crossed the border into the Black Forest.

There was a familiarity in how she touched him. Or maybe she was just handsy with every man she met. I didn't recognize her, though. I didn't believe she was from Seolia. Had he brought her here with him? Was that the woman from Reales? He had brought her *here* to my kingdom. He came here and seduced me; little had I known, he didn't even need me.

What about her going to Cade? Were they trying to break us apart? Had the depths of our friendship somehow become a threat, and now we were being sought out and distracted by beautiful people sent here to rip us apart?

My magic sizzled against my skin, coming to life farther into the forest I walked. The trees pulsed against my hand as I touched them like they had a heartbeat of their own.

"Excuse me, miss?"

I jumped when I heard a voice and turned toward the sound. I stilled as a man walked out from the dark, smiling at me. Though it seemed genuine, chills ran down my spine.

"Can I help you?" I asked him, curling my fingers at my sides.

"I was wondering if you have any food you could share."

I didn't, but I knew how to get into Isla's cottage and could scrounge something up for him. "If you follow me, I can show you to some."

He again smiled at me, baring his teeth. "I would greatly appreciate it," he said, taking a step forward.

As I went to turn, I heard him lunge, and his fingers wrapped around my wrist. "But I see something much more delectable," he whispered, pulling me to him roughly. He snaked his arm around my waist and leaned forward to sniff my hair.

I rolled my eyes. "Thanks, I use a shampoo with pear extract," I replied dryly. With his tight grip on me, I knew he was expecting me to scream or flee, which meant this wasn't the first time he had tried this. But it would be his last.

My feet remained planted firmly on the ground. "You have one chance to let me go, as my answer is a very hard no."

He pulled his head back from my hair to look at me with an evil grin, tightening his grip on me as he cackled. "I don't let good things go when I catch them."

I sighed, annoyed. I cocked my head as I traced the outline of his face with my eyes. He was probably attractive once, but his years of being a complete asshole had worn on his features. "If only everyone felt like you, I probably wouldn't be such a bitter bitch."

The pathetic excuse for a man raised his eyebrows at my response. Before he could do or say anything else, his eyes suddenly widened as he looked down at his hand gripping my wrist. I had turned it to ice. He screamed, but I flicked a finger and froze the inside of his throat. Gurgled noises tried to escape him. He wouldn't be able to breathe for long.

"You fucking fool," I said, shaking my hand free of his icy grip and shattering his hand in the process. "When a woman says no, she means no. It's not left open for your own interpretation."

With my hand now free, I shoved it into his pants and wrapped my hand around his very shriveled length, giggling. "Were you going to try and fuck me with this thing?" I started to freeze it but stopped before it was completely iced over. I didn't want it to be numb. He needed to feel what was going to happen next.

He tried to stumble backward from me, grasping at his throat with the only hand he had left. I clicked my tongue. "Not so fast." I flicked my fingers toward the ground and encased his feet in a block of ice. I walked around him in a circle, looking him up and down. "I can only guess I'm not the first woman you've tried to force into something against her will. And I doubt I would've been the last."

His eyes were wide, the look of defeat crossing over his face.

"You know, typically, I'm a generous person, but I don't feel like you would have given me the same respect if I had pleaded with you to let me go." I wrapped my hand around his icy nub again, freezing it just enough to shatter it but not so much that he couldn't feel his manhood being obliterated.

I leaned forward to whisper in his ear as I continued to squeeze, feeling as it broke apart in my hand, "Is this how you like it?"

His body shook against me as cries tried to escape from his mouth. Crumbling into me, I removed my hand from his pants and continued my dome of ice around his body, moving slowly up from his feet to his knees, his waist, and wrapping it around his chest. I left his shoulders and head exposed, but I wasn't even sure he was still awake anymore.

I took a step back and admired my work. I loved using my magic for the greater good. "I was going to bake you muffins," I pouted. I snapped my fingers, encased his head in ice, and snapped again. Now he was just a snowman.

"Fuck, that felt good. Let's keep going," I said to the snowman and closed my eyes, letting Blaze finally come out to play. Heat crawled over my ice, thawing it, and I shivered. I welcomed my fiery red bob and opened my bloodred eyes, glaring at the snowman.

I raised my arm to graze over his head, leaving a small trail of fire that melted into the snow. "They never learn, do they?" I asked the trees, sighing. I shook my head to answer my own question and snapped my fingers, turning the snowman into a pile of ash at my feet.

I kicked at the pile and smiled to myself.

And then I heard it. That deep voice.

"Raven, what the fuck?"

CHAPTER ELEVEN

Raven

I slowly, so slowly, turned toward the voice.

Zeke stepped out from a clearing behind the trees and looked back and forth from me to the pile of ash at my feet.

"I know how this may look…." I began, biting my lip.

"I just… watched you…." he stammered, slowly taking steps closer to me. Like he was afraid.

I couldn't do anything but nod and look at the pile of ash scattered at my feet. "I don't know how to explain this." Well, that wasn't true. It was actually a very simple explanation. But, that still didn't make it lean in my favor.

He stopped a long distance from me, most likely fearful of getting any closer. I watched as his eyes darted over my body, taking in this fiery side of me. "I don't think this is a disguise."

I shook my head and held my arms straight to the side, twirling slowly to give him a complete look. I tugged on my hair, revealing to him that I was not, in fact, wearing a wig. I didn't even own a fucking wig. "All me."

"That's why I couldn't pull it off," he muttered.

I rocked back and forth on my heels. "Not sure where we go from here."

He ran a hand through his hair, mussing it up.

"In my defense, in this particular situation, this man…." I gestured behind me and then looked down at the pile of ash again, wrinkling my nose. "…I guess he's not really a man anymore, but he was going to try and assault me."

He took another step toward me at that like he could somehow still protect me.

A small smile tugged up on my cheeks. "He didn't do anything. I got to him before he could get to me."

He relaxed a little but cocked his head. "Now you want to explain all of this?" He gestured toward my body.

I looked down at myself and pursed my lips, nodding absentmindedly. Where to start? "Well, remember when I told you that the Black Forest has magic? I meant me."

"You're going to have to give me more than that."

I swallowed and looked around, walking to a tree. "Sorry, this will only take a second," I muttered to it before I held out my palm and set it ablaze. He took a step closer, but I held up my finger, and he stilled.

Before the tree could truly burn, I shifted into Frost and released ice from my hands, drowning the fire and leaving thick, icy shavings on the bark.

Still holding my finger up, he gave me a quizzical look. "Yeah, I'm not finished yet."

I shifted into Terra. He had the tiniest smile at seeing me again like this, my violet hair resembling the same night we met. I beckoned wind forward, and it lifted my hair as it whirred past. I moved my arm in a circular motion to create a small tornado, guiding it close enough to the tree to lift the icy shavings off it.

With the shavings twirling in a snowy tornado, I took a step toward him, and he remained completely still, letting me push the tornado toward him. He lifted his arms as they danced around him, the shavings coating his clothes until I snapped my fingers, the tornado dissipating into thin air.

When I finished, I looked at him. He remained still, waiting to see if I had anything left. I shook my head, and he gave me a slight nod. He rested his hands on his hips, looked back and forth from me to the ice on his clothes, then to the pile of ash, and sighed. He pinched the bridge of his nose with his fingers and massaged the skin. I remained still and waited for him to finish processing all of this. It couldn't be easy knowing one of the women you'd been sleeping with had dark magic coursing through her veins.

"So, you're a witch."

"Ah." I gave him a slight shrug. "I don't know."

He nodded and blew out a breath. "Does anyone else know?"

"Cade. Recently, my advisers because John exposed me at breakfast. Apparently he's known since I came to the castle, but didn't feel like sharing that with the rest of the group."

"You've really been holding back on me."

217

"It's not exactly something you tell someone on a first date. Or first fuck in our case."

"Or second or third. Or earlier, when I asked you about how you became queen." He was partially shouting at me, starting to pace.

I held up my palms to him. "I'm sorry for not telling you. I don't walk around sharing that I possess dark magic. It brings up too many questions that I don't have answers to. I didn't even know the king knew I possessed magic until three days ago. Me becoming queen because of it is just as new to me as it is to you. And also, I don't have to explain myself to you. I'm the fucking queen of these lands. And you're not exactly the most forthcoming person, either."

At that, he stopped pacing and turned to face me, narrowing his eyes. "Are you actually comparing this…" he waved his arms around manically, "to me not wanting to talk about another woman with you?"

I threw my arms up in the air. "Excuse me for wanting to know who the man I'm fucking… is fucking! And oh yeah, how about that? Didn't realize you brought her *here*. To *my* kingdom. Where has she been this entire time? Trying to fuck Cade? Did you not see them together at the pub?"

He scoffed at me but didn't seem bothered by that.

"It doesn't matter. You don't belong to me, and you've made that abundantly clear. Just do me a favor and stop fucking me while your girlfriend is here," I snapped.

"She's not…" he started, but his tone was clipped. Instead of answering, he turned and started walking away from me, back toward the forest border.

"Is that just it then?" I shouted after him. "Meet your word count for the day?"

He didn't answer and left me standing there. Still fuming.

I spun on my heel and stomped off in the opposite direction, kicking my way farther back into the forest. I cursed under my breath, hitting trees with my fist as I passed. Blinking, I shifted from Terra to myself. Staying in the caves tonight seemed like a plausible idea. More than ever, I needed space, away from Zeke, Cade, John, responsibilities, all of it. I needed time to clear my head and not be distracted by the intoxicating scent of Zeke at every turn. Why had he even followed me from the village? He was obviously in fine company. They were probably together now. In his room. In my castle.

I cut through the trees into the clearing, where the spring still rested peacefully under the moonlight. I stopped, leaned down, removed my boots from my feet, and walked barefoot to the spring. Sitting on the ledge, I lowered my feet into the warm water, cursing myself for already missing him. I drew in a deep, unsteady breath and leaned back on the palms of my hands, tilting my head back to look up at the stars sparkling brightly, like they didn't have a care in the world.

"How I wish I could be a star," I muttered, the heaviness of the last few days finally settling on my shoulders, making my bones ache. As a shooting star quickly crossed the sky, I closed my eyes and made a wish for answers. I didn't need anyone to solve these problems for me. I was strong enough to do it on my own.

Before Cade, I learned to rely on myself often. I'd become too comfortable having someone by my side all the time, helping me make all my decisions. There had to come a point where I trusted myself. And only myself. I was letting too many other people seep in and cloud my judgment.

I'd always thought that nothing about me could push Cade away. But he left at the first sign of a struggle and immediately found someone to bury himself in. Just mere days ago, we were fine, and now I was confused about how I felt about him. Wanting to chase after him as soon as he walked away.

But lately, Zeke was always there to stop me.

I cocked my head, recalling that he had successfully put himself between Cade and me since the day in my throne room. He made sure I missed breakfast with Cade again this morning, asking if I'd be in trouble. And at the pub — his perfect timing after I had thrown the bucket of water on Cade. Pulling me back before I could chase him after the banquet. He'd torn us apart almost every time we were together over the last few days, guilting me if I tried to leave him for Cade.

The wedge between Cade and me wasn't just because of us. It was because of Zeke, too.

But why? He had someone here. He was possessive, but he seemed hellbent on making sure I wasn't near Cade. Or if I was,

I was always furious with him about something. He only just asked me if something was happening between Cade and me.

He looks at you like he's in love with you.

If he hadn't wondered about that until tonight, why had he spent his entire trip trying to pull us apart? Why was he at the Festival of Dreams? Why was the blonde? He said he spent his whole first day exploring the Black Forest, but he just happened to stumble upon me that night. A stroke of luck? No one was that lucky. Finding me out in public was a rarity. Plus, I was shifted into Terra. Cade just happened to bring the same woman Zeke traveled with from Reales to his room?

There were too many coincidences.

Unless they really were trying to split us apart.

Alienate me.

The rumors were spread by someone trying to turn my people against me. No.

Fuck, fuck, *fuck*.

I jumped up from where I was sitting and grabbed my boots as I took off into a run, zigzagging through the trees, looking behind me every few steps to ensure no one was following me. I pushed myself into a full-on sprint, my lungs crying. I was really out of shape. I passed by Isla's cottage and flew down the pathway that led into the castle, snow kicking out from underneath my feet. The guards at my gate looked alarmed as they saw me running toward them and pulled open the doors quickly, letting me fly past.

I had to find Cade before Zeke found me again.

I threw my boots down near the door at the castle's entryway, my feet pounding to the floor as I climbed up the mounds of stairs that led into Cade's wing. My forehead banged into the door as I tried to stop abruptly, immediately replacing it with my fists. "Cade, CADE," I shouted, never letting up on my fists against his door.

Finally, he swung his door open and grabbed my arm, yanking me inside. "Raven, what the hell—"

I held my hands up to him and doubled over, trying to catch my breath. "It's him. It's Zeke," I croaked between gasps.

"What is? Raven, what are you talking about? Here, come here." He took my elbow and led me into his sitting room, pushing me into a chair.

I palmed my eyes as I leaned back, trying to calm my breathing as my brain slowly refocused. He returned to my side and tapped my hands with the bottom of a glass. I grabbed it and raised it to my lips, gulping down the icy water in one long swallow. I could feel him staring at me. "Raven, tell me."

I threw my glass to the floor and stood, grabbing his shoulders and shaking him. "You were right about Zeke and how he just showed up. He's here for a reason. He's not just here because of the king. The mysterious stranger in the village? I think it's him. He's here with that girl, the one I made you kick out the other night, the one from the pub. I think they're trying to separate us, alienate me."

He was quiet, staring at me like I had completely lost it.

"I saw him talking to John in the courtyard earlier today. They were whispering about time and someone being impatient, and me."

He opened his mouth to say something, but I continued before he could. "And tonight, I saw him in the village with her...."

"Jeanine," he interrupted.

My eyes flared. "Yes, *Jeanine*. And he didn't deny it when I confronted him about it later. They're together. I think like, *together* together, but I'm still fuzzy on that detail. He saw me shift. He knows. He knows, and he took off."

As soon as I said the words, tears stung my eyes.

He saw my magic. And he ran.

Cade nodded, slowly catching up to what I was trying to tell him. "You think he came here to separate us, but why? What would that accomplish?"

"I think we're a threat together. It's well known by every kingdom that we're close. You're always by my side during visits. It makes me seem weaker if we're not side by side constantly. I'm unprotected. Or if anyone knows they can get to you, hurt you, I would be easier to control. Don't you see it? They're trying to turn my own kingdom against me. John was right. I think there's a war brewing, and he could be part of it. I don't know how, but he knows Zeke somehow."

If fumes could have sprouted from anyone besides me, they would be coming from Cade. His jaw was tight, and his fists balled up to his sides. "They tried to pull us apart."

All I could do was nod. I felt sheepish for falling for this trap laid out for me. I felt like a mouse looking for cheese, only to get my hand bitten off by a cat. He had successfully turned me against Cade, the only person who'd been there consistently since I took the throne as queen.

He wrapped his arms around me and pulled me to him. Tears immediately fell down my face as we embraced. "I'm so sorry," I muttered between sobs. He only held me tighter, pushing his lips against my forehead. I almost lost him. If I hadn't realized what was happening, I would have.

I would not make the same mistake twice.

What felt like hours later, I woke up and looked around, meeting the eyes of Cade, sitting in a chair across from me. I looked down and realized I had fallen asleep in his bed after hours of trying to figure out where to go from here.

I'd been too afraid to return to my room, especially since I showed Zeke how to get into my room through the hidden corridors. We didn't have a plan yet, but I had an idea brewing that I was sure Cade would disapprove of. "I have to keep pretending that I don't know anything," I finally said, my voice still heavy with sleep, but there was weight behind my words.

Cade rose from his chair to move toward the bed, shaking his head. "Are you crazy?"

"Yes, but we still don't know the full scale. Right now, they can deny everything. I need to know how far this goes and who is involved. If this reaches all the way to the kingdom of Reales. To Mira."

He sat on the edge of the bed, his head falling into his hands. "It's too risky."

"It's a risk we have to take. I don't see another choice."

He turned to me and scooted back to lie down next to me, resting one of his arms behind his head. I rolled to my side and threaded my fingers through his. "I didn't sleep with her, in case you wanted to know."

I wasn't wondering, though maybe I should've been. He clearly hadn't been as gullible as me.

"Though I don't think I can say the same for you."

"Cade," I sighed, covering my eyes with my hand. "I didn't know his intentions."

"I tried to warn you." There was a slight snap in his tone.

"Only because you were jealous," I snapped back.

He was silent for a moment, and I was partially irritated. I still felt defensive over Zeke, and that only frustrated me further.

Quietly, he asked, "And if I was?"

A beat of silence passed between us, and I brought my arm down. His eyes were on mine, waiting for a response. All I could think to do was raise to my elbows and gently press my lips to his cheek. It was soft, maybe too soft to really count as anything, but when I pulled back, his eyes were closed, and he was smiling.

I didn't have it in me to offer him anything else. And he wouldn't push me. That was the best thing about Cade. Everything, at the end of the day, was always my choice.

———————

As was the decision to go with my idea.

After a couple more hours of arguing back and forth about it, he eventually relented. It was honestly the only thing to do. Confronting Zeke or John about it would only tell them we knew what was happening. It didn't get to the root of the problem and definitely didn't answer the why.

I would continue acting lovestruck, though; I wasn't sure I even had to act. I'd pretend like everything was fine between Zeke and me. Cade would continue tracking John, informing every guard to let him know exactly where he was at all times. And we'd both stay the hell away from Jeanine.

The plan would remain between the two of us. We'd already risked too much lately, and we couldn't afford someone else finding out about it.

Cade had his own condition. I would have to sleep in his room every night from now on. He wasn't thrilled that I shared with Zeke how to enter the castle undetected, especially into my room. He didn't push as to why I let him in, and I was grateful for that. And I was happy to agree to sleep here. It was the only place I felt safe. I'd need to move some of my dresses and clothes in because being alone in my room would be risky.

The only problem with this plan was I had no idea where Zeke was. He disappeared, and we didn't have anything planned together in the days to come. I hated how desperate I'd appear trying to seek him out, but it was my only choice.

Luckily, it didn't have to come to that. Because as I entered my throne room the following day, he was there waiting for me.

CHAPTER TWELVE

Zeke

That was her magic. She inhabited the elements. And damn, she looked good as a little demon with her fiery red hair. But, like I had told her before, she could wear a burlap sack, and I would still want her. Now there were four of her. I had wondered why I couldn't pull off her blonde hair earlier, thinking it was a wig. I yanked it pretty rough, wanting to only fuck her as herself, but it didn't budge. And her eye colors… those had been changing, too, and I never wondered how. Or why. I was too enamored to be in her presence to care.

She had quite the arsenal in that small, delicious body.

Fuck, I wanted her. I should circle back and take her again in the spring. That was the last place I saw her stomping off when I left her. I hadn't wanted to leave her. I knew she struggled with acceptance, but I couldn't stay and make her feel… loved. Walking away from her at that moment had to be the hardest thing I'd ever done. She needed me, and I let her down.

I rubbed the creases of my forehead as I walked into the castle and up to my room. I could be irreparably damaging my relationship with her by becoming her evil. I may push her too far to where she'd never look at me the same.

I stopped in front of my door and leaned my forearm against it, hanging my head. Maybe I could afford a couple more days with her before I had to turn on her. Before she'd start to hate me. I didn't want her to ever feel like she wasn't someone I could love because of what she possessed. And I hadn't exactly been doing my part, fucking her three times already today. I was supposed to be shoving her off, not pulling her closer. I couldn't end our day like this, though.

I pulled up from the door and jogged back downstairs. I needed to find her. I knew I shouldn't. I knew this was my idea, but I couldn't leave her, not like that.

Before I could pass the gate, Jeanine stopped me by walking in front of me, and I almost smacked into her. "Where are you going?"

I huffed out a breath, desperate to leave her. "Out."

When I asked her to bring Cade to the pub but not sleep with him, I worried she thought that was from jealousy. When, in fact, I didn't give a fuck who she slept with if it got her off of me. I made it clear to her from the beginning that whatever happened between us wasn't serious. I needed to know what Mira was up to, and Jeanine gave me pieces of information. Now, the thought of touching anyone but Raven made me sick.

Jeanine grabbed my arm, and I tensed, looking down at it. "Want to come to my room?" She fluttered her eyelashes as she asked in an attempt to entice me.

I shook my head. "No, Jeanine. I told you that we're not doing that anymore."

She released me and threw her arms in the air. "You need to make up your mind. You wouldn't let me sleep with Cade, and now you're saying you don't want me?"

"Don't you have a job to do?" I asked her, becoming more annoyed the longer I had to stand here and talk to her.

"That's all I've been doing since we arrived. There's hardly anyone left to tell. This isn't exactly a big place."

She was correct about that, but I needed to keep her mind occupied and off of me. And I needed to find Raven. "Just... keep up the good work." I sidestepped around her and took off again toward the forest border.

———

I jogged until I saw the clearing and picked up my speed, only slowing down once I reached the edge of the spring. I looked around. She wasn't here, but I could smell her, which meant she had been here. I ran into the cave, ensuring she wasn't hiding there. Her scent lessened the farther I went.

I exited the cave and jogged to my ship, hopping onto the deck. I threw open the hatch and lowered myself into the hull. It was dark, and I couldn't smell her anywhere. Where was she? I climbed the ladder and stood on the deck, racking my brain for places she could have gone.

As I stepped back onto the dock, I stopped. That black cat was sitting on the edge and staring at me. It looked... worried. Why would a cat be worried? I took a step toward it, and it peered up at me with its green eyes, purring and turning its head, looking back toward where I came from. "I'll find her." I reached down and patted its head before taking off, jogging again through the trees.

I stopped again as I reached the border, looking first at the cottage that bordered it. Raven seemed to know this place, and I recognized the front door from her memories. A light inside flickered to life, and I saw an older woman moving around. I peered around from my vantage point but didn't see Raven.

I looked past the cottage and down the pathway that led to the village. Maybe she was at the pub. Perhaps she was waiting for me, knowing I go there every night. I took off in a sprint, ignoring the looks from the guards at the gate as I passed them. Desperate times, boys.

I practically flew through the door as it opened in front of me, a patron stumbling to the side from me, interrupting their exit. "Arthur!" I called to him, briskly walking to the bar and sitting on a stool. He was already pouring me a glass of rum, but I shook my head, breathless. "Raven."

He slid the glass in front of me and nodded to it. "Drink. Calm down first."

I swirled the glass in my hand and threw it back, setting it back down. "Was she here?"

Other patrons looked at me like I was crazy for suggesting the queen would come here. Arthur looked around at their curious faces. "Mind your own damn business," he said to them, leaning over the bar. "I haven't seen her since this afternoon. Everything okay?"

I shook my head again. "No. I fucked up."

He poured me another glass, and then what he said started to register. "Wait... what do you mean you saw her this afternoon?"

I was with her all afternoon. And she was her little... icy figure.

His eyes scrunched at my question, and he took a deep breath.

"You know, don't you?"

He hesitated before slowly nodding. "I've known for a while."

"Did she tell you?"

"No, but every so often, a young woman would come in. She always looked different, but her voice was the same. And so was her kindness. And her sadness. She was always down about something, and I'd try to cheer her up. When rumors began to circulate about... you know." He looked at the drunks on either side of me, glaring at them until they diverted their attention away from us. "I figured it out. That girl... such a pure heart."

I stared at my glass. "Even the purest of hearts can find their darkness, Arthur." My voice carried a heavy sorrow.

He gave me an assuring smile. "You'll find her. She'd never abandon her kingdom."

No, she wouldn't. I knew she was around somewhere. I dropped some gold coins on the counter, and Arthur tried to stop me. "Between friends," he said.

I grinned and dropped another gold coin. He rolled his eyes. "If you see her…." I trailed off.

He nodded. He knew what I was asking. I waved as I exited the pub and walked down the cobblestone street, peering into the bakery where she had practically drooled over chocolate pastries. And where she saw me with Jeanine. I sighed outwardly. I had planned that. I needed her to see me with someone else, assume the worst. I didn't know how, but I felt I'd see her in the village. I was learning that she couldn't be alone for very long without drowning in her own mind.

But the look of betrayal on her face… I hated myself for it. I saw her disappear into the crowd and waited outside to watch her return to the castle, but when I saw her take off to the forest alone, I had to make sure she was okay — which she could clearly take care of herself.

I laughed softly as I recalled her turning that man into a snowman. She was so confident in herself. It was refreshing to see.

It was getting late, and businesses were starting to close. I hung around for a bit to see if she filtered out of one of them, but she never did. I looked toward the castle. It was the only place I hadn't checked. My eyes settled on the barn that was tucked against the castle wall. If I tried to pound on her door, she might not answer. I'd have to use her corridor to go to her room.

I walked to the barn and pulled open the rickety door. It was dark, but I didn't see any sign of her. I looked up at the loft and immediately missed her warmth in my arms. That was the night I decided to break her. And even without giving it much effort, I was already succeeding. I cursed as I pulled open the hidden doorway and walked inside.

When it split, I looked toward the opposite hall. Was my little demon hiding in the dungeon? I chose that corridor first and threw open the door, padding to the back of the room while peeking into every cell. My dick hardened at the memory of fucking her against the bars. Hell, I needed to find her. Bury inside her. Kiss her until she forgave me for leaving her in the forest.

I left the dungeon and went back into the corridor, taking a left toward her chambers. I crouched down and felt for the small door, shoving it open. I hated this thing. I crawled through, grunting as it squished my body. I never would've done this for a woman before I met her.

I stood to my feet and dusted my knees off, looking around. I couldn't smell her here, either. I walked through her bedroom and threw open the doors to her balcony, peering over to look for any trace of her but only saw guards. I walked through her office, bathroom, and lounge, growling as I went. I was growing frustrated. She was pissed at Cade, so I didn't think she would be there. I spun in a slow circle. Where. Was. She.

I left out of her bedroom door and wandered through the castle, peeking into random rooms but not finding her. I walked out through the courtyard, dipping into multiple breezeways, and she was nowhere.

I felt like I was going fucking insane. Did she have some sort of invisibility magic, too? What else was prowling around in her veins? Why couldn't I *feel* her?

I walked out through the gates. One of the guards raised an eyebrow at me, probably curious as to why I kept popping up.

"You wouldn't happen to know where Raven went, would you?"

His mouth thinned into a straight line as he stared at me.

"Queen Raven, I mean."

He shook his head and averted his eyes.

Fucking liar. I could smell it on him, but he wasn't going to tell me. His allegiance was to her, and I respected that. "Thank you for protecting her," I said.

He glanced at me again quickly, giving me a curt dip of his chin.

I clenched and unclenched my fists; my anxiety of not knowing where she hid was starting to make me panic. I walked back into the forest. She said she loved it here at night. Maybe she was exploring it, deep within.

———

I was exhausted from our nefarious activities this afternoon, but my adrenaline pushed me on. I didn't stop for miles, walking until my legs were sore and until I heard crashes of water against rock. I was approaching the island's edge, opposite where the harbor was. It was pitch black, only light from the moon illuminating the ground.

The caves were up ahead. Maybe she was in there.

I stopped at the entrance of one and called her name. It echoed back to me. I walked to another and did the same, getting the same result. But then I heard whispers from the third, and my eyebrow lifted as I slowly strolled to it. "Hello?" I bellowed out, and the whispers ceased.

I took a step into the opening of the cave. A gust of wind hit my back. I turned my head to see if it was from Raven, but no one was there. And then it started slowly, tickling my ears. All around me, her name was being whispered. It wasn't my voice. This was not an echo. I turned in a circle, trying to locate the source, but it was only me.

"Where is she?" I asked the whispers. They immediately silenced. I wasn't fearful. Perhaps I should have been. But I felt an understanding within these stone walls. Whoever voices these were, they loved her as much as I did. "I just want to find her."

More silence followed. I was about to give up when I heard a quiet purr. I looked down at my feet as the black cat came into view, sitting and staring at me. "Who are you?" I wasn't sure if I was asking the cat or myself, but it tilted its head at me.

I crouched down. "Your eyes look like hers." It purred again. I was losing my goddamn mind. "Can you take me to her?"

It stared at me for a moment as if contemplating my question. I had exhausted all other options. Following a cat may have made me certifiably insane, but I didn't know where else to look. I'd been all over the forest and the village, everywhere I knew to look for her.

The cat stood and stretched before trotting out of the cave. The things I did for this woman. I sighed, hanging my head as I stood and followed the animal out.

The sun was starting to break over the horizon. I'd been trying to find her all night. No wonder I was willingly following a cat. I was a little delirious.

It led me through the trees, never looking back to ensure I was still there. And I just… continued to follow it. When the castle broke over the tree line, I rolled my eyes. "I've already been here." And the goddamn thing hissed at me. It certainly had Raven's sassiness; I'd give it that.

We crossed the border, and the gate came into a clearer view. John came out of it, walking straight toward me. "I don't have time…." I started.

He held up his hands to stop me. The cat walked right to him and rubbed its back along his legs. I looked from the cat to him and back to the cat. "You know this cat?"

He chuckled and nodded once. "The longer magic lies dormant in that forest, the hungrier it gets to awaken."

"This is a… magic cat?" I rubbed my eyes. I had to be dreaming.

"I don't know. But I know the people of Seolia have long feared dark magic returning here when they haven't realized it's been reigning over them the entire time." The cat disappeared back into the forest. "You were looking for her, weren't you?"

I fisted my hair in my hands and started to pace. "I can't find her, John. I've looked everywhere. I checked the village, the forest, the castle... I even peered into her cottage like a fucking creeper. I don't know where she is."

"Isla's cottage."

I sighed, rubbing the back of my neck. Everything hurt. "Who?"

"That cottage belongs to her aunt. Isla."

"Aunt?" I ran my hand through my hair. "She said she has no family."

"Isla adopted her, or well, took her in. That's the cottage where Raven grew up."

I looked toward the cottage, nodding. I knew that part from her memories. "As much as I'd love a lineage lesson, I really need to find her."

"She's with Cade."

I stopped pacing, nearly pulling my hair out of my head. "*What.*"

John sighed and beckoned for me to follow him. He was walking back toward the forest, and I stopped, crossing my arms. "I am not going back there. There's some strange shit in those caves."

He turned to face me, dipping his chin toward the guards watching us. "There're ears everywhere, son."

I glanced back at the guards and waved. The one from last night merely glared at me. I was making so many friends here.

"Raven is with Cade. She came back last night in a frenzy. I don't know what happened or why, but she stayed with him."

My fists clenched at my sides, and he noticed. "It's never been like that between the two of them, Zeke. You have to get a grip on your anger."

"I've pushed her to him. It'll be like *that* between them soon."

His eyebrows drew in. "Why?"

"You know why. I can't trick her. I can't hurt her, not like that."

"There's so much you don't know yet."

I opened my mouth to speak, but he shook his head. "We don't have time for that right now. I'm being followed very closely by the guards. They're reporting my movements back to Cade. They think we're the enemy."

"We *are* the enemy."

"We're not, Zeke. This has gone too far."

He rubbed his hand over his head, and I sighed, looking back toward the castle. She was in there the entire time.

"Listen, do whatever you need to, but you must do it quickly. They're getting suspicious, and Raven needs to feel a sense of normalcy return before she can let her guard down."

That meant I needed to end it with her soon. I had to let her go. I looked back to John and nodded.

He sighed, patting my arm. "She will forgive you, Zeke."

My shoulders sagged. "How do you know?"

He waited to answer, looking back toward the forest. "Because she's not her mother."

CHAPTER THIRTEEN

Raven

My heart pounded wildly in my chest at the sight of him. It'd only been a day, but I missed him. And I hated that. I needed to cut him loose. I needed to stop myself from falling deeper for him. But even after realizing why he was truly here, my heart still fluttered when he turned to look at me. He looked exhausted like he hadn't slept the entire time we were apart, even wearing the same clothes.

It was all an act. I had to tell myself that over and over as I approached him slowly. We were technically still in a fight, so feigning anger was not difficult. Especially since I was angry most of the time anyway. "I'd like an audience with the queen," he said quietly as I walked by him and took my seat on my throne.

I leaned back into it coolly, resting my elbow on the arm of the chair, and dipped my chin once at his request. He approached my throne and fell to his knees in front of me. My eyes widened at him. He looked absolutely devastated. But I remained still, though my heart was pounding so hard in my chest that it may spill out on the floor in front of him. He'd just stomp on it.

Grief-stricken. That was the only way to describe the look on his face. I wanted to kiss it away and ice over his pain. But I couldn't. "What can I do for you?" I asked, lowering my eyes to him, groveling on the floor at my feet.

His eyes lifted to me, resting back on his heels. "Forgive me."

Forgive him for what exactly? Fucking betraying me? Making me fall for him? Trying to pull me apart from Cade? But I didn't say any of that. Instead, "Please continue."

"I was an ass to you. I need you to know how sorry I am."

Well, that much was true. And as much as I would have liked to see his groveling continue, I had to pretend I was still as crazy about him as before. And I was. That was the worst part about this. I turned my palm toward the ceiling and motioned for him to rise. "You may approach me."

He stood quickly and took long strides toward me. I stood, raising my arms to wrap around his neck as he enveloped me in a tight embrace. He kissed my temple over and over. "Please forgive me. Raven, I couldn't sleep. I went to your room, but you weren't there. I haven't stopped looking for you."

"I stayed in the Black Forest. I didn't come back until early this morning."

He stiffened at my words. I wondered if he could tell I was lying. Maybe he had tried to look for me there, but the forest was huge. I could have been anywhere. "You were there this entire time?"

Mistrust was heavy between us now. This was going to be tricky. "I needed some space. I know the forest well. I was safe." I needed to convince him. Distract him. I leaned on the tips of my toes and kissed the corner of his mouth. "I missed you."

He melted into me, peppering my face with kisses until I giggled. "I love hearing that."

I had missed him. I wasn't lying about that. I missed him still, and he was holding me.

"Let me take you somewhere," he begged, pressing his lips fully against mine. His tongue teasingly pushed against my bottom lip, but I broke from him. He seemed to deflate.

"I can't right now. I have meetings, and I need to hold an audience." I tipped my chin to the people slowly trickling in.

"Always such a giving queen," he murmured. "Can I stay?"

"Stay here? You won't be bored?"

"Bored? I could sit and watch you all day." His gaze moved to the completely healed bite on my neck.

I gave him a slight shrug. "I can also heal myself."

"How am I ever going to permanently maim you?"

I laughed softly. "You have. You just can't see it."

He frowned. My eyes fell to the ground between us. I'd already given myself away. I inhaled softly and lifted a hand, rubbing the pad of my thumb over the dark circles under his eyes. "Are you sure you want to stay? It'll be hours. You should go rest."

A beat of silence passed between us. His eyes pierced into mine. "I can't…" he said, sorrow flooding the shadows behind his irises. "I can't sleep without you."

My shoulders sagged at his words, my forehead falling against his. How could our addiction already be so lethal? "Baby," I breathed.

His entire body was heavy as he leaned into me. He kissed me deeply, passionately, and I let him. Maybe I should let him rip me apart. He could carry my broken pieces around with him.

When he pulled away from me, he looked like he wanted to say something but didn't.

"Stay," I whispered.

So he did. He watched me as I listened to what my people need. I would steal a glance at him between each person, falling apart bit by bit as he looked so ravaged. He became especially attentive when Cade came to join me, constantly moving his eyes back and forth between the two of us.

We had to pretend like we were still warring with one another, which was difficult to do when everything between us was healing. I would have loved one of his reassuring squeezes on my shoulder, though I could've killed him when he started smiling at a woman making eyes at him in the audience.

A small part of me was annoyed that while claiming to want me, Cade shouldn't have been doing that. And though Zeke had someone else, he had never once made me feel like he wanted anyone more than me. It only added to my devastation and confusion about him.

But, I remained placid, not sparing a glance at Cade when he walked out. As soon as I finished, Zeke came immediately to me, again begging to take me somewhere.

"Let me change, and I'll meet you out in the courtyard."

"Wear that."

He really didn't want to let me out of his sight.

I looked down at my heavy dress and shook my head. "I'll be quick, I promise."

He wrapped his arm around my waist and pulled me flush against him. My backstabbing self craved him. He leaned down and gently grabbed my bottom lip with his teeth, nibbling. I whimpered at the contact, warmth spreading through my core.

He was too good at this. He knew how to send me over. When he released my lip, my mind felt cloudy. I wondered if I was under some sort of spell. What an irony that would be.

"I'll be outside when you're ready," he muttered against my mouth, releasing me from his grasp.

My heart tugged as I watched him walk away.

I pretended to be walking to my own chambers before ducking quickly into Cade's wing, quietly unlocking his door with my key. I shut it behind me and shoved him as he walked toward me. "Ow, what the hell?"

"Maybe *don't* flirt with the women in my audience."

"I didn't *flirt.*"

"Don't give me your definition of flirting."

He took a tentative step toward me, and I narrowed my eyes.

"It's kinda cute when you're jealous."

I wanted to burn him alive.

"Except for when you're throwing ice-cold water on me."

"That was a mild reaction."

He held his hands up in defense and took another small step. "Where are you going?"

"I don't know. He wants to take me somewhere."

"And you feel okay about this?"

I shrugged, moving past him to grab one of my lighter dresses that cut beneath my knee. I removed my shoes to slip on boots laced up in the front, cutting my midcalf. I was making it a requirement that I only wore things that were easy to move in. "I feel like I'm doing what I need to do."

I gathered the hem of my heavy dress in my fingers and slowly raised it over my head, extending my arm and dropping it to the floor. I watched as Cade's eyes slowly took in my body. He'd seen it before from our nights swimming in the harbor, but it'd been a few years since then, and I had turned into a woman, my girlish features falling away.

I slowly spun on my toes, allowing him to see every exposed inch of me. "Is this flirting? You'll have to tell me."

He inhaled a shaky breath.

I grabbed my new dress from his bed and slid it on.

His tongue rolled over his lips, a low rumble escaping his throat. "You're not playing fair."

I closed the distance between us. "Don't make eyes at other women in my presence, Cade."

"You're kissing him," he bit back.

"I *have* to." I wanted to, but I couldn't say that.

His frustrated growl was like thunder. He threw his arms in the air. "This isn't fair, Raven. I have to accept this guy touching you, and you're pissed at me for smiling at someone?"

My need to possess could be unfair. I ran my hands through my hair and exhaled, irritation growing in the pit of my stomach. Struggling to settle my feelings about Cade made everything about this more complicated than it needed to be. I didn't even know how I truly felt about him. I was hung up on another man.

I could only think of one way to make this easier. "Maybe we need to take away the expectation of us."

His expression was one of pain.

"I don't know what else to do, Cade. I have to play his game. I have to pretend that I'm still his." And fuck. I was.

"You are not his." He grabbed my chin with his fingers. "You are not his," he repeated. His eyes flicked to my lips. I watched how his face twisted at the internal battle he had within himself.

I wanted to pull away. I didn't want to kiss anyone else. Neither of us was ready yet, but that didn't take away from how our hearts called to one another, beckoning, trying to soothe. Our connection was deep-rooted, and we'd spent years protecting it. The last few days tested us, and we almost failed. It was going to take time. We just needed time.

He let out a deep breath through his nose. It tickled my eyelashes, making my eyelids flutter. That made his eyes snap to mine. "There's no one else I want," he whispered.

I gave him a slight nod, my chin still trapped in his fingers.

I desperately wished I could promise him the same.

———————

I left Cade, knowing that if I waited any longer, Zeke would grow antsy. I could tell he was on edge. And a little clingy, barely letting me out of his sight all day. I had to find a way to calm him down, to assure him that we were fine, or else finding a way into Cade's room every night would be impossible.

I walked out into the courtyard, waving to the gardeners who tested when they could plant seeds to welcome new flower growth in the upcoming spring months. That meant that my birthday was less than three months away. I didn't feel like celebrating for the first time in over a decade.

I didn't see Zeke anywhere, which was odd since he'd promised to be here waiting for me. I wandered through a small breezeway that connected the courtyard to a smaller grassy area that housed benches and water fountains, which weren't currently running.

I heard Luisa's voice coming from around the corner. She was speaking to someone, and I felt guilty for eavesdropping. Nothing about Luisa's allegiance had ever given me any doubt. Even still, I froze and held my breath.

"*Surprise.*"

"*Secret.*"

"She'll *just love it.*"

It was Zeke conversing with Luisa. I quickly picked up my feet again and turned the corner toward their voices. My sudden appearance made Luisa jump, but Zeke flashed me a coy grin. I lifted an eyebrow at both of them and waited. Luisa gave me a small curtsy before speedily walking to me and grabbing my hands. She leaned forward, pecked my cheek, and my eyes widened in surprise at our sudden embrace. "You lucky, wonderful girl." She winked at me before scurrying off into the castle.

I looked to Zeke then, confusion written all over my face. "What was that about?"

He smiled again and shook his head, coming to me and putting his arm around my shoulders, pulling us into a walk. "I have a surprise for you, but it won't be for a couple months. Luisa is helping me."

"A couple months? Aren't you leaving in a couple *days*?"

"I am, but I plan on coming back."

"Queen Mira would be okay with you returning after just returning?"

He went quiet at my question and dropped his arm from around me, stopping. That caused me to stop, and when I looked at him, his face was twisted in a sneer. "Do you not want me here?"

I shook my head quickly, furrowing my brow. "Of course I do. But you have people—" I dragged out the word. "Waiting for you."

"Would you let that go?" His tone was sharp, irritated.

"I don't think I can. I'm not a sometimes girl, Zeke. You can't have me here and someone else in Reales. I won't be one half of what completes you."

"You have no idea what completes me."

"You're right. I don't." Now my own voice oozed with acid. Why were we even talking about this? We couldn't be together. Period. He was the enemy.

We stared at one another. I crossed my arms over my chest. I wouldn't budge on this. I'd spent days hanging on his every word, wishing we could find a way to be together, but he'd already made his choice, and it definitely wasn't me.

Finally, his face softened, and he loosened a sigh, closing the space between us. I had to tilt my head back to look at him. "Please, just let me give this to you. We can figure out the rest later."

There wasn't anything left to figure out. I couldn't accept anything from him. But I nodded, relenting to appease him.

He smiled and grabbed my hand, pulling me back into a walk. Away from the village and castle, heading straight toward the Black Forest.

"Where are we going?"

"You'll see."

"I'd like to know."

"You've never had trouble trusting me before." More edge in his voice.

That was before I knew he was part of the problem. I bit my lip as he continued to pull me, turning my head to give a sidelong glance at the castle. Maybe this wasn't a good idea. Cade was correct; we were risking too much. Being alone with Zeke was a possible danger. But he'd know if I stopped and told him to take me back. I had to keep going. For my kingdom, for my throne.

And if anything went awry, I was my own greatest weapon.

———

The evening was upon us, and I squinted my eyes as we plunged through an area of the forest that was covered in the setting sun's rays. I recognized where we were going. He was taking me back to the spring, but he would've told me if that was his endgame. There had to be more of this, which made me skittish.

He'd been quiet for a while now, glancing back at me every few steps. I would just smile at him. Things were awkward, not just because of our current situation, but because he walked away after I revealed my magic to him. The fact that he could just walk away after something like that, especially after our last few days together, hurt. I was stupid to believe it meant more than it did, but I was just a means to an end.

I expected him to stop as we approached the clearing, but he kept plowing through. I looked around, trying to spot where else he'd take me. I tugged on his hand as we passed the makeshift cave that housed the spring. "Zeke?"

He only grinned as he looked back at me. I couldn't help but give him a genuine smile at how cute he looked. He was still devastating to look at, regardless of how much I hated him. And hated that I didn't actually hate him.

He finally slowed our walk and pointed up ahead. I followed his finger. He was pointing at his ship, knocking gently against the wooden dock. "Are you taking me somewhere?"

He shook his head. Our boots clunked against the boards as we stepped onto the dock. "As much as I'd love that, we'll stay put."

What was there to do on a ship? I followed him, taking his hand as he helped me onto the deck. The weight of our bodies made the ship rock underneath our feet. I lost my balance and stumbled into him. He caught me with a chuckle, straightening me up. "Plant your feet."

I widened my stance, resting my hands on the ship's rail. I took the time to look around, realizing it was bigger aboard than I thought it'd be. I guessed it needed to be since Reales was across the channel and could sometimes take days to sail, depending on the water. "It's been a long time since I've sailed," I admitted to him.

"Do you know how?"

I shook my head. "I've never had the time. And when I need to travel, I have a crew."

"Maybe one day I can teach you," he offered.

The pain of his words hit me unexpectedly, and I had to turn my head away. I hadn't considered that yet. Before I discovered who he was, a future for us had always been in the back of my mind. A possibility. But now, that door was slammed shut. There was no future for us.

"Hey," he said quietly, placing his palm on my cheek and turning my gaze back to him.

My eyes were somber, and I blinked back tears threatening to fall from how he looked at me.

"Come back to me," he whispered, sincerity dripping from his voice.

I nearly broke.

When I hatched up this brilliant plan of mine, I only weighed the risk of physical harm. Not emotional. And now I was warring within myself, trying to push down the part that still desperately called to him. And then an even smaller part that was confused about Cade. And the smallest piece of me wished I didn't want either of them and could remain in my naïveté about both.

He moved closer to me, aligning our bodies to face each other, his hand still on my cheek. I should fight this, turn away from him, leave, anything but remain still and silently beg him to close the gap. He kept his eyes glued to mine as he leaned into me, resting the tip of his nose against mine. The heat between us was palpable.

The tip of his tongue glided gently across my bottom lip, asking for permission. My thoughts went fuzzy, and I remained frozen in place, not pulling away. He had his answer.

His tongue pushed into my mouth, and I opened it for him, hungrily tangling my tongue with his. Couldn't we stay like this?

Ignore the rest of the world and freeze time. If only I could. All this ice was running through my veins, and I couldn't even freeze moments. I'd freeze this one. I'd never feel like a traitor to my crown, and he'd never have to cut the string from which he had my heart dangling.

He shifted against me, and suddenly his hands were grasping at my face, pulling at my hair, cupping around my neck, like he was frantic for me. Hungry. Like he knew we only had this moment — like he knew our time together was ticking away.

And then he was gone, breaking our kiss and taking swift steps away from me. I was left standing there, breathless, and he was pacing, trying to inhale deep breaths at an alarming rate. "I can't even be near you without needing to touch you." He was talking aloud, but it wasn't to me. It was to himself.

"Is that such a bad thing?" I asked him with a light-hearted tone. We'd never get through this night if he started to brood.

He stopped moving and looked at me. Really looked at me. His gray eyes were the color of charcoal, and his jaw was locked. He looked at me like a predator stalking his prey. And I knew the answer to my question was *yes*.

"Let's just… regroup," I offered, taking a step toward him, but abruptly stopped when he took a step back. He was determined to not touch me. Super. "You brought me here for a reason. What is it?"

He put his hands loosely on his hips, casting his gaze to the floor like he was rethinking the entire night. Maybe he'd take me back, and we wouldn't have to face one another before he left. But that thought made my stomach fall.

"This way," he grunted and turned to walk to a latched door in the floor, bending down to grab a circular handle and raise it. He was going to brood anyway. And we had come so far.

I drew a small breath and followed him to the door, peering down into the barely lit hole. Some stairs led down. He nodded at me and then at the stairs, which I guessed was my cue to take the first step. I sucked in a deeper breath and took a step onto the trim ladder, not glancing back to see if he followed. I'd gotten myself into this mess, and I would face the consequences if he decided to lock me in.

My feet hit the floor, and I tried to find a wall to cling to as the boat continued to rock at the weight shift. It was a good size ship, but he was a good size guy. He clunked down the steps, the rocking only settling as I heard him land beside me.

There was no light. We were masked in complete darkness. Which, in our case, usually led to fucking, but he was still keeping a good two feet between us. I knew that because when I reached out to find him, I couldn't.

I willed fire to my fingertips and lit them ablaze, holding them out in front of me to make out something. Anything.

"You're a living candle," he grumbled.

I rolled my eyes at his grumpiness. He held a candle up to my fingertips, waiting for me to light the wick. Being a *living candle* was okay as long as he had use for it. I was tempted to not help him, but I also wanted more light. I stuck a fingertip to the wick and watched it come alive in his hand.

He stepped away and spread the fire from the candle in his hand to other candles lying around the hull. I was finally able to make out a bed and a small table with wooden crates on the floor next to it that held some nonperishables in them.

Sitting atop the small table was a wicker basket. I looked at him and then moved to the basket, lifting the flaps to peer inside. "Did you make a picnic?"

He shrugged at me and leaned back against the wall, crossing his arms over his chest. "Technically, your village made it. That's what I picked up yesterday. There are pastries in there from your bakery and some cheeses. A bottle of wine."

Yesterday. When I saw him in the bakery with Jeanine.

"Yesterday," I mumbled aloud. Envy heated the fire in my belly.

"Don't," he warned.

My eyes narrowed as irritation crept over my skin. "Why am I here, Zeke? You have someone. Where is she?"

"Not here."

No shit. "*Why am I here?*"

He was annoyed at me. I could tell by his piercing stare. When he didn't answer, I cursed under my breath and reached into the basket to pull out a pastry as big as my hand. It was doughy and soft, filled with chocolate, and covered in a sugary glaze. It was the one I wanted on our date.

I lifted it and bit the corner, chocolate immediately spilling into my mouth. I sighed, running my tongue across my lip to catch the filling. I heard him inhale sharply, tracking the movement of my tongue across my mouth.

This was how I could draw him out.

I did it again, taking a more significant chunk of it with my teeth, letting the chocolate pour over my mouth. I slowly lapped it up with my tongue. He dropped his arms from his chest and hung them loosely at his sides, his eyes glued to me.

I took another bite, but instead of licking the chocolate from my mouth, I let a drop of it fall to my neck, clinging to my skin. A ghost of a smile played across my lips. "Can you get that?"

He looked like he wanted to eat me alive. His jaw was still clenched like he may combust. At first, he didn't move. And neither did I. Who would prove to be more stubborn? He watched as the chocolate continued to drip slowly down my neck, like a siren beckoning a sailor to his demise.

He slowly pushed off from the wall and took a step toward me. Then two. My insides clenched at the sight of him coming to me only surrounded by candlelight. Did he have to be so goddamn mesmerizing? He was intentional with his movements, knowing the anticipation was killing me. It frustrated me that I wanted him — that I was still here.

When he was within inches of me, we stared at each other. His fingers wrapped around my wrists as if he wanted to keep me from touching him as he cautiously leaned forward to my neck. I tilted my head to the side, exposing my throat to him. My entire body felt hypersensitive to his touch as the tip of his tongue licked up the side of my neck, removing the chocolate from my skin.

All that was left was the feeling from his tongue. When he drew back, he blew out a breath on the spot he had cleaned. I shivered. He straightened and dropped my wrists, retreating again until he was back against the wall. I narrowed my eyes, glaring at my enemy, displeased with how easy staying away from me seemed to be for him. "Do you have a problem?" I asked through gritted teeth.

He chuckled huskily. "You."

"I'm *your* problem?" I couldn't help but laugh at the irony. "Your tongue was just in my mouth. Is that how you deal with all your problems?"

His lips pursed at my question.

"My mistake. Of course, it is." I loathed how bitter I sounded. "Do you think about me when you're with her?" I could turn around, walk back up those stairs and leave. Every instinct was telling me to. "Do you wish I'd think about you when I'm with Cade?" If looks could kill, I'd be dead. My fire pushed under my skin, his gaze on me awakening my need to fight or flee.

I didn't want to do either. I just wanted him. I discarded the pastry sloppily back into the basket and pulled out the bottle of wine. Corked. I fingered through the basket, looking for a way to open it, but I grew impatient. I took the bottle and banged the top against the table until it broke off and fell to the floor.

A KINGDOM OF FLAME AND FURY

"Whoops," I muttered. I tipped it to my mouth and kept it away from my skin, catching the liquid with my tongue. I took as much as possible before lowering the bottle and swallowing.

He remained still, watching me.

So I did it again and again. I didn't even understand why he was so angry with me. I was the one who should be angry, but I was more resentful of the fact that he wasn't touching me.

I drank the wine too fast, and now I felt gooey. And more confident. "Why'd you even bring me here if you were just going to act like a little bitch?"

No answer. I seethed. I raised the bottle again and poured the liquid into my mouth while taking a step toward him. "You really know how to give a girl whiplash."

His eyes remained on me, though I swore I saw a ghost of a smile sweep around his mouth. Nothing about this was humorous. It was infuriating.

I needed to go. He didn't want me. I was playing right into his hand. I shook the bottle. I'd drank it all. There was nothing left for me here. I stared at him. He stared at me.

And then I hurled the bottle at him. It broke against the wall next to his head, and he straightened, but I didn't care and didn't watch him long enough to see his reaction.

Instead, I turned on my heel and made a mad dash for the stairs.

CHAPTER FOURTEEN

Raven

I hurtled up the ladder and heard him behind me, his long strides catching up to me quickly. I pushed open the door and felt his hand try to wrap around my foot, but I yanked it from him and took off onto the deck, jumping down to the dock. He was behind me, starting to chase after me.

I tore into the woods, passing the spring and glancing behind me to see him right on me. I leaned over to the side, brushing my fingertips across the ground. It shook underneath us, and he stumbled, growling as I gained a little more distance from him. "You can't outrun me, baby!" He shouted to me.

I cursed under my breath. I was growing tired, my lungs trying to take in deep breaths, and I nearly fell as that black cat emerged from behind a tree. I stumbled, trying to stop my run as it stared at me. "What the fu—" I started to say when I felt his arms wrap around my waist from behind. I pummeled his arms with my fists, trying to get him to drop me.

He overpowered me quickly and threw me over his shoulder, slapping my ass as I kicked him. "Thank you!" he called out.

I pushed my palms up against his back and leaned up. "Did you just thank the cat?"

He didn't respond as he carried my flailing body back to his ship. He crouched down to grab the latch, and I kicked him again, but it did nothing. This man was unbreakable.

Once we were back in the hull, he threw me down on the bed. He glared at me, and I returned it. I tried to stand back up to leave again, but he shoved me back down.

This shouldn't be turning me on so much. He knew I could find a way to escape him if I really wanted to. He saw me turn a man into a fucking snowman. But we both knew I wanted him to catch me. And if he wanted to let me go, he would've.

When I tried again, he lunged for me. His body crashed into mine, and his weight pushed me back flat against the bed. I wrapped my legs around his waist on instinct, and he snarled at the contact, moving his hands to my thighs and pinching my skin between his fingers. I yelped at the sudden burst of pain and tangled my fingers in his hair, tugging it roughly.

And then his tongue shoved into my mouth, and I opened for him, warmth spreading down my core, wanting him everywhere. But no. I pushed him off me and rolled out from underneath him, panting as I stood. "No," I bit out.

I didn't recognize the man in front of me as he stood and prowled closer. I took steps back until I felt the wall behind me. A dangerous grin was on his mouth. "No?" His voice was hoarse.

I shook my head slowly, my resolution wavering.

He pushed his fingers into my waist and ground his hips against mine. "What do you mean 'no'?"

"I mean…" I said, baring my teeth. "You can't have me."

It would have been him if a person could inhabit the depths of midnight. Everything about how he looked at me was dark. Dominating. Possessive. "My sweet baby."

I wanted his voice burned into my skin, forever on replay.

"I already do." And then his lips were crashing into mine and he bit down on my bottom lip until my flesh tore under his teeth.

I groaned and shoved him back, but he didn't move. His tongue lapped up my blood. He started to suck out more like he wanted me to keep his own black heart pumping. I could feel how hard he was for me, but I was full of so much envy and despair that I put all of my strength into pushing him off of me again. He took a step back, and I swiped the back of my hand across my mouth, wiping the blood off.

"You're using me," I growled through gritted teeth.

His eyes flared for a second until they narrowed.

"I am *nothing* to you." It hurt to say it. Everything about this was hurting me. Breaking me down.

He took a step forward, our bodies touching again. I swallowed the lump in my throat as I peered up at him.

"Raven," he whispered. "You are everything."

His mouth pushed against mine and my hands cupped around his face as I finally returned his passion. But it was over quickly as he broke from me and caged me in with his arms.

"You are my melancholy." His eyes bore into mine like he'd been starved and wanted to savor me.

That wasn't the alcohol I inhaled that made me feel wobbly. It was all him. The way he talked to me was informal like we'd been playing this game for years. I wondered if I always lost.

"But you're not mine," I whispered as my voice broke. I desperately wanted this man. My soul clung to him, wound up tight within his web of deceit. I wanted to stay there, let him crawl all over me, beg for him to end me.

He reached down and started to bunch the hem of my dress as he slowly raised it up and over my head, dropping it to the floor. He unbuckled his pants and let them fall to his feet while I kicked off my shoes. I pushed up at his shirt and he yanked it over his head, wrapping his hands around my waist and moving us back to the bed where he guided me gently down onto my back. He was on top of me, our chests pressing together, his hand in between us as he aligned his tip with my entrance and watched my face as he slowly filled me.

He wanted to ruin me.

Break me.

Make me yearn for him in every possible way. And I did.

And then he was gone, pulling out of me completely. I sat up on my elbows, frustrated by his absence. He walked to the basket and sifted through, bringing a fresh pastry. He crawled back on the bed and leaned over me on his knees, shoving the corner of the pastry into my mouth. I bit down, and he dribbled the chocolate on my mouth and watched as I licked it clean. His gray irises are almost black. Full of contempt for me.

We knew we were enemies. He wasn't supposed to want me. But, here we were — our very presence together threatening everything.

He turned the open end of the pastry up so it stopped dripping into my mouth. Pulling up slowly, he trailed the chocolate over my breasts, my belly button, across my thighs until it ended on my core. I whimpered, begging for his tongue on me. He tossed the pastry to the floor while admiring what he'd done. All I could do was gawk at the devil on his knees in front of me. Something inside him broke as he leered at me, and he brought his eyes back up to mine, searching for answers I couldn't give him. Secrets that lay deep within us.

Slowly, he lowered down, placing his palms on either side of me, locking me in. I wanted to be at his mercy. He dipped his head to my breasts and circled his tongue around one of my nipples, licking off the chocolate. I moaned softly, drawing in a heavy breath as he moved to the next one and nipped at the skin.

His tongue traveled downward toward my navel, dipping into the crest of my belly button. I sucked in my stomach from the contact, reaching for his shoulders to either pull him up or push him down; I wasn't sure. As his tongue glided to my thigh, he tilted his chin just enough to meet my eyes again. We stared at one another, even as he licked up one of my thighs. He nipped at the skin, tugging it between his teeth, then soothed the pain with feathery kisses.

Goose bumps rose over every inch of me. I bucked my hips against him, wanting this tease to end, but he moved his hands to cover my hips and pinned them down against the bed, stilling me.

He was trying to kill me by sexual torture. This would be how I'd go. And I would have for him. Goddamn him.

He gave me one last hard stare before his tongue finally pushed into my cunt, moving in and out quickly, taking what was his. His fingers pressed roughly into my hip bones as I tried to move again, but he wouldn't let me. His tongue moved everywhere, all at once, and I felt dizzy from never having the same sensation twice. He sucked on my clit and nibbled at my skin before he'd plunge his tongue in. Over and over, he tortured me, bringing me to my peak only to shove me back off.

I screamed for him, cupping the back of his head and pushing him harder toward me, urging him to continue while trying to thrust against his mouth. I was so close, but he didn't want me there yet. "Please," I begged aloud.

He groaned against me before he dove in again. My walls tightened around his tongue as I came fiercely, the force of my high making me roll to my side, but he still had a grip on my bones and pulled my hips against him, making me fuck his tongue until I had nothing left to give.

My hand fell from his head and moved to my forehead, trying to wipe the sweat away. I was mentally and physically exhausted, but he gave me no time to recover. "You're not going anywhere," he growled, not allowing me a chance to adjust to his body weight as he pressed our chests together and filled me again.

He pushed roughly into my core, and I cried out, lifting my legs to lock around his waist as I tried to adjust to how swollen he was for me, but he didn't want me to. He wanted the pain to constantly remind me of him. He bucked into me repeatedly, never letting me catch my breath. My core tightened at the feel of him in me, on me, his tongue pushing into my mouth as he devoured me all over again.

I tasted me on him and let him coat my tongue with it. I dug my nails into his back and scratched deep until I felt his blood. He groaned from the pain, but it was nothing compared to how he was tearing apart my insides and heart.

He was hungry for me. I was ravenous for him.

This was an addiction. A dangerous game we played.

An obsession that was built on shaky ground.

He continued to drive into me, deepening our kiss. My cheeks were wet from the tears falling from my eyes. Tears from how much I needed him. Tears from how much I didn't want this to end. He pulsed and filled me with his release, spurring my own again, moaning against his mouth as I tumbled.

As he steadied his movements and I felt our hearts connect with their matching rapid beats, I realized he'd already won.

I had fallen in love with him.

And he would be my undoing.

When our breathing had calmed and the ferocity of what just happened settled, I loosened my legs from around his waist and let them fall against the bed, completely spent. How could I let this happen? I'd fallen for the enemy. The very man sent here to destroy everything I had built. The logical thoughts tried to push through what I was feeling. I shouldn't have made this plan. I shouldn't have followed him.

But when he raised his head to stare into my eyes, I knew I was putty in his hands. He could burn the very ground I stood on, and I'd beg him to do it again. I'd offer him my own fire. The fire coursing through my veins, urging me to run, stop this. But instead of listening, I kissed him in an attempt to pour all of my feelings into it. Make it better, I begged him silently.

Please choose me.

When he broke our kiss, I knew that one of us would have to destroy the other. We were from different places, his allegiance sworn to another queen. A queen that may be the driving force behind all of this.

He studied my face, my cheeks stained with dry tears. He looked as miserable as I did and dropped his forehead to mine. "This wasn't supposed to happen. We weren't supposed to happen," he whispered, his voice breaking.

I just nodded. I knew it was his way of trying to warn me, the only way he could. We both knew this was over. Our time was up.

"I didn't mean…." He trailed off, and I just turned my head from his. He rolled off me to his side, wrapping his arm around my waist to pull me back against his chest. We laid there, and he let me cry while he leaned over and kissed away the tears falling down my cheeks.

I needed to tell him. I knew I shouldn't. I knew it would make no difference. But I was exasperated, always keeping everything I felt buried inside me. If this was my last night with him, what else was there to lose? "I fell in love with you," I breathed.

His lips pressed against the back of my head, his body crumbling into mine. He was quiet for a moment, and second by second, I withered. And then, "We can't."

He'd chosen his queen. It wasn't me.

And every piece of my heart shattered.

————

Our walk back to the castle was one of silence. We didn't touch. He would look at me from the corner of his eye, but I didn't return it. I couldn't. He was another person who didn't want me. I had let him in, despite everything in me that told me not to. I had let my guard down. Allowing myself to feel protected. And now he was leaving.

When we entered the courtyard, I moved to leave him, but he called my name quietly, and I froze. He lightly touched the sensitive part of my wrist as he turned me around to face him. I couldn't meet his eyes, so I stared at his collarbone, remembering how many times I had touched him there. Another tear fell down my cheek.

"Raven," he whispered, wiping my tear away with his finger.

All I could do was shake my head, never meeting his gaze. He leaned down and pressed his lips to my forehead in a feathery kiss. I closed my eyes, soaking in the last moment.

"Goodbye, baby," he murmured. His voice broke on his nickname for me. And then he was gone.

———

I knew I should've returned to Cade's chambers, but I needed time to work through everything that happened, which was how I ended up running a hot bath in my own bathroom.

I leaned back against the tub, skimming my fingers over the water. I had no proof that Queen Mira was involved in this, but it wasn't too far-fetched. I doubted Zeke decided to seek me out on his own, especially if his claims about not knowing my name were true. I still wasn't sure how John was involved or how far this truly went. Thoya and Perosan were peaceful kingdoms, quiet like Seolia. Their rulers seemed just as desperate to keep the Circle of Peace peaceful.

But I didn't know Mira. Could she have the same thirst for power as her ancestors? Her father maintained the peace for many years; what would make her want to change that? And what did it have to do with me? And how would Mira know I possessed magic? Unless John was the one who relayed that information to her. Which still led to the question: how was John involved in this?

He had been closest to King Leonidas, which would mean that he'd want to honor his wishes in keeping me protected. Why wait fifteen years with me as queen before deciding to take the throne? And what did any of this have to do with Zeke?

I splashed my hand down against the water in frustration.

Every inch of my body was sore, and yet I'd do it all again if he were to walk through my door. But I knew he wouldn't. He was going home because he knew I was aware of why he was here. I could have had him arrested. I could have killed him myself. But how could I kill someone who felt like one half of me? I raised my palms to my eyes and pressed hard against them. Maybe I could scrub his memory clean if I could somehow shove them into my brain. But I didn't want to. I wanted him permanently stamped on me.

And as much as I wanted to, I couldn't stay in the bath all night. I needed to get to Cade's. I wasn't safe anywhere anymore, even in my own castle. Traitors walked within the walls.

I sighed and stood slowly, letting the water drip off me before reaching for my plush robe. Maybe I'd get some sleep tonight since my body was exhausted. Or perhaps I'd never sleep again, constantly plagued by my heart that beat unevenly now.

I wrapped the robe around my body and padded out of the bathroom and into my bedroom, but stopped short and looked around. Something was off. Someone had been in here. There was a presence that hadn't been here when I returned.

I breathed through my nose, catching a whiff of a distant scent. Pine. My favorite. My heart started to ache all over again.

Zeke had been here. He used my tunnel. I fell to my knees and crawled to the hidden door, yanking it open. I peered down the dim hallway but didn't see him. I shut it and stood, looking around my room until my eyes fell to the bed.

Lying on my bedspread was a single rose, freshly cut with its bright red petals matching the color of my bloodred eyes when my fury was brought to the forefront.

I grabbed the rose by the stem, one of the thorns piercing the skin of my finger. I didn't react. I just watched as my blood dripped onto my quilt. I curled my fingers around the stem and let the thorns break the skin of my palm, blood pooling within my grasp.

Just like how my heart bled for him. I welcomed the pain. I was his rose, and he was the very thorn that pierced me. He took my heart with him. Now it was time to see who I was without one.

I opened my hand and the rose fell to my bed with some of my blood, the wounds in my skin already mending. I lit the rose with a flick of my wrist and watched it burn.

Hell hath no fury.

I gathered more of my clothes to take with me to Cade's. I wouldn't be back here. Not until this was all over. They wanted my throne; they'd have to pry it from my dead, cold hands. Even then, I'd still be burning. I'd lost the man I loved. He used me, made me fall in love with him, and then discarded me.

He would return to Reales, and I'd spend my time hardening my heart against him, against anyone who wanted me gone. I may not have earned my place on the throne, but I was going to keep it. They could have their war.

I didn't spare my room another glance before I left.

But little did I know that he had watched me hidden in the shadows of my balcony. He watched me burn his rose. He watched me leave for another man's room. Naked under my robe. Beautiful. Thirsty for his blood. A dangerous game, indeed.

———————

Hours later, while Cade slept, I snuck down to the dock by our spring and watched from behind a tree as Zeke and Jeanine loaded onto his boat and pulled away. I contemplated, briefly, freezing the water to prevent him from leaving.

Instead, I shifted into Terra and stepped out from behind my tree. I didn't know how, but he sensed me and leaned over the railing to stare at me. I held my palms up and loosened a gust of wind from them, listening as his ship groaned against the new weight spurring them faster away from my island.

He hung his head, realizing that I was only there to aid them in going. "I love you," I whispered.

His head snapped up at that like he could hear me.

"Now get the fuck out."

PART TWO

CHAPTER FIFTEEN

Raven

Four weeks.

Four weeks passed, and I spent them performing my normal daily duties — talking with my subjects, meeting with my advisers with no news, and discussing John's movements with Cade. The thought of moving Isla into the castle crossed my mind at one point, but I decided that since I never introduced her to Zeke or showed him where she lived, she'd be safer to remain distant from me. Nothing was out of the ordinary, but Cade and I decided on two things.

One, we were going to comb through our libraries again and look for anything that could prove helpful. We weren't sure what that could be at this point, but whether it was sharpening our knowledge of Reales or the origin of dark magic, we were going to find it.

And two, we needed to train. Cade would work with me and our small legion of soldiers. We needed to brush up on our fighting techniques. We'd spent the last few weeks working on my hand-to-hand combat, just in case there ever came a day when I couldn't use my elements. How naive we'd all been — to think we would never need any of this.

Cade and I planned to visit the Black Forest every night, starting tonight, to sharpen and hone my abilities, maybe learn how to wield all three at once. But today, it was my monthly excursion into my village to greet new residents and check in with all the shop owners to make sure everyone had what they needed from me for their businesses to thrive.

I sent out for new fabric almost immediately after permanently abandoning my chambers. I had new outfits fashioned from lighter fabric, specifically soft cotton and silk. I'd wear my fitted leathers to continue training, but I wanted the ability to move quickly around and out of the castle at a moment's notice. My dear seamstress had worked around the clock for me, and today, I was wearing one of my brand new ones.

It was light blue in color and fell to the ground with long sleeves and cuffs of gold silk wrapped around my wrists. The colors of Seolia's crest. Light blue and gold were the colors of most of the fabric I had ordered. I wanted to represent my kingdom daily, showing that I was not going anywhere.

My diadem sat on my black hair braided like a fishtail, glistening in the sunlight that rose higher each morning, beckoning spring forward.

Snow was starting to melt, and I was ready to kick this dreary weather to the side and let my soul welcome the sunshine. I needed a rebirth. Winter had always been my favorite, but it reminded me of him, and I needed to move on.

But even still, after four weeks without him, everything still ached. I'd catch a slight scent of rum or pine and immediately look around, hoping he had come back, even if it was to destroy me. I'd close my eyes every night to fall asleep and remember his raspy laugh and how I was the only one to hear it.

He was always so serious around everyone else, but he finally started letting me in. For me, he had pushed his darkness aside. And then he left, and I'd find myself crying throughout the day. Cade just watched, unable to help, knowing I was still lusting for someone who was never truly mine.

But, he'd given me space. He knew I needed time. Every night, we'd fall asleep with me in his arms. He comforted me and kept my dreams away. Because I didn't want to dream about Zeke. They were too real, and I'd wake up in pain all over again, feeling like he was truly there, holding me in my mind, even as scattered as they'd become when I'd wake up.

I could always sense him there, hiding in the depths of my subconscious, clawing it softly when I missed him. But, the more I was with Cade, the more I slowly started to swim up from the shadows of my depression. And he would look down at me from the surface with his blue eyes, so blue that I could easily drown in them if I wanted to — instead of the gray ones that still seemed to call to me.

Cade would be by my side every step of the way today, flanked by two guards. It wouldn't be a mystery to the villagers as to why I suddenly had an increase in security. We'd passed the point of maintaining decorum. The secret of my darkness was creeping into every corner of our four kingdoms as whispers became louder.

As we stood on the breezeway that led us to a small bridge that connected the palace to the village, Cade faced me and put his hands on my shoulders. I gazed into his eyes and gave him a small smile. So much had changed in such a short amount of time. Usually, we'd be skipping in excitement over the bridge. We lingered, unsure of what we'd face on the other side.

"Are you ready? You look beautiful. Every inch the queen you are."

My smile broadened at his compliment. I inhaled and exhaled a deep breath. He gave my shoulders a reassuring squeeze before he dropped his hands and took his place two paces behind me. I had to start walking on my own. My people needed a strong queen.

I took the first step, and my entourage fell into step behind me. The clicking of the guard's boots behind me on the bridge added an extra level of reassurance that I wished I didn't need. As emotionally spent as I'd been since Zeke left, I wasn't sure how much fight I had in me if something were to go wrong.

I approached the end of the bridge and heard cheers and saw people waving from the crowd formed on the street in front of us. I beamed at all of them. If I was proud of anything in my life, it was this. Serving them. Earning their trust.

I returned their waves, extending my arms as I approached some to shake their hands, leaning forward to accept their pecks to my cheeks. Behind some adults, I saw a tiny Eva jumping up and down, trying to catch a glimpse of the commotion around her.

My face was already hurting from smiling, but it grew wider as I walked to Eva. The adults blocking her moved to the side for me to kneel in front of her. "Hello, sweet one," I cooed to her.

Eva had only seen me as Terra, but a look of realization passed over her tiny eyes, and she raised a hand to my cheek. I covered her hand with mine and fought back the tears threatening to spill over. "My butterfly," she whispered.

I laughed softly. The crowd around us grew silent as they watched our interaction unfold. "My queen is my friend!" Eva squealed in excitement.

I nodded to her, a single tear escaping and falling down my cheek, pooling against her tiny hand. "Always."

Her eyes grew softer as she felt the tear. "Don't cry, butterfly."

She wrapped her arms around my neck, and I wrapped mine around her tiny frame, and we stayed like that in a tight embrace. This was the little girl I needed to fight for. She deserved the life she wanted, and I wanted to give it to her. I wanted to give it to all of them.

I kissed her temple before we released one another, winking at her as I stood and met her father's eyes, Theodore, whom I hadn't seen since we danced together at the banquet.

"Hello, butterfly," he greeted me in a whisper with a secretive smile on his face. A look of understanding passed between us, and then he bent at the waist in a bow.

I took another step and saw Arthur waiting for me. My eyes filled with tears again, and he gave me a small smile. He opened his arms to me, and I stepped into them, letting him wrap me up in a hug. He smelled like his pub, and another hot tear fell down my cheek. "Look at me, Raven."

I raised my head a little bit, wiping my tears off. I met his eyes, and the kindness behind them calmed me.

"I liked him, too."

I choked back a sob as I nodded. I'd been holding down all my feelings, but I had someone in front of me who understood and saw what we had. He winked at me, and I returned it with a small smile. "Give your heart time. And come see me soon." He bowed to me before he took his leave.

After the crowd had parted, I continued my tour of the village, stopping at The Stag Shack and listening to the owner's story about how one of his tables randomly burst into flames.

Cade snickered behind me, and I turned to narrow my eyes at him before returning my attention to the pub owner, promising a replacement would be delivered tomorrow.

We walked past the bakery, and I paused, staring into the window as I recalled the awful memory of seeing Zeke with

Jeanine. Cade came up behind me and nudged me with his elbow. "Are we going in?"

I hesitated -- the anguish in my bones from missing him still fresh. But, this visit wasn't about me — it was about ensuring my village was well supplied with everything they needed. So I nodded, and Cade pulled the door open, beckoning me inside with his hand. The smell of chocolate-filled biscuits immediately hit me, and I licked my lips, taking a deep draw of the scent, wanting it all to myself.

"My most popular pastry," an older woman huffed, pulling one from the display and passing it to Cade. The pastry chef then gave me a quick curtsy.

Cade handed me the pastry. "I don't like chocolate," he muttered.

I rolled my eyes and took a small bite, bracing myself for the chocolate to spill. I caught it with my tongue before it could.

"I can hardly keep them before someone comes in and buys all of them. One woman, in particular, comes in every morning and buys the whole lot. Must have a big family to feed, but she takes them all, and I have to rush to start baking more."

I smiled at the woman, who I remembered went by Lara, and enjoyed how informal she talked to me. "Is there anything you need from me?"

A quick shake of her head. "Not a thing, m'lady. We're well stocked with ingredients. I appreciate how you keep the ships moving."

I was about to bid her goodbye when I noticed a young woman sitting behind the counter, reading a book.

"Don't mind her. She gets lost in her books. In another world." Lara whipped at the young lady's leg with a towel.

The girl looked up abruptly and noticed me, immediately dipping into a curtsy.

I beckoned her to rise with my palm. "What's your name?"

"Grace, Your Majesty."

I could tell she was nervous. She was cute, probably not older than eighteen, with bright red hair that fell in frizzy curls over her deep brown eyes. "Do you enjoy reading?"

"Understatement of the year," Grace responded in a mutter.

I grinned. Lara whipped her again. "I have libraries in my castle that are a mess. Ancient texts are out of place. Texts I need. Are you interested in a librarian position?"

Her mouth fell open. "You're… you're asking me to come work for you in your libraries?"

I nodded, shrugging. "There's plenty to read during breaks, as long as you can organize for me. And if you're not needed here. You'd be home every night in time for dinner."

"She's not needed," Lara said. "All she does is read. I'll make her little brother do all of the heavy liftings."

I heard a boy groan from the back room, and I smiled. "You can start tomorrow morning. I'll inform one of my advisers, Luisa, to be looking for you. She'll show you to the library and explain what we need. I'll find you tomorrow afternoon."

Grace clapped her hands in excitement, bouncing on her toes. "Thank you, Your Majesty!"

Cade and I waved goodbye as I walked out the bakery door, still listening to Grace squeal as it fell closed behind us.

"Great idea," Cade said, nodding back toward the bakery. "That'll help us."

I took another bite of the pasty, and Cade laughed as I tried to stop the chocolate from dribbling down my chin. "These are so good, but I run a risk every time I eat one." I wiped the chocolate off with the back of my hand and gave the pastry back to him. "Only freaks don't like chocolate."

He hesitated before he took a small bite. "Not bad."

"I told you," I replied, doing a double take as I looked down at a table in front of the bakery. For lying atop of it... was a single red rose. I grabbed it, the thorns biting in my skin, but all I did was stare. I felt my heart in my mouth, threatening to spill onto the ground beneath me.

It had to be a coincidence. He was gone, but that didn't stop me from looking around, the hairs on the back of my neck rising. All I saw were my villagers bustling through town.

"Everything okay?" Cade asked, coming up beside me after finishing the pastry. He looked down at the rose in my hand as I wrapped my fingers around the petals and shredded them, dropping the rose to the ground.

I linked my arm through his and gave him a big, albeit fake smile. "Let's go home."

A few hours later, Cade and I dressed in our training ensembles. I had upgraded my usual leathers for a leather jumpsuit that hugged my curves and helped make my motions fluid and more controlled. Cade was in fitted leather pants cuffed around his ankles and a long-sleeved black shirt. We were both in laced-up canvas boots that met midcalf. I had sent out for them when Zeke left, and I could understand why he always wore them. They were lightweight and comfortable, easy to trample over people's hearts. And I couldn't lie. I felt badass walking around in the jumpsuit like I was ready to go to war.

Against my pleas, he was insistent that we practice with swords. My jaw dropped at the weapons inventory when he unlocked the castle armory. Not once had I ever visited here. I sighed as I ran my fingers over the fuller of swords while I walked through the armory. "I had hoped we'd never need these."

He came beside me and removed my hand from the sword, bringing it to his lips in a gentle kiss. "We still may not, but it's always smart to be ready for anything." He dropped my hand and moved his hand to cup my cheek. "I know you want to do this alone. But people want to fight for this kingdom. For you."

I closed my eyes at his words and smiled while he rubbed my cheekbone with his thumb. "I'd go to war for you," he whispered and pulled me to him by my waist, wrapping me in a warm embrace.

I rested my head against his chest. "I'm just so tired. I want all of this to be over."

He kissed the top of my head softly, slowly rocking me back and forth in our embrace. "It will be. We'll make it through." He released me and chose two swords, handing me one.

I looked at it and wondered if the blade in my hand had taken any lives in the last war. If I'd take any.

What our story together would be at the end.

———————

"When's the last time you were in the forest?" I asked him as we crossed the border in the black of night.

He looked around, keeping his eyes peeled for any sign of trouble. "Ah, probably not since the time you brought me out last."

My mouth fell open. "Cade, that was five years ago."

He shrugged. "Never saw the point. It's creepy in here."

I threw my head back in a laugh. "It is not creepy. It's beautiful here, especially at night."

He turned to look at me. "You're beautiful. This is a bunch of trees."

I reached out and shoved his shoulder. "Stop flirting. We have to be tough."

He bent his arm and flexed, his muscles bulging through his sleeve. "I am tough."

I wrinkled my nose and pinched the skin of his muscle. "I don't know. You seem out of shape."

He rolled his eyes and lifted his shirt, exposing his stomach. My eyes fell to it, sheepishly roaming over the lines of his abs. He smirked smugly. My cheeks were hot as I averted my eyes.

"Exactly," he bragged.

I shoved him again.

He tossed the swords down to the ground, confident that we were far enough into the forest for no one to find us. The sky was pitch black, and we blended well beneath the treetops, still bare with dark, deadened leaves.

"We'll start with you. You want to wield all three at once. What stops you?"

If I knew that, I wouldn't be here. "It tires me out, trying to pull from them. I can't seem to hold two without feeling like collapsing."

He tilted his head to the side, waiting for me to elaborate.

"Imagine this. You're swimming in the channel and go under for ten seconds. No problem. So, you extend it. You push yourself to twenty seconds, and it starts to hurt a little more. It burns inside your chest, right?"

He interrupted, "You can only hold your breath for twenty seconds?"

I rolled my eyes. "When you come up to gasp for air, even that's painful. Now imagine pushing yourself for thirty seconds. You're dying under there, and even after coming up for air, you're still disoriented, like your brain can't function with all that pressure. That's what it feels like. I can wield one, no problem. I can hold two, but it's uncomfortable. I want to pull in air. If I try for three, I feel like I may *literally* combust from the inside out."

He nodded at my explanation. "Let's start with two then. We won't get anywhere if we don't try. Start with Frost and Terra. Let's not bring Blaze out just yet."

Yeah, because she was fucking insane.

"Start as yourself. See if you can wield without shifting."

I widened my stance and planted my feet. Willing my ice forward, I opened my hands to create sharp icicles on my palm. Simple, like breathing. With the icicles in my hand, I closed my eyes and pulled at earth, creating wind around me. Sweat beaded along my temple, but I held out.

With my free hand, I created a column of wind and lifted the icicles from my hand until they dangled in the air. Now for the most challenging part: I had to try and combine them. I drew in a deep breath and raised my hand, trying to move the icicles horizontally with my palm, aiming the sharp ends at a tree.

My chest was burning. With a lot of effort, I drew my hand back, still balancing the icicles in the air, and launched my arm forward, sending the icicles flying toward the tree. They pierced the tree trunk, and I collapsed on the ground, gasping for air.

"Again," he commanded, coming to me and pulling on my elbow until I was standing. "The more you try it, the less it will hurt. It takes practice."

So, I did it again. And again. Again. Until my lungs felt like they were bleeding.

"Now, shift into Frost and try to maintain the same stamina you have with Terra."

I closed my eyes and shifted into Frost. When I opened them, I held my hand again and created the icicles, but bringing forth my wind wasn't as simple as before. I hurled the icicles, but they shattered before they reached the tree.

Cade bristled. "You're stronger as yourself when you want to wield two. That's important to know. What else can you do as Frost?"

I raised an eyebrow. "What do you want to see?"

"Walls."

"*Walls*?" I crowed.

"Yeah, Raven," he replied like I was dopey. "Build a wall of ice."

I stood still and cocked my head to the side as I contemplated how to raise a wall of ice. I'd been able to create singular blocks. But a whole wall in one take?

I crouched down, put my arm to the ground, and slowly brought it back up. A thin layer of ice followed as I did, but it was only as wide as my arm. I kicked it and the icy wall shattered under my foot. I crouched again and repeated the motion but added in my other hand. I drew the ice out, expanding it horizontally until I was standing behind a wall of ice that was at least my body length if I were to lie down.

I heard him grab a sword from the ground, and I quickly started reinforcing the wall with more layers, jumping when he stabbed through it. As he punctured it, I made a block of ice around the point of his sword that protruded from the wall. When he went to yank it back, it was stuck. He left the sword dangling from the wall and walked around to where I was, chuckling at my creation. "Clever."

"It'll only prove useful if I'm dealing with one person, though. I don't think I could hold off any more than that."

He nodded in agreement. "What can you do with Terra?"

A lot. Besides pure destruction with fire, earth was my most substantial ability. If I focused hard enough, I could shake the very foundation of a cottage.

Shutting my eyes, I willed Terra to the surface, my icy blonde hair shifting into violet. My golden eyes sparkled in the moonlight, and he stared at me, mesmerized. "You're drooling," I said, snickering.

He mocked me and ushered me to start. I crouched again and put my palms against the ground. An eruption of dirt spurred into shallow ditches and stretched out from my hands. The ditches grew into deeper trenches as they continued down their paths swiftly, uprooting trees in their way.

I removed my hands once I couldn't see the end of them. As his back was turned to examine my work, I tiptoed behind him and stomped my foot. The ground beneath him shook, and he fell backward, catching himself on his palms. He looked up to where I stood, sticking my tongue out with my hands on my hips.

"I am going to make you pay for that," he threatened, jumping quickly to his feet.

I took off into a run, squealing as I heard loud footsteps behind me. Laughing as I weaved through the trees, I glanced back to see how close he was to me. He caught up quickly, and I shrieked as he tackled me to the ground. He pinned me down on my back, wrapping his hands around my wrists and putting them above my head. "Now what, Your Majesty?" His tone dripped with sarcasm, a smug grin plastered on his face.

I quickly lifted my legs and wrapped them around his waist, rocking my body and twisting until he was under me and I was straddling his waist. I laid my palms flat against his chest as he gripped my waist. "Don't fucking try me, adviser."

His eyes moved down my body while he grinned.

I placed my finger on the tip of his nose. "Boop."

He howled in laughter, and I giggled, yelping as he used the leverage from his grip on my waist to twist us again, pinning me with his body. "Did you just... *boop* me?"

I nodded and bit my bottom lip to keep from erupting with laughter. He leaned down to my face and nipped the tip of my nose with his teeth. "Boop."

We both erupted, our bodies shaking with laughter.

When we started to catch our breath, our gazes met, and we stared at one another. All the tension that'd been lying dormant between us bubbled at the surface. I couldn't help but feel guilty and relieved that when he leaned down, it was only to press our foreheads together before he rolled off and stood, reaching out his hand to mine. I grabbed it, and he pulled me up, gently squeezing my waist. "You did great tonight," he assured me as we walked back to find our swords.

He grabbed them with one hand and used his free one to lace our fingers together, leading me back to the palace. The only sounds we heard were the swords clanking against each other every few steps.

"We'll come back tomorrow night and use these things." He nodded down toward the swords.

"We need to let Blaze out at some point. I need to learn to control her," I told him.

Something that resembled fear crossed over his face.

"Tell me."

"The last time I saw Blaze, you were so pissed at me."

"I won't be pissed at you tomorrow night. Unless you try to make me jealous first."

"Were you?"

I looked at him, my eyebrows rising in surprise. "You know I was."

"Why?" he dared me.

I cast my eyes at the ground and sucked in my bottom lip, gnawing at the skin. "You'd left me that day, and it was hard seeing you with someone else."

"Why?" he emphasized the question, stopping.

I lifted my hand to rub at the creases in my forehead. Was I really ready to have this discussion with him? It'd been years of pent-up feelings and only a few weeks of realizing those feelings. Not to mention that my heart was still tangled up in Zeke's.

He watched me as I sorted out my thoughts. I finally raised my golden eyes to his and gave him a slight shrug. "You know why."

The answer was enough for him, and he returned it with a small smile. It was all I could give him right now. I was mending. But I wanted to let him in. I just needed more time. At least, I hope that was all it took. But, as we started to walk again, I couldn't help but think about Zeke.

And I wondered if time would ever be enough.

———

After we had dropped the swords off at the armory, we returned to Cade's room to bathe and try to sleep. It didn't come easily to either of us lately. We were both on alert for any noise that seemed irregular.

After I had moved out of my own chambers, we stationed guards at my door, and the only people allowed in or out were Cade and me. The barn that housed our secret tunnel was also being guarded. That had surely raised some eyebrows, but we'd have to figure out what to do about it later. I didn't want to lose my ability to move in and out freely and undetected, but our only option may be to burn it down and close the tunnels.

I was disappointed in myself for ignoring my better judgment and showing them to Zeke. It was another thing I was trying to resolve within myself. I'd spent so many years hiding who I was and ignoring my own instincts that I didn't know when to trust myself. I was learning to embrace who I was, darkness and all. It was something I tried to explain to Cade after Zeke left. I said that John had been right, and there was darkness looming inside of me, and I needed to learn how to accept it. I couldn't be ashamed anymore. It was part of me, and he needed to accept it, too. According to him, he would.

Zeke embraced it. He was as dark as me.

I let Cade bathe first tonight. I wanted to sit on the balcony and watch my village below. It was very late, only a couple hours until morning, so there was no life down beneath me except for my guards.

I leaned over the balcony, resting my elbows on top of the wall, and caught movement in the corner of my eye. I whipped my head toward it and squinted, trying to determine when it could have been. Candlelight along the wall illuminated the path below, and I moved my eyes along it but didn't see anything.

I straightened when Cade called my name, telling me it was my turn to bathe. I glanced down once more, and my heart stopped. I could've sworn, even if it was just for a millisecond, that a pair of gray eyes stared back at me. When I blinked, they were gone. Great, now I was hallucinating. He'd really done a number on me.

After I finished bathing, I pulled on one of Cade's shirts that was more like a short dress on me and climbed into bed beside him, snuggling down under his quilt. His back was turned to me, and I pushed mine against it. He rolled over and scooped me up in his arms, pressing his chest against my back. And as he smoothed my hair back, my eyelids fluttered shut. Combining my abilities had worn me out, and when he kissed my temple, I expelled a deep breath and felt him smile against me. "Sleep now. I have you."

So I did.

And for the first time since he left, I dreamed.

———

I dreamed of haunting gray eyes that followed me through the Black Forest, never fully forming — but they stayed with me at every turn. "Go," I said, but they just stared at me. I felt heat rise across my skin, itching to be closer to him. "I smell you," I whispered, inhaling softly as his scent filled my nostrils.

I heard his raspy chuckle, and I groaned, the sound making my bones rattle. "Sweet baby," he purred.

"Baby, baby, baby," I whispered.

CHAPTER SIXTEEN

Raven

A week later, I excused myself from the meeting we scheduled with Luisa and John. Cade could handle it on his own. I was tired of hearing that there was nothing new multiple times a week — and absolutely sick of looking at John's face on the opposite side of my table. He'd been on his best behavior lately, hardly ever leaving the castle and being overly friendly with me.

The behavior change was odd, but since we didn't have a legitimate reason to remove him, we decided to keep him close. He may do more danger without constant eyes on him.

We'd been training every night, still working on Frost and Terra. The swords and Blaze hadn't come out to play yet. Since my heart was recovering, I hadn't felt my fury as often. I just felt... sad. Lost. I didn't understand why this was happening — why anyone would want to go to war with us. We were small, our army only containing maybe fifty soldiers. Controlling us would be easy, but why would anyone want to? I'd been queen for nearly fifteen years, and it'd been quiet.

And I couldn't understand why I felt so… out of place without Zeke by my side. Sure, there had been some strange connection to him, but why did I feel so… unstable?

I wandered into the library to find Grace sifting through books on a high shelf. "It's a mess, isn't it?" I called out, smiling when she turned to look at me.

"Oh! Your Majesty! Uh, I can't…." She looked down at the ladder and tried to bend her knees. "I don't know how to greet you from up here."

I laughed and shook my hands. "No, don't try, please. I don't want to explain to your mother that you fell off the ladder on your first day. You're doing everything you need to right now. Have you found anything of interest?"

She nodded toward a pile of books on the table. "All the ones I want to read. But I'll only read them here, I promise."

I shrugged my shoulders as I combed through the books she'd chosen. "I'm just happy to see someone reading them. Cade and I don't have the time."

Grace blushed at the mention of Cade's name.

A corner of my mouth lifted. "Yes, he's sexy." I winked at her, saying what she was thinking out loud.

"Are you two, well are you… you know, are you…" Grace stammered, but I knew what she was trying to ask.

"Cade is way too old for you, dear," I replied, finding this entire interaction amusing.

"Oh! Gosh, no, I wasn't suggesting that. You're just two beautiful people, and you'd look like a couple out of a fairy tale if you were… you know."

I smiled at her compliment and heard Cade's voice from behind me. "I'm way too good for her, I'm afraid."

I rolled my eyes, and Grace blushed again, turning her head quickly to begin sorting through the books again.

"But darling, we'd be like a fairy tale."

He snorted in response.

I leaned against his knees as he pulled himself up to sit on a table. "Anything?"

He grabbed my hand and rubbed my knuckles with his thumb, frowning while he shook his head.

I sighed. "Did we dream this up? It's been quiet for too long."

"We didn't dream it. It's quiet because they're planning something. I just don't know what it is or how to find that out. John keeps going on about how he's here for '*our queen.*'" He rolled his eyes as he said it.

I giggled at his sarcasm.

"So dreamy," Grace muttered under her breath.

I snorted. "She has a crush on you," I whispered to him.

He laughed. "She's not the only one," he countered, raising my hand to his mouth and kissing my knuckles one by one. "You jealous?"

I watched him, biting down on my bottom lip as I grinned. "I'm seeing *green*."

"As long as it's not *red*." Cade smiled and dropped my hand, pulling me to him by my waist. He pressed his lips to my cheek and gave me a light kiss before he released me to slide off the table. "I have to leave you ladies. Luisa has requested my presence."

I pouted. "Already leaving me for another woman. That didn't take long."

He laughed again and nipped at my nose with his teeth before leaning to whisper against my ear, "Luisa bakes better."

I fake gasped, holding a hand to my heart in mock pain. "They always say that a way to a man's heart is through his mouth."

"Bake me a pie, and then we'll talk." He didn't spare me another glance before walking out of the library, but not before he yelled over his shoulder, "Apple!"

My laugh carried him out.

After he'd gone, I turned my attention back to Grace. "Grace, darling, do me a favor?"

She turned again to look at me, waiting.

"If you find any books on magic, specifically dark magic, will you start a pile for me?"

I was about to leave when I heard her ask, "It's true then?"

I froze and arched my brow. "What's true?"

"That you possess dark magic."

My stomach felt like jelly. "Grace, where did you hear that?"

"I was at the bakery about to deliver a basket of pastries to Keaton, the flower shop owner."

I nodded, knowing who she was referring to.

"A person was standing outside the shop. They had a hood on, and I didn't recognize their voice. They were saying that our queen possesses dark magic."

"Did you tell anyone what you heard?"

"No, because I don't care."

I cocked my head at her, and she sighed, smacking her forehead with the book she was holding. "I'm awful with words even though I read a lot. By not care, I mean, *who cares?* It'd be awesome if you had magic."

A small smile tugged at my mouth. "You think so, huh?"

"I think that magic chooses its people."

"What do you mean?"

"I've read a lot of books, some about magic. Back when dark magic supposedly flowed through the kingdoms, only a select few could wield it. If magic wasn't special, everyone would have it. If you possess it after all these years, it's for a reason."

I blinked back wetness pooling in my eyes. "Thank you, Grace."

––––––––––

Long after I had left the library, I became curious about where Cade and Luisa were. When I couldn't find either of them, I went to wait for him in his chambers. I pushed the chair on his balcony to one side and laid down on the ground, closing my eyes as the sun hit my face.

Winter was so close to being over, and it was starting to warm up. I had missed the feel of the sun on my face, though I was partial to winter. I looked forward to it every year, but this one had been hard. The sunshine might help me overcome my need for Zeke and his darkness, which seemed to replicate winter's gray tones.

I was about to doze off when I felt a body lie beside me. Shielding my eyes with one hand, I tilted my head toward Cade. "And where have you been?"

He hesitated. "I'm not supposed to tell you."

"Fat chance of that." I giggled. "You can't keep a secret."

He gasped. "I can keep a secret, you little shit."

"You always end up telling me."

He remained quiet for a moment and then snapped his fingers, rolling over to his side and propping up on his elbow to look at me. "When you moved into the king's quarters, I switched the pillows in your room with mine."

My jaw dropped at his admission. "You *what*?!"

He nodded and shrugged. "I liked yours better."

"You *stole* my pillows."

"You're sleeping on them, so you got them back in the end."

I knocked on his shoulder with my fist and shook my head. "I could've had neck pain all these years, and it would've been your fault."

He just shrugged again. I sat up quickly and stood, marching to his bed, and started grabbing the pillows off.

"What do you think you're doing?" He followed me to his bed and laughed at me, trying to hold multiple pillows in my arms.

I stomped one foot. "I'm taking my pillows back."

He continued to laugh and yanked them out of my arms. "Like hell you are. These are mine now."

"You're a *thief.*" I tried gathering them up in my arms again, shrieking as he tackled me to the bed. I snickered in amusement and tried to shove him off, but he pinned me again.

"Don't take my pillows. Please," he begged, sticking out his bottom lip.

"You mean *my* pillows?"

"Compromise. *Our* pillows?"

I smiled at that. "Our pillows."

He dipped his face to mine and fluttered his eyelashes against my cheek. I giggled at the tickling until he raised his head, giving me a lopsided grin. His proximity to me made me ask again, my need to possess everyone I loved rearing its ugly head. "Where were you?"

He sighed, and dipped his head again, resting his forehead against my shoulder. "Luisa will kill me."

"I won't let her," I promised.

"I guess turning twenty-five is a big deal, and she wanted to inform me that we're having a ball in your honor."

I groaned. He smirked in response, lifting his head.

"I don't want a ball. I want our picnic on the balcony."

He smiled and pretended to be deep in thought about something. "How about this… if you dance with me, I'll have a picnic with you after the ball?"

I rolled my eyes. "Some bargain that is."

He pretended to be hurt. "My picnics are incredible."

"I was talking about the chance to dance with me," I retorted.

"You're such a smart-ass."

"You love it," I said smugly, wiggling underneath him.

His eyes fell quickly to my mouth and lingered there for a second before rising again to meet my eyes. He was asking for permission. It had only been five weeks. My heart rate picked up, but I didn't stop him. I needed to move on.

Steadily, he dipped his head to mine again, never breaking my gaze until, so gently, his lips pressed against mine. The feeling was like being wrapped in a warm blanket. Comforting. Safe. Cade.

Hot tears pooled in my eyes because it didn't feel right. But Zeke didn't want me, and Cade did.

I tilted my head slightly, parting my lips. He took advantage, tilting his head and moving his lips against mine leisurely as our kiss deepened. It felt good. Foreign, but good. I had missed being kissed like this. And while it may not have been the fiery passion I felt for Zeke, this was reliable.

His body relaxed into mine and I brought a hand up to his cheek, gliding my thumb across his cheekbone. The tip of his tongue touched mine, and I hesitated briefly but opened for him, letting our tongues slowly dance together. Every thought in my head went hazy, and the tension in my body loosened for the first time in weeks.

If I was fire, he was the cool waters that calmed me.

But I felt like I should be kissing someone else. I wanted him erased, buried deep inside of me. I wanted to heal.

When he pulled back, I puckered my lips in a pout. "Believe me, I want more, but we're not going to rush this. I've wanted this for a long time. I'm going to relish it."

I could understand that, but I needed this dull ache in my heart to go away. "Kiss me again," I whispered, looking at him through my lashes that felt wet from my glassed eyes.

"Raven…"

I pushed a finger against his lips. "Just kiss me. It doesn't have to go farther, but that wasn't long enough."

He grinned against my finger and kissed it before I removed it from his mouth. He brought his lips to mine, and I immediately pushed my tongue against his, sighing softly into his mouth. His fingers moved lazily over my ribs. My body began drumming back to life.

He nibbled on my bottom lip, and I threaded my fingers through his hair, pushing his head harder against mine, wanting to taste a little more of him and forget how another man tasted. His breathing quickened. I knew I was taking it too fast, even for myself.

Zeke's presence still lingered around me like a ghost.

But, Cade. He wanted to fix me.

I loosened my grip on his hair and slowly broke apart from him. He pressed his forehead against mine and sighed. I felt how hard he was against my thigh. "Maybe we don't *have* to savor it," he offered.

I smiled. "No, you're right. Let's take our time. It'll be sweeter that way."

He sighed again but gave me a nod of acknowledgment and begrudgingly lifted off of me. He grabbed my hand and pulled me off the bed to stand in front of him — and then his mouth was on mine again, more greedily than before. I welcomed it, but it only lasted a few seconds before he was gone again.

"Stop teasing," I whined.

He snickered. "I couldn't help myself."

"Well, now I may have to help *myself*," I countered.

His eyes darkened. "You evil girl."

"I'll let you watch if you behave."

He growled and took a step back from me. "I have to walk away from you now."

I feigned innocence with wide eyes. "I don't know what you mean."

He shook his head as he continued to back away. "You know exactly what you're doing to me." He grunted while walking into his bathroom.

I followed him and laughed as he turned the faucet in his bathtub to splash cold water on his face. He flicked some at me, and I yelped, jogging out of the bathroom. As he chased me out, piece by piece, I felt my heart try to mend itself back together.

———————

We were back in the Black Forest that night, practicing sword-fighting techniques. Straight, down, up, diagonal right, diagonal left, again, again again. We'd been out here for hours, and muscles in my arms that I didn't even know I had were screaming. I massaged the tricep of my arm currently holding the sword, and rolled my neck side to side. "I'm a much stronger weapon on my own. You're making my arms cry," I pouted, pushing my bottom lip out.

"Stop making me want to kiss you," he said as he lunged with his sword.

I took a step back, raising mine to block.

"You'll thank me for this."

I grumbled and stuck the point of my sword into the ground, leaning down on the pommel. "You're just using this as an excuse to flex your muscles."

His mouth turned upward in a cocky grin. "So you have noticed."

"You're incorrigible."

He ignored me and nodded toward my sword. "Knowing you, you'll never need this on the offense, but if anyone finds out that steel is your weakness, you'll need this on the defense."

I rolled my eyes, scoffing. "It's not a weakness."

"If it slows you down, it's a weakness."

I huffed and pulled the sword out of the ground. "Fine. *Offend* me."

He stacked his feet, one in front of the other, and raised his sword. I braced, keeping my sword down by my side. I needed to train my muscles to be able to lift the heavy steel blade at a second's notice. He didn't make sudden movements, and I became bored as I waited.

"You sure are pretty," he said.

I rolled my eyes, and that was when he lunged. I raised my sword barely quick enough to block his blade from cutting my shoulder.

"Always remain alert, Raven. Don't let sexy men like me divert your attention."

I kept my blade pressed against his and smirked before releasing and spinning, aiming for his waist as I swung the sword around. He grunted as he moved his sword to the side, catching my swing with his blade. "Who said you were sexy?"

He laughed and took a step back, nodding in defeat. Dropping his sword to the ground, he raised his palms to me. "Touché."

I followed suit and dropped my sword next to his, smiling as he wrapped his arms around my waist and pulled me against him. "I just want to keep you safe," he uttered.

I pressed a light kiss against the corner of his mouth. "Likewise."

He sighed softly and leaned his forehead down against mine. I wrapped my arms around his neck. We stayed like that for a moment, just swaying and listening to the sounds of the rustling leaves. Soaking each other in.

"Savoring may be my worst idea yet," he whispered.

My body flushed at his words. I pressed my lips softly against his while his hands gently brushed my ribs. As I was about to deepen the kiss, twigs crunching separated us. He stretched his arm across my stomach and pushed me behind him.

We both looked around, unsure which direction the sound had come from. His body was tense. I circled my fingers around his wrist, drawing closer to him. I knew I was his first priority, and he'd lay down his life for me, but I'd do the same for him.

We were stronger as a pair, but now that we were becoming closer, the emotional ramifications of possibly losing him made my stomach clench, and my fire raged inside me. Just thinking about someone watching us, plotting an attack, had small flames dancing across my palms. The need for blood coated my tongue, and I clenched my jaw, silently daring someone to come out from the dark.

Feeling the sudden warmth beside him, Cade turned and looked down at my hand. But instead of looking alarmed, he just stared at my face with admiration. His body relaxed, and he kissed my cheek, wrapping his arm around my shoulders. I relinquished my flame, letting it simmer back down into my skin. I clenched and unclenched my fist as I stared at my hand, immediately longing for it again.

"We'll let her out soon," he promised, squeezing my shoulders.

Good. Because I wasn't sure how much longer she could be sedated.

We made it back to the castle without incident. Whatever we heard had scattered, or we were just idiots for fearing the sound of a squirrel stepping on some twigs. Too bad the adrenaline rush of our night still coursed through our veins. We were both lying in bed, wide awake, trying to calm our nerves and attempt to sleep. "Stop moving so much," he grumbled, shoving at my shoulders.

I shoved him back and exhaled a long sigh. "I can't sleep."

He had been attempting to sleep on his stomach. He rose up to his elbows. "That doesn't mean the rest of us shouldn't try."

I snorted and shoved his elbow, making him topple partially onto my chest. "Tell me something. Anything," I demanded softly.

He kept still on my chest, his cheek resting against my heart. His fingers lazily drew shapes on my stomach through the fabric of my shirt. I ran strands of his hair through my fingers.

"I remember the first time we snuck out," he began. I felt him smile against my chest, his voice heavy with sleep. "For the first time since you came to the castle, I saw the excitement in your eyes. You always looked so solemn, so overwhelmed. I knew I needed to get you out before it overcame you."

I frowned as he spoke but remained quiet. I remembered it, too. I was sixteen and had spent my first six years as queen, never leaving the castle, too fearful of meeting anyone new outside these walls. By then, I had become a little more confident in my ability to lead an entire kingdom. We spent almost every day in the libraries, trying to retain as much information as he wanted to give me, and then we'd practice my magic behind closed doors. It was like he breathed new life into me when he took me out.

"I led you to the channel, and we watched the boats rock against the docks after we swam. It was so peaceful. I would look at you, and you just seemed so content. Finally. I had doubts that you'd ever feel at peace in your own skin, especially here. You were so young, but there's always been an air around you, Raven. That night, at that moment, I knew I'd destroy anything that tried to touch you. Anything that tried to disturb the tranquility you deserved."

He raised his head from my chest and rested his chin against it, his eyes searching mine. The only light in the room was from that moon that shined through the glass of his balcony window. "I need you, Raven."

My hand was still in his hair, my heart picking up its beat against his skin. He crawled up a little more, closing the space between our faces. His lips pressed lightly against mine, and he pulled back again, whispering against my mouth, "I don't feel whole unless you're in the same room with me, sharing my space."

Let him have you. Open your heart to him. Silent pleas to myself. Those haunting gray eyes shot into my mind, bringing tears to my eyes. A sole image of him could steal my entire atmosphere, pulling me away from the one man here, begging me to love him, wanting to savor me, worship at my feet.

"Cade," I whispered, my voice breaking.

He pressed his forehead against mine, nodding once. Understanding. Never pushing me. "I'm here. I'm not going anywhere. I'm just sorry I waited too long."

Zeke wasn't here anymore, and he was stealing my moments, my thoughts. Precious time was ticking by.

CHAPTER SEVENTEEN

Raven

The following day seemed to rise in a flash, the sun beaming down on us as we slept. I wanted to stay here, not open my eyes, wish away the day. Cade was resting against my chest, having finally passed out after our hours of tossing and turning. He fell asleep with my heartbeat in his ear, and I fell asleep to the sound of his steady breathing.

I didn't want to wake him. He looked heavenly as he slept. His mouth was slightly open, his long lashes resting soundly against his skin. His blond hair looked golden with the rays of the sun beating down. He was everything good, everything pure. The light to my darkness. He inhaled a deep breath, his broad back muscles expanding and falling. I gently traced them with my fingertips, moving across the divots in his skin.

So many other hands had been here before, petting him, writhing with him, pleasuring him. The thought made me crazy. And I could've had him. We had wasted so much time. So many years of playful teasing and just standing by while we cured our loneliness in the arms of others.

And then... Zeke.

He stole my mind. My body. My heart. In our very short time together, I fell for the first man to give me his undivided attention. But it wasn't just that. We brought something out in each other. I quieted his darkness. He encouraged mine, coaxing out the rage I'd kept buried for many years. I was only a game to him, and he succeeded at his task if it was to pull me away from Cade. Distract me. Make me doubt the one constant at my side. How was it possible to love both? But I was *in* love with Zeke. Deeply. Painfully.

I sighed and leaned my head against the headboard of his bed, continuing to idly draw across his skin. Sometimes I felt as if my mind was slipping away from me. I never felt in control anymore. How could I defend my kingdom if I couldn't harness every depth of my magic? There was still so much I didn't understand about myself. How desperately I wished to know my identity. To know where I came from.

Butterflies embrace change. If I was going to forge ahead into unfamiliar territory, I needed to embrace it. Stretch my wings; champion for their colors, even if they were dark and sometimes ran together in a mess of emotion. Back when I was dropped on a porch in a basket, who I was then didn't matter anymore. Not now, not when so much was at stake. I couldn't keep asking others to accept me if I couldn't even do that for myself. I needed to be my own clutch, the driving force for saving everything I loved.

Cade kept his slow breathing. He made me feel serene when we were safe together, nuzzled in each other's arms, but brought out envy when the thought of him with anyone else but me was threatened. It was the same way with Zeke. Knowing that he had someone waiting for him in Reales, someone who knew his body the way I did, made me want to wreck worlds beyond ours. The idea that someone else would be on my throne while I still lived, taking it from me, nearly brought me to my knees.

It was always when the risk of something I loved being taken from me arose: my anger was needed, never on the offense. That was what Cade had said to me. My darkness has always been used to defend. When I was young, the little girls at the festival, passed out drunks in the street that I kept warm... Magic, John had told me as he exposed me at the breakfast table. King Leonidas... had seen all of it.

The king had watched me. He wanted me to protect his kingdom. *He* chose *me*. He needed my instinct to protect. He needed my darkness. He knew this was coming. Why shouldn't I want to possess what was mine? So much was taken from me in the beginning. I had the right to want, to keep. I shouldn't have expected that everyone would leave at some point. I deserved more than that.

"Cade," I whispered, shaking him. "Wake up."

He opened his sleepy eyes, groaning as the sunbeams hit him.

"Cade." I shook him again.

He raised his head to look at me. "There are better ways to wake a man up, Raven," he grumbled, rubbing the sleep out of his eyes. "I was dreaming of you. And apple pies."

I shoved his shoulder, trying to get him to move his body. "I'm flattered. Off."

"I have never once been kicked out of my own bed," he growled, sitting up.

"I promise to try not to make it a habit, but we must go to the library."

"We? Don't you know how to read by now?"

I rolled my eyes and stood, patting his cheek gently with my hand. I walked to the wardrobe I had removed all his clothes from and placed all mine in instead. "You sleep. Find me later." He didn't say anything, but I looked at him again and saw his eyes close, his chest rising and falling steadily again. I smiled at the sight of him, my heart warming.

I would protect him even if it killed me.

I was in the library only moments after leaving Cade's room, wearing another light blue cotton dress with a gorgeous sweetheart neckline and puffed short sleeves. It ballooned out at my waist and felt like I was wearing air around my legs. My long hair was piled in a messy bun at the top of my head, fastened with a modest gold tiara. I felt radiant as I sauntered into the grand doors of the library.

As I opened my mouth to greet Grace, who was, again, on a ladder way too high, I stopped and glanced down at one of the tables. A mixture of flame and fury rushed through my veins as I took small, tentative steps toward the table.

A bright-red rose with thorns sat atop it.

I carefully picked it up by the stem and studied it — like it'd give me an answer to where it came from and what it was doing in my library. "Grace, darling," I called out, my eyes never leaving the rose in my hand.

Grace's head turned at the sound of my voice. She beamed. "Good morning, Queen Raven! Your pile of books is on the table there," she responded, pointing toward a table.

"Grace, did you bring this?" I cocked my head at the rose.

"No, Your Majesty, I didn't see it when I came in."

I placed the rose in my palm and set it ablaze. Where the fuck were these coming from?

Grace's eyes drew open, her jaw falling slack. "Not a fan of roses?"

I watched the flower wilt into ashes in my hand. "No, darling. Not a fan of men who give them to me." I wiped my hands together to dispose of the ashes on the floor.

"Can I… see that again?"

My eyes lifted to hers, a grin replacing my previously irritated frown. I nodded, grabbed a piece of paper off the top of a pile on a table in front of me, and lit it up in my fingers. I held it out to Grace as she descended the ladder and watched in amusement at the look on her face as the paper burned.

As flames continued to encase the paper, I released watery frost from my fingertips, the fire sparking in a beautiful purple as it mixed with the cold. Grace continued to watch, perplexed and amazed.

Once the fire was put out by the icy water, I gathered air from the room and used it to spin the paper around us, the charred piece dancing in circles around our bodies. We both laughed until the paper landed back on the table, its corners black and wrinkled from the flames.

"That was incredible!" Grace squealed, her eyes still on the piece of scorched paper.

"That's not even the full scale of them," I explained. "I can shift into each one, fully becoming the element."

Grace clapped her hands together and fixated her gaze back on me. "Can I see?"

I giggled and shook my head. "Not today. I'm still trying to learn how to control one of them. I can't contain my emotions when I fully let my fire out."

Grace started to pace back and forth, her fingers on her chin like she was deep in thought. "Where were you feeling when you burned the rose?"

Fire brimmed at my skin's surface again as I recalled my emotion from seeing it on the table. "Fear. Fury."

"Would you say those are your strongest emotions?"

I nodded, tilting my head curiously at her questions.

"That's your answer then."

I shook my head in confusion. Grace spoke in riddles.

"Harness your fear, your fury. Is it easy to spark?"

I chuckled at her question. I felt like a walking volcano, waiting to erupt at any moment. "Yes," I replied flatly.

"Then, if you practice, try thinking of something that makes you angry. Or something you fear. If your feelings are passionate enough at that moment, then..." she trailed off and shrugged.

I understood what she was trying to say. And it made sense. My fear and fury had always seemed like a lethal combination. My fear of losing my kingdom, being abandoned, the ones I chose not choosing me back. The fury of someone trying to steal my throne, Cade leaving, Zeke wanting another. Those were always the first ones to boil over and were the ones I pushed down, not wanting them to overtake me.

Maybe I needed to let them.

But, first. I needed texts on Reales. I asked Grace to find me a couple, and she had them on the table in front of me less than ten minutes later. Quite efficient, my little librarian.

The pile she had started for me on magic were all books I had read before, and it was nothing about its history. They were simply folktales, rumors of what magic could have been.

I flipped through the pages of the first book, brushing up on my history of Reales.

It started similarly to Seolia, Perosan, and Thoya. King Alaric had escaped his country, and with royalty in his blood, he created his own empire. To sustain it, he started importing iron and then, later, steel. He was savvy and used every resource at his disposal, eventually able to manufacture it within his own kingdom.

When the other three kingdoms were erected, they relied heavily on his inventory of materials to create their own weapons needed for their protection.

Reales had always been the biggest of the four kingdoms, even though Perosan and Thoya had vast land of their own, but manufacturing something that each domain relied on for various things bred a thirst for a little something more. Alaric's son, Leopold, took the throne after his passing and became cocky that Reales held so much of what other kingdoms needed, which turned into lust. If the other kingdoms needed Reales so much, then why shouldn't he rule over all of them? So, Leopold invaded Perosan, who had been unprepared.

Up until that point, the kingdoms had existed peacefully, so no one suspected that anything was coming that would be the complete opposite. Perosan's king was held hostage as King Leopold ordered his soldiers to murder any of Perosan's residents who didn't pledge allegiance to him as their king. Hundreds of lives were lost. No one wanted one king to hold so much power over two kingdoms. It would make dealings between the four too complicated, and trading between the kingdoms might have ceased, essentially starving Seolia because we relied so much on the other three kingdoms to bring shipments through.

Even without large armies, Seolia and Thoya became involved. Through sheer luck, because the numbers definitely weren't there, the armies invaded Perosan, where King Leopold was still stationed, and he was overpowered. It was interesting, even now, that two small troops could take down the size of one like Reales had. I believed that when you threatened free will, people would start to fight back, and they carried that threat with them when they fought Leopold's army.

At the threat of Reales being invaded next, King Leopold agreed to sign the treaty to keep the peace between the four kingdoms. And that was one hundred years ago. King Leopold's son-in-law maintained that promise his entire reign, showing nothing but kindness towards both King Leonidas and then me.

I moved to the next book, which went into further detail about King Leopold's family. He was married but had only one daughter: Celestina. Celestina went on to marry Rudolf. There was a watercolor sketch in the book of King Rudolf and his queen. Rudolf had a goofy grin on his face, but Celestina looked solemn. She had dark hair and olive skin, similar to mine. I continued to flip through the pages, trying to learn about Mira, but there wasn't anything about her. Not even a sketch.

I sat back in my chair and palmed my eyes, a slight headache building behind them from all my reading over the last couple of hours. Had it been that long? Surely Cade wasn't still asleep. I was getting hungry. Maybe I could find him, and we could dine together.

I bid farewell to Grace and thanked her again for all the advice and books, and set off to find Cade. I checked his chambers first, then the dining hall and the courtyard, and he was nowhere to be found. I meandered past the throne room, peeking in, and narrowed my eyes at what I saw.

Cade wasn't alone. He was having a conversation with Jeanine. What the fuck was she doing back in Seolia? And why was she here, in my castle, and why was Cade smiling at her like a buffoon? She was the enemy, and he still had to pretend like she wasn't. I told myself that, but it still didn't answer the question: *why was she here?* Was Zeke here? I saw them both leave. I helped them leave.

Suddenly, Cade's eyes lifted and met mine. I glared, my fingers warming at the jealousy brewing inside of me. The need to ignore my urge to set him on fire only made my irritation grow. I turned on my heel and set a fast pace as I left them in the throne room. I muttered curse words as I marched through a door. She shouldn't even be welcomed back to Seolia.

I asked him to find me when he woke up, but that simple instruction had obviously been too difficult for him to follow. Why were the men in my life so stubborn?

I pounded down the stairs, my anger fueling my pace until I stared into the face of one of my kitchen maids. "Your Majesty!" The maid jumped and immediately bowed into a curtsy — as did all the other maids bustling around the kitchen.

I felt foolish for bursting in on all of them like this. I wasn't even sure where I was going, only seeing red.

I bowed my head to the maids and apologized for frightening them. "If you're not too busy, would you mind if I had the kitchen to myself for a little while?"

They curtsied to me and left me to my raging thoughts.

I paced the length of the kitchen, my hands on my hips. He was just talking to her, Raven. But why was she here again? Would I always have competition with that woman? I was the queen. Surely I would be someone's first choice.

Did we need to search for Zeke? Would he come to find me if he came back with her? Were they still together? All questions I wouldn't get answers to.

I grabbed an apron off the table and wrapped it around my waist. I needed to use my hands. I needed a distraction from marching back upstairs and setting something on fire. Setting Cade on fire.

I baked plenty of times as a child with Isla. The smell of burning dough was still implanted into my brain as Isla rushed around our cottage, throwing open all the windows to let the smoke out. I had just laughed and laughed. And then she let me try again. And again. Until it was perfect.

Recalling the memory was working. A calmness started to creep across my bones. I rolled my neck side to side as I kneaded the dough under my fingers. I giggled at the thought of hitting Cade with the rolling pin. He could be so infuriating. Him and his fucking apple pie.

I peeled the apples and combined them into my bowl of sugar and flour, pouring cinnamon on top. I recalled another time that Isla had taken me into the village to buy some fruits from one of the booths set up during one of the farmers' markets. She taught me not to buy any apples that looked bruised or smelled funny.

I laughed out loud, remembering when Isla had demonstrated by sniffing every apple at the booth, throwing my head back in hysterics at the annoyed face the merchant made at us the entire time.

It'd been weeks since I had laughed so hard. Over a month since the Festival of Dreams, I last felt so light and joyful. The past few days had contained some good, but I was always thinking about what Seolia was about to face as a kingdom. I missed Zeke and continued to make myself miserable over it.

We only spent a matter of days together, but I felt like I'd known him my entire life, but he pulled me apart. And Cade had been there, attempting to put me back together. He'd been at my side, almost every waking moment, training me and repairing the parts of me that felt shriveled up.

We'd spent the last couple of weeks becoming reacquainted, only this time as two people who could actually fall in love. We had loved one another for years, but it never pushed past the point of no return. Our touching was purposeful. I found myself missing him when he wasn't there. He was fulfilling my emptiness.

I wondered if Zeke even cared if someone else was trying to replace him. Or if I was just the crazy queen from Seolia who fell in love with a man in a matter of days. Or was I even more insane for falling for my best friend and depending on him to heal me?

When would I be able to heal myself?

How could someone with dark magic feel so human?

I worked for two hours, pulling good memories from the recesses of my mind and trying to reason with myself until I finished baking the pie. I stared at its golden crust. It looked delectable. I used the tip of my finger to sear the edges of the crust, bringing out its natural flavors. The smell of crisp apple filled the kitchen, and I felt proud as I stared at the pie in front of me, nearly jumping out of my skin as Cade called my name from the doorway.

"I have been looking everywhere for you!" he rumbled, crossing his arms over his chest.

"Finally tear yourself away from your company?" I asked, refusing to look at him.

"Fuck, Raven. You would've seen Luisa with us if you had gotten there a minute earlier. Jeanine is helping with the ball. I don't know why. Maybe Luisa asked her before *he* left. As soon as you saw us and ran, I excused myself and went after you, but you were gone."

I shrugged and leaned my palms on the table. "You don't owe me an explanation."

I heard him sigh as he leaned against the door. I chewed on my bottom lip. I was too much for myself most of the time, so I could understand if I exasperated him.

"Fuck this," he grumbled.

I expected him to leave, but his body crashed into mine seconds later. His mouth found mine, and he pushed his tongue against my teeth until I opened for him. I brought my hands up to the back of his head, pulling threads of hair between my fingers, tugging them.

He groaned against me and broke our kiss, backing me into a wall. "You're absolutely maddening." His voice was a low growl, dripping with irritation. "How else can I tell you you're all I want?"

I didn't know. Because such a large part of me wasn't ready to move on. And because of that, I couldn't give him what he wanted to hear. But instead of waiting for an answer, his mouth found mine again.

His hands grasped at me hungrily, never stopping, like they'd never have enough of me. He bent and cupped his hands under my ass, lifting and twisting to set me on the table. I wrapped my legs around his waist and brought him closer to me, our tongues fighting together, trying to spill over a decade of feelings out.

My head tilted to the side as his mouth moved down my chin and neck, peppering me with kisses until I was dizzy.

This was okay, I told myself. I wasn't doing anything wrong.

He bent again and grabbed the hem of my dress, raising it over my knees and bunching it until it was pooled at the base of my hips.

This was okay, I repeated silently. I needed Zeke gone. I needed his touch replaced.

He cupped my ass again and scooted me to the table's edge. His fingers found my core, and he pressed the tips of two fingers against my clit, groaning at how wet I was.

"Cade," I breathed.

That was all it took. He broke through the walls we'd built and let himself have me. He unfastened his buckle, his pants falling, and I leaned back a little to push my hips closer to him. He wrapped one arm around my waist to steady me and took his dick in his hand, pushing into me.

I cried out from my walls trying to expand to accommodate his length. He peppered my neck again with light kisses. I just nodded, encouraging him to keep going.

Erase him, I begged silently.

Make me forget, I pleaded.

Everything inside me screamed. The broken pieces of me scattered. I let myself feel that pain. I couldn't heal if I didn't try. I couldn't move on if I didn't open myself up. Hot tears pushed against my eyelids. I tried to blink them away. I had to let him go. But this feeling. I felt as if I was betraying my own heart.

I felt numb.

It was like Cade could hear my silent pleas because the pace of his thrusts increased, claiming me roughly. I looked down between us and watched him pound me, my hips trying to buck against his. "Come for me, Raven," he demanded.

But I couldn't. I couldn't get there because it didn't feel right. I'd already been claimed. He didn't seem to notice because he released his cum hot and vast like he'd been saving it all for me. I would be filled with him for days, but he didn't have me, which frustrated me. I hadn't found any release since Zeke left.

Our chests rose and fell quickly as we stared at one another, trying to catch our breath. Fifteen years. We'd been best friends for fifteen years, and now we had crossed a line.

I leaned forward and grabbed his mouth with mine again, claiming him back. Greedily, eagerly. All the jealousy I had felt for years, watching him with other women, poured out of me, and he drank it up.

When I broke from him, I giggled at the remnants of flour from my hands all over his hair. I raised a hand and put it against his cheek, marking him.

He shook his head but grinned. "You are such a little shit."

I raised an eyebrow at him, running my thumb over his bottom lip. "Do you talk to all of your ladies like that?"

He rolled his eyes and bent down to pull up his pants. I straightened my dress back over my legs but kept my eyes on him. "You have to stop with this jealousy shit, Raven." He brought one of my wrists to his mouth and kissed it. "You have more than enough personalities for me."

I scoffed and tried to pull away from him, but he brought me back. He cupped the side of my neck, and I tilted my head, meeting his gaze. "I'm in love with you, you wicked woman."

My eyes closed at his words, tears pushing past my eyelids and falling down my cheeks. "I love you," I whispered, and I meant it. I had always loved Cade, and it was growing deeper by the day.

But why, when I said it, did I see those gray eyes?

We sat at the table in the kitchen, eating the apple pie I baked for him. I explained to him what Grace had said, and he agreed that it sounded like a plausible idea if I could learn how to harness my anger. "You seemed to today," he said, nodding toward the pie.

"But that was hours of trying to calm me down. I won't have hours if someone attacks us."

"We'll just need to practice more. It's going to take time. We've never had to prepare for anything like this, and I'm still unsure what to expect."

They were taking their time if someone was trying to ignite something against us. Nothing had happened since Zeke left, and I wondered if I had made the entire thing up. Why would Mira invite me to Reales if she planned on invading? She would've just done it by now.

He took another bite and leaned back in his chair. I bit my lip sheepishly at the sight of him. Everything was different between us now. Maybe someday, I could let him have me the way he wanted me. And when he saw the look on my face, a smug grin plastered across his mouth. I rolled my eyes and flicked the pie on my fork at him. "Shut up."

"How much I want you is bad, Raven. I don't know how I'll be able to think of anything else. I won't ever be sated."

His fingers dusted across my lips, and the tip of my tongue licked at their ends. He pulled me into his lap and started kissing along my neck, but I shook my head. "We can't spend all day fucking in the kitchen."

He scoffed. "Why not? It's our kitchen."

I stood from his lap. "We have a kingdom to save. Unfortunately, fucking is not the way to do it."

He stood and towered over me, lifting one of his shoulders in a shrug. "Maybe it should be with the way you fuck."

I shoved him. "You need a cold bath."

He lunged at me and wrapped his arms around my waist, lifting me until I dangled over his shoulder. He slapped my ass and started toward the stairs, shaking me with each step he took.

I pounded on his back with my fists. "What the hell are you doing?!" And why did every man insist on toting me around like this?

He was silent at my question. I kicked my feet, hitting his stomach. I pushed up on his back with my hands when I heard a door open, trying to sneak a peek at where we were. We were back in his chambers and headed toward the bathroom. "Cade, I swear."

He ignored my warning and simply tightened his grip on me while using his other hand to lean over his tub and flip on the faucet. I hit him with my fists again, wiggling against him to try and get him to drop me, but he was too damn strong.

He kicked off his boots one by one and at least had the decency to remove mine. I took the opportunity to kick at his hands. He took the opportunity to slap my ass again.

"Behave," he snapped, but there was amusement in his tone. He put one foot in the tub and adjusted me on his shoulder as I started to slip off him from the sudden movement. And then his other foot joined him.

"Cade!" I squealed. One last attempt to try and change his mind.

He kneeled, and the ice-cold water hit my feet. I kicked again. "Gods, you're squirmy," he said as he slid my body down until he sat in the tub with me on his lap. He gasped at the cold temperature.

I was the one grinning smugly now as I spread my warmth over my body, bringing my fire to the surface of my skin. "I said *you* need a cold bath." I wiggled in his lap as proof. His erection was hard against my ass.

"A cold bath won't even solve it if you don't stop your wiggling," he gritted through clenched teeth. His clothes were sticking to him. The skirt of my dress was also sticking to me, making it hard to move. He relaxed his grip around my hips, and I moved to dodge, but he caught me and pulled me back down. "You're not even cold," he grumbled.

"I'm a living inferno, Cade." I cupped my hands together and dipped them under the water, creating a pool of cold water in my hands. I raised them to pour over his head.

He inhaled through his gritted teeth, narrowing his eyes at me. I snickered, repeating the motion. "I'm just trying to cool you down."

"It's your fault I'm so heated," he replied, grabbing my face between his hands and bringing my mouth to his in a rough kiss.

My body relaxed into his, and I returned his feverish kiss with matching intensity. His fingers pushed into my waist. He couldn't stop touching me like he'd been deprived. The cold bath was the exact opposite of calming him down when I was the warmth he craved.

"Cade," I breathed.

He pushed his hips up against me.

"*Cade*," I said again, shaking my head.

"One more time," he pleaded.

"One more time? That's all it's going to take?"

He licked his lips and tried to catch my mouth with his again. I leaned back quickly and put my hand to his mouth to stop him. He sighed and leaned back against the tub, though his eyes moved up and down my body, taking in the way my nipples were hardened against my dress.

"*Cade*," I dragged his name out.

A small smile tugged on the corners of his mouth as he slowly raised his eyes back to mine.

"We have to get dressed and get ready to train. It's getting dark outside."

He just sighed in response and nodded.

"Exude self-control, soldier," I said, giving him a small salute. He chuckled.

It was what his dad used to say to him when I'd watch them practice in the training yard. The memories of watching Cade getting his ass beat by his own father were still some of my favorites. I loved his dad like I'd probably love my own if I had one. And his mother, too. They welcomed me into their family.

"I am going to go hang my dress over the balcony. I refuse to believe that you've ruined it. It's become my favorite," I pouted, pulling the soaked fabric off my legs so I could stand. I could tell he wanted to reach for me again, but he didn't, and I felt relieved, which also made me feel guilty.

"I'm sorry," he said, his forehead creasing from guilt.

Before I stood, I leaned down and gave him a quick peck on the forehead. "You can make it up to me later." I winked at him and took a sloppy step out of the tub.

He grunted in a brooding response as he watched me go.

I trudged along the floor, pulling the heavy dress with me as water dripped all over the floor. I pulled it up and over my head before stepping out onto the balcony, slinging it over the wall that reached my waist. Raising my arms over my head, I stretched my naked body, enjoying seeing the sunset over the horizon and letting the foreign feeling of ease settle on my shoulders.

And then tears fell. One by one, down my cheeks.

I had betrayed him. Betrayed us. Even though I hadn't seen him in weeks, even though he had left me, I forced myself into something I wasn't ready for yet and hated myself for it.

I quickly wiped away my tears when I heard Cade walking up behind me. I turned my head to glance over my shoulder as he came up, pressing his bare chest against my back, and wrapped his arms around my waist. "My eyes only," he whispered against my temple as he walked us back into his room, throwing the doors shut as we went.

I still didn't find a release.

As we walked into the courtyard in our training leathers, our hands were linked together and idly swinging between us. We kept throwing one another timid glances as we walked. He was being adorable, and he'd fought me on going out this evening.

But tonight, it was going to be all about Blaze.

He wrapped a hand around my waist and pulled me to him, trapping me in a kiss as he walked back through the gate. Pushing me back against the wall, he deepened our kiss. As I was about to remind him that we needed to go, we heard screams from the village. We both snapped our heads at the sound and took off in a sprint, guards joining us.

That was when we saw it. Flames rising up into the sky.

We flew down the street, trying to find the source. All I heard were the frantic cries of people lining the cobbled streets. They were all pointing toward the same place, and I followed their guidance, freezing in fear when I saw it. The bakery. And it was up in flames. Without a second thought, I raced in, ignoring Cade's demands for me to stop.

I coughed as the smoke hit me. This fire wasn't my magic. I couldn't stop it. I looked around for buckets, anything I could use. And then I knew what I had to do. Right here, in front of all of my village.

I held my hands out and willed my ice forward, shooting it in every direction. I pulled Terra through and used wind to spur the ice faster, swallowing the flames engulfing the structure.

Tired. I was so tired.

I pushed through, feeling blood dripping from my nose as I held my palms up, giving it everything I had. I tried to pool all of my anger and shoved it out. I thought of Zeke first. Always Zeke first. I still missed him, even as another man's hands claimed my body. I thought of my parents and how they left me somewhere unfamiliar. I let it grow and swirl inside of me.

I remembered Zeke walking away after I told him I loved him. I grabbed at the fractured memories of my childhood, feeling like I wasn't ever enough. Enough to stay. Enough to love. It was never enough. And I let it stir, awakening my soul.

I screamed. And screamed.

Frozen ice blended with air, causing it to rain inside the bakery. Flames slowly started to choke and drown. My eyes squeezed shut as I continued to push out all the pain of my memories, my body physically shaking as tears fell down my face.

Embrace the pain, Raven.

Zeke, Zeke, Zeke. All I saw was Zeke. All I wanted was him.

When I couldn't see any more orange through my tear-filled eyes, I dropped my arms, doubling over. I couldn't stop shaking, couldn't catch my breath. I heaved as I tried to push my pain back down. Hands grasped at me, and I fought them, tears never ceasing. The strong arms wrapped around me, and I breathed in Cade, falling against him. He held me, crying, shaking me gently until my face lifted to his. He kissed my tears away, smearing the blood that had fallen from my nose to my mouth and chin.

Grace's mother rushed in, followed soon by Grace. Grace immediately wrapped herself around me, and I curled my arm around her, pulling her into our hug. I kissed the top of her head, and she looked up at me tearfully, silent gratitude in her eyes.

Lara thanked me for saving what I could. All I could do was nod in response as Cade promised to send help out immediately to repair the damage. My body was exhausted and heavy. Out of the corner of my eye, I caught movement. I turned my head to see the eyes of what had to be every villager staring at me, mouths gaping. The rumors about their queen were true.

With Cade's arm around my shoulders, he led me out of the crumbling structure and onto the street as they all stared at us. He never dropped his arm from around me, showing everyone that we were still a team. My gaze settled on Cade's parents in the middle of the crowd, smiling at the two of us together. I gave them a slight nod as Cade's arm tightened around me. Somewhere in my hazy stupor, I found it odd that they didn't seem surprised at what they had just witnessed.

I opened my mouth to speak, but nothing came out. What was there to say? My eyes met Theodore's, and little Eva was next to him. She broke from her father's grasp and ran to me, throwing her arms around my legs. A sob escaped my throat as my hand curled around the back of her head. A child wasn't scared of me. No one else had any reason to be.

I stared at the silent crowd around me, tears still falling down my face. Here is your queen, Seolia. Take me or leave me.

It started with Theodore as I saw him bow. One by one, people followed him and bowed to me in gratitude, in surprise, in allegiance; I didn't care what their reason was. They weren't revolting and weren't grabbing their pitchforks. They accepted me. And that was all I had ever wanted. Ever needed.

I looked at Cade, whose own tears coated his cheeks. He leaned down and kissed my temple and then my lips. I heard claps from the crowd, growing in volume. I smiled, trying to laugh through my sobs.

I walked through the crowd, accepting hugs and handshakes of gratitude and acceptance. I would save every building in our village if it were on fire, even if it killed me. Maybe they understood that now. Maybe the questions of why I'd been chosen to rule over the kingdom were answered.

I would be its savior and fiercest protector. Nothing mattered to me more than keeping our kingdom safe. I didn't need their gratitude, but I accepted it and gave it back. Gratitude for accepting me.

A wave of warmth washed over my tired body. As I took another step through the crowd, I staggered and fell. Pain. I felt pain everywhere. Cade called my name. I saw golden locks of hair racing toward me. I tried to smile. If he was the last thing I saw, I'd die happy. Because that was what it felt like. It felt like I was about to exhale my last breath. A hooded figure in the shadows stared at me. Then I saw a flash of gray eyes.

And then it all went black.

CHAPTER EIGHTEEN

Zeke

Raven had successfully blocked every way into the castle, making it nearly impossible for me to get in. But what she didn't know was that in Reales, scaling was one of the traits I taught my soldiers. And scaling her balcony at night was easy. When I'd enter her room, I would use her hidden corridors to exit the dungeon without anyone seeing me. She thought she could keep me out — keep me away from her — but that would never happen.

I would always find my way to her.

I dusted her bedspread with my fingertips, touching the dried blood on her quilt. I wished I could taste her. But now she was thirsty for my blood, wanting to hurt me the same way I hurt her. "My love, if only you could understand," I muttered, sighing as I walked to her wardrobe and threw open the doors. She had moved everything except for some extremely fluffy dresses, which I assumed were used for balls or other fancy events. I had never seen her in any of them. They seemed rather heavy for someone as delicate as her.

She was in Cade's room now.

I gripped the fabric between my fingers as I recalled seeing them sleep in the same bed, her body curled into his — the way she had been curled into mine. It'd been weeks since I left her, but I hadn't seen anything more from them.

Not that I didn't believe it was coming. I watched them one evening, training in the woods, wrestling on the ground. I sensed nothing but pure want — pure need — brimming from Cade, but felt only shame on Raven. That was the first night I revisited her dreams, expecting to feel nothing but hatred from her, but instead, she wanted me to come closer. I was crouched next to her, watching her sleep, and she could smell me.

That was the night she saw me. After watching her train, I wanted to see her, and she obliged me, coming out to Cade's balcony. She was itching for answers, wanting to be freed from her ivory tower. I had followed her eyes to Duck's and knew she was thinking of me. When I stepped out from the shadows, her eyes flickered at me, and I wanted her to see me. I wanted her to know I was still around. Though, when she had tipped so far over the balcony, I almost shouted at her to go back inside. I didn't understand why I was doing that to her. I couldn't keep leading her on. She didn't deserve it, but I couldn't let her go.

She was still hanging on to me, which was not part of my scheme. I needed her to move on and believe I was an unhealthy addiction for this plan to work. For weeks, I'd watched her wither away, a fraction of herself, of the enchanting creature I had come to know.

I had stood by as she walked into the village, more of her self-doubt etched into her features. Her eyes were sunken in, and the color drained from her cheeks. I saw her smile only when Arthur approached her and pulled her in, clearing some of her darkness for a brief moment. I wondered what they were talking about -- if she had told him that I abandoned her, or if he already knew.

I should've stayed away, but seeing her so broken, so hesitant to walk into the bakery... I needed to send her a message, let her know I was never truly going to leave her. So, while she was inside, I left a freshly cut rose for her on the table and stood at the window, watching as she ate the chocolate pastry we had enjoyed together just weeks before.

When she came out and handed Cade the pastry, letting him share that piece of us, a part of me broke. And then she saw the rose on the table, and I could sense her fear. And her hope. It was cruel, and when she ripped the rose to shreds, I couldn't help but smile at the anger I felt brewing inside her. I needed that brought to the forefront, and if being cruel got her there, then I'd be the most brutal bastard within the four kingdoms.

I sensed her in the forest the night she thought I was leaving. I knew she was lingering somewhere, watching me go. When she appeared behind the trees, it was like being part of my own extinction. She was exiling me, pushing my ship onward, farther away from her island of indecision. She didn't know that all we did was circle around behind the caves and anchored there.

The one bed was a problem, seeing as Jeanine would still pout at my lack of need for her, but she eventually relented, realizing that I was forever bound to another. I allowed her the bed, and I slept on deck, falling asleep to the thought of the woman who put the stars in my sky.

Jeanine had worn her hood to go into the village and grab food for us twice a week, continuing her dirty deed of circulating rumors of Raven's dark magic. I wanted to stop her, tell her she'd done enough, but I couldn't risk her going to Mira when we returned home.

Home. My home was wherever Raven was.

I reached into my coat pocket and fumbled for the engagement ring I was supposed to give her. I pulled it out, letting the moonlight bounce off it. It was my mother's ring. Even though I insisted she not give it to me before I left, she said she had a feeling. What feeling, I had asked her, and all she did was smile. I never imagined I'd come here and find the reason my heart beat.

The diamond on the ring was cut like a pear, which was what Raven's hair smelled like. She told me I loved her best in the dark, and the small diamonds along the band were cut like stars. This ring was made for her, and it was the very ring that John had given my mother when they married many years ago.

I released a long breath, staring at the diamond in my fingers. I was betraying Raven the same way John betrayed my mother. The thought made me sick to my stomach. But, I was not doing it for personal gain. I was doing this for her. It killed me that when I presented this ring to her, she'd look upon it in disgust. I slipped it back into my pocket and walked to the balcony.

I peered over, looking deep into the forest. They typically trained around this time, and I wanted to see how she was progressing with her magic. I descended down her balcony and dropped to the ground. Pulling up my hood and looking around, I didn't spot any guards nearby before taking off into the forest.

I drew in a breath through my nose. She'd been here recently, either to walk into the forest or back out. As I walked in farther, I heard the faint sound of swords. I advanced slowly, quietly, toward the sound and saw her. My smile was broad.

She was trying to block Cade's swing, grumbling something. I had to bite my knuckles to keep from laughing out loud. She rubbed her arms, sore. She had never needed to prepare for any conflict, always relying solely on her magic to keep her safe. Watching her try to wield a sword was charming. And sexy. She was wearing her leather one-piece, and it made me nearly come apart every time I saw her in it.

I watched as Cade lowered into a fighting stance, grinning at her boredom. My fists clenched as he called her pretty, even though it was true. He swung at her and nearly cut through her shoulder, but she raised her sword just in time to stop him. She'd have to be faster than that. My soldiers were trained to kill.

She spun and nearly cut Cade. I was partially impressed, partially disappointed that she failed. They dropped their swords, and he wrapped his arms around her waist.

I stilled. I wasn't breathing.

She kissed his cheek. I braced myself. And then it happened. Their lips touched. Nothing but fury coursed through me, and I took a small step toward her, twigs snapping under my feet. I froze, silently cursing myself. This was what I wanted to happen. It had been weeks since I left her. I needed her to move on. But seeing it actually happen… They were looking for me, trying to find the source of the sound. I remained still.

They wouldn't find me. I knew how to hide in the shadows. The flames dancing in her palms were because of her instinct to defend. But Cade wouldn't allow her to let that part of herself go, making her extinguish her anger whenever it surfaced. He didn't appreciate her like I did.

Luckily, I did not have to witness any more of their public display as they disappeared into the castle. I lingered at the border, watching her go.

I walked along the shadows until I was outside Cade's balcony, waiting a long time before scaling it. My feet were silent as I landed on his deck, flattening myself against his wall. I peered inside. She was awake, unable to sleep, and I wished I could wrap her in my arms.

Cade was talking to her. I silenced my thoughts and closed my eyes, wanting to hear what he was saying. He was talking about the night they went swimming. The memory I pulled from that night in the barn. All I felt from her was sadness as he spoke about it. He whispered pretty words to her, and my eyes rolled, looking at them again just in time to see him kiss her. The veins in my hands constricted. It was like they knew I was here and only did this shit when I could see it. He wanted more from her, but she couldn't give it to him. I sensed trepidation in her. I didn't know how much longer she could hold on to me.

I slid down the wall until I sat, stretching my legs out and crossing my ankles. I'd sit here until she fell asleep.

———————

Every now and then, I'd peer over. Cade was asleep, but she was still lost in her mind, absentmindedly running her fingers through his hair. What were you thinking about, my love?

For the thousandth time since I started this, I went over my plan again in my head. Was it really necessary to leave her? I couldn't stay with her, let her fall into an irreversible love with me, agree to bind our kingdoms together out of fear of losing me, and then declare war on Thoya and Perosan for ultimate power.

Or, maybe I was giving myself too much credit. Perhaps she wouldn't have chosen me. Either way, this would have ended in heartbreak, and she wouldn't know the truth about Mira, how dangerous she was. She'd learn to lean on her instead and possibly agree to war to not lose her sister.

No. This was still the only option. She had to hate me, let her anger pull through, and I needed to keep invading her dreams, showing her glimpses into her past. I would need to propose and not give her the option of saying no, even if she loathed me.

It was time to send Jeanine back in. Luisa was expecting her back to help plan Raven's birthday celebration that Reales was paying for. With the help of the seamstress back in Reales, Raven's dress should be delivered any day now. I sent her a letter the day I pretended to leave with an idea for a dress for her. I didn't have an address living on a ship in the middle of a channel, hidden behind caves that still whispered her name every night, so John should be receiving it soon.

I leaned against the wall and closed my eyes, thinking about my mother and Luca. I hoped they were okay without me. Hopefully, I'd return in a few weeks with Raven, and maybe Mira would be so overcome with gratitude that she'd let them go. Let me free. I shook my head against the wall, knowing that would never happen. She had come to rely on my abilities, and I had become addicted to blood running through my fingers.

But then I smiled, pulling my memory of Raven in the dungeon to the front of my mind. She savored death the same way I did. She wanted to steal life, make it her own. That was her mother's darkness living inside of her. Instead of thirsting for power like her mother, she thirsted for justice, wanting to use murder as retribution. My sweet little demon.

I needed to invade her dream. I opened my eyes and sat up, looking at her again. Her eyes were closed, and her fingers had stopped moving in Cade's hair. I slowly rose up and whispered her name, and she didn't stir. I stood and ambled to her, smiling at her beauty in the moonlight. She was devastating anyway, but seeing her only lit up by the moon's light was like the feeling one may get while watching the sunrise.

I looked at Cade, still asleep on her chest, and fought my urge to choke him. His lips had been on hers. My eyes flickered to her mouth. That mouth was mine. I took a deep breath, trying to calm my murderous instinct.

I crouched beside her and pushed into her mind, filtering through some of her memories. I needed to be cautious in my choice. I wanted to remain in the ones of us, smiling at how we laughed together on our way to the barn the night of the banquet. But I continued, falling deeper into her depths, shuddering at the torment of her earlier days in the palace, trying to find out who she was, where she belonged.

With me. She belonged with me.

There were only a select few memories with Mira in them, as Raven was only days old when she was taken. But I stopped on one and brought it out, pushing it into her subconscious. She twitched in her sleep, and I continued to move it forward until her mind's eye focused on it. Her eyebrows drew in slightly in her sleep.

I closed my eyes and my mind entwined with hers.

———

I grabbed her hand and pulled her through Mira's castle as she stared at me in bewilderment. She couldn't understand how she always found me in her dreams. I guided her into a room that had a white cradle in the middle with a mobile of stars and moons hanging over it. We heard cooing in the cradle, and she stopped abruptly, staring at the noise. I tugged her again, and she shook her head at me. Her subconscious was beginning to not trust me, knowing I'd broken her.

"It's okay, baby," I whispered to her.

Her green eyes could pierce through my soul, still trying to find our connection. She took a tentative step toward me, then another until I could bring her closer to the baby in the cradle, trying to reach for the shapes above her. Raven peered over, and everything about her seemed to recoil. I lifted an eyebrow.

"Raven, what's wrong?"

She stared at the baby in the cradle before slowly bringing her gaze back to me. "She's here," she whispered.

Her fingers wrapped tighter around mine as a little girl bounced into the room behind us, coming to pick up the baby from the crib. Raven stared at the girl. Mira.

'*Little bird*,' Mira said to the baby, bouncing her in her arms. And then movement in the corner of my eye had me drawing Raven closer to me.

"Why do you keep bringing her here?"

I pulled Raven behind me at the eerie voice. Celestina was standing up from a rocking chair in the corner. How had I not sensed her here? But Raven had, and I felt her fear as she wrapped her arms around my waist from behind, burying her forehead against my back. I had to get her out of here, but I couldn't. I looked around the room that seemed to be shrinking as Celestina stared at us, slowly taking a step toward me.

I shook my head, narrowing my eyes.

"Raven," Celestina called.

Raven's hands dug deeper into me. We needed to leave, but there was resistance when I tried to shove out of the memory.

"Raven," she called again, her voice softer than before.

Raven's head moved, peeking around my side. I pushed us farther back, trying to get us to the door.

"Mother," Raven whispered, loosening her grip around me.

Fuck, she was going to want to stay. Celestina's resolve weakened at Raven's voice, and I flung us out, stumbling a few steps back as I did.

———

I froze as Raven's eyes snapped open, her chest rising and falling from the sudden thrust out of her mind. She inhaled through her nose and exhaled with a tear falling down her cheek. She could smell me.

I wanted to go to her. Comfort her from that memory. I didn't know Celestina was there. All I saw was Mira. Celestina was trying to reach Raven through her memories, and I'd become a catalyst.

Raven's head rolled to the side toward me, and I took a tiny step back, hidden in the dark of Cade's room. Another tear fell down her cheek. She was withering, and I couldn't help her. Her eyes fluttered shut, trying to find sleep again. I shouldn't. I knew that I shouldn't, but right when I felt her on the brink of dozing, I whispered so low that she may not have been able to hear, "I love you."

Another tear fell as a small smile sent her off to sleep.

Walking back into the forest, I yawned. I had to spend daylight hours on my ship so I wouldn't be seen.

I stayed with Raven for an hour longer after her dream, wanting to make sure that her sleep stayed peaceful. I knew I needed to leave her when the black sky started to lighten. But I'd see her again tonight.

Before I left her, I snuck into the library to leave her one of my roses that I knew she'd destroy, but I couldn't stop my incessant need of wanting her to know that I was still around, missing her, wanting to console her.

Choosing her memories was becoming trickier now that Celestina knew what I was doing. Celestina was more dangerous than Mira, and I couldn't allow her to get to Raven. I would have to comb through her memories carefully, which was irritating since we didn't have much time.

I reached the caves, and the black cat came trotting out of one. My eyes narrowed on it. It sat in front of me, staring at me with its big green eyes. "If you're who I think you are, stop causing trouble." The cat hissed, leaving me standing there.

I grumbled, rolling my eyes at the whispers of Raven's name in the caves. "Don't you ever have anything else to talk about?" I asked the voices. They silenced before a gust of wind came out, making me stumble sideways. I raised my middle finger toward the cave as I walked past it. Too many witches, too much attitude.

I needed to get off this forsaken island. I needed to murder someone, but no one ever came into the forest, which meant all my pent-up rage was directed toward Cade, who kept touching my girl. Which was exactly what I needed him to do.

Fuck Mira. This was all because of her.

I jumped across the large rocks that led to my ship and landed on the deck as it rocked under my feet. The water was restless today. Jeanine heard my steps coming out of the hull, and I nodded at her in greeting. "How is she?" she asked.

My eyebrow rose in question.

She gave me a slight shrug in return. "I like her. I know she hates me, but she's kind. Her villagers are very protective of her."

I was quiet, but I nodded. Sadness loomed over me. "Then why are you doing it?"

Jeanine sighed and came to stand beside me, looking out over the water. "Because Mira will make my life hell if I don't."

I laughed softly at that. "Why don't you leave?"

Her face fell at my question. I hoped I hadn't offended her.

"It's not my intention to hurt you. That's not why I asked."

She shook her head. "That's not it." She turned to face me, crossing her arms over her chest. "Mira wasn't always so... ruthless."

I thought back to before Rudolf became ill. Mira was tolerable. She was always drawn into herself, rarely stepping foot outside of the castle.

"But then something snapped in her when Rudolf started to get sick. All she could talk about was her mother, how she had a sister in another kingdom that was snatched away from her. The more she talked about it, the more it seemed to eat away at her."

"Why did she send you here? What's the point of it?"

Jeanine shrugged again, expelling a deep breath. "I honestly don't know. All I could get from her was that she wanted the people here to fear Raven. I've never understood why she'd want her sister's kingdom to turn against her."

I was quiet while I thought about it. I knew Mira wanted Raven back in Reales to manipulate her into a war, but Raven would need the help of her people to form an army to invade other kingdoms. How could she do that if they feared her? Unless they thought going against her wishes would result in their loss of life. But Raven told me that she never ruled her kingdom like that. She never used anyone for her benefit.

"Mira doesn't realize that their greatest motivator is love." I met Jeanine's eyes. "Her people will do as she asks because they adore her. They don't need to fear her to fall in line." And it would destroy her if she had to ask that of them.

Jeanine asked, "What do we do?"

I pinched the bridge of my nose. Either way, we had to get Raven back to Reales. That always had to be the end result. "We stick to the plan. You said you've told everyone in the village?"

She nodded.

"Just focus on the ball now. Help Luisa. Go to the castle today, and let Raven see you with Cade. I need her jealousy to turn into fury. She keeps burying it down. I need her to let it out."

"What are you going to do?"

I looked back toward the palace, hidden behind the caves and miles of forest. "I must keep making her hate me until the ball. And then I'll give her as little information as I can before we get to Reales. I can't tell her everything. It'll shock her too much, and when she gets overwhelmed, she shuts down." And I needed to keep invading her dreams, but I didn't say that out loud. I trusted Jeanine when she said she liked Raven, but I couldn't give my entire plan away in case Mira found a way to break Jeanine down.

I felt Jeanine's hand on my arm. I looked down at her, and her face was composed, understanding. "You love her, don't you?"

Love was not strong enough to describe how I felt about Raven, but I nodded. She wrapped her arms around my waist, and I put my arms around her, letting her. Just weeks ago, I was fucking her for information, using her the same way Mira did. "I'm sorry," I muttered.

She looked up at me.

"For using you. For hurting you."

She stared at me for a moment, and then a smile brightened her face. "It was fun while it lasted."

I chuckled, shaking my head.

She released me. "Raven is a lucky girl."

"I'm the lucky one."

She nodded again, still smiling. "Yes, you are."

I smiled with her, feeling lighter for the first time in weeks.

Jeanine and I ate breakfast together, which consisted of fruits she had picked up from the market in the village. I took a bite of pear and immediately craved Raven, and I finished it just because it reminded me of her. Jeanine left me shortly after to go to the castle and talk to Luisa about the ball. "Remember to get Cade alone," I reminded her as I walked with her back to the palace.

She nodded in response before giving me a small wave and disappearing over the border. I knew Cade would be hard to hold on his own, aware of Raven's rage, but Jeanine could do it. She was bubbly in person, and people found it hard to ignore her.

I gazed longingly at the castle. Raven was in there somewhere. And then I looked at Duck's. I missed my rum. And he said he kept secrets. I pulled up my hood and kept my eyes averted from the guards as I strolled past them, keeping a calm composure. I didn't know if Raven had told them to keep me out or not. If she had, and they noticed me, they may say to her, and all of this would have been for nothing.

But they didn't say anything as I glided past. I relaxed my shoulders. My hood remained on even as I pulled open the door and stepped into Duck's. There were a lot of patrons. I pushed through to the bar and sat on a stool at the end.

I felt a glare at me, and I finally raised my eyes to see Arthur standing before me. "You," he said, his ordinarily jolly demeanor missing.

"Listen…"

He whipped my arm with a towel. I could feel the zing of pain, even through my coat. "Uh, ow," I grumbled, rubbing my arm.

"I told you to keep her safe," he grunted.

I winced. "I *am*," I replied, my voice tired. "I am."

He stared at me hard for a long time before he reached below him and pulled out a glass from underneath his counter, filling it with rum. I sighed, dipping my chin to him in gratitude. I threw it back, relishing the taste of it burning down my throat. He poured me another before leaning his forearms down against the counter, sighing as he watched me swirl the rum around in my glass. "You don't look good, kid," he muttered.

I nodded before I tossed my second drink back.

"She misses you, you know."

My eyes burned. "I miss her," I breathed.

He poured me another.

"You can't tell her I was here."

He blinked. I knew he was contemplating it.

"It's important, Arthur. She can't know."

Finally, he nodded once. "She doesn't come in here anymore, anyway. Cade won't let her."

My forehead creased. "*Let* her?" She was the queen. He didn't have the right to control anything she wanted to do.

Arthur nodded. "He doesn't let her out of his sight. I saw her one night trying to come this way, but he caught up to her. Dragged her back."

He held her there, only letting her come out if he was with her. He was trying to control her. Keep her only for himself. And I was helping him. The free will she was so desperate to give others, he wasn't giving her. I tapped my fist on the counter twice and stood up from my stool. "Thanks for the drinks, Arthur. And keeping my secret."

He tipped his chin to me.

I dropped coins on the counter. "Between friends."

———

The evening was falling, which meant Raven and Cade would leave for the forest soon to train, and I wanted to see how they interacted together. I lifted my chin as I passed by Cade's balcony, freezing as Raven breezed out, naked. She stretched her arms over her head. Even from where I stood, she still took my breath away. I wasn't particularly fond of her strolling out onto the balcony where other people could see her, but it was her body

when it wasn't mine. She wiped tears from her eyes, and I
frowned. What was I doing to her?

And then, everything stopped. Pain that I didn't know I could
experience shot through me. Arms wrapped around her waist
and pulled her back inside, throwing shut the doors. I turned and
vomited the contents of my stomach on the ground. All the rum,
the pears, I needed it out.

He won her over. She let him possess her.

I wiped my mouth with the back of my hand and jogged
toward the forest. That image of them was going to plague my
nightmares every night. Her beautiful body belonged to him now.
I had to stop my jog to lean against a tree and vomit again,
coughing as my eyes watered. This was what I wanted. I needed
it to happen. But fuck, it hurt. Seeing my girl with someone else,
the way I used to have her.

Tears fell down my cheeks as I returned to my ship, wiping
them off quickly as Jeanine appeared from the hull. Her brow
wrinkled when she saw me, and she walked quickly to me,
grabbing my arms. "What is it? What happened?"

I shook my head, swallowing a lump forming in my throat. "It
worked," I rasped, shaking myself from her grip and leaning over
the boat's edge. Nausea rolled through me. "You with Cade. It
worked."

She must've understood because she came up and started
rubbing my back. "I only talked to him for a few minutes before
she saw. But it wasn't lust in her eyes, Zeke. It was only anger. I
don't think she wants him, not the way he wants her."

I was shaking as I hung my head. "I pushed her to him."

"But why?"

All I could do was laugh through the despair. "Because I needed her to get over me. Find someone else." And she did. My little demon did exactly as I wanted.

Jeanine was quiet behind me.

I cleared my throat, needing a distraction. "How's the ball going?"

"Good. Raven will love it. John had her dress, and he showed me. It's very her."

I felt relieved at that, at least.

"You smell like rum. Did you go into the village?"

"Just for a little bit, to Duck's. He won't tell her."

"You should try and sleep." Her voice was soft.

I knew that I should. It'd been a couple days since I had. I nodded and straightened, squeezing her shoulder once before descending into the hull and falling down onto the bed. I needed this to happen, and that was what I had to keep reminding myself. I left her so this exact thing could happen... but I wondered if she thought of me still. If he gave her the same pleasure that I did. If she screamed for him.

The image of them together did indeed become my nightmare.

It felt like hours before I woke up, my head heavy from regret and rum. I ran my fingers through my hair as I climbed the ladder to the deck, but then my nose wrinkled as I smelled smoke. I looked up to see it stretching over the caves.

"Jeanine?" I called out, but she didn't answer.

I jumped out of the ship, climbed over the rocks, and ran toward the smoke. Raven. Was she okay? Did she cause this?

The guards at the gate were gone, and I looked toward the village. It was coming from there. Raven wouldn't have done anything to harm her people. This was something else.

I pushed through the crowd of people, throwing up my hood. I stopped when I saw the bakery and Cade standing outside of it, frantically yelling Raven's name. No. I pushed farther into the crowd, trying to get to her, but then I saw a flurry of ice inside the bakery. The silhouette of her body was pushing through the smoke. She was trying to stop it.

Everyone around me stared at her, watching their queen obliterate the fire with her own dark magic. And I was bewitched by her, too. Her body shook as she pushed out her ice and wind, trying to calm the raging flames. I wanted to speak to her, tell her to breathe, but I didn't want to throw her off, risk her falling apart.

All I could do was wait. Rather impatiently.

As the fire died out, Cade rushed in. She collapsed into him, her face covered in blood and tears. The baker and a redheaded girl ran in, and Raven wrapped her arms around the young girl. I tilted my head. That was her librarian. The one I saw coming in not long after I had left the rose on the table.

When Cade pulled her outside, I felt her self-doubt, even from the back of the crowd. She was afraid they wouldn't accept her. A little girl ran up and hugged her legs, and I smiled at the relief that stretched across her face. And one by one, her people bowed, and I bowed with them, promising to always accept her, always love her.

I took a few steps back, disappearing into the crowd. She wouldn't train tonight, and I couldn't continue watching her with Cade.

I was almost out of the village when I heard screams. I turned, watching as Raven fell to the ground. An arrow was piercing her side. My eyes burned with tears as I took another step toward her, but someone gripped my arm roughly and pulled me backward. I thrashed against the arm, needing to get to Raven and help her.

"Zeke, stop. She's going to be fine."

I heard John's voice, and I turned to him, my eyes narrowed at the bow strapped across his back. "You shot her." Nothing but rage coursed through me, and I pulled my arm back, punching him square in the jaw. He stumbled back a step, but I was on him again, holding him up by his shirt. I tossed him back behind a row of buildings. "I'm going to fucking kill you," I growled.

He stood and put his palms up, spitting blood on the ground. "I did it for her own good," he mumbled.

I balled my fists at my sides. I should have ended him where he stood, but instead, I stared at him. "What do you mean?"

John sighed as he massaged his jaw. "They needed to see who she was. She's kept it a secret for too long."

"*Why*? Why did they need to see it?"

He looked at me like I was missing something. "Didn't Jeanine just tell you that Mira wants her people to fear her? Some of them do. I'm in the village almost every day, and while most of them love her, there are a few who are afraid of magic returning to the island."

I waited, unsure of what his point was.

"They needed to see for themselves that there is no evil in that girl, not when it comes to them."

"So why shoot her?" I growled, itching to get back to her.

"Because they needed to know that she's not invincible. If her darkness threatens them, there's a way to stop her. And they needed to know that if a war comes, they'll be useful to fight for her. I'm doing all of this for her. We're running out of time."

"You could have killed her."

He shook his head. "I know what she can handle. I was close to Leonidas, son. He trusted me enough to tell me things. His blade the night he killed Celestina was covered in poison. He wanted to destroy her magic, let it die with her, but it counteracted and bled into Raven instead."

I nodded. I already knew that.

"It won't kill her. But she will have nightmares, son. Her magic will be paralyzed for a little while, but you must let her feel that. She needs to feel the pain of not having it."

"Why?" I asked him again, running my fingers through my hair.

"Because she is fading without you. There's no fight left in her. She doesn't come to meetings and does nothing but walk lifelessly around the castle. Cade is the only person keeping her going daily, and she shouldn't even be trusting him."

At that, I dropped my hands. "What do you mean by that?"

John chuckled as he shook his head. "You're desperate to be the villain in her story when she already has one."

I looked back toward the village, unable to see Raven or Cade.

"He's known about who she is her entire life."

I nodded because, again, I knew that.

"But she doesn't know that."

I slowly turned my head back to John.

"He's never told her, but Leonidas informed him of everything on his seventeenth birthday. I knew that Raven would need someone young in the castle to rely on, to get close to. I'd become friends with August, Cade's father, who told me that Cade saw him bring Raven in as a baby. So, I told Leonidas to bring Cade to court, make him protect her, make her feel safe."

I was going to be sick again.

"Cade made the decision to never tell Raven. Instead, he followed her around for a year with Leonidas, learning her quirks and what she could do. He's known exactly who she is her entire life, but he wanted her to rely on him. She might have tried to leave and go to Reales herself if he told her. He didn't want to let her go."

"And I pushed her to him." I turned from John and walked back toward Raven, stepping just far enough around the building to see her still on the ground, still passed out.

John came up beside me and patted my arm. "I promise she'll be okay. But you have to let her feel the pain, Zeke. She needs to figure out who she is without anyone else trying to tell her. She needs to find her fight again, or she'll never survive Mira."

Cade was on the ground with her, shouting back and forth at the redhead girl, trying to figure out how to wake her up.

"I have to get to her. Bring her back."

He sighed next to me.

"John, she may not want to come back if what you're saying is true. If there's no fight left in her, she may not feel like there's a reason to return. I have to." I shook my head slightly. "Arthur warned me about this."

"About what?"

"Twin flames," I sighed, glancing at him. "We're twin flames. And he said that twin flames go mad if they're apart after they've been found."

"Twin flames," he repeated, awe in his voice. "That's… that's something else. A pairing. It's been… well, a very long time."

"Please… please don't tell Mira," I said, my trust in him long diminished. "Raven doesn't even know. I can reach her, but I need to do it now."

"Son, I wouldn't…" he trailed off but nodded from the corner of my eye. "Find her, and then you have to leave her. I mean it, Ezekiel."

I winced at the use of my full name. He always called me that as a child when I was in trouble, which was often, and it still held weight behind it.

"She has to figure this out on her own. She has to see that she doesn't need Cade or anyone else."

I nodded, and he left me to reach her. I was far from her, which meant I couldn't pull a memory, so I'd have to shove into her subconscious. I focused on her body, closing my mind while I tried to search hers. It was quiet. I couldn't find her. "Come on, baby," I gritted through my teeth, reaching for her.

And then I was in a black room. I saw her far away on the opposite side. She started to walk closer, and I followed her lead, meeting her in the middle. There was a glass pane between us. She placed her palm on the glass and watched as her skin faded. "I'm dying," she whispered.

I nodded slowly, putting my palm against hers. "What do you want, Raven?"

Her eyes lingered on her vanishing skin. "You." Her voice was quiet, like a bird fluttering in the wind. She slowly moved her eyes to mine. "All I ever wanted to do is love you, but you won't let me."

I leaned my forehead against the glass. She rose to the tips of her toes to try and mirror me. She was so faint like she was slipping away. All I wanted to do was let her love me. All I ever did was love her. "Come back to me," I murmured. I slowly took a step back, beckoning her to follow me.

She pounded her palms against the glass, trying to regain her strength. She pressed her cheek against the pane, her body too tired. "Always leaving me," she whimpered.

I nearly broke. I couldn't make her do this. She needed to choose to live. "Come on, baby," I called out to her.

She screamed. The glass shattered.

CHAPTER NINETEEN

Raven

I awoke with a gasp and tried to sit up, but jolts of pain shot across my body. Strong hands pushed me back down to wherever I was. I thrashed, tried to kick, tried to flail my arms. I screamed. My skin, everything inside of me, felt like it was on fire, but it wasn't my own fire. This was something different: it was suppressing my magic, pushing it down. I desperately tried to fight through the pain and bring it back.

I'm sorry I ever doubted you; I pleaded with it.

It screamed with me.

Please don't leave me, I said over and over in my mind.

I heard voices trying to break through my screams. Familiar voices, but when I tried to open my eyes, my back arched, and I started to cry. Silent tears fell down my cheeks, soaking into my skin. I tried to scream again, but there was nothing left. Hands were on my shoulders, arms, and legs, trying to keep me still.

"She can heal herself; why isn't she healing?!"

Cade. Yelling at someone.

I wanted to find him. He would make it all go away. I tried to summon my ice to the surface, but I had exhausted all of it. And whatever was burning through me wasn't letting it form. "It's aconite!" Someone else screamed. Another familiar voice. Grace. "The arrow was laced with it!"

"Why the fuck would aconite be doing this to her!?" Cade yelled again.

"Because it's used to kill witches."

Witches. Witches. Witches.

And it was coursing through my body, killing me.

I was a witch. Though I felt like I was dying rather quickly.

The word repeated over and over in my head.

And then I faded away.

———————

I dreamed of being in a dark kingdom, a kingdom that wasn't my own. I ran toward a gray castle that seemed too big for the sky. Death was at my feet. I jumped over bodies while hands of the undead tried to grab my feet and bring me down. Screaming, I ran faster. Reaching the castle seemed like the most important thing I'd ever do.

The smell of pine and rum settled on my body, making me tear through the black streets faster as they turned into one steep hill. I climbed and climbed, falling to my knees as I started to crawl. I was so tired — my body sore from exertion.

I cried his name, and he came out to stand on the castle steps, cocking his head at me. He didn't know I'd be here — but he always knew. How had I gotten here alone?

"Go home, Raven," he said.

My tears blinded me, but I kept crawling. I couldn't speak. All I could do was shake my head before he extended his head to me. I felt a surge of energy thrumming through my veins as I grabbed his hand, giving me new life.

"I love you, I love you," I told him.

His own tears slid down his cheeks. "Wake up, Raven."

I grasped his fingers tighter, trying to pull him to me. If I could just kiss him, maybe he'd come back. Maybe he'd let me stay here among the dead and dying because it was where we belonged together. His face twisted as he pulled his hand back. I knew he was about to push me out of wherever this was — wherever he kept finding me. "Go home, baby."

And then I was thrown, and it felt like flying out of a picture in slow motion.

———————

It felt like months had passed when I finally opened my eyes again. I kept trying to drown myself in nightmares, but they always ended. I squinted as sun rays temporarily blinded me. A sharp pain pinched at my side when I tried to raise my arms. I groaned as someone gently pushed my arms back down.

I fluttered my eyes open, making out his form as he stood before the rays. "Angel," I muttered, blinking until my vision cleared. I saw his jaw first, then his lips, until I could find his eyes, which were flooded with relief and wet with tears.

"Raven," Cade whispered, brushing his hand against my cheek.

A calm settled over me momentarily, and then I remembered. I pushed up, trying to shove at his arm holding me down. Pain shot through me. I wasn't used to feeling pain. I was typically able to heal myself fast enough to hardly feel anything.

"Slow. I'll help you."

He wrapped his arms around my chest and gently pulled me up until I sat against the headboard. I tried to roll my neck, but it was stiff. I needed to defog my brain, so I kept going until it loosened. The last thing I remembered was feeling immense pain and burning, and... witches.

"Witch," I tried to say aloud, but my voice was barely a whisper.

He chuckled softly. "You're a witch, I guess."

It made sense, and it explained the dark magic. Witches were extinct a long time ago. I didn't understand why they'd rebirth with me. "What happened to me?"

He sighed and lifted one of my hands, cradling it between his hands. He was quiet for a long time, and I just stared. "You were walking down the road. When I saw you go down, you'd gotten a few feet away from me. I didn't know what had happened. I ran to you, but you were already passed out. I saw the arrow piercing your side when I tried to pick you up. I pulled it out, but there was so much blood, Raven." His voice broke as he nodded to where I felt the throbbing pain. "Grace came rushing to us next. Her bookish brain figured out that it was aconite coating the arrow and that it was used to kill witches. We ran you to the infirmary and realized it wasn't enough to kill you because your body eventually started burning through it, and your wound started to close."

"Hurts," I said.

He nodded. "It's been slow healing. Much slower than usual."

I tried to draw a deep breath, but my lungs felt like they were on fire. "I can't feel my magic," I muttered softly, trying to call on Frost to soothe the burn.

He hung his head, a tear escaping down his cheek. "It's there, Raven. It's just a little paralyzed right now."

But he couldn't know that. It could be gone. I felt nothing. Empty. Maybe all this time, I had known who I was. I was an orphan with a rare set of abilities. An orphan who became queen because of them. And without them...

I really didn't know who I was.

It'd been a week, and Cade never left my side. Luisa would come in every now and then to keep him up to date with everything going on. Our soldiers were scouring the small countryside trying to find whoever did this, but they had not found anyone yet. They were long gone, having jumped on one of the departing ships.

Isla visited, but I asked her to go home. It was the only way to keep her safe. She tried to fight me on it, but I begged her, and she reluctantly agreed.

I had stayed in bed, only getting up to bathe, and then he would make me lie back down. It was something I'd try and fight usually, but I felt nothing but emptiness in my bones, always cold, constantly tired.

The night would fall, and I'd try to sleep, but nightmares plagued me. I'd feel the punch of the arrow all over again, but my entire body would be paralyzed, and I'd have to watch it happen to everyone I loved and cared about. It would take them down one by one, and I'd wake up in a panic, screaming. Cade would be there, rocking me back to sleep.

I'd see a faceless queen sitting on my throne while Cade kneeled at her feet. I'd start to cry in my sleep until he'd shake me awake, soothing my fears. No one would take my throne; he'd repeat until I would close my eyes again.

And then, I'd dream about those gray eyes — the ones that haunted me every day, in everything I did. Those same ones kept me from surrendering myself to Cade. His hand would reach for mine, a dream within a dream. Our fingertips would brush, and an explosion of energy would push us apart.

'Go home, baby,' he'd continue to say, and I would beg to stay with him, but he was always unattainable.

I would cry until I had no tears left — my anger had been replaced by fear. I never thought I would miss the need for blood, the need to destroy. It fueled me, and kept me going. It instilled hope in me that I had something to fight with. Now, all I did was lay in Cade's bed and feel sorry for myself while I waited for my body to try and heal. I silently begged my magic to return and give me one more chance, but it didn't respond.

It was gone.

After over a week, I started begging Cade to let me out of the room. He argued heavily with me, but I told him that I needed to visit the village — they needed to see that I was okay and that we could bring as many guards as he wanted, and it'd be during the daytime. He relented after I started crying and helped me into one of my light dresses.

I thought I'd be more excited, but all I felt was heavy.

I braided my hair, wincing whenever I needed to lift my arm. He watched me, again trying to talk me out of going. But I merely shook my head. He led me out of the room, holding my hand. Guards bowed as we passed. I kept my eyes straight, my mouth in a thin line. I was ashamed. And cautious.

I dropped his hand and clasped my fingers at my waist, but he found me again and palmed the small of my back while guiding me out of the thick oak door of my castle. We were flanked by three guards on each side. I rolled my eyes. It was overkill, but I told him he could. We used to travel with zero into the village, and now we had six.

We started across the bridge, and his hand never left me. It made me uncomfortable since I was the queen and the leader of this kingdom, and I was being guided along by my adviser. I glanced up at him as we approached the cobblestone road. "Cade, you have to let me go."

He met my eyes, shaking his head. "No."

"You can't tell me no, Cade." My voice was quiet, but it had a bite to it.

His eyes narrowed. "No." And he wrapped his arm around my waist, pulling me closer to him.

I muttered a curse word under my breath.

I saw Eva running to me from down the street, but when I tried to bend down, he pulled me back up. "You think little Eva is the one who shot me?" I asked him, trying to shove his hand off.

"I don't know who the fuck shot you, but it's only been a little over a week. You can't expect me to just let you walk around," he snapped.

"You don't *let* me do anything." I uncurled his fingers from my waist and dropped them.

He stiffened next to me as I bent down just in time to catch Eva in my arms. She was crying wildly, and I pulled her head back to look at me. "I'm okay, Eva. You don't need to worry about me. I just… may not be a butterfly anymore." I choked down a sob that threatened to spill.

"You'll always be my butterfly," she whispered, throwing her arms around my neck.

Theodore came up, and a guard stepped closer to my side. I shot him a glare, and he stepped back again. This was out of hand. I couldn't remember the last time I was alone.

I stood with Eva still in my arms, pushing down a groan. I didn't want to scare her. Theodore gave me a small smile. "She hasn't slept much. She's been worried."

I rubbed her back. "You should've brought her to the castle. I would've seen her."

Theodore glanced quickly at Cade and then back to me. "You tried."

He only nodded.

I sighed, squeezing Eva tighter. "I will handle that. Don't ever hesitate to bring her by again. And as for you…." I trailed off, ticking Eva's sides until she looked at me. "Don't fret. I will be good as new soon." Empty promises. I felt nothing good.

She sniffled and allowed Theodore to take her from my arms. I gave him a small smile before turning my heel to face Cade, crossing my arms over my chest. "You wouldn't let that little girl see me?"

He only glared at me.

"You don't tell someone no without talking to me first."

He nodded once, but his fists clenched at his sides.

"Calm the fuck down." My voice was low as I looked at his fists. "If you don't stop, they will think I'm weak, and I'm not."

"I *love* you," he growled at me, taking a step closer. "Someone tried to kill you, Raven. It's my job to protect you."

"Protect me, but don't suffocate me."

He faltered at that, retreating a step.

I took a moment to study him. His eyes were darker, his lines harsher. That night changed us all. And I hated that I had hurt him, but I needed to do this alone. I turned again and walked toward the bakery, waving to Grace and Lara as I approached. "It looks great!" I shouted to them.

Grace ran to me. She was one of the select few that Cade had let into his room to visit me, but seeing her always brought a smile to my face. A guard came to my side again, and I groaned, taking a step away. I opened my arms to Grace. "It looks like you'll be open for business in no time."

Grace nodded, pulling back a little from my embrace. "It didn't reach past the front room. Cade sent men to help us rebuild the counter and the frame. We should be open by next week!"

My smile widened. "I can't wait for more chocolate pastries."

———

I continued my tour around the village, greeting the shop owners. They would all hug me. My guards had finally taken the hint and stayed back. As we were about to leave the village to lock me away again in the castle, I stopped at Duck's and stared at the front door. I wanted to go in. The last time I tried, Cade had found me and dragged me back. I wanted to see Arthur.

"I'm going to go in here," I said, not looking at Cade. "I won't be long."

I heard him sigh, but I ignored him and stepped inside the pub. I immediately felt heavy again. As Arthur approached me, I wiped a tear that fell down my cheek with the back of my hand. One look from him and I crumbled, a sob escaping me as he wrapped his arms around me.

"Raven, there, there." He patted my back, letting me cry on him while guiding me over to the end of his bar.

I sat on one of the stools and dropped my head. "He won't... let me be alone." I sniffled between sobs, putting my face in my hands. "I can't think straight. I never have a second to just... digest. And I miss *him*."

I heard him set a glass down in front of me, and I pulled my hands away from my face, watching as he poured rum into it. Zeke's rum. "Someone tried to hurt me, Arthur. And I can't... it's gone." The tears continued to fall, blurring my vision.

He patted my arm. I rubbed the tears out of my eyes with my hand. He nodded to the glass, and I lifted it to my mouth, throwing it back. It burned going down.

"You're not eating."

I followed his gaze down to my body and shook my head. My dress was hanging off my bones, swallowing me like my fear. He sighed and poured me another glassful. "You're an old soul with a young heart, my girl."

I sniffled again, raising my eyes to his.

"That means you feel... everything. If you give in to it and let it overcome you, you won't make it. You need your magic."

I flinched as he said the word aloud, but then it settled into my bones, and I welcomed it. I didn't have to hide anymore. That was the first time I had realized it in over a week.

"Find yourself, Raven. Don't let others do it for you." He dipped his chin toward the door.

I knew he was talking about Cade. My gaze lingered on the door, and I saw movement from the corner of my eye. I turned my head, but Arthur patted my arm again, bringing my attention back to him. "Drink."

I tossed the drink back and set it down, giving him a slight nod. "I should go." As I stood to leave, I realized I had no coins. "I'll have Cade come and pay you," I offered.

He shook his head. "Don't send him in here. Just come back."

A small smile was all I could manage.

As I turned to leave, I looked over to where I spotted movement earlier and stopped. I took a small step and then another until I was in front of a small table in the back corner. I grabbed the fresh rose on top of it and smelled the faintest scent of pine. I turned back to Arthur with a raised eyebrow. He simply shrugged. My eyes rolled. Bartenders and their secrets.

So, he was back then. I wasn't hallucinating.

"I hope you told him he's an asshole," I said to Arthur.

He laughed, giving me a slight nod.

Holding the rose flat in my palm, I tried to call on my fire. I frowned and wrapped my fingers around it, extending them again. Burn.

Breathe, Raven.

I heard him in the back of my mind and closed my eyes as a tear fell down my cheek, letting his raspy rumble wash over me. So, I did. I inhaled a deep breath and tried to will it forward again but felt nothing. I was nothing.

I dropped it back down to the table. He was here, somewhere. He'd come back for the rum but not for me. I really had read too far into everything.

"Where are you?" I gritted out through clenched teeth as another tear fell. I crouched down until my chin rested on top of the table. I stared at the rose — the first one I hadn't destroyed since he started leaving them. "Why do you keep leaving these?" I asked aloud, though I knew he wouldn't answer. I wasn't sure he was still around. "I miss you," I whispered, pressing the tip of my finger against a thorn.

I heard footsteps behind me. Fingers wrapped around my elbow, pulling me up harshly. Arthur came out from behind the bar. I sighed and held my hand up to him before turning to Cade. "I'm fine."

With his grip on my elbow, he pulled me to him and kissed me roughly. My entire body went rigid, but I didn't want to cause a scene, so I let him. When he broke from me, he laced our fingers together and didn't say a word as he pulled me out of the pub and toward the castle.

I turned my head to look back inside the pub. I wanted Arthur to know I was okay. But as I did, goose bumps pimpled on my skin. I could've sworn I saw a pair of gray eyes staring back at me from the shadows. When I opened my mouth to say something, Cade pulled me closer and kissed me again, never letting me look back.

Three days had passed since my awkward excursion through the village, and I started getting restless again. Cade let me leave his room to roam around the castle, but he was always with me. I didn't understand his need to protect me within my own walls, but he didn't listen when I asked him to stop. I felt suffocated, but I'd given up. I had let him have me, and now I was all he wanted, and he was making damn sure that no one could come near me anymore. Or ever again, I guessed.

I didn't attend any of my meetings. I didn't have the energy anymore. I felt utterly useless — more useless than I usually did on any given day. The reason I became queen was gone, and I wasn't sure what my point here was anymore. I couldn't protect my kingdom. We didn't have an army to do so if there were to be an invasion. I had let everyone down.

I had attempted to hold an audience today, but Cade stationed guards along the walls, and the villagers seemed too frightened to ask for anything. I would encourage them, but they'd wish me well and leave. When I asked Cade if all of this was really necessary, he only kissed me in response. That was all he ever did, and it had become rather unenjoyable.

It had been a week and a half, but we'd had no threat since the night I was shot. They hadn't found who did it, and I worried that until they did, this was how Cade would remain.

I wished I could shift, but I still felt cold.

I rolled over in bed and stared at Cade, who was sleeping beside me. I knew he'd hate me if he woke up to find me gone, but I needed to breathe without him.

I very carefully, very slowly rose up from the bed and looked down at myself in his shirt. I couldn't go out looking like this, but I couldn't rifle through drawers for my leathers. I looked around the floor, saw my discarded dress from earlier, and grabbed it, padding quietly into his lounge. I removed his shirt and tossed it down before I slid my dress back on. I didn't have my heat anymore, so I needed a coat. I found his on the floor and pulled it on.

I stared at the doorknob. His door creaked if you pulled it open too fast. I twisted it and gently pulled it open inch by inch, just enough for me to slip through it and closed it behind me. I loosened a sigh of relief and looked down the halls, hurriedly rushing down the stairs until I was in the open courtyard.

I spun as I looked up at the night sky. Hello, air.

I wondered if Duck's was still open. The guards stared at me as I passed by, but I ignored them. It was still my kingdom, and I could do as I pleased. I walked past the gate toward Duck's, freezing, when I heard a voice behind me. "Where are you going?"

I turned on my heel to see John. I nodded back toward Duck's. "I just want a drink."

A small grin tugged on his mouth. "Allow me to accompany you."

I shouldn't. I didn't know if we could trust him, but walking with someone in the dark would be safer. I glanced up at Cade's balcony. He would kill me, if someone else didn't, when he discovered I was gone.

"Take advantage while he slumbers."

My eyes met John's. I guessed everyone had noticed that Cade followed me around. John extended his elbow, and I took it, walking with him in silence to Duck's. I didn't have anything to say, but I did find myself leaning on him as we walked. I was so tired all the time.

Duck's light was still on, and I felt genuine joy for the first time in weeks. John pulled open the door and ushered me inside, Arthur starting to laugh when he saw us. "Raven, we need to talk about the company you keep," Arthur said.

John laughed behind me as we walked up to the bar.

I asked, "You two know each other?"

"Longtime friends," Arthur replied, grabbing two glasses.

They did look to be around the same age. He poured Zeke's rum into my glass and a clear liquid into John's.

"I caught our Raven here sneaking out of the castle," John told Arthur.

Arthur chuckled while shaking his head at me.

"You're always here, Arthur." I took a sip of my rum. It was the only thing I wanted to drink for the rest of my life if it kept me connected to him. "Do you live nearby?"

Arthur pointed up to the ceiling. "I live up there."

I nodded, glancing up. "Are you married? I'd love to meet your spouse if you are."

A sad glance was exchanged between Arthur and John.

I squeezed my eyes shut. "I'm sorry. I shouldn't have asked."

Arthur patted my arm and nodded toward my drink. I took another sip. "She passed away a few years back. You would've liked her. She was rebellious, like you."

I gave him a small smile before finishing my drink. John did the same with his but didn't ask for a refill. "I saw Jeanine here today, helping Luisa," John said quietly.

I didn't look at him, swirling my freshened drink around in my glass.

"Did you know she was coming back?"

"She's been back for a while." There was a bite in my tone.

"Did you know they were together?" At that, I looked to John.

He raised an eyebrow at me. "How would I have?"

"Because you are *all-knowing*."

Arthur snorted at my sarcasm. "There's our Raven."

I looked at Arthur next. "Is he here? Are you hiding him somewhere?"

At that, Arthur frowned and sighed at me. "No. He's not here, Raven." He grabbed my hand with sorrowful eyes. "But I bet he wishes he could be."

"I bet not," I whispered.

John cleared his throat. "You two…" He glanced at Arthur before he continued, "You two seemed to have a connection."

"Not a strong enough one, apparently." I threw the rest of my drink back and set the glass down. I shook my head when Arthur grabbed the bottle. "I don't want to run you out. I'm not allowed to do anything anymore, so I don't think I could reorder it for you immediately." I was snippy. These poor men. What company I was lately.

John asked quietly, "It's not back, is it?"

I shook my head, staring at my empty glass.

"It will. It's in you, Raven."

I looked at him again, hot tears in my eyes. "I should go," I whispered, hopping off the stool.

"Do you want me to walk you back?"

I looked out the window at the darkness ahead of me. I used to relish it. I'd spend all day wishing for it, so I could be alone in the forest. But now, I was fearful all the time, and I didn't want to be anymore. I wanted my freedom back.

So I shook my head. "I'll be okay. John will cover my drinks." I patted his back and waved goodbye as Arthur laughed at me. I stepped outside and shivered within Cade's jacket, pulling it tighter around me. I kicked at the melting snow at my feet as I walked.

I saw a hooded figure staring at me when I was close to my gate. I stopped, my pulse pounding in my ears as fear crept over my body. I looked back toward Duck's. I could get John again, but I was too far away. Whoever this was would catch up to me before I could. I called on my magic again, but it was silent. I growled.

The hooded figure cocked their head at me. I stared at them, narrowing my eyes. They started walking backward toward the forest, and my eyes followed them. I knew that walk. I took a step forward, and he took another step back. Again. Again.

I stomped my foot. His raspy chuckle sent chills everywhere.

"Why are you here?" I called out, my voice carrying in the empty air. "Why are you doing this?"

"Come here, baby," he responded, his voice predatorial. He turned and started to run.

And I chased him.

CHAPTER TWENTY

Raven

He was fast. My body was tired. But I followed him, sprinting to keep up with his long strides. He zigzagged through trees, and I groaned, slapping trunks with my hand as we zipped by. He didn't let up, didn't slow down, and I wondered how long I would have to follow him. And why I was following him.

He glanced back at me every so often to ensure I was still behind him, and I'd flip him off. I could see the outline of his smile, and it made me want to smile, but I didn't.

Cade's jacket felt a hundred pounds heavier, and I discarded it, dropping it to the ground. The chill of air bit at my skin, and I willed my fire forward, but it was stagnant. Tears pressed against my eyelids and stuck to my skin as they fell. We reached the clearing to the spring, and I slowed down. I started shaking my head as it came into view, slowing down to a walk.

I looked around. I lost him.

I fell to my knees and wrapped my arms around my middle, sobbing. "You're a coward!" I shouted into the air, unsure if he was still close enough to hear me.

I fell forward, putting my forehead against the cool rock of the spring. I tried to call on Blaze again and felt a ghost of her before it disappeared. I slapped my palm against the stone repeatedly, screaming, trembling.

"Where are you?" I cried, unsure if I was asking my magic or Zeke. Both, maybe. I couldn't even keep my magic from leaving me; now I was truly alone.

I crawled sloppily toward the spring and lowered myself, still fully dressed. Wading into the middle, I sank down until my head was covered. The hot water on my frozen skin burned. I could stay like this. I wouldn't have to face anything else. I wouldn't have to miss my magic or the man who didn't want me — who kept torturing me with his absence.

My lungs burned, but I held myself down.

It was so warm, and I was so cold. I sank lower and lower until I was on my knees at the bottom and wondered if I could burrow a hole into the earth and find a new world waiting for me on the other side. One that could take me away from this one. I clawed at the floor, opening my mouth to scream as the flesh on the tips of my fingers tore. No breath left as I closed my mouth again, tipping sideways to lie down for a little bit.

Suddenly, a body was next to mine. He wrapped his arms around me and pulled me up. Before breaking the surface, I knew who it was, which wasn't who I wanted.

I gasped for air, my lungs screaming as my brain tried to defog. I coughed as Cade pulled me out of the water. He wrapped the jacket I'd thrown down around my body and pulled

me into his lap, stroking my hair as I sobbed again. "Raven," he
murmured.

I curled into him, my cheek pressed against his chest.

"They're gone," I whispered through my tears. "They're all
gone."

He shushed me, squeezing me tighter against him. "They're
not, Raven."

He kissed the top of my head and stood with me in his arms,
cradling me to his chest. He weaved us through the trees. I
picked up on his scent, and my tears continued to fall. He didn't
want me to find him. He was toying with me, and I hated him for
it. He saw that I was alone out of the castle and wanted to know
if I'd still follow him. And I was the idiot who would. He knew
the power he held over me. And I had Cade, who loved me so
much that he wouldn't let me out of his sight, and I couldn't ever
escape him.

He guided us through the gate, mumbling gratitude to the
guards. My eyes rolled. They had tattled on me. We entered his
chambers, and he set me to my feet in his bathroom, turning on
the water in his bathtub. I watched as the steam rose.

He came to me, lifting my heavy dress from my body, and
grazed his fingertips over my scar. His eyes met mine, and he
kissed me softly for the first time since I was hurt. His kisses had

been hungry lately, rough. Like it was somehow my fault that I was shot and didn't want him following me around.

He hadn't had me since the accident, and I didn't think I was ready yet. "Bathe with me," he whispered.

I hesitated but nodded.

I stepped into the hot water and slid down into the tub. He discarded his clothes and followed me in, leaning back against the tub wall and pulling me back against his chest. He was hard against my back, and I knew how much he wanted me, but I was so tired.

He massaged soap in my hair, bubbles falling down my face, and I blew them off. "You're using too much," I said, patting the blob in my hair. I started to sink, ducking my head under the water to wash it off, but he quickly pulled me up.

"Don't," he sighed, holding me tightly against him.

I had frightened him in the spring. I wasn't sure what I was trying to do, but I didn't want to be found. Surely I would've eventually let myself up, but the burning felt good. I needed to find it elsewhere if I couldn't have my own fire running through me.

"Raven," he whispered. "Let me fix you." He slowly ran his hands down my arms, kissing the side of my head.

He wanted to feel close to me again and wanted us to feel connected. I hadn't found any release since Zeke left, and maybe it would help me relax. Maybe I wouldn't feel so empty if he filled me.

I put my fingers around his thighs, and he put his hands around my waist, lifting me up just enough to glide down onto his length. He groaned and thrust up gently, fully sheathing himself in me. It was painful, and my walls tried to expand for him, but he thrust again. My eyes wetted from the ache.

His mouth was on my neck as he started kissing me, working his way up until my earlobe was between his teeth. Tears burned under my eyelids as my mind wandered to Zeke.

Cade's fingers pressed into my hips as he guided me on him, rocking me.

I thought of Zeke's raspy chuckle and moaned, my head rolling to the side.

Cade continued to buck into me while his fingers found my clit.

I recalled hearing Zeke's voice in my mind at the pub, telling me to breathe, trying to help me find my fire again.

I rolled my hips quickly as Cade bit my ear again.

Zeke's head between my legs at the spring.

I whimpered, biting down my lip.

Us in the dungeon.

My walls tightened as I rocked. Cade groaned as he pulsed inside of me.

Those gray eyes.

I cried out as I came, my eyes falling shut as I rocked my hips, riding my wave. I found my release, and my entire body relaxed.

And it was still because of Zeke.

Cade's arms wrapped around my middle again. He stayed inside of me, pushing his lips against my neck. "I missed you," he murmured against my skin.

I stayed quiet, only nodding, breathless from the man who haunted my mind. Guilt settled on my shoulders, and I turned my upper half toward Cade, pushing my mouth against his — a silent apology for coming to the thought of another man.

I lifted myself off of him and stepped out of the tub. He followed close behind me, drying us off with a plush towel before he scooped me up and carried me to his bed.

He pulled me against his chest, holding me tightly to guarantee that I wouldn't disappear from him again. I stared out at the balcony, knowing Zeke was out there somewhere. Jeanine hadn't come back alone. He came back with her. They were still together. That had to be why he hadn't come to see me.

Cade breathed heavily behind me, already asleep. I knew I should sleep to prepare for my day of doing absolutely nothing again. I closed my eyes, exhaling softly, and ignored the tugging of my heart as I slowly drifted off.

And then I dreamed.

I was in my favorite blue dress and walking through my village, alone for once, beaming at everyone as I passed by. I looked ahead and saw Zeke at the end of the road, breaking into a run and lunging into his open arms.

He spun me once and kissed the top of my head as he let me down. I smiled so broadly that it hurt, even in my subconscious.

He returned it, leaning down to crash his mouth to mine.

"Why are you here?" I breathed, my voice soft as it left my lips. Here, in my dream, in my village, in Seolia.

"I just needed to see you smile again," he said.

He kissed me again. I didn't want to leave, but I could feel him fading away. I pulled him closer, shaking my head. "Let me stay," I begged, my eyes glistening.

"I can't, baby. You have to go back."

I put my hands on his face and kept him to me, kissing him again until I was dizzy. And he let me. He wanted to stay, too.

"We can be together here," I offered to him.

He sighed into me, pressing his forehead to mine.

"You can keep us here, can't you?"

He nodded slowly.

"Stay with me," I whispered, kissing him again.

His arms wrapped around my waist, and he let us stay wrapped up in one another for a moment before he pulled away again. All I could do was stare at him as he took steps back, one by one, distancing himself from me. "Wake up, Raven."

I shook my head, watching the village blur around me. I whimpered, tears rolling down my cheeks. "There's nothing for me there."

He didn't stop. Landscapes began to scatter around us. I leaned down and pushed my palm against the ground, the ground rumbling beneath us.

His eyes widened. "Raven, stop."

His voice was a warning, but I didn't listen, feeling strong from the magic pulsing through my veins again. I put my other palm down, the stones of the street cracking underneath my fingers. He ran to me, pulling me up to him. "You have to stop. If you change what I created, we'll get stuck."

"I want to be stuck," I bit out, pulling him to me again. I clamped down on his bottom lip with my teeth.

He groaned, threading his fingers through my hair.

"Stay with me."

"This isn't real, Raven," he murmured to me.

I stared at him, pleading silently with him to let us find a way to be together.

"Wake up, baby. Please."

"Why don't you love me?" I whispered.

His face broke.

And then I was thrown, toppling backward out of my mind.

My eyes snapped open, and I sat up in bed, Cade's arm falling from around me. I threw the quilt off and bounded up, grabbing Cade's shirt off the ground and pulling it over my head as I raced to the balcony. I peered over and saw a hooded figure running to the border of the Black Forest.

He turned around to glance at me before he disappeared.

A week passed by, and I didn't dream anymore. I didn't leave the castle anymore because Cade wouldn't stop watching me. When we slept, he'd stay beside me and jolted awake whenever I moved.

I leaned over the wall of his balcony, looking down at the castle beneath me.

Cade left me alone to meet with John and Luisa, and I was enjoying the time to myself. I kept trying to sweet talk my magic to the surface and would feel a ghost of warmth or my icy haze, but then they'd fade away.

I had to get out of this room. I refused to be weak and stay secluded until I died. I'd need to sneak out. Again.

I straightened and padded quietly toward the wardrobe. He wasn't here, but I felt like he could hear me anyway. I threw open the heavy doors of the chest and immediately grabbed my aching side. I would need to move swiftly but gently.

I pulled out my fitted jumpsuit and dropped my robe to the floor, glaring at the wound underneath my rib cage while I stuck one leg in the jumpsuit, followed by the other, groaning as I pulled it up over my body. I rolled my neck and raised my arms above my head, the skin tugging where the wound was trying to close. I'd have to ignore that.

I tiptoed to Cade's door and quietly pulled it open, sticking my head out to look both ways down the hall. There were guards everywhere, but even with Cade's strict orders to keep me in, they couldn't stop me. I was still the queen, and I trumped Cade. That, however, didn't mean they wouldn't *tell* Cade, which meant I had to walk quickly through the castle and as fast as I could to the border of the Black Forest.

"Buy me time," I whispered to the guards outside my gate, who always saw me move in and out. I heard one of them snicker behind me, and I couldn't help but grin for the first time in a week. They'd tell him, just like when I ran after Zeke in the forest.

As I walked, I resisted the urge to press against my wound and forged ahead, keeping my hands down by my sides. I crossed the border and immediately walked to a tree, pressing my forehead against it. Placing both hands on the trunk, I sighed into it, tears dripping down my cheek. "Please," I whispered to the tree, banking on our connection that it was listening. "Please give it back to me." I stayed there for a moment, drawing in a breath before I released it and continued deeper into the forest.

I was exposed here and knew it was a risk, but it was necessary. I closed my eyes and stayed very, very still. And I waited. Slowly, I beckoned forward my fire. Your turn to play, Blaze. But nothing came. I tried again, curling my fingers at my sides as panic grew. "Where are you?" I whispered.

I inhaled and held my breath. Leaves rustled around me. Wind brushed through my hair. *Come back to me.* I felt the pain of not having him everywhere. I thought of how it felt to never be good enough for anyone to stay. I pulled from the pain. Warmth started to flood the bottoms of my feet. I was a fisherman trying to reel in my prize. It flowed up to my calves, and I kept coaxing, promising to not push it down this time.

I'm enough, I kept saying to myself.

I could do this on my own. I didn't need Zeke or Cade to fix me. There was nothing to fix. My broken pieces mattered. I mixed strength with my pain for everything I had overcome my entire life. My magic wasn't something that needed to be hidden.

It was something to be proud of.

I would never push it down again. Please just come back.

It spread over my legs and belly, pushing past the wound in my side. I moaned as it slowly overtook my every sense and felt the weight of my long, black hair gone and the ends of my fiery red bob whispering against my jaw. As I extended my open palms toward the sky, a smug grin found its way to my mouth.

My bloodred eyes snapped open.

And flames danced along my palms.

I squealed as I saw the flames, rocking on my heels, balling my fingers over the fire, and making a fist. I drew my arm back and launched it forward, throwing the ball of fire into an open clearing. It came to life on the ground. I repeated the same motion with my other hand and relished the feeling of seeing something burn to ash in front of me. I did it repeatedly, raised my arms into an X, and brought them down quickly, extinguishing every flame in front of me.

I beckoned forward Frost and ice swarmed over my warmth. I welcomed it back with open arms, working on my icy walls. I shifted back into Blaze again and threw balls of fire at the ice walls, trying to learn how thick they'd need to be for anything to break through. I shifted into Terra and shook the ground underneath the ice wall, shattering it to the ground. And then I'd do it all over again, repeating the same movements repeatedly until my body felt familiar with my magic again.

———

I closed my eyes and shifted into myself. I needed to practice wielding all three again. I needed to find my fury. I closed my eyes and pulled from my nightmares — the woman sitting on my throne. Falling in love with Zeke — how our darknesses fed one another's. I brought forth the memory of him walking away from me in the courtyard. '*Goodbye, baby.*'

I recalled everything in my mind, my heart in anguish again. I yanked at the fragmented pieces of my dreams, searching for his face, but they all ended with him walking away from me.

I welcomed it, nodding for it to keep going. I didn't let myself be numb to any of it.

I pulled the harrowing memories of lying in a bed as a child, wondering why I hadn't been enough to love.

My anger pooled in my belly, accompanied by my fear of being left, and I held on to it.

I held out my palms again, created the two balls of fire, and hurled them, quickly shooting ice to encase them. As I was about to pull the wind, the balls of fire fell and shattered. I'd have to be quicker. I tried again. I launched the fire and covered it quickly with my ice. My wind almost caught it before it hit the ground, only sustaining it for a couple inches before it shattered.

I fought hard through my exhaustion and aches. I put my hands on my hips and inhaled, exhaled, inhaled. I planted my feet to keep from stumbling.

And then I started again.

I was learning that the larger the ball of fire, the harder it was to encase, which made the ice too heavy for the wind to catch. I palmed two more petite balls of fire and threw them, quickly wrapping them in ice. My wind picked them up and launched them farther. I guided the wind with my hands, knocking the balls into two trees that sat far apart.

As time passed, I enlarged the balls of fire and launched them farther until I couldn't see where they landed. Over and over, my strength only grew. I jumped in the air for my victory, pumping my fists. No one would want a ball of ice landing on their face, let alone one that erupted into flames.

I had an actual weapon of my own creation to use.

————

When night fell, I looked around and realized I'd been alone for a long time. I was shocked that Cade hadn't tried to find me. I poked my tongue against my cheek. He had been watching me so long that not having him nearby was unsettling. I huffed, crossed my arms over my chest, and heard a chuckle from behind the trees, whipping around to the noise. Cade strutted behind them, not far from where I'd been practicing all day. "How long have you been there?"

A playful grin crossed his mouth. "Since about ten minutes after you left the castle."

I smiled at him, and he returned it. We both walked toward each other at the same time and lunged. I wrapped my arms around his shoulders, and he pulled me up by the waist until I was snaked around him. He spun us around twice, and I giggled, pressing my forehead against his.

"You did it," he said.

I beamed at him and nodded before pressing my mouth to his. He inhaled sharply at our touch and pulled his head back, frowning at me. I pulled back as my cheeks flushed. "I feel like I did something wrong."

He shook his head and walked us toward a tree, pressing my back gently to it. His eyes were full of guilt as he looked at me. "I'm scared of breaking you."

"Cade," I whispered, cupping his cheek.

He leaned into it and kissed my palm, keeping his lips there for a moment. "You have no idea what it's felt like these last few weeks. I was helpless. I didn't know what you needed."

He loosened his grip around my waist, and I slid down his body, trying to search his eyes. Two weeks ago, he couldn't stand not being able to touch me, and now he was back to treating me like I was made of glass. "I saw you dying, Raven. And then in the spring... you weren't coming back up. I realized then that if you died, I wanted to die, too. I don't want to live a life without you."

A tear slipped down his cheek. I put both hands on his cheeks and shook my head. I wanted to take away his pain.

"To live without your touch," he continued, taking my hands in his. "Without your heart." He moved a hand to my heart. "Your smart-ass mouth."

I giggled at that.

He gave me a slight grin, but there was still a pain in his features. "To never get to feel you again. Hear you giggle. See you roll your eyes at me."

I tried to kiss him again, but he turned his head away from me. It stung, and I frowned.

"I'm so madly in love with you, Raven. I can't live without you."

"Cade," I whispered his name again. A lump formed in the back of my throat. "I don't want to live without you, either."

He sighed and rested his palms beside my head against the tree, caging me in. He pressed his forehead against mine, and I lifted my face, the tips of our noses touching.

"After this is all over, Raven... I'm going to demand that you spend your life with me."

My eyes widened.

"This is a very informal proposal. Tomorrow isn't promised. I don't know if we will make it through whatever is coming. But if we do, if we're still standing at the end of this...." He was stuttering now, his breath shaky. "I'm going to ask you to marry me."

I opened my mouth to say something, but he shook his head. "I don't want you to answer. This doesn't count. And I know it seems quick. But it's not. Not really."

I inhaled my own shaky breath and puffed my cheeks out. Marriage. He squeezed my cheeks, a puff of air blowing out on his face. He chuckled before smashing his lips against my smushed ones. "Let me take you home."

I nodded, turning his words over in my mind. Marriage. Marriage to Cade. Proposal. I felt overwhelmed. We had only been together for a couple weeks, and now he wanted to marry me. Nausea rolled over me, but it had to be from nerves.

He linked our fingers and swung our hands between us as we walked back. He cleared his throat, and I side-eyed him. "Gods, what now?" I asked, preparing myself.

"Your, uh, ball is tomorrow night."

Fuck. I had forgotten all about that. Had it really been three months since all of this started? Had it really been almost that long since Zeke left me? I was turning twenty-five, judging by the night sky, it may be soon. "I have to stop by my room first, then. I didn't move any of my ball gowns to your room."

Cade winced. "You're getting a new one."

I groaned. "Of course I am."

"You'll like it. I made sure it wasn't too poofy."

I snorted and shrugged. "At least let me choose my own diadem then. What color is the dress?"

A grin from Cade. "Red."

"I know the perfect one then."

CHAPTER TWENTY-ONE

Zeke

I watched Raven as she fell to her knees in the spring. I ducked behind some trees, controlling my urge to go to her. I hadn't planned to bring her here, but after I saw her walk into Duck's a few days ago, I couldn't stand by and watch her wither away. And Cade was letting her. He wanted her to rely on him; he wanted to be the one to fix her. Control her.

I looked behind me. It wouldn't be long until he found us. There was still snow on the ground, and he'd notice our footprints. I turned back to Raven and listened to her scream.

Feel it, baby. Bring your pain back.

She had become so numb to everything lately. She was giving up on herself. I did a great job of making her angry, and I was hoping that her chasing me and not being able to catch me would bring some of it back. But all she was doing was decaying.

"Come on, baby," I whispered, taking a step forward when she immersed herself in the water. I hadn't expected that.

Half a minute ticked by, and she wasn't coming up. I took another step forward. Thirty more seconds. She was going to stay under. I took another step to run to her, but something caught in the corner of my eye, and I froze. Cade was here. He threw himself into the water and pulled her out.

I sank back against the tree, my chest heaving in panic. She was curled up in his arms, sobbing. I bit my fist to keep from losing it. I didn't anticipate her falling apart. I set something in motion that she was never going to recover from. It seemed like she was coming out of it slowly, but John was right. Something was missing behind those green irises. She relied on someone else to fix her, and he gladly took the bait. And now, he was controlling everything she did.

I thought with her sneaking out tonight that her fearlessness was peeking its head out, but I was wrong. She was full of self-doubt before she lost her magic and now she was just… gone.

We had stolen that from her.

Jeanine walked up behind me, patting my arm as she watched Raven cry in Cade's arms.

"I broke her," I whispered.

She shook her head. "No one can break Raven but Raven. Give her time."

I pointed to Raven, turning my body toward Jeanine. "It's been weeks now. Look at her."

She put her hands on my arms and looked up at me. "You have no idea what she's going through right now, so I'll spell it out for you."

My eyes narrowed at the disdain in her voice.

"The man she fell in love with leaves her. Her best friend, who up until you showed up was *only* that, suddenly wants her. She didn't want him, but you shoved her to him, and now she has to sit with the guilt of tainting what the two of you had."

I turned my head, watching as Cade carried her through the trees.

"And then, as she's trying to learn how to fight for her kingdom, *she gets shot*. With a poisoned arrow."

I put my palms up, shaking myself free of her grip. "Okay, I get it."

"No, you don't. All the men in her life are putting pressure on her to be so many different people and no one is letting her breathe. No one is giving her the space to figure that out. And now, she doesn't even have the confidence to find her magic."

"I didn't know Cade would be such an asshole!" I exclaimed, walking back toward my ship.

She followed behind me. "But he is. And you're still letting him possess her. She's not going to know how to stop now, Zeke. She's learned to rely on him for everything. And then you're going to show back up, and what do you expect to happen? She's going to run back into your arms?"

I shook my head, curling my fists at my sides. I didn't need to hear this.

"She won't know which way is up, Zeke. She won't know who to trust, who to believe."

I growled, fisting my hair in my hands as the damned caves whispered her name. I was going fucking crazy.

"You have to get her away from him, Zeke. Or he's going to bury her."

I slowly turned to face Jeanine. "What do you mean?"

She sighed and looked toward the caves. I wondered if she could hear it, too. "I've talked to John about Cade, who he is. He was trained as a soldier before Leonidas brought him to court; did you know that?"

I shook my head.

"He learned how to torture. His dad was a general and taught him how. He knows how to break people down. He knows how to manipulate them. And he spent a year learning who she was before she became queen. He's kept her close for fifteen years, and when a threat came in to take her away, he reacted. If she leaves him now..." she trailed off.

I was uneasy as I looked toward the castle.

"I don't want to imagine."

"Why didn't John do something about this before?"

She shrugged. "He didn't need to. Raven seemed content to stay inside the castle, only sneaking out at night. John says that Cade didn't know she used to drink at Duck's until he caught her. It was the only time she had to herself. John's purpose was to keep her safe, and he has."

"Why does he share this with you but not with me?"

She snorted. "You can't be serious."

I supposed I wasn't. I sighed and pulled Jeanine into a hug, which she returned. She had become one of my closest friends, which was not something I would have expected given our history together. "I have to go see her," I said upon releasing her.

She nodded. "Be careful," she called out to me.

I gave her a small wave as I walked through the trees and back to the castle.

I threw my hood on and scaled the outer wall, dropping to the courtyard ground below. John came out from the castle and stared at me, shaking his head as he disappeared back inside. I followed him. "Why didn't you tell me about him?"

He stopped and faced me. "Because you'd kill him."

I leaned against the wall, nodding. "I still might."

"You can't yet. It'll destroy her, and she can't handle anything else. I told you to leave her alone. I see you heeded my advice."

I ignored that. "Why is her magic taking so long to return?"

He shrugged. "That's on Raven."

I sighed, rubbing my forehead.

"She's in there. She snapped at me tonight in the pub. She said more than I'd heard her say in a long time. She asked me if I knew you and Jeanine were together."

I stared at him.

"I wasn't aware you were."

"We're not," I mumbled. I ran a hand through my hair to shake off my guilt. "Anymore, at least."

Now he stared at me.

"I needed to know why I was being sent here, and I thought sleeping with Jeanine would get me an answer. But all it did was

A KINGDOM OF FLAME AND FURY

complicate things and got me no answers." I was screwing everything up left and right.

John sighed, moving his gaze to the stairs that led up to Raven's chambers, even though she wasn't there. "And she knows about the two of you?"

I frowned, sullen. "Yes."

"That's another risk we'll take when returning to Reales. When Raven meets Mira, she could say something."

I groaned, hitting my forehead against the stone wall. I hadn't thought of that.

"Our only saving grace is that she's not vengeful. If it comes out, it won't be out of spite."

I realized that Raven was too good for any of us. None of us deserved her. "Is she safe with him? If she's not, I need to end this and get her out."

He contemplated it, looking from me to outside. "I don't believe he'd hurt her, but he does want her to himself, which is why he's following her around. We just need to watch how things progress with them."

I wanted to stop talking about Cade. "I need to see her."

"Scaling his balcony then?"

I grinned. It was surprising how well he knew me, considering I hadn't seen him in so many years.

"Don't get caught."

"Never do," I said as I walked back outside. I went to the wall beneath Cade's balcony and grabbed hold of one of the stones that jutted out, making my way up and onto his terrace.

I peered inside, and they were both asleep, his arm wrapped around her naked body. I cringed at the mixture of their scents. It wasn't pleasant. Ours smelled much better.

I crouched in front of her, sighing as I stared at her. She looked crushed, even in her sleep. "Where are you, baby?" I closed my eyes and created a dream for us. No memories this time. No more trauma. She needed to recuperate.

I pushed into her mind gently, casting the dream into her mind's eye. I smiled when she appeared, catching her as she lunged for me. She was smiling. Beaming.

It was the most beautiful thing.

We couldn't stay too long, or she'd accept it as her reality, but she was kissing me, and it felt so real. She felt so right in my arms. She begged me to stay. She looked heartbroken when I told her I couldn't keep her in the dream. I was so tired of being the reason for her pain. Maybe we could stay. There'd never be any worries, any pain.

But I needed to walk away from her. I let her go and took a step back, but her stubbornness prevailed, and she put her hands on the ground, shaking it beneath us.

Well, shit. If she changed my landscape, we could get lost. I told her to stop, but she did it again. The landscape was crumbling around us. I ran to her and brought her to me, trying to explain that we couldn't stay. She bit my lip, and fuck, I even wanted her subconsciously. I would have to throw her, and she would wake up as soon as I did.

I stood beside her bed, the connection between us wavering. "Wake up, baby." I took a few steps back. "Please."

As I was about to throw her, she asked why I didn't love her, and everything inside of me, all the walls I'd built to keep from breaking, did. I worried she'd never be able to understand.

I looked into her eyes one more time before I severed our minds. I ran to the balcony and jumped, practically sliding down the wall, cursing as pain shot through my legs from landing. I heard her feet pounding against the floor above. She knew.

I ran through the gate, not giving a damn if the guards saw me, and took off toward the forest. I glanced back at her and saw her watching me from the balcony.

Fuck, maybe I spoke too soon when I told John I never got caught. Leave it to Raven to be the first one to do it.

But now, I needed to give her a break. She would be waiting for me every night, knowing I was here and always seemed to be in her dreams. I didn't have time to scatter that one as much as I usually did, so she would remember it better.

I rubbed my eyes. I needed sleep, needed to digest this information about Cade and how I was an idiot for sending her to him. Surely he wouldn't harm her, not physically. I'd made it nearly impossible for her to leave him now.

I passed the caves, which were quiet for once, and circled around to the back, climbing over the rocks to my ship.

Jeanine was standing on the deck with a basket in her arms. I jumped on the deck and looked to her basket, then to her.

She asked, "Breakfast?"

I smiled and opened the latch door, leaving it open so the sunlight would light the dark cabin. Jeanine followed me down, setting the basket on the table. "More fruit today, and…." She pulled a sack out. "Muffins."

"Muffins? How did you score that?"

She shrugged. "I was the first one there today. I didn't even know she had muffins."

I laughed as I took a seat on the edge of the bed. She threw one to me, and I peeled back the paper and took a bite off the top. "I don't recognize the flavor."

Her eyebrows drew in as she took a bite of hers. "Cinnamon?"

I took another bite. "Apple?"

She took another bite, starting to giggle. "Are we just going to name every flavor?"

"Something has to stick."

She threw her back in a laugh, and I laughed with her. Whatever it was, it was good. Doughy and soft.

"Save me one for tomorrow if you have extras."

She nodded as she looked in her basket. "I bought six."

I nearly choked on my swallow, coughing. "Did you buy her out?"

She nodded again. "I want to help her out. Since she lost work because of the fire."

"The fire you started?"

Sighing softly, she nodded. "John said it was for Raven. I couldn't say no."

"Why do you like her so much? I love her, but she hasn't exactly been nice to you."

Staring down into the basket, she chewed on her lip. "When I would go around the village, her people had nothing but wonderful things to say about her. They would go on about how she helps them, visits them, knows their names." She came to sit beside me on the bed. "And I remember back when Reales used to be like that. It was lively and bright. It's always been gray, but your mother...."

Looking at me, she frowned. "She used to sew the most colorful dresses. All the girls wanted them. There would be a wait for them." She linked her arm through mine. "And then Mira happened, and everything just... died. Now it's kill or be killed. But Raven takes care of everyone. And if I can help maintain that, even though I was sent here for the exact opposite reason, I won't feel so... evil."

"You're not evil, Jeanine. You just fell into bed with a hungry ruler. You let her use you, control you, turn you into something you're not."

Compassion was behind those blue eyes. "Like Raven."

My head hung forward, regret heavy in the air surrounding us. "Like Raven."

It had been three days since Raven nearly caught me in Cade's room. Three days of her staring over the balcony multiple times a day to catch a glimpse of me. I had stayed low, hidden in the forest's shadows, but I watched her. I knew where she was at all times, which was always in the castle. Cade hadn't let her out since the night in the spring.

Her birthday celebration was just days away, and I wasn't sure she would even come at this point. From my understanding, she would rarely leave Cade's chambers. Without her magic, she would not feel like celebrating, and if there was no ball, then all of this would have been for nothing. I would have to return to Reales without her and face Mira's wrath, which would most likely include something with my mom and brother.

This plan I created clearly was not the right choice. I should have told her what was going on. I shouldn't have shown back up in her life; I shouldn't have led her on. But if I hadn't, that would mean that Cade would keep her locked away. I had spent weeks watching them interact, watching her hesitancy around him, which made her giving into him that much more confusing. Unless she was just determined to move on.

"She still won't come to meetings," John said as he sat on the deck of my ship. "She won't come out, period. Cade does everything now. He refuses all of her visitors."

Jeanine asked, "Have you tried talking to her?"

He nodded but then shrugged. "She came out once to go to the library to see Grace, but Cade was with her. When I would ask her questions, he was the one to answer for her."

"Zeke, stop pacing."

I glanced down at Jeanine, who was seated next to John. "Can't," was all I replied. It was my fault she was relying so heavily on him. "I need to call all of this off. I need to leave or tell her what's going on."

"You can't," John replied. "Not only will you risk her, but you'll risk your mother and Luca. If Mira finds out that you've told her and this doesn't end in her favor, they will be the ones to suffer for it."

I hated when he talked about them. I knew he visited them when he could, but we wouldn't be in this predicament if he hadn't told Mira about my abilities long ago. They would be safe. Instead, we were all moving pieces in this ridiculous game for power. And I was hurting the one person I loved more than anything. "Why didn't you tell me I was supposed to marry her? Why didn't you tell me that was the plan?"

"You refused to see me every time I came to Reales. How was I supposed to tell you? I knew once you saw her, you wouldn't object. Men have been trying to court her for years."

I growled as I glared at him.

Jeanine laughed. "Does that shock you?"

No, but I didn't want to hear about it. "She was never interested in them?"

John stared at me like I should already know the answer to that question. "Do you really think he would let her meet anyone else? I was surprised he even let you in."

"I bet he wishes he hadn't now," Jeanine said.

"He'll really regret it when I'm finished with him," I snapped. I stopped pacing and rolled my neck, trying to shove down my need to find him and end it all. "I need a drink. I'm going to Duck's."

"He has a drinking problem," Jeanine said to John as they both looked at me.

I rolled my eyes but grinned. I only had a drinking problem when my true addiction was locked away in a castle like some fucking damsel in distress.

"Well, you were right," I said, staring at my empty glass. I had gone through an entire bottle and still didn't feel any better. "I'm going fucking mad without her."

He slammed a book down on the table in front of me. It was large and had yellowed pages that seemed bent, preventing the cover from laying flat. I looked from the book to him. "I am not in the mood for reading right now, Arthur."

"It was my wife's. Do you want to learn about twin flames? It's all in there. There are even earmarked pages for you. Go upstairs. Read. I'm cutting you off. Rum isn't going to bring Raven back to you right now."

I grabbed the book and stood, swaying. I had built up a high tolerance, but my inability to sleep lately and missing her was more potent than the alcohol. Combined, it was lethal.

"I love a man who reads," a woman said as she came up to me, nodding toward the book.

I was about to deny her, but Arthur patted my arm and shook his head. "You don't want this one. He belongs to the queen. Go sit at the bar, and I'll serve you in a moment."

Pouting, she walked away. But I grinned so sloppily that I doubted any woman but Raven would ever find me attractive. I belonged to the queen and liked that he freely told everyone that. It hadn't been the first time a woman approached me at his pub, but he was always quick to shut them down. If I didn't know any better, I'd say that Arthur liked the idea of me with Raven.

I had drunkenly told him everything that was going on. Luckily, John and Jeanine had been in here with me and could explain it to him soberly. Unbeknownst to me, Arthur and John had been friends for a very long time, and Arthur trusted that we could handle it. We made him swear his bartender's oath that he would keep it to himself, but now he seemed to think that he needed to make sure I didn't somehow kill myself while in one of my drunken stupors. I nearly did as I climbed his stairs, slipping on one of them.

I heard him sigh from behind me, and he whipped my arm with his towel. I growled and nearly threw the book at him, but he did it again. "Get your ass upstairs or oath or not, I'll go get her."

The threat sobered me enough to make it up the stairs without further incidents. I collapsed on his sofa, the book falling onto my chest as I did. I groaned and rubbed my eyes, a headache forming in the back of my skull. This was another reason I enjoyed drinking from Raven more: she never gave me headaches. I was hard while thinking of her taste, my mouth wetting. But I refused to find any release until I could be back inside of her. Nothing could ever measure how it felt to have her writhing with me.

I looked around the room. It didn't seem like Arthur had changed anything since his wife died. For a bossy bartender, floral portraits and brightly colored embellishments were not what I would have pictured for him. I had been up here often lately, using it as a place to hide when I didn't feel like walking the long trek back to the ship.

Grabbing the book from my chest, I rested my head on the arm of the sofa, propping one leg up with the other hanging off. I used one hand to hold my hair back out of my eyes while the other opened the book and propped it up on my chest.

'Divine Counterparts' was the book's title and made me smile. Raven was divine. I flipped through the pages. The words were blurred as my mind tried to sober up, but I stared at the sketches of the different kingdoms in our realms. Books on any sort of magic were destroyed long ago, so the fact that I was holding one right now seemed like another gift from fate.

Before magic was banned or destroyed, finding your flame or mate was considered a sign of goodwill from the gods. It meant you were blessed and in Aphrodite's favor. When magic disappeared, so did the celebrations. Rules became stricter about leaving your kingdom once you pledged your allegiance, making it difficult to meet anyone new.

I chose one of the earmarked pages and blinked a few times to regain my vision. I saw the word 'pain' first and frowned. Pain was associated with all flames, and you needed to use your connection with the other person to learn how to grow from it. I felt nothing but pain all the time without her.

But when I got to the part about feeling like you'd know your flame from past lives, it only further confirmed that Raven was mine. And then I laughed aloud as I skimmed over where it said that finding your flame would result in a rapid transformation, changing your entire life to be near the person.

My life before finding her only consisted of murdering and fucking. I was immature and unaware of how my choices affected others. And I didn't care. Until her, I believed I only had one purpose in life: to kill for Mira and hopefully find freedom for my family.

My life still consisted of murdering and fucking, but it was only for her. I would do anything to keep her safe and could guarantee that I would have no one unless I had her. I would spend every day following her around, even if it meant we couldn't be together. I was never going to love anyone else.

"The greater good," I read aloud. Our connection could be used for fixing the universe and helping people. Since it was rare and a gift, we were expected to use it to assist others. Which is what we were doing, but it would take a while. It would take a lot of moving parts, and so far, I was doing a shitty job of making sure they moved smoothly. But for her, my family, and our kingdoms, I would find a way to make this right.

———————

I woke up and groaned, covering my face with my hands. It'd been a week since I created a dream for her. Without fail, every single time I slept, I missed her as soon as my eyes opened. I missed her when I fell asleep, wanting her body next to mine. I always dreamed of her, but they turned into nightmares when my memories of her with Cade came to the forefront. I always woke up in a sweat when that happened.

I looked around the hull. It was dark. Surely I hadn't slept all day. I usually woke within a couple hours of falling asleep. I sat up and stretched my arms, yawning.

Raven's devastation was beginning to creep into me, and it was heavy. I reached down to the floor and grabbed my shirt, tugging it on as I stood and walked up the ladder, throwing open the door.

I looked around and didn't see Jeanine anywhere. The sky told me that it was mid-afternoon. I slept at least five hours, and the lack of sleep lately made me feel dazed. I slid on my boots and grabbed my coat, shrugging it on.

Tomorrow was Raven's birthday. And the day when I would face her again. I climbed over the rocks and jumped onto the island. It was time to see where my girl was. I threw my hood up and kept to the edge of the border as I walked toward the village.

Maybe I had time for a glass of rum before returning to the forest to wait for Raven. Arthur had started cutting me off after three drinks, but that was still enough to numb some of the pain. I glanced up at Cade's balcony and immediately stepped back into the shadows. She was up there, leaning over the wall as she peered down at the village, but she looked unfocused. A look of resolution crossed her face before she disappeared into the room.

What was she up to?

I returned to her favored gate and stood behind her aunt's cottage to watch. And waited. And then I saw her muttering something to the guards as she set off onto the path toward the forest. Alone.

I followed her, sticking to the inner edge of the tree line as she hurtled off into the middle of the forest, stopping to lean her forehead against a tree. I listened to her plead with it, my head cocking to the side. The caves. The whispers. She was connected here somehow. Her magic lived here.

I stayed behind her as she drove deeper into the forest. She stopped abruptly and stood very still, and I smiled at her calm resolve. I quietly walked in a circle around her, wanting to see her face. I'd missed seeing her in that jumpsuit. She was the most enchanting creature. But she looked…. pained. I shouldn't. It was an invasion, but I needed to know what made her so sorrowful.

I thrust into her mind and closed my eyes, remaining as still as she was. She was thinking about me. I stumbled back until I was leaning against a tree. She replayed how I walked away from her the day I left her. What she felt. My voice in her mind. She was letting herself feel her pain. Alone. She wanted to fix herself. A tear slipped down my cheek as she pulled memories from her childhood, wondering why she was never enough for anyone. She believed she wasn't enough.

I left her mind, frowning at her.

She was absolutely everything.

Her eyes snapped open, and I glanced at her palms. Her flames. Her magic was back. I wanted to rush to her, love her, tell her that I knew she could do it. But she didn't need me. She needed herself now.

Cade approached from behind her.

Don't you fucking dare, I wanted to shout. Leave her be.

I swore I'd kill him if he interrupted her right now. He noticed her flames, and his face was torn.

Leave her alone, Cade. Let her have something that doesn't include you.

He sighed and walked behind a tree, watching her.

I slid down the tree I was leaning against and propped my knee up, stretching my other leg out. I wished I had something to eat. I stared at my favorite flavor, watching her become familiar with her elements again.

My little demon was doing so well.

I'd missed seeing her like this.

———

Hours passed, and she kept going. She was trying to combine them and kept messing up. She paced, flailing her arms around in frustration. She was tired, but I smiled.

A body sat down beside me. I looked to Jeanine, who handed me a bunch of red grapes. "Thank you," I whispered, taking them from her. I popped a grape in my mouth as we watched Raven together. "Where have you been?"

"Party planning," she said with a sigh. "It'll be quite the affair."

It was getting dark outside. I was surprised Cade hadn't popped out from behind his tree yet. He must not have had a death wish. I sensed confusion in Raven as she looked around. She wasn't used to being alone. She wasn't used to having peace.

Jeanine looked at me, wanting to know what Raven was feeling. "She's wondering where Cade is."

She nodded.

Ironically, given that Jeanine wanted Cade for herself not too long ago, we both stiffened as he came out from his tree, laughing. He wrapped her up around him. I needed to stop eating when they were together. It always made me nauseous to see them. "Stay here," Jeanine whispered.

I gave her a quizzical look as she stood and disappeared behind the trees. I brought my attention back to Raven, who looked to be discussing deeply with Cade. I wished I could hear them. I didn't want to pull the memory. It was enough to see them together in person. I didn't like seeing it from her perspective. I didn't like seeing her with him at all, ever.

Unease poured from her, and I tilted my head curiously. What was he saying to her?

Jeanine returned next to me as Cade dragged Raven off back toward the castle. "He proposed," she said. "Or is going to. He told her that he wanted to spend his life with her."

I was almost positive that my pulse had stopped. I didn't know what to ask or say. My mouth felt dry. The cold air felt extremely warm. I shrugged my jacket off. "And what did she say?"

"Nothing. She said nothing. She just looked…."

"Uneasy?"

She nodded. "You can't let her."

"I don't *let* her do anything. And I can't stop her. She's free to make her own choice."

Jeanine groaned.

"*What?*"

"You're infuriating, that's what. You didn't even give her a choice to miss you."

I hung my head. "I'm beating myself up every minute for setting this plan in motion, okay? But it's too late. They've become close. I can't make her love me again. And I can't make her stop loving him." It tasted bad on my tongue as I said it.

"You can at least help her try. If you're dead set on maintaining this ruse you've created, you can at least change how it ends. Let her see that you still love her."

I let Jeanine's words soak in before I responded. I wasn't planning on letting her see me until the ball, but maybe Jeanine was right. Perhaps I should make an appearance, wet her tongue.

Keep her mind on me. But I couldn't be nice about it. She still needed to hate me, for her sake and when she met Mira.

Mira couldn't know we were in love.

I nodded and stood. "I'll see her tonight, but she won't like it."

"Don't be a complete dick."

I snorted, grabbing my jacket from the ground.

"She said she needed to go to her room first and pick a tiara for the ball tomorrow night."

"I need a rose."

CHAPTER TWENTY-TWO

Raven

The guards stationed outside my chambers assured Cade that they'd seen no one enter from this door or the door that housed the secret corridors. With their assurance, Cade agreed to stay in the hall while I went in. "I'll just be a minute," I promised him.

I entered my chambers and sighed. They didn't feel like mine anymore. I had allowed a stranger in, and he'd broken me and forced me to leave. They were tainted with our memories. Eventually, I would need to move into another wing. Or just stay with Cade, as I doubted he'd ever let me leave.

Now that I was alone, I had time to consider everything he said to me in the forest. I walked room to room as I replayed his words in my head. I touched the cold faucet of my bathtub, my fingers idly grazing over it. He wanted to marry me.

My life could be perfectly content with Cade. If we were to ever have children, I knew he'd make a great father, and I could be the mother to my children that I never had. We could travel the countryside and see things I'd yet to see, even as queen of my kingdom. I would have an heir, and my legacy would live on. Maybe I could breed a little witch of my own.

I walked into my office. The dust I had wiped off the top of
my desk had returned. I rested my palms on top of it. Yes, all of
it sounded like a dream, and I was sure that if he asked, I would
say yes. Did I have a reason to say no?

I left the office and touched the doorframe of my bedroom.
The nagging feeling of my heartstrings tugging reminded me.
My spine started to crack from the pressure of his memory. Of
course, I had a reason to say no.

Because even as much as I adored Cade, I wondered if I
would always think about Zeke. If I would always wonder where
he was if he'd fallen in love with someone else. If he ever loved
me. If I haunted him like he haunted me. If I could ever let
myself fall in love with Cade.

I walked to my bed and stared down at the faded stains of my
blood from the rose he had left for me so many weeks ago. Right
after he decided to walk away from me.

Our last time together on his boat, throwing the bottle at his
head. Him chasing me through the forest. I raised my fingers to
my lips and remembered our last kiss and the way he held me as
I cried. "He chose his queen," I mumbled aloud, running my
fingers over the stained blood on my quilt.

I had to move on. I had a man who loved me, and wanted a
future with me. I had to let go of the man who didn't.

I padded to my wardrobe and threw the doors wide open. I
looked over my shelves of tiaras and spotted the exact one I
came here for — it was a plated gold one, and the cold chill of it
in my fingers sent shivers across my skin. I reached for it and

pulled it down to admire it. Sitting in the center, atop an intricate headband of shapes and small white-gold diamonds, sat a bright red ruby glistened in the moonlight. It was perfect.

I heard a knock on my door and turned my head toward it as I shut my wardrobe doors. Cade called my name.

"I'll be right out," I yelled back to him.

I went to my vanity to grab the matching gold necklace with a red ruby dangling from the end. A matching set.

I was about to leave when something from the corner of my eye caught my attention. I looked toward my balcony as I placed the diadem and necklace back on my vanity. Slowly, I walked through the glass doors to the terrace.

I chilled to the bone when I saw what was waiting for me on the terrace wall. A freshly cut rose. I looked over the balcony wall and tried to spot him. I could smell him. His strong scent of pine. And an even stronger scent of rum. But how?

"Where are you, my love?" I whispered, picking up the rose.

"Not going to burn this one?"

My eyes widened as I inhaled his scent again. The smell that awakened my very soul. I whirled just as two hands grabbed my shoulders and spun me, slamming me into the wall of my balcony, hidden within the shadows.

I stared at his face, only lit by the moonlight shining down. He only loved me in the dark. I made out the outlines of his jaw, his mouth. My booming heart cracked all over again. His gray eyes searched mine. The ones that had been in my scattered dreams. He was devastating, and as I stood with him, I realized I was still devastated.

"You're the one who shot me with the arrow," I spoke slowly as the realization dawned on me. I remembered seeing a flash of his gray eyes before I passed out. He had been there.

He frowned. I tried to push out from underneath him, but he didn't let me budge. "You let him touch what's mine." There was no kindness in his voice, but there was pain.

I glowered. "I'm not yours. You *left* me."

He chuckled darkly. "I never left you." He pushed his hips against mine.

I whimpered softly, hating myself for coming alive at his touch.

"You still want me," he growled, his voice low.

"I don't *need* you," I replied flatly.

His nostrils flared. "Tell me, baby. Do you scream for him like you did for me?"

"Does *she?*" I asked through gritted teeth, my envy awakening my fire.

"I love it when you're enraged." He leaned down and took a deep inhale of my skin. "I never told you that my favorite scent is pears and jasmine."

Mine.

He nibbled on my earlobe, and my traitorous body pushed against him, feeling how hard he was against my thin fabric. "Do you love him like you love me?" He asked quietly. Painfully. His entire demeanor had changed when he asked. It was no longer the threatening one but the broken one. The one I fell in love with.

A single tear slipped down my cheek. No. And he knew it.

"You're a cruel, hateful bastard."

He chuckled again, the sound swimming across my skin. "*On the contrary.*"

"You starved my heart for too long, and it had to learn to feed from another." I brought my fire to the surface of my skin, letting heat spread across me.

His hands loosened at the sudden warmth, and I slid my hand up, wrapping my fingers around his throat. He remained pressed against me, moaning at the heat. "Don't stop," he growled.

I didn't want to. I wanted to hurt him like he hurt me. And the fact that he enjoyed it… it made me thirst for him differently. When that thought crossed my mind, I immediately released him. He sighed into me, disappointed.

"Let me go," I demanded, only half-meaning it.

Instead of listening, his mouth crashed into mine. He bit down on my bottom lip with his teeth, and I cried out at the sudden rip in my skin, tasting my blood pool.

"Still so sweet." He groaned against my mouth, licking it up.

Gods, I wanted him.

"Tell me you love me, baby. Tell me about how you see me in your dreams."

My mouth fell open, but instead of answering, I grabbed the collar of his jacket and brought his mouth back to mine. He inhaled sharply through his nose but gave in to me, roughly grabbing my chin in his fingers. I wanted to pour everything into the kiss. I wanted to keep him here with me.

Neither of us moved to break, the tips of our tongues gliding together. I loved him, I loved him. So much that it made me crazy. So much that I was convinced I was under a spell, maybe one of my own makings somehow.

The sound of my door being thrown open had him sighing through our kiss. I wasn't ready to say goodbye to him. He broke from me, kissing me softly once more. "Happy birthday, baby," he whispered against my mouth.

And then he was gone, disappearing over my balcony. And I was convinced it had all been a wonderful, chasmic dream.

Cade called my name, but I couldn't answer. I was frozen to the wall with want. With hate. With soul-shattering love. And all I wanted to do was die. My body immediately missed his when he released me. Our heartbeats matched.

Cade ran out to the balcony and turned, seeing me standing against the wall with blood dripping from my mouth. He frantically pulled me to him, studying my face. "Raven, what happened?"

I just stared at him until a look of understanding crossed his face. And then fury. Guards ran in behind him and peered over the balcony, trying to find where he had disappeared. "How did he get in here? How did he find you?"

I stared at the wall he disappeared over, my voice flat as I answered, "He has a knack for finding abandoned things."

Cade was quiet, waiting for me to continue.

428

A ghost of a smile played across my mouth as I brought my fingers to my lips. "He's a hunter. And I'm his prey."

———————

Cade walked me back to his room and held my elbow the entire time, knowing I was still heavy within a daze, or maybe because he didn't want me to bolt again. He laid my diadem and necklace on his bedside table and stationed guards at his door, and then he was gone. What I didn't tell him was that Zeke never used the door.

Cade would spend the night trying to find him with a handful of our soldiers. They wouldn't find him.

I laid down in Cade's bed, brushing my finger back and forth over my bottom lip. I could still feel his bite. The way he sank into me deep with his teeth. He wanted to make his mark. Reclaim me. Now he was the last one to kiss me. Cade was erased. All the time we'd spent trying to purge him from my body, gone. He lived in my very bones again, my body was raw.

And now, the scar from his arrow would stake his claim on me forever. He knew exactly where to shoot and not kill. He was making a point. I was his. He wasn't going to let me go without a fight. And a part of me wanted him here. I yearned for him. The way we fit together was like a puzzle finding its last piece. Our darkness was twisted, binding us together.

I didn't want to sleep. I wanted to see him again. It was him here the other night — the last time I dreamed. He had been here. All those nights I smelled him. He was nearby. But why wasn't he showing himself? Why always only in the dark?

My body was fighting me — begging for a reset.

It was tiring today, combining my magic, using it after weeks of silence. But it was back, and it was a comfort to feel a sense of self again after only feeling empty for so long. But now I was hollow without him. He left too soon. I had so many questions that I craved answers to.

Warmth. I craved warmth. I shifted into Blaze just because I could. Heat spread across my bones as my eyes fluttered shut.

———

I dreamed of the gray castle again, but now I was inside. I slowly walked room to room, flames dancing in my hands. I was somewhere I shouldn't be, yet it called for me. Portraits lined the wall, and I walked to one of them. Staring back at me was a woman with deep green eyes like mine.

"You're familiar," I said. But how could that be?

To my left, Zeke came to my side. I met his gaze, and he held out his hand. I grabbed it, that same deep connection thrumming through me again. He pulled me into a dark hallway. Both of my hands were still lit with flames, but it didn't bother him. He wouldn't let go of my hand.

He stopped in front of a long mirror. I stood in front of him, looking between my face and his. He placed a soft kiss on my neck and my eyes closed. "Open your eyes, baby."

I did, but we were no longer in the mirror.

Instead, a small girl with big green eyes and dark brown hair was staring back at me. She stared back at me, reaching out her small hand. I reached back for the tiny stranger, who looked eerily familiar. "Hello, little bird," the girl said to me.

My eyes widened, a foggy memory tugging at the back of my mind. And then she scattered away, and Zeke returned behind me. "Who was that?" I breathed.

"You look beautiful as you sleep with your raging blood."

My eyes opened the following day. I moved my arm to the side to feel for Cade beside me, but the bed was empty. I was still lying atop it, never having made it under the covers. I slowly sat up. I felt I had drunk too much, but I was completely sober. I rubbed my forehead as broken images from my dream tried to piece back together.

Zeke's ship had been gone for weeks. Where had he been staying? Was that how Jeanine came back? Had they both been here? All great questions, Raven. But I wouldn't get a fucking answer from the most elusive man in the universe.

I stood from the bed and rolled my body slowly, trudging into Cade's bathroom to draw myself a hot bath. I was still in the jumpsuit from last night. How had that only been last night?

I unzipped it and tugged it down, groaning as I stepped out of it. Why did it feel so difficult to move my legs? The tub filled higher and higher, and I watched as the steam rose from it. My mind flashed back to the spring, and I cursed under my breath. Everything reminded me of him.

I finally stepped into the tub, leaning over to turn the faucet off, and sank into the hot water. I relaxed my neck against the rim, sinking so low that only my face remained. I wondered if Cade or his soldiers had picked up any trace of Zeke. Anything to tell us how long he'd been here. All those roses he'd been torturing me with were fresh. He'd been in the flower shop in our village, and we'd been naive for weeks.

I groaned and put my hands over my face. It'd been him. The hooded figure in my village. And maybe if I had told Cade about the roses earlier, we could've figured out that he'd been here and prevented last night from happening.

But I wouldn't have wanted to prevent it.

My head rolled to the side when I heard the door to Cade's room open. He walked in, looking defeated, frustration coating his features. He stood in the bathroom doorframe and watched me, raising his arm to rest against the frame. We stared at one another, out of words, and then I realized I was still shifted as Blaze. And my anger, that part of me, belonged to someone else. I blinked and shifted into myself. He didn't like my anger, anyway. Always wanting it shoved down.

He removed his shirt, his boots, and his pants. My eyes moved slowly up his body, and he grew hard under my gaze. I sat up in the tub, scooting forward, and he stepped in and sat down, pulling me back against his chest as he settled in. I wasn't going to press him for information. Not yet.

My fingers moved idly across his knee. He sighed, pushing my hair to the side, leaning down to gently kiss my neck. Once, twice. And then his tongue licked along the shell of my ear. I shifted against him, goosebumps rising on my skin.

I was mentally spent, but he needed this.

He was throbbing against my lower back. His hand moved across my shoulders and down my chest, his fingers twisting one of my nipples. A sigh fell from my lips. He moved across my chest and repeated the movement with my other nipple, both hardened by his touch. His mouth continued its tease on my neck and behind my ear. I tilted my head to the side to look at him and raised my hand to cup the back of his head, pressing his mouth down to mine.

My mouth opened, and he tangled his tongue with mine, his hand sliding from my breasts down my stomach. My heartbeat picked up as he lowered his hand to my core, pushing one finger against my clit, groaning at the slickness. He glided his finger up and down against my clit, and I pushed my hips up against it, encouraging him to add another. He did and pushed them inside of me, moving quickly in and out.

His gentle kisses were quickly dissipated by the roughness of his fingers inside of me. He wanted this to hurt. He was hurting. And he wanted to hurt me because of it.

His fingers suddenly left and wrapped around my waist, pulling me up to my knees in the tub, the water resting around my thighs. He bit down on the sensitive skin between my thigh and ass, and I groaned as he tugged at it. "Turn around," he growled, his voice unrecognizable.

I twisted and turned until I was on my knees before him. He leaned back against the tub wall, not touching me, only staring as he rested his arms on the rib. His eyes stared at mine and then dropped down my body inch by inch. I flushed at the intensity of his gaze on me. There was so much animosity under his features, his eyes dark and unreadable.

"Do you love him?"

My mouth fell open at the question.

Please don't make me do this.

He waited, never moving, his gaze resting on my sex.

"I love you," I whispered, urging him to look at me. But he didn't. Because that wasn't what he was asking, and we both knew it.

"Do you still want him?"

Another question that I didn't want to answer. A single tear fell down my cheek. "Cade," I cried as my voice broke. A tear fell and dropped into the water. The look on his face was breaking my heart. He was fighting a battle. We'd only just found our way to one another, and now he knew that I didn't belong to only him.

He inhaled a deep breath and let it out through his nose, slowly sitting up and wrapping his fingers around the back of my thighs. I stayed utterly still, unsure if he wanted me to touch him.

He tilted his head back just enough to look at me, and all I saw was outrage in his eyes. I was suddenly afraid.

The tip of his tongue pushed against my clit. I threw my head back, not realizing that his mouth was moving to my belly button. He nipped at my skin and tugged it between his teeth, causing me to gasp and bring my chin back down to see him.

"Keep your eyes on me," he demanded.

I bit my bottom lip and nodded.

His tongue returned to my clit. My fingers gripped the tub's rim as his tongue moved so teasingly over my bud. He squeezed my thighs before he plunged deep into my core, teasing over and over, bringing me close to the edge and pulling out quickly, never giving in.

It was not enjoyable. He was trying to punish me for something that couldn't be helped. I didn't ask Zeke to come to my balcony. I didn't ask to love another man. I never wanted to hurt him.

I threaded my fingers through his hair and tugged roughly at his strands, making his face tilt to mine. "If you want it to hurt, then just do it already."

His eyes narrowed on mine as his hands left me, shoving himself up and out of the tub. He cupped my elbow and pulled me up, water sloshing everywhere as he yanked me from the tub.

"Get on your knees," he bit out.

I stood there, my fists balled up at my sides. "Make me," I replied through gritted teeth. The fight I still had left in me didn't want to submit to him.

His fingers pierced the skin of my waist as he hoisted me up until I was wrapped around him. He stomped out of the bathroom while I grabbed his hair again and pulled, trying to keep his mouth away from my skin. A low rumble escaped from his throat as he threw me onto the bed. I fell onto my palms, but he didn't give me time to recover before he grabbed my waist again and flipped me to my stomach.

He found the front of my thighs and yanked my bottom half up until I was on my knees in front of him, and then he drove his cock right into my pussy, pummeling me roughly until I had to ball the fabric of his quilt in my fingers to keep from falling forward. "Say it, Raven." His voice was hoarse.

I could barely comprehend what he was telling me. He slapped my ass hard with the palm of his hand. "Tell me who you belong to."

I lifted my head off the mattress just enough so he could hear my cries. "You."

I was lying, and my eyes watered from the unbearable weight of that silent confession. He groaned and pinched my waist, pulling out. I buried my face back down, hitting the mattress with my fist. He wanted me to feel this. He wanted me to know how much it killed him that I wanted someone else.

He shoved at my hip until I was on my back with him on top of me, burying my body farther into the bed by his weight. His mouth crashed into mine, and he bit my bottom lip. I screeched from the pain as he repeated it over the exact spot where Zeke had been the night before.

My flesh split, blood coating my tongue, but he did it again. I tried to turn my head, but he wouldn't let me. He kissed me, cupping my throat as he pushed back into me.

"You're making me go crazy," he growled against my mouth. I couldn't breathe. I needed him back. I needed his anger to subside, or we would never get past this. I needed this to end.

I put my palms on his cheeks and lifted his head until our eyes met. "I'm yours," I whispered.

His face crumpled, his forehead falling against mine. He wrapped a hand around my hip as his thrusts slowed, allowing me to catch my breath. "Say it again," he breathed, hot air against my mouth.

A single tear slipped down my cheek. "I'm yours," I cried.

That triggered his release, filling me quickly. But my body couldn't react to his. I felt numb as I fell back down from my peak, never reaching my brink. His breathing was heavy, and mine was fading, dizzy with his weight.

All I tasted was blood.

"Again," he muttered, his tears falling on my cheeks.

"I'm yours," I rasped.

Lies. So many lies between us.

CHAPTER TWENTY-THREE

Raven

We were on our backs, panting and trying to sort through what just happened. He was making damn sure I knew that he had no intention of sharing me. He'd always been protective of me, but this was something new. This was purely primal.

After a few moments of silence, he rolled on his side and stared at me. The pad of his thumb brushed against my bottom lip, and my head jerked back from the pain. He dropped his thumb, the darkness in his eyes returning.

"I was on such a high last night, Raven. Until I let you in that room, and he found you."

Always letting me.

I turned to my side and propped up on my elbow, licking over my broken lip. I didn't know what to say. Zeke was always going to find me if he wanted to. So, I just stayed silent.

"I can't stand the idea of anyone else's hands on you." His voice was quiet, but it dripped with disdain. "We didn't find him," he said, falling down to lay on his back.

I knew they wouldn't. But again, I didn't have anything to say. There was nothing I could say to improve this — and my lip hurt, making moving my mouth feel like a chore. I needed it to heal, or this conversation would be over really quick.

I leaned down and kissed the corner of his mouth. "I love you."

His eyes widened. It was the first time I had said it on my own. His body immediately relaxed, and I gave him a small smile.

"Raven." He wrapped a hand around my head and pressed our foreheads together. "You have no idea how good it feels to hear you say that."

I waited, but he was silent. I pouted and leaned away from him again. He chuckled and chased me, leaning over me. "You fucking know I love you."

I just shrugged and turned my head away from him.

"You're fucking infuriating," he grumbled.

"Tell me again," I demanded, refusing to look at him.

He grabbed my chin and turned me back to him. "Raven, I am so desperately in love with you that I think it may make me deranged."

"Again," I whispered.

He pressed a light kiss to my mouth. "I love you."

I wanted our future together. Somehow. I didn't want to be the cause of his anger. I didn't want him to hurt me anymore. "Yes."

His eyebrows rose. "Yes, what?"

I gave him a slight shrug. "I'll marry you."

A wide smile formed on his mouth, but then he shook his head. "Raven, no. I didn't ask you. We're not counting that as a proposal."

My arms crossed over my chest. "Fine. Ask me then."

He shook his head again, releasing my face from his grip. "No, not like this."

I rolled my eyes. "Why the fuck not?"

"Because Raven, you need fucking flowers. Or some kind of romantic shit. Not here, all sweaty, after we just fucked."

I threw my arms up in frustration.

"I'm going to marry you, Raven. But let me ask you the way I want to ask you."

I grumbled something inaudible, and he caught my mouth with his, shutting me up with a soft kiss. He pulled up just enough to nip at my nose. "Happy birthday, Raven."

We stayed like that for the next few hours, reminiscing on our last few years of birthdays. We'd laugh and recall always passing out from drinking too much, only to be woken up by Luisa banging on Cade's door.

'*I swear I serve such children*', she had grumbled to us once, and then we erupted into laughter all over again. We'd always been child-like together, never fully grasping the concept of having to grow up and run a kingdom. But as the years passed, we'd wake up before Luisa could knock on the door, and we'd be in the dining hall, ready to solve any issues. At some point over the last two years, we grew up. I'd always felt as if Cade was meant to be in my life, one way or another. Only within the last few weeks did I realize that being more could be an actual possibility. I'd always be grateful that we found our way to one another, even through these circumstances.

When my heart still called out to another.

Marry. Cade. Marry Cade.

The entire idea seemed like such a fairy tale like it couldn't possibly be real. Everything had happened so fast over the last few weeks that I didn't feel like my heart and brain had a chance to catch up. Our friendly love had blossomed into something deeper, more permanent. And even if I couldn't say I was in love with him, I knew I could be.

But I had to battle with my heart to heal and piece it back together. I had to let go of Zeke. But why did it feel like we were so connected? Our hearts felt like one whenever we were together. Like we'd only been one half of a whole until we met. And when I was with him, I felt whole. How could something like that just go away on its own?

But I couldn't spend my life dwelling on the what-ifs anymore. Cade said it best: Tomorrow isn't promised. But with Cade, it was. I could tell by how he watched me with longing and hope that my tomorrow would always be promised. He wouldn't leave my side and hadn't for fifteen years.

After only a few days together, Zeke was gone. I wouldn't be able to live my life like that. Always wondering when he was going to disappear and then show up, wrecking me all over again. He was a puppet master, and I was his puppet, and he liked cutting my strings, letting me fall into a heap of self-doubt when he finished with me. Cade was here. And for over a decade, I'd always wanted him by my side, and he wanted to be there. And he loved our kingdom, our people.

I had to let Zeke go.

But even as I told myself all of this, fragments of my dreams tried to come together and remind me that it just wasn't that easy.

———

I finally convinced him that we had to get out of bed to get ready and promised we could return as soon as it ended, but only after our annual picnic on the balcony. He tried to make another bargain to eat me instead, and I shoved at him.

"You promised an *incredible* picnic if I remember."

He wrapped his arms around my waist and pulled me against him. "You are my incredible picnic."

"Do you need another cold bath?" I asked him, shaking my head at how needy he was for me — like if he didn't have me right now, he never would again.

"I'm in a tux, but I can quickly take this off if you want to join me." He took a step toward the bathroom.

I laughed and pulled him back.

"Wait here," he said, leaving me and disappearing out of his bedroom.

I heard him shuffling around in his office, but I stayed put. I turned to the table beside the bed and ran my fingers across the ruby attached to my diadem.

Last night came flooding back to me like a harsh wave, threatening to drown me.

My thoughts were interrupted by a sound of shuffling, and my eyes returned to the door, gasping as Cade returned with the most gorgeous dress I'd ever seen.

When I put it on, Cade had tears wetting his eyes.

It was a deep red and made of the softest velvet. The skirt was floor-length and ballooned out, accentuating my waist and wrapped tightly around the curves of my breasts. The sleeves were long and clung to my arms, exposing my shoulders and neck, curving into a slight sweetheart neckline.

It was absolutely sinful. And I never wanted to wear anything else. I placed the gold diadem on my head, fastening it to my long hair that cascaded down my back. He secured the matching necklace around me and pressed his lips lightly against the top of my spine. "There will never be a woman more beautiful than you, darling," he whispered against my skin. "I'm so madly in love with you."

I felt one of his tears drop on my shoulder, and I turned in his hold, my thumb wiping away another tear as I looked into his eyes. He was so desperate for me. And I so desperately wanted to belong to him. I rose to my tippy-toes and pressed my lips to his in a soft kiss.

He balanced his hands delicately on my waist, staring deep into my eyes. My mouth slowly widened into a smile.

He leaned in and pressed his lips to mine again, his hands moving gently over my ribcage. "You're mine, forever. Let's go celebrate another year of Raven."

I rolled my eyes at the thought of celebrating myself. Our celebrations were typically so small. It seemed foreign to go to a ball held just for me. It was something I'd normally discourage, but from the hints I had received from Cade about what to expect, it would be quite the affair with everyone from the village attending.

I had told him that I also wanted servants and staff to have a chance to attend. We could serve ourselves. He promised to relay all of my requests to Luisa and *Jeanine*.

Before leaving his room, he walked me to the balcony and pointed toward the village. My eyes followed his finger, and a broad smile spread across my face as I saw people lined up at the gate, filing in one by one to celebrate with me. They looked so dapper dressed up, and I could see Grace's bright red hair bopping through the gate to enter the castle. I even saw a tiny little human who resembled Eva skipping through the gate.

"Can we go?" I asked, clapping my hands together in excitement, which was not an emotion he expected to see from me tonight.

He laughed and grabbed my hand, threading it through his arm as he led me out. I licked my lips, tasting the red lipstick I had painted on my mouth. My hair swished across my back, a little more pep in my step than usual.

"We'll let them get situated in the grand ballroom before we enter. I'll go in first and announce you, and you'll come in after me," he explained.

I frowned at him. "We won't walk in together?"

He stopped walking and turned to me, cupping his hands around my face. "I'd be honored to walk in beside you, Raven, but I don't think it's appropriate until we've announced our upcoming engagement. After all, I am just but a lowly subject," he said, falling into a deep bow.

I pulled up at his shoulders, laughing at his mockery. "Fall to your knees tonight. For now, just get me there."

He straightened again and linked our arms once more. "With pleasure. On both accounts."

Half an hour later, we stood outside the grand ballroom doors, giving all the guests time to enter before we did. Luisa came up to us, holding a gold box in her hands, smiling at me as she extended it. I looked at Cade, who grinned. I peeled back the lid, and sitting on white tissue paper was an intricate masquerade mask. I gasped as I stared.

It was two-toned in color, made of gold and red. The area around the eyes was gold, blended into the red with magnificent swirls, pointing out at either end in ruffled curves. From the top of the mask, over the right eye, were two long, silky feathers. One black, one red. I very gently lifted it from its box. "Did you do this?" I breathed, asking Luisa.

She shook her head in response with a coy grin.

I looked to Cade next, who just smiled.

"Can you put it on for me?"

He nodded and took it from my hands, standing behind me as he lowered it over my face, tying the two red ribbons around my head. I lifted my fingers to brush across the mask, which seemed made exclusively for me as it fit snugly on my nose and perfectly across my eyes. And then he produced a plain black mask from his jacket pocket, tying it over his eyes. Luisa did the same with a mask made of blues and silvers.

"It's a masquerade?" I asked in a squeal.

Cade and Luisa both laughed. "We have baskets full of masks inside for the villagers. Lots of surprises in store for you, Raven," Luisa answered. Before turning back inside, she pulled me into a tight embrace. "I am so proud of you, Raven. I am honored — absolutely honored — to celebrate you tonight. I can't wait to see what else you accomplish in your reign."

I was moved to tears by her words and returned her hug, whispering my gratitude. She squeezed my hands and kissed my cheek lightly before disappearing inside.

Cade turned to me, and I shook my head. "You're going to make me cry; I already know it."

He smiled at me and took my hands in his, drawing a shaky breath. "There's not much that I can say that you don't already know, but I have to echo Luisa's sentiment and say that I am so proud of you. For being a wonderful queen, and overcoming your fear. For accepting who you are." He raised a hand to my cheek to brush a tear away. "You are loved, Raven. So very loved."

I could tell he wanted to say more, but his throat bobbed, pushing down a sob. I placed my hands on either side of his face and drew him down to me, pressing my lips against his gently. He enveloped me with his arms and kissed my forehead. I brushed off the red lipstick stain on his lips, but he pulled back. "Leave it," he said. "I want everyone to know who I belong to."

I dropped my hand from his mouth and kissed him again.

After one more moment together, he released me to disappear behind the doors. I inhaled deeply, suddenly very nervous to walk in alone. Every eye would be on me. But I felt beautiful, my dress swaying around my legs. And the man who loved me was right inside. And he wanted to marry me. I had security in my future.

I smoothed my hands over my waist and evened out the dress across my shoulders, wiping away leftover tears from my eyes and shaking my hands to alleviate some of my nerves. I couldn't stop fidgeting.

When I heard Cade announce my name, the doors opened, and I closed my eyes, taking that first step. Then another.

Gasps surrounded me, and my eyes opened, my jaw falling open as I took in the room. Ivory tablecloths covered golden tables with matching golden chairs. Atop the tables sat flower arrangements in golden vases that had to be almost as tall as me. And they were all filled with... red roses.

In fact, as I started to spin, roses were everywhere. Red rose petals were scattered across the floor and across the buffet tables. My stomach tightened at seeing them, panic closing in on me. My chest rose and fell quickly. All I saw was red. Warmth spread across my skin, awakening at my increased heart rate.

Breathe, Raven.

I heard him in my mind, and I jerked at the sound. I was hallucinating again. I spun but saw nothing but red and gold blended together. I heard claps from the crowd, thinking I was spinning for their benefit. Why were there so many roses?

I started aching for him, sweat beading at my temple.

I stopped spinning, and my eyes fell on Cade, standing in the center of the room, smiling at me. The panic started to settle as I kept my eyes locked on his, letting his presence settle me. *I love you*, he mouthed to me.

Sounds stopped mixing together as I gained focus.

I could do this.

I suddenly felt weight against my legs and looked down to see a tiny person pushing against my dress. I smiled as I leaned down to Eva and scooped her up to balance on my hip. Her little mask was made of purples. "Are you asking me for the first dance, Eva?"

Eva nodded, giggling. "Spin me, butterfly."

So I did. As the music played, I spun my tiny best friend around the room, dipping over so she'd fall backward against my hip and erupt into a plethora of giggles.

Grace ran up, and I set Eva down as we all held hands in a circle, spinning and laughing until we were dizzy. Grace spun Eva away so Theodore could take their place. I barely knew this man, but I felt a kinship with him. He and his family could be part of my extended chosen family.

I laughed as he spun me around the room, trying to dip me in my poofy dress. "You're heavier this time," he said.

My face hurt from the amount of laughing I'd already done, and it was only the beginning of the night.

Cade walked up to dance with me next, but an arm flew out between our bodies. When we looked to see who was on the other end, smiles spread across our faces at Cade's father. "Move, kid," he said, shoving Cade away from me.

I raised my arms in a shrug, and Cade pretended to look defeated, backing up a few steps to dance with his mother instead. August danced slower with me than the others had. "He treating you well?" he asked.

I looked over at Cade, grinning as I nodded. "He wants to marry me," I said.

He guffawed, leaning forward to peck my cheek. "We'd be honored to have you as a daughter."

I beamed at him. "I've always known I'm your favorite."

"Seems like fate, the two of you," he said.

My eyebrow arched. "Oh yeah?"

August just nodded, seemingly hiding something in his eyes. He didn't get a chance to continue before Cade interrupted us, shoving at his father's shoulder. "Can I get my girl back now?"

August released me and handed me off to Cade, returning to his wife. My eyes followed him, and he glanced at me, winking.

My forehead dipped toward the floor in slight confusion before I looked to Cade, who beamed at me. "I never thought I'd get a chance with you."

I laughed as he spun me around the room, trying to dip me. "I don't think this dress is made for that," I said.

He laughed before he tried again, getting me halfway down before pretending he would fall. "How many apple pies have you been eating?!"

I slapped his arm, giggling as he brought me back up. I stuck my tongue out at him, and he did it back to me. "I make them for all of my boyfriends."

"As long as I'm your favorite."

I shrugged. "I'll kiss them and let you know."

At that, he growled playfully before attacking my face with kisses. "You're such a little shit, even at twenty-five."

I laughed again as his kisses moved down to tickle my neck.

The doors to the ballroom opened, and a giant cake was rolled in on a table. The music died down as Cade smiled at me, grabbing my hand to lead me over to the monstrosity. It was five layers tall, covered in white icing with rose molds decorating each layer. Seeing it pulled at my heart, and I sighed as the crowd cheered.

The chef lit a candle on the top of the cake that was way too tall for me to reach. I shook my hands in front of me. There was no way I could get up there. A chair squeaked beside me, Theodore laughing as he held his hands up in guilt and backed away.

I groaned and took a step up. Cade's hands balanced my waist as he helped me pull my other foot up. I rose to my tippy-toes and blew out the candle, the crowd cheering. "Get me down," I said through gritted teeth, looking down at Cade.

He couldn't stop laughing as he grabbed my waist and pulled me off, kissing my cheek before he released me. "At least I know you'll always keep me around to reach things on the top shelf."

I pouted at him, but it was immediately replaced by a huge smile as a plate with a piece of cake waved around my face. Grace handed me my first piece, and I took some of the icing off the top with my finger and rubbed it down Cade's nose. He gasped, sticking out his tongue as he tried to reach his nose to lick it off.

"I thought you were better with your tongue than that," I said through my giggle.

His mouth dropped open, and I immediately regretted it as he charged at me, rubbing his nose all over my face, icing spreading across my cheeks. I pushed him away, and Grace grabbed my hand. Cade chased us around the cake while people started dancing in the crowd surrounding us, the music filling the ballroom once again. We joined them, all three of us bouncing and spinning to the song.

I had never been happier than in this moment right here.

And then the music was suddenly quieted, and Luisa stood in the middle of the ballroom. I turned to Cade, and he shrugged.

"Our dear Raven," Luisa started, shouting over the crowd. "We are so happy to celebrate this special year with you."

Claps. Cheers.

"And as much as I'd like to take all the credit for this beautiful ball, I have to thank Jeanine, who came all the way from Reales to assist me."

My eyes narrowed slightly on Jeanine as she came up next to Luisa and curtsied to me. Cade wrapped his arm around my waist, pulling me to him, assuring me.

Luisa continued, "And I have been sworn to secrecy about this next surprise for months. This birthday celebration has only been possible because of him."

Him. My mouth fell open as I followed her hand that was motioning toward the entrance. I stepped toward the door as Cade tried to hold on to me.

"No..." I breathed as the doors opened.

Standing coolly at the entrance was Zeke.

CHAPTER TWENTY-FOUR

Zeke

After leaving her, my mind and body were in a frenzy. It was the first time I had touched her in weeks, and she wanted me to. She didn't want me to go. I could sense her contempt, but she still radiated so much love. I underestimated her heart.

I didn't go far after leaving her on the balcony. We were running out of time for me to pull memories. There weren't many left with Mira in them, so I needed to start pulling from my own to collide with hers. I hid in the shadows of the courtyard as I saw Cade and a handful of his soldiers follow him to find me. I scoffed at the idea that he believed he could.

I scaled the wall to his balcony and pulled myself over, peering inside. Raven was shifted into Blaze, and I smiled at my little demon. She was accepting herself. Her eyes fluttered shut, and I waited, looking over the balcony for Cade. I hoped Jeanine would stay put on the ship. I didn't know what he'd try to do if he found her and not me. If he was trained to torture and knew we came here together… I shook my head. He couldn't be that desperate yet.

I padded slowly to Raven, kneeling in front of her. My eyes watered at the sight of her. For so long, I had watched as she shriveled away, unable to accept her pain. Unable to grow.

I gently brushed my fingers over her red hair, and her mouth pulled up slightly. Her subconscious could sense me here. And I knew she was waiting for me since there were no guards on her balcony. She didn't tell Cade that I'd been finding her that way.

I wanted to pull her into another happy dream and stay with her there for a bit. I wanted to tell her how proud I was of her. But I couldn't. We were running out of time.

I'd been cautious with her dreams lately in fear of Celestina finding us. I should be pulling from her memories, but I couldn't risk her again. Not yet.

I closed my eyes, filtered through my mind, and shared it with hers. I pulled her into one of the dark hallways of our castle in Reales. Her palms were lit with her flames, and I grinned in and out of her subconscious. She was staring at the portrait of her mother. I held my hand out for her to grab. She could sense our connection, and awe danced behind those red irises of hers.

I pulled her into an empty room that contained a tall mirror and stood behind her as she stared at herself and then at me. I couldn't resist her. I leaned down and brushed my lips to her neck, her eyes closing as her body awakened at my touch.

I couldn't let this go too far. I wouldn't want to stop. "Open your eyes, baby," I whispered to her.

They snapped open, staring back at the small girl from her memories. Mira stared back at her like a reflection; the only difference between them was their hair. "Hello, little bird," Mira said to her.

One of my distant memories was watching Mira interact with Raven as a baby before she was taken. And though she didn't know what it was, Raven tensed in my arms. She didn't like this.

I scattered Mira and returned behind her. She glanced at me, asking who that was. I couldn't answer. I kissed the top of her head gently, regretting having to leave her again.

"You look beautiful as you sleep with your raging blood."

I gently pulled out of her mind, not wanting to wake her up. She needed to sleep. Her body needed rest after the afternoon she had relearning her abilities. But I couldn't let her go yet. So, I sat in front of the bed, resting my chin on the mattress.

I knew it'd be hours before Cade returned. He wanted to kill me. "I love you," I breathed, my voice barely a whisper. And in the silence and the darkness, I tried to tell her.

I told her that I hadn't wanted to hurt her — that I was sorry for making her feel like she wasn't enough for me. I kissed the tip of her middle finger, listening to her breathe soundly. I wished I could hold her, promise never to let her down.

But I couldn't do that because I would let her down. She was going to hate me for not telling her who she was. She wouldn't understand. Jeanine was right: Raven wouldn't know who to trust. But I had my risks to weigh. I had a mother and a brother who relied on me to keep them alive. And this was the only way I could keep all three of them safe. I had to complete my mission. I had to get her to Reales, and then I'd need a new plan. I'd have to keep creating as I went. Keep trying to warn her.

And she thinks I shot her. I had let this go too far if she thought I could be the one responsible for trying to maim her. I guessed my catastrophic idea was turning out just the way I needed it, too.

I sighed, and strands of her bright red hair blew back. She whimpered softly in her sleep. She could still smell me. I needed to go. The light was starting to dawn behind us, making her skin glow the most delicious way. Now that I'd tasted her again, keeping my hands off her was difficult.

My heart betrayed my mind, and I leaned forward, softly brushing my lips against her cheek. "Happy birthday," I whispered against her skin before I stood and took slow steps back. I drank her in until the last drop, descended down Cade's balcony, and flipped my hood up.

John stepped out from behind a breezeway. He had been waiting for me. He nodded toward the wall I always scaled to return to the forest. "They're right outside. We'll have to find a different way out."

I followed him as he led me back into the castle and through the dining hall, both of us looking around to make sure no one saw us. No one could know about our connection yet.

He asked, "Is she all right?"

My brows drew in. He'd been showing more concern for her lately. "She's better. Her magic is back."

His shoulders sagged in relief.

I didn't ask him why he was so curious because I couldn't handle anything else right now. I needed to focus on making tonight happen smoothly. "How can I get in tonight?"

John pointed up ahead. "I'll show you."

He led us down winding stairs until we walked through a large pantry. A maid looked up at us as we passed but didn't seem to care that we were here. I sensed lust coat her skin as she stared at me and shook my head. I was so taken that I didn't think there was a word for it.

John pushed open a door. I followed him into a tunnel and looked around. This tunnel looked like one of Raven's. "Does Raven know this exists?"

"No. And neither does Cade."

"You've never trusted him."

"He was too obsessed with her. Once she turned sixteen, they were inseparable. He never touched her, but he made sure no one else could, either." He led me through the dark tunnel as he spoke.

My jaw was clenched as I listened.

"When she turned twenty-one, he started looking at her differently. There's not a word for it. She's always been cute, and even as a confused kid, she was bubbly. But... you've seen her. She looks like her mother, but...."

"Beautiful doesn't even begin to cover it," I finished for him.

He nodded. "And Cade put her so high up on a pedestal that she never hungered for anything else. He'd allow her to go out to festivals and at night."

I grinned as I remembered seeing her at the festival.

"And she'd... sew her oats."

My grin disappeared.

"I needed a way to get her out if necessary. If he ever reached a point of truly locking her away, I'd have a way to save her."

"Why do you care so much? Leonidas murdered your queen."

"Raven is my queen. Celestina was my sister-in-law, and I loved her. I wanted to avenge her death, and the best way I could do that was to protect Raven. When Mira suggested binding our kingdoms together, I thought that would be a good way to settle it. Make it right. But then I started noticing traits in Mira that I saw in Celestina. She wants revenge. Raven is the best way for her to get that."

"And Leonidas became your friend."

John sighed, climbing up a wooden ladder. "And Leonidas became my friend."

He pushed on a wooden door and pulled himself out. I followed him and blinked, looking around. We were in the Black Forest. "This is how you'll get in. Remember where you are.

Make a trail, do whatever you must, but Cade will ensure you can't find a way in tonight."

I extended my hand to him. He looked at it, surprised, before reaching for it, giving me a slight shake. "Thank you," I said.

He cleared his throat, nodding once. "Go get some sleep," he said before crouching down and disappearing back down the ladder.

I closed the door for him and looked up from where I knelt, trying to sketch a memory of what I saw. All that surrounded me were trees. I didn't see the caves or the spring anywhere nearby, which meant I was on the opposite side of the forest.

I sighed and stood. I had nothing to mark the trees, nothing to create a trail. The snow was melting, so I couldn't make footprints. I looked down at my clothes. I thought about shredding them, but I was getting low on things to wear.

I blew out a breath. I was going to have to use nothing but a memory. I started heading south. The caves should be in the middle of the tunnel and the spring. If I could find those, I'd be able to make my way back tonight.

I'd been walking for half an hour and was beginning to doubt my sense of direction. I saw something on the ground up ahead and squinted my eyes. Bodies. I was coming up on dead bodies. I tilted my head as I approached them, noticing their decaying skin looked… burned. And then I smirked, shaking my head as I kept going. Those men I saw her burning when I first came here —little demon.

I'd use their corpses as a guide — it took me thirty minutes to get to them and forty-five minutes from there to reach the caves. I'd need to leave plenty of time to get to the ball in time. It was late morning now, which meant I'd only have time for a couple of hours of sleep.

I jumped on the deck of my ship.

Jeanine was there waiting for me. "Eat before you sleep. You'll need your energy." She tossed me a muffin.

I nodded and pulled the paper off, taking a bite from the top. "When do you leave?"

"After I make sure you eat. You're running yourself ragged."

I snorted and took another bite, shrugging. "I'm addicted."

"John is meeting me at the gate to ensure I can get in. I guess you've set Cade off. They'll watch who comes in tonight to ensure you're not one of them."

"I have a way. Don't worry about me."

She tossed me another muffin after I finished the first one. I raised my eyebrows at her.

"You need to stay bigger than Cade."

My eyes rolled, my mouth full of food as I responded, "I am bigger than Cade in every way."

"I wouldn't know. Raven saved me from that wreck before I got a chance to ride."

We both started to laugh, my head shaking at her. She bent down and pulled out a bottle of my favorite rum, handing it to me. "From Arthur."

I grinned and unscrewed the top, taking a drink. "Are you trying to get me fat and drunk before seeing her?"

"I'm trying to calm your nerves. You're bouncing."

I looked down at my feet. I hadn't realized I was. I inhaled a deep breath through my nose as I took another drink, taking in enough to let the liquid infiltrate my bloodstream.

"It'll be okay," she told me, her voice gentle.

"She's going to hate me, Jeanine. It's only a matter of time."

"We won't know until we try. She may surprise you."

She already had. She still loved me, even after everything I'd put her through.

"I'll see you tonight. Get some rest."

She moved to leave, but I held out an arm and gave her a small side-hug. "Thank you. For helping me. For seeing the good in her."

"It's too late for one sister's soul, but not hers," she responded.

I let her go, watching until she safely crossed over the rocks and landed on the island. I took another big chug of my rum and started into the hull, kicking off my shoes before falling into bed. I stared up at the ceiling.

I was proposing to her tonight. And I wouldn't even get to marry her. I groaned, rolling over to my stomach. She wouldn't want to marry me after this. She may not want anything to do with me. I needed to prepare myself for that — for having to live without her if she chose that. For her, I'd suffer the worst of fates if it meant she stayed safe. If Seolia stayed safe.

———————

I woke up and sat up quickly. The light wasn't peeking through my hull. Fuck. I jumped up and ran up the ladder, throwing open the door. It was evening. The ball was going to start soon. I planned on making a late entrance, but not so late that everyone had left. It would take me over an hour to walk that damned tunnel.

I disposed of my clothes quickly and pulled my black tux off the hook. Jeanine had insisted that I hang it up so it wouldn't look wrinkled. I rolled my eyes as I pulled on the pants. Like I gave a shit about that. But it did look nicer. Maybe I didn't get her enough credit.

I pulled my black shirt over my shoulders and left it unbuttoned at the top because it made Raven crazy. My socks matched her dress, and I slid on much nicer shoes than she'd ever seen me in, lacing them tightly. They were going to hurt like a motherfucker while walking through the forest.

I opened a drawer in my trunk and grabbed my mother's diamond ring, staring at it. It looked like Raven. I tucked it into a pocket inside my jacket, pulled it on, and drew in a shaky breath. Everything had led to this point -- to getting to her, proposing to her, and bringing her back to Reales. And it wasn't even the end. We still had so much ahead of us.

I ran my fingers through my hair to keep it slicked back. I needed to look somewhat decent while waltzing into this party. Crossing rocks in these shoes wouldn't be fun. Jeanine wasn't all dressed up when she left. She was probably getting dressed there. Damn, I should've done that. I grunted as I crossed over the rocks, my feet threatening to slip on the smooth stone.

I made it across and checked my pocket to ensure the ring was still there before I started my long walk toward the tunnel.

Fucking Cade. He and Mira could both burn. They ruined everything. I didn't anticipate him busting in on us last night. I should have since he never fucking left her alone. My fists were clenched at my sides, and I needed to relax. I should've finished off my rum before I left.

I just wanted to see her. I'd be fine once she was in my arms.

The sky was darkening, and I knew the ball had already started. John and Jeanine would kill me if I didn't make it in time. I threw open the tunnel door and climbed into the dark corridor, wishing I had Raven and her fingertips to light the way through here. She was right. It did get darker here during winter. And I doubted this tunnel was ever used until John needed to sneak out, so he hadn't kept up with the lighting.

I felt down the wall to ensure I was heading in the right direction. When I heard voices, I pulled open the door that led into the pantry and was met with bustling maids and servers.

They didn't even look at me as I cut through them, focused on ensuring the party upstairs had everything it needed.

They yelled at one another to finish so they could join the party, which made me smile. Raven had invited them. I climbed up the winding stairs, and John stood at the top. "Took you long enough."

I shrugged.

He led me back through the dining hall and stopped at the door, peering out both ways before he beckoned me to follow him. "He's locked it down," I said.

John nodded, constantly turning his head.

"John, I'll be fine. I can handle myself." I'd trained hundreds of my soldiers. I was sure I could take down several of Seolia's untrained crew.

But John just shook his head. I could see where I inherited my lack of words.

He stopped abruptly, and I nearly stumbled into him, but his arm shot out to catch me. He dipped his chin, and I followed it. My breath was nearly knocked out of me.

There wasn't a word that any scholar would ever invent to describe what I was looking at.

Raven stood at the ballroom door, her lengthy hair shiny and moving as she did. Her olive complexion was flushed from her nerves as she twisted her hands in front of her. The dress hugged every part of her perfectly, and I was instantly swollen for her as I stared. Her head tilted as she rolled her neck back, exposing her throat to me and causing my mouth to water.

Her face turned slightly toward me and I saw the red of her lips. I wanted them on me. Her green irises were bright under that mask of red and gold that I had designed for her — a black feather representing her name, red for how I burned for her.

She was delectable. Perfect. Mine.

"Take me to her," I whispered.

The doors slowly opened, and she inhaled deeply, slowly walking into the room. When the doors shut, John let me go, and I followed behind him to the doors. I could see her through the crack of the door. She was frozen in the center of the room. I didn't know why, but I could see colors of gold and red surrounding her—the roses. Jeanine had come through for me. Raven saw roses. I closed my eyes, trying to connect to her.

She was longing for me, trying to find me.

I whispered into her mind: *Breathe, Raven.*

Her breathing calmed.

"Wait a little bit before you go in," John said, breaking through my thoughts.

I nodded in response as I continued to watch her.

Someone approached from my other side. "She's exquisite, isn't she?"

"And she doesn't even realize it," I whispered, watching her dance with a small girl. I couldn't stop looking at her. "How long do I have to wait?" I was itching to get to her.

"They're bringing her cake out in an hour. I'd wait until then," Jeanine answered.

"I must stand here and watch her dance with other men," I bit out.

Jeanine snorted as John patted my arm. "You don't have to stand there like a creep. You can go wait in her room," Jeanine suggested.

I considered that for a moment before I shook my head.

"What's your plan?"

"To propose," I said.

John chuckled. I gave Jeanine a sloppy grin.

John asked, "And if she says no?"

"I won't give her a chance. And she won't say no."

"Does he get that cockiness from you, or?" Jeanine asked John.

I pulled away from the door, pacing.

John asked, "Do you have a ring?"

I stopped. I hadn't told him. I pulled the ring from my jacket pocket and held it out to him. He took a small step toward me and sorrow settled on his face. "Mom said she had 'a feeling' I would want this."

"I had that made for her." His voice was quiet, and his eyes glistened.

Jeanine came up beside him, her mouth falling open. "I'll marry you," she said.

I couldn't help but laugh as I looked down at the ring. But then I looked back to John. He seemed genuinely heartbroken, and I couldn't understand why. He chose to leave us. He chose to damage our relationship and tell Mira of my abilities.

I tucked the ring back into my jacket pocket, and John retreated to the door. There was nothing left for us to do but wait.

———

When the cake rolled in, we knew it was almost time. I watched as Raven climbed on a chair to blow out the candle. I chuckled softly and tensed as Cade wrapped his arms around her to bring her down. It would feel so good to take her from him.

"You'll need this," Jeanine said, holding out my mask.

I grabbed it, grinning, and tied it around my head.

"John and I are going to go in," she said, tying her mask on. "Luisa is going to announce you after they're done eating."

My fists were clenching and unclenching over and over as I tried to calm my nerves. Jeanine put her hand on my elbow. "It'll be fine, Zeke. This will all work out."

All I could do was shrug.

John dipped his chin to me, and then he and Jeanine disappeared quietly inside the ballroom. Now I was the one nervously twisting my fingers together. I had to remain calm when I walked in. Collected.

I heard Luisa's voice breaking over the crowd. Raven seemed perplexed. When Luisa thanked Jeanine, Cade brought Raven closer to him, and my eyes rolled. He was a fucking piece of work.

She introduced me. My throat cleared. John would make sure the doors opened for me. I rolled my neck and relaxed my body as Raven stared at the doors. I smiled, counting down the seconds until I held her again.

And then they opened.

CHAPTER TWENTY-FIVE

Raven

Zeke straightened the lapels of his jacket, tugging to adjust the cuffs of his sleeves as he sauntered into the ballroom, his sinful grin pinned to me. My gaze was held captive as he didn't look anywhere but right at me, his walk full of intent. His strides were long, cool. My world froze. Sounds died out.

He was the only one in the room with me, stealing my air.

And he was devilishly handsome. His black hair was slicked back, curled under his ears. His jacket and pants were the deepest blacks I'd ever seen, and he had on a black button-down shirt that was unbuttoned to the third button, exposing his smooth chest. His shoes were slick and shiny black, and underneath, I saw the deep-red socks that perfectly matched my dress.

But his mask.

As he neared me, I could see that his silver-plated mask was detailed with one single black outline along his left eye. An outline of a raven. Me.

I have a surprise for you, he told me.

I should've realized it sooner. Cade's hand was on the small of my back, and I didn't turn to him, keeping my gaze strictly on Zeke. "You knew about this," I whispered with a harsh tone.

He hesitated before he answered, his voice low, "I didn't know he'd be here, just that it was his idea. I can have him removed."

I shook my head, never breaking our intense stare. "Don't make a scene. No one knows what we do. It has to stay that way."

Zeke approached me and bent at the waist, bowing to me. He grabbed my hand and brushed my knuckles with his lips on the way up. My insides melted at his touch, my body calling to him. And he answered, tugging on my hand and pulling me flush against him. "Dance with me," he demanded with a husky voice.

I was putty once again in this man's hands.

He wrapped his hand tightly around my waist and squeezed, extending our arms straight to the side, and then we were moving, twirling gracefully around the room as the music played. I needed to say something, anything, but my mouth was dry. His eyes were the color of charcoal again, and I wanted to lose myself in them. "Why?" was all I could get out.

His chuckle caressed me like the velvet of my dress. "I told you I have a surprise for you," he replied. His eyes were still on mine, flicking to my mouth for a second. I silently dared him. "Here? In front of Cade?"

My eyes widened, immediately biting down on my bottom lip, which had finally healed.

He tracked my movement. "Let's not tease, baby."

I glared at his use of my nickname. There had to be more than this. He wouldn't have done all of this for one dance. I tried to push through the dark haze of my thoughts and studied his face. His lines looked harder in the light than when he left me three months ago. He continued to spin me, watching me stare at him. He was trying to convey so much through that look.

"But I *saw* you leave," I argued with what he said to me last night about never having left.

He simply shook his head slowly. I couldn't understand any of this. I needed to. I could feel Cade's eyes burning into us, but I didn't care. He'd chosen to hide this from me. "Do you like the dress I chose for you?"

He chose this dress. Not Cade.

All I could do was nod, my mouth falling open.

His hand squeezed my waist again. "I do know you well."

"Give me something. Anything," I pleaded with him.

His eyes darkened at my request, and he dipped me down, our mouths inches apart. "I'm going to," he promised, but his words were laced with something dark.

The song was ending. No. I needed more time with him. He'd leave me again. I squeezed his hand, and for a second, his features softened. "I didn't know," I began, tears pushing behind my eyelids. "I…" I trailed off. There was so much I wanted to say, but I couldn't get it out.

The look he gave me could kill. "You move on quickly, baby."

At that, I glowered. "You told me that we couldn't happen."

"We weren't supposed to happen. But we did," he purred, his mouth finally closing the space between us as he pressed it against mine.

The world around us fell silent again as he pulled my hand between our chests, letting me feel how our heartbeats were thundering together in the same rhythm. He'd realized it, too.

He broke our kiss and left me breathless as he released me from his grip. My emptiness returned — an emptiness I'd been clawing to fill with Cade. But when Zeke let me go, I realized that I'd never feel fulfilled without him.

"Don't go," I breathed.

He didn't move, blinking like he wanted to say something.

"Please don't leave me again."

His mouth pressed against mine again, and I placed my hand gently on his cheek. I love you; I love you, I told him silently. His hands were wrapped around my waist, gripping me tightly, and when he went to pull away, I pulled him back. "Kiss me," I whispered.

Something was conflicting in his eyes.

"Stay with me." My scattered dream. Him. "You should've let us stay," I cried, my voice breaking.

And then his mouth was on mine again, and I didn't care who was watching us. Let them. I didn't care about anything — I just wanted him.

His tongue pushed into my mouth, and I tangled mine with it. His chest rose and fell rapidly, and I didn't understand why he wouldn't let me have him — why we couldn't be together.

It was Cade shouting my name over and over, breaking over the music. And before he could reach us to pull me away, Zeke broke from me suddenly and dropped to one knee. My eyes widened as he looked at me with something sinister behind his. "The fuck are you doing," I bit out.

"Queen Raven," he began, his voice loud enough for everyone in the room to hear.

I shook my head, but he ignored me and continued, brandishing a ring from his jacket pocket. I gasped at the sight of it. It was beautiful with its gold band and white-gold diamond sitting atop it. As I peered closer, I noticed that small star-shaped diamonds were fashioned to line up on either side of the larger diamond in the center.

"Marry me." He wasn't asking, and he wasn't going to let me answer. He took my left hand and slid the ring up my finger.

I felt like my voice box had melted away somewhere because I was speechless. And light-headed. I felt like this was one of my dreams that didn't make sense.

He stood and wrapped his arm around my waist, holding up my hand to show the crowd. Claps and cheers sounded from all around us. I pulled my hand down and was about to decline all of this when his mouth crashed into mine again, silencing me.

When he pulled back, it was to whisper against my mouth, "Let me take you home, Raven."

I was taken aback by that, my head jerking back. "Home? I am home."

He shook his head, frowning. "You're not."

Cade was beside us now, shoving Zeke off of me. Zeke just looked at him and cocked an eyebrow, daring him. He kept his hand on my waist, unfazed. "Not here," I said through clenched teeth. I stepped away from them both, bowing my head in feigned gratitude as people reached out their hands in congratulations.

Arthur stepped in front of me with conviction in his eyes as they met mine. "What do you know?" I asked him.

He gave me a small smile and placed his hand on my cheek. Tears pooled in my eyes. Tell me your secrets.

"I know that you are a brilliant young woman. And that you will listen to both sides."

I sighed, leaning my head into his hand.

"Keep your wits about you." He gave me one of his warm smiles and released me.

I excused myself and left the ballroom, knowing that the two infuriating men would follow me.

———

I kept silent until we were in the library, then slammed the doors behind us, putting my hands on my waist as I paced. Zeke leaned against one of the tables and crossed his feet at his ankles, crossing his arms over his chest. Cade leaned against one of the library shelves. We all removed our masks, though I still felt like I was staring at strangers.

"First off, what are you *doing* here?" I finally asked, looking at Zeke.

He nodded to my ring. "Isn't it obvious?"

I pulled my hand up and looked at the ring. Damn. It really was beautiful. Focus, Raven. "What did you mean about taking me 'home'?"

This time, Zeke nodded toward Cade. "Ask your boyfriend."

I whirled to Cade and looked at him. "Cade?"

He sighed and took a step toward me. I took a step back and shook my head. He stopped and licked over his bottom lip, inhaling like he didn't know what to say next.

"Tell her," Zeke said.

Cade's fists balled at his sides. "Raven..." he began, but then clenched his jaw.

"Here, let me," Zeke said.

I spun to face him again.

"Your boyfriend knows who you are. He's always known."

I shook my head in disbelief, backing away until I bumped into a table. The opposite of fury pulsed through me. I felt my eyes shifting into blue as I felt nothing but cold.

"Raven," Cade said again, holding his palms up to me. "It's not what you think."

I didn't know what to think.

"All I remember was one night when I was eight years old; I woke up to my father yelling something about a baby. I saw my mother holding one. You. He was telling her that she needed a home. She's the one who chose Isla."

If I had eaten anything, I would've vomited it right then.

"I… didn't know who you were then. I didn't know who you were until I was seventeen."

Seventeen. One year before I was whisked away to the castle.

"King Leonidas made me follow him around the Festival of Dreams to watch someone. Watch you."

I couldn't even look at Cade. My body was heavy with his betrayal.

"I swear I didn't know who you were, Raven. But your black hair and green eyes reminded me of the baby I saw my mother holding. And the king, he made me promise to protect you. He told me that you'd be queen. And then he made me a member of his court."

He tried to take another step toward me, but I held up my hand to stop him. He sighed before continuing, "I didn't want to. I hated that first year. But when you showed up, there was something in your eyes; I knew I needed to make good on my promise. I wanted to *protect* you."

I stared at the ground like I could burn a hole in it. And I felt like it, my fury returning as I realized that Cade had been hiding things from me for a very long time. I was convinced he couldn't keep a secret, and I had never been more wrong.

"You're from Reales. And he knows that," Zeke said.

My eyes snapped up to his. I just shook my head again, blinking my eyes. This was too much to digest.

"You are. I'm here to take you home."

"You're not taking her anywhere," Cade argued.

Zeke's eyes never left mine, but he answered Cade, "That's not really up to you, is it?"

And he was right. Cade had tried to control where I went for too long.

"But... why? Why now?" I asked, finally finding my voice.

"Mira will explain it all," Zeke answered.

My headache was starting to return. "Mira?" I sighed, not wanting any more pieces of the puzzle.

Zeke just nodded, and I'd had enough.

I lit flames in my hands and curled them into fists, hurtling small balls of fire at them both. Zeke barely moved an inch to the side as one whizzed by, and Cade ducked. The flames extinguished behind them. I palmed my eyes, my skin still hot from the fire. "Tell me why Mira will explain everything."

Zeke shook his head. "I can't. It's not my place to say."

"You have to tell me something, or I'm not going anywhere. We've been under the impression that you were sent here to incite a war. To pull me away from Cade. Make me weaker. And now you're proposing to me and telling me that I'm from Reales and that I have to see *your* queen to get answers?"

Zeke scoffed and leaned back slightly. "I'm not the enemy, Raven. Pulling you apart from Cade was just a fringe benefit."

Cade growled at that, but I silenced him with a stare.

"You *shot* me," I bit out.

Zeke shrugged unapologetically. "I let my jealousy get the best of me."

I held up my left hand and waved it around manically.
"And *this*?"

He shrugged again, and I swore I'd kill him. "Come to Reales and find out."

I laughed, but not from amusement. I laughed from shock and irritation. "Fuck you."

"You've been dreaming of me. Don't you want to know why?"

My eyes shot back to his, and I felt Cade's burning into me. "You dream of him?"

I winced. "My dreams are like shattered glass, Cade. I never have all the pieces."

"Yes, she dreams of me," Zeke answered for me.

I really needed to get out of this room. "I need... space. I need to breathe on my own." I straightened from where I'd been somewhat melting into the floor and smoothed out my dress, straightening the crown on my head. I wasn't going to fall apart here. I walked toward the door, but Cade stepped in front of me. "Don't," I warned.

He put his hands on my arms and held me still.

"You're touching my fiancée," Zeke spoke up, amusement in his voice.

Cade's eyes slowly tore from mine and landed on Zeke, and I had no time to stop him before he was headed right for him. Zeke remained cool, only raising an eyebrow. "She is not your fiancée," Cade snapped, balling his fists again.

Zeke looked at me but was again only talking to Cade. "How does it feel, Cade? To know you had to beg to kiss her, but she was begging me to fuck her?" Zeke uncrossed his ankles, his fingers wrapping around the table's edge. "To know she's done nothing but think about me since I left? It only took me a matter of days. It's taken you fifteen years."

Cade's arm pulled back, and punched Zeke in the jaw, but Zeke barely leaned to the side from the blow. He stood then, towering an inch or two over Cade, and exhaled a bored sigh. "I'm not going to fight you, Cade."

Cade shoved at his shoulders, trying to agitate him. "Why the fuck not?" I could practically see steam rising from Cade.

"Because I'll fucking kill you," Zeke replied smoothly.

I rolled my eyes and walked out of the library, hearing Cade follow after me. I continued down the hallway, ignoring his calls for me to stop.

Once in the courtyard, I took off in a run, my dress swishing behind me. I knew he was following me, but I didn't care. I kept running, taking deep breaths, trying to clear the fog from my brain. When I crossed the border into the Black Forest, I fell to my knees, burying my face in my hands.

I was from Reales. I had a beginning somewhere.

And Cade knew that. He could have told me this entire time that his parents knew who I was instead of letting me feel abandoned when in truth, it was Cade's mother who had left me in a basket on Isla's porch.

Cade caught up to me. I stood and spun, shoving him as he approached me. He let me. I swung my fists at his chest, pushing him repeatedly, tears spilling down my face. He continued to let me and stood there, taking all of it. I swung my arms until they hurt until I had nothing left, and then I fell into him.

He wrapped his arms around me, holding me up. "I'm so sorry, Raven."

I sniffled and raised my head, piercing his eyes with mine. "I can't trust you."

His whole face broke as he shook his head over and over. "Raven, you can."

I choked back a sob and pushed away from him. "I can't. I'm questioning everything now. All those years, you listened to me go on about how I wished I knew who I was. You had the answer the whole fucking time."

He was quiet. There was nothing left for him to say. He couldn't defend this.

"August told me tonight that you and I are fated to be together." I raised my palms to either side of my temple and shook my head. I felt like I was going mad. "Because he knew. He knew that you knew about me. He thinks we're fated because he's the one who kick-started this whole fucking thing."

"We *are* fated, Raven," he shouted, his voice breaking.

I fell to my knees again and wrapped my arms around my waist, screaming. He was so desperate to help me. He fell to his knees in front of me and tried to pull me to him, but I resisted. "How do I even know you're not fucking someone else?"

He looked betrayed at my question.

"You do have a thing for blondes. And apparently had enough conversations with Jeanine to know that Zeke is the one who planned this whole thing. And you kept that from me. What else are you keeping from me?" I didn't care if he was fucking someone else anymore. He'd been deceiving me for fifteen years. The one person I'd come to rely on for everything had been holding my answers the entire time.

Cade just shook his head in disbelief at my words. I was in disbelief, too. I didn't know what was real anymore. "I didn't share it with you because I knew the mention of Reales would make you think of him. And I only slept with blondes because I wanted you so fucking bad that I needed the opposite of you in my bed so I wouldn't think of you."

I started to cry again, choking on my sobs. I was trembling, completely broken in a nightmare-like state. Not the kind of nightmares I looked forward to every night, hoping to see Zeke. The type of nightmare that could completely rip apart your soul and have you screaming for release from the mental hell they put you in. Nothing made sense anymore.

"Raven, please," he begged. "Just come home with me."

At that, I sucked in a breath and slowly looked up at him with narrowed eyes. "I don't have a home," I replied, my voice flat.

His mouth fell shut.

We remained like that, on our knees in the Black Forest.

The only place I'd ever felt like I belonged.

After what seemed like hours, my eyes became heavy. My body started to crumble, but Cade caught me and lifted me into his lap. He stood, cradling me in his arms, and walked us back to the castle. I had no fight left in me to try and stop him.

Our picnic on the balcony. That wasn't going to happen for the first time in fifteen years.

In the span of a few hours, my entire life had changed. Everything we thought we knew about Zeke, wrong. Everything I thought I knew about Cade, wrong. Everything I thought I knew about myself, wrong. Wrong, wrong, wrong.

Tonight was supposed to be magical, but now it'd live in infamy as the night I discovered that my life had been a lie.

When we returned to the castle, Cade muttered something about Zeke, and my head rose from his chest.

"Let me down," I said.

He reluctantly did.

Zeke approached me, stopping an arm's length away.

"Leave us," I told Cade.

He shook his head.

I turned to him, putting weight behind my tone, "*Leave.*"

Cade's nostrils flared as he stared at me, his fists clenching at his sides. I didn't back down. Cade glared at Zeke, but Zeke's eyes never left my face. "Don't touch her," Cade told him before disappearing inside the castle doors.

"Walk with me," Zeke said, giving me a chance to decline before he grabbed my hand and pulled me with him.

So much for Cade's warning.

I let him steer me away from the castle. He kept my hand in his, pulling me through the dark village, silent from everyone still enjoying my birthday celebration at the castle.

He pulled me down the grassy knolls stretched out in front of the harbor. Boats rocked against the docks, their sails swaying in the wind. I closed my eyes and felt the breeze circle around me in a hug. I sighed against it, letting it comfort me — the element being one of the only constants in my life.

Zeke just watched me, understanding.

He pulled me down until we reached a dock and dragged me across it until we were at the end before he released my hand, motioning down, asking me to sit.

I pulled my dress up enough to lower myself, my feet dangling over the edge. The moonlight danced across the water as it rippled. I heard him draw a soft breath, but my eyes remained on the water.

"I knew you," he began.

My head slowly turned toward him at his words. I swallowed but stayed silent. It was his turn to give me answers.

"I knew you when I was young. I can't give you every detail because it's not only my story. But I was five when you were taken." He never looked at me, his gaze remaining on the water. "For years, I wondered what happened to the baby with black hair." He laughed softly, shaking his head. "You were magic, even then. Not a soul in Reales didn't want a peek at the baby with the deep green eyes and hair black as night."

I watched him, still mesmerized by how he looked in the moon's light. But mostly, I was just perplexed.

"I was sent here to bring you home."

I opened my mouth to plague him with questions, but he just shook his head. I shut it, exasperated.

"I wasn't sent here to fall in love with you." And at that, he finally turned to meet my stare. "But I did, Raven. It was like… suddenly everything in my life made sense. Like I had a purpose greater than the one I had been serving. You made it all seem worth it."

I fought back the tears, watching how pain skated across his face.

"My heart…" He raised his hand to his heart, silver lining his eyes. "It beats because of yours."

With a shaky voice, I asked, "Why'd you tell me goodbye then?"

He exhaled, and my eyelids fluttered when his breath reached my eyes. "We can't happen, Raven."

It was the same answer he always gave me. I nodded, turning my head away from his to watch the boats sway. Tears flooded my cheeks.

"But I need you to know," he whispered.

It took every ounce of strength I had left not to look at him again for fear of falling apart.

"I need you to know that I will never love another the way I love you. I will never love another, ever. I need you to know...." He trailed off, his voice hoarse now. "That you are the very blood that runs through my veins. You are every breath, every whisper. Every dream, every nightmare. The ghost of you will forever haunt me. The ghost of what could be."

My chest heaved at his words, caving in on me. I raised my hands to my eyes, wetness pooling against my palms. "I would've burned the very soil of this world for you." My voice was barely a whisper, and I wasn't sure he could hear me.

But then he spoke, and his voice had a sense of finality, "I will find you in the next one."

CHAPTER TWENTY-SIX

Raven

I was spent and had nothing left to give after Zeke dropped me off at Cade's room. I had considered returning to my chambers since the threat against me had seemingly disappeared. But who I was when I lived in the king's quarters was no longer the person I was. Until a few hours ago, I was excited that a future for us seemed like a possibility. I was trying to talk myself into saying goodbye to Zeke. But now... I was just tired. The last three months had aged me, not only mentally but physically.

I stared at myself in the mirror of Cade's bedroom, having discarded the gorgeous red dress from the ball and was back in my plush robe. Cade sat behind me on his bed, his fingers gripping the edge as he watched me.

I cocked my head, holding my hands out in front of me, and stared at the engagement ring wrapped around my finger. It shimmered in the light, the diamond stars sparkling as they did in the night sky — the very stars that accompanied the moon every night I spent with Zeke. The ring was loose on my finger, and I used my thumb to spin it around, pressing hard on the diamond that resembled the shape of a pear.

His favorite scent.

My eyes tracked up to my wrists. My skin looked stretched across the bones. I moved my gaze back to the mirror as my hands glided up my arms to trace my collarbone and the plate of my chest that seemed hollow, lingering on the gap between my breasts.

Cade inhaled a stuttering breath behind me, but I ignored him and kept my eyes only on myself. Only me. For once.

My hand rose slowly and circled my neck, winding my fingers tightly around my throat. I squeezed, closing my eyes as my air felt trapped, making a cloudy daze fall over me. I released and gripped again tighter, trying to draw deep breaths as my brain screamed.

I heard Cade rise from the bed, and my eyes shot open, snapping to him in a warning to stay back. He stopped his movements but kept his eyes glued to my hand wrapped around my throat.

Again, I released, my chest quickly sucking in air to push into my lungs. I felt light on the balls of my feet as my brain grappled for it, taking it greedily.

My hand glided up my throat, and the other joined to pat at my hollow cheekbones, protruding from the skin my skull was wrapped in. The half circles under my eyes were darkened, making the green of my irises pop, and I saw shadowed flecks within them.

The pad of my thumb drew across my bottom lip, remembering how it felt to have Zeke's mouth on mine. And then Cade's. I sucked on the tip of my finger, tasting a whisper of them both, still tattooed on my skin from weeks of letting them invade my body.

They were permanently a part of me. They wormed their way into my very being, taking pieces of my soul as they pleased. Keeping secrets from me. Whispering sweet promises against my ear and then devouring me like I was their last meal.

For so long, I'd felt nothing but guilt for being torn between two lovers, wanting them both simultaneously. Never able to give my heart entirely to either of them. I'd been split into two, and they each took their half of me, dragging my limp body behind them. They lied to me, never revealing the full scope of the truth. Giving me what they thought I needed to hear, let me cast self-doubt upon myself every day.

And now here we all were, under one roof again, no closer to the answers I craved than I was three months ago. My answers were in a kingdom far away, hidden in the depths of another throne taken by another queen.

My long black hair still laid against my back, mussed and tangled from my night running and screaming outside. I sifted it through my fingertips, the blackest pieces matching the darkest nights. Ebony.

When I dropped it, it fell against the opening of my plush robe, covering up exposed skin. When my eyes lifted again in the mirror, I sighed softly, staring at the stranger I'd become. The woman in the mirror thought her existence was finally starting to ebb and flow like that of a sated river. She was letting herself feel anger and joy. Now the woman in the mirror was staring back at me with nothing left behind those green eyes and lost as I was on that fateful night when I was left on a porch twenty-five years ago. My eyes were dry, no liquid left to pour for the lost soul staring back at me.

Cade came up behind me, his chest pressing gently into my back. My darkness, the invisible blackness of my soul, enveloped us, binding us together. My Cade, who had always been the calm to my rough waters, had secrets of his own. He was no longer my pure, honest confidant. He was my enemy, his thread of dishonesty now tying knots around my broken soul, casting shadows on everything we had built together.

His cheek rested against the side of my head, and our eyes met in the mirror. I felt like I was meeting him for the first time. "I love you," he muttered painfully, the sound piercing into my skin. His eyes bore into mine, the depths of his blue threatening to drown me. His arms wrapped around my waist, his fingers pulling apart the ties that kept my robe wound around my body. The palm of his hand flattened against my stomach, his fingers splaying open across my skin.

This was forbidden, just a short time ago. Our bodies hadn't found one another. Our sweat hadn't combined into our own kind of scent. We were just two people, the threat of our demise never blanketing across our tongues.

With his hand on my stomach, he pulled me back tighter against his chest, the hardness of his length pushing against my lower back. I was nothing to him, just something to own. To possess and control was exactly what he'd been doing for the last fifteen years—holding my secrets in his hand, always dangling them in front of me like meat to a starved dog. I scented them, searched blindly for them, and then he'd pull them back again, keeping my truths out of reach.

His claim was heavy on my weakened body, but I could not stop it — because I'd come to rely on him for everything. Every decision, every thought, my own body hummed when he was near, immediately wanting release. And he took it without a second thought, stealing everything I had to give, knowing I needed someone to love me. And he gave that to me.

His hands pulled at the open tabs of my robe, yanking it down, and it fell to my feet. My naked body felt the sudden chill of the air as it danced upon my skin. I didn't bother to will my fire forward to warm me. I wanted everything about this to hurt.

His hands found my hips next, his fingers digging into my hip bones as he dragged us backward toward the bed, our steps in sync. I was the perfect puppet on my strings.

I heard the sound of his pants falling to the floor and the feel of his chest leaving my back as he sat on the edge of the bed. With one of his hands still on my hips, he guided me down, the tip of his hard cock pushing into my core until he filled me.

With his grip, he moved my hips against him, and I watched him in the mirror, his eyes staring down between us as my ass pushed against his abs. His forehead fell against my back as he moved me into a grind against him, his hips roughly pushing against me. Two of his fingers circled the cradle of my hips to my clit, and he groaned from the wetness drowning them.

He knew my body. He knew how to coax out a climax. I'd let him overtake me too many times.

He moved his fingers against me, building me up higher and higher. As I felt his cock pulse and release into me, my walls tightened around him, and I came to the feeling of Zeke's mouth on mine, my eyes closing at the rapid intake of blood rushing to my brain. He peppered light kisses on my spine, repeating those lies against my skin.

The ones that used to give me butterflies.

I hated myself. And I hated him.

I dreamed that night of being in a room full of large windows and golden rays of sunshine that seemed to fill every inch of the room. I turned in a slow circle, my body covered in all black. Black diadem, black dress, the opposite of the golden rays seemingly avoiding my very being.

I felt him first and then inhaled his familiar scent. His lips whispered against my ear and sent shivers down my spine. "Come back to me, Queen of Darkness," was all he said. And then he was gone.

My eyes fluttered open, the dream scattering into oblivion, joining all the others that always seemed to fade when I woke up. Cade was asleep beside me, and my head turned to drink in the achingly beautiful man. I wanted to feel his blood running through my fingers. It would be thick with years of deceit. But I couldn't kill the man who held half of my heart, or I may die alongside him.

I felt between my legs, still slick with his cum from the night before. I wiped my fingers along his quilt, trying to remove him from me, not wanting to feel his falsehood on me any longer.

I sat up and stretched my naked body, letting the bright sun rays pour onto me from the open balcony doors. I stood and walked toward them, begging them to lift me and take me away from this place — make me part of the beams that heat the earth.

Surely some part of the world that was always dark and cold could use some of the fire raging inside me.

Just like me.

I quietly walked to the balcony's deck and leaned my palms down on the waist-high stone wall. Below me, doors opened, and footsteps mirrored what I had just done.

Zeke. He was right beneath my feet. Pieces of his face from my dream were trying to come back to me, trying to remember why he had been there, but it remained fragmented.

I bent carefully over the balcony wall to look down below. All I could see were his hands and forearms that rested against the railing of his balcony wall. I wanted to see his face. I wanted to know if he slept. I tried and leaned forward, just an inch more...

"*Raven.*"

I heard the sharp call of my name and straightened quickly; Cade's voice nearly made me tip over.

"What are you doing?"

I bit down on my bottom lip. "Just stretching," I replied, my tone dry.

"Stretching? Naked? Hanging over the side of the wall?" He asked, his eyebrow arching.

I heard a dark laugh from below, and I pinched my eyes shut. "I'll see you at breakfast, baby," Zeke called to me from his balcony and then closed his doors as he disappeared back into his room.

"Un-fucking-believable," Cade muttered, leaving me to stand out there alone.

I rolled my eyes at his remark and followed him inside. "What?" I didn't know why I cared or bothered following him inside. He didn't have the right to be upset with me about anything for the next hundred years or so.

"We made love last night, and then I find you nearly killing yourself to see *him.*" His voice was heavy with disgust, his fingers pinching the bridge of his nose.

"I'd hardly call that making love," I retorted, walking to the wardrobe and pulling out my favorite blue dress. I was relieved to see it hadn't been ruined by Cade's sudden need to bathe me the other day.

He drew in a frustrated sigh and then took steps toward me. I whipped around and held up one of my hands, using the other to hold the dress against my naked body. "Enough." There was enough weight behind my word to make a man fall to his knees.

"Enough?" Cade repeated slowly, shaking his head. "Enough *what?*"

I didn't answer him; instead, pulling the dress over my head and smoothed it across my body. I really did love this dress. It made me feel youthful. Gleeful. Everything I currently wasn't.

"Enough *what*, Raven?"

"Enough touching me. Enough loving me. *Enough*," I bit back.

The look on his face at my words would have broken me if I wasn't already broken. Anger etched across his features, closing the gap between us, his hands finding my shoulders and pinning me against the wardrobe. My mouth remained straight, the look on my face calm, unbothered.

"You are *mine*, Raven. You *will* be my wife. We *will* get through this." Demands.

I held my left hand in front of his face, wiggling my fingers. My ring sparkled in the sunlight, and his eyes bulged at my cruel gesture. "Should've proposed when you had the chance."

He glared at me. "So, that's just in then? You're done with me?" His voice was dark, his tone dripping with fury.

I shrugged in response. His grip on my shoulders tightened as he pressed me farther into the wardrobe until I felt like I was part of its structure. His face closed in on mine, and his lips pressed against the corner of my mouth. He took a deep breath of my scent, and I turned my head away from him, but his mouth was next to my ear. "You don't love me anymore?" he growled, his hips pressing against mine. I felt how hard he was through the fabric of my dress. He wanted me even when I wasn't sure I wanted him anymore.

"I don't even know who you are," I replied evenly.

A low, guttural rumble came from the back of his throat, his fingers surely leaving marks on my skin from how hard he shoved them into me. "I'm the man who isn't letting you get away." he roared against my skin. "I'm the same man who's loved you, protected you...."

"Lied to me, kept secrets from me, *used* me," I interrupted.

His head lifted at that, catching my eyes with his. His fingers loosened on my shoulders for only a second before a dark grin spread across his face, and the pressure was back. "You let me put you back together once. You'll let me do it again."

He released me, my skin biting from the loss of pressure. I looked down at my shoulders and saw the yellow bruises forming under my skin. He stared at them, too, his features twisting at sight. "Is this how you want me, Cade? Bruised by your anger?"

I shoved past him, pulling at my shoulders sleeves to try to cover what he'd just done. Still, I couldn't find the effort to cry. "I am allowed to be hurt by what you've done." I whirled, facing his back now as he still stared at my wardrobe, where he just had me pinned. I inhaled a steady breath, trying to pull at the small remnants of my confidence. "Of course, I still love you. But I also hate you. And you will not put your hands on me like that again, or I will have you removed and banished."

The man who turned to face me was a shell of Cade. His eyes were dripping tears, regret coating his features. "I'm sorry," he rasped, lifting his hands to stare at his fingers.

I knew he hated himself at that moment, being the one who brought me pain. But he had still done it. Brought me pain. Emotional and physical. I couldn't let him off the hook — not yet. But my heart still broke again, seeing him there, scared of losing me, losing us.

I took a small step toward him and then another until we were an arm's length apart. I stood there until he dropped his hands to meet my eyes, his shoulders sagging. "Just give me time. You owe me that," I whispered.

His body shook as tears fell down his face. He wanted to reach for me but stopped, fighting to keep his arms to his sides. "Don't leave me, Raven." He fell to his knees in front of me, wrapping his arms around my lower back, his face falling against my thighs.

Still, I could not conjure up emotion. I just rested one hand on his head, feeling like an empty vessel. "Please believe that I don't want to," was all I could manage. I didn't know if that was true.

———

We stayed like that until I told him we needed to try and eat something. He reluctantly released me and stood, holding his arm out to ask permission to lead me there. My body felt heavy, so I took his arm and linked mine through it. We started toward the dining hall like we'd done so many mornings before.

The memories of happier mornings weighed thickly on my shoulders, sore from the bruises on my skin. He would steal a glance at me, but I kept my eyes forward. He wanted something out of me that I couldn't give him.

Reassurance.

———

As we entered the dining room, I heard the scuffle of chairs. My eyes lifted to see who we'd be dining with this morning. I met Zeke's eyes first, who was staring at my dress. My dream. It was a blurry mess, but I was wearing this, and he was there. His gaze on me was soft as he met my eyes. I wanted to go to him, but Cade grabbed my wrist, and I flinched, keeping still.

Zeke's eyes narrowed as he noticed.

My eyes left him and moved to John. "*You*," I bit out. I wasn't sure why I was so upset at the sight of him, but he knew Zeke, and he had kept that from me. I knew their conversation in the courtyard was more than what he had told me.

"Raven," he said, already compiling his list of defenses.

I pulled my arm from Cade's and stomped toward where he stood next to his chair. Quickly, Zeke hopped in between us and held his palms up toward me. Cade was beside me quickly, glaring at Zeke. "Hear him out first," Zeke said before he took a tentative step to the side.

I folded my arms across my chest and waited for how he could possibly explain being involved in any of this. I waited for the sack of bullshit he was about to throw on me. Instead, what he said nearly knocked me on my ass.

"Zeke is my son," he said upon exhaling.

My eyes widened, shock written across my face as his words washed over me. What could I even say? What questions could I even ask? "I literally cannot with you people anymore," was all I managed before I turned on my heel and took my seat at the head of the table. All three men were silent as they took their seats after me. My eyes moved back and forth between John and Zeke, trying to see a resemblance and figure out how I could've missed this. "You look nothing alike."

"He looks like his mother," John grumbled in response.

Zeke's jaw tic, and his knuckles went white around the apple he held. I turned my gaze to Cade, who shook his head at me, silently telling me he had no idea. I watched as he studied the two men. I didn't have it in me to ask any more questions because I just didn't fucking care. I was surrounded by too many men, and I wondered if that was why I always had headaches.

Another few moments of silence passed by before I cleared my throat, and six eyes snapped at me. I met Zeke's first. "I have decided to accept your invitation to visit Reales."

Cade slumped against his chair.

"But I don't want to travel alone. I'd like Cade to accompany me with a handful of our soldiers. They can follow behind us on one of our ships since I presume your ship is still here somewhere?"

Zeke shot me a pompous grin.

I glared. He wasn't going to tell me where. "Great. I will be sailing with you."

Cade sat up and slammed his fist on the table. "Over my dead body," he snapped at me.

"That can be arranged," Zeke replied unhurriedly, taking a bite of his apple.

I ignored him and looked at Cade, rolling my eyes as his narrowed on me. "Cade, I am not going to be on a ship full of men for a week. That's too much man."

"I bet she never says that about you," Zeke piped in.

I exhaled an annoyed breath.

"You can stay below deck in my quarters," Cade countered.

I knew exactly what he was insinuating and why he was doing it here, in front of Zeke. I was not in the mood for their pissing contest over me. "Zeke's bed is comfortable. I'll be fine for the week." The look on my face remained cool, even as jealousy spread across Cade's face, imagining how I could know that detail about another man's bed.

Zeke snorted. Cade remained silent.

"Good. It's settled, then. We can leave this evening before the sun starts to set."

The tension in the room was so thick that I was surprised none of us had suffocated yet. John kept a weary look on his face. And it was about to get so much fucking worse because as I leaned forward to reach for an apple, the fabric of my sleeve fell down my shoulder, revealing the yellow pigment bubbling under my skin. I cursed under my breath as Zeke's eyes snapped to my skin, and I closed my eyes as pure rage crossed his face.

I peeked one eye open to see his hand curled into a fist, dropping the apple he'd eaten to the table. His eyes slowly moved from my skin to Cade as his forearms leaned against the top of the table. "Did you do that?" His voice was low, his jaw tightening and releasing as he tried to keep his fury in check until he had confirmation.

Cade was silent as he met Zeke's stare. I knew exactly what was about to happen. John met my eyes. We both braced.

Before I could take another breath, Zeke's chair flew out from underneath him as he stood, and then he was across the room, pulling Cade up from his chair and pinning him against the wall with his forearm across his chest.

He slammed him again, and Cade's eyes went out of focus for a split second before settling on Zeke's face again. "You bruised her," Zeke snarled.

Cade's eyes flashed to my skin quickly and then back to Zeke.

"If I knew it wouldn't destroy her, I would fucking kill you where you stand." He released Cade, but only to pull his arm back and shoot it forward, connecting his fist with Cade's jaw.

I jumped at the sound of flesh meeting bone and watched as Cade stumbled sideways, wrapping his hand around his jaw as he tried to catch himself. Zeke didn't give him time to recover before he gripped him by the collar and pushed him back against the wall. "But I swear, Cade..." his voice could cut glass, "If you ever fucking hurt her again, not even Hades himself will let me into hell for what I will unleash on you."

He released Cade, who stumbled forward from the punch, and release of pressure from Zeke's hold on him. Zeke walked to me and reached his hand to wrap around mine, pulling me from my chair. He dragged me behind him as we exited the dining room. I didn't know where he was taking me, but I had to put forth a lot of energy to keep up with his long strides.

He noticed and stopped, wrapping his arms around my waist and pulling me up to cradle against his chest, his entire body shaking with rage as he started walking us again.

He dropped me to my feet once we were out in the open air of the courtyard. He started pacing, his hands tangling in his hair as he looked at my yellowed skin. He couldn't stand to see me in pain, which was ironic since he shot me with an arrow not too long ago. My mouth fell slack as the realization fell on me like snow during a winter storm. "You're not the one who shot me," I breathed, my eyes going out of focus as I stared at the wall.

He stopped pacing but kept his hands in his hair, his chest heaving with rapid breaths. "I'm not the one who shot you."

CHAPTER TWENTY-SEVEN

Raven

I paced, my hands palming my eyes until I could see colors. I was starting to get delirious from the amount of information my brain had to take in the last twelve hours. "Then why... why did you say that you did?" I asked him through clenched teeth.

"Technically, *technically*," he said.

I slowly lowered my hands from my eyes to narrow them.

"I never did. I just didn't deny that it was me."

I threw my arms up in frustration. "How is that any better?!"

He quickly closed the space between us, and I took a half-step back. "You needed me to be your villain, so I became it. And..."

I shoved his chest. "*And?*" I drew out the word in frustration.

"And if you knew who it was, it would've foiled our entire plan."

I growled and shoved him again. He didn't move, and that only made me angrier. "Stop talking in dribs and drabs. Just answer a question fully."

A tiny smile played on his lips at my anger.

I growled again, fisting my hair in my hands. "I feel like I'm going fucking crazy."

He drew in a breath and looked to the ground, contemplating. "It was John."

I turned on my heel to walk back inside, but he grabbed my wrist and pulled me backward. I shoved at him again, but he didn't let go. "Please just trust me when I tell you that I handled it," he said while trying to get a grip on my flailing arms.

"I can handle it!" I barked, trying to turn again.

His arms wrapped around me, and he lifted me off the ground, carrying me toward the gate. I thrashed and warmed my hands with my fire, hitting his arms with my fists, but it did nothing to him. "Why can't I burn you?!"

He didn't answer, and I started kicking my legs in frustration. "You need a break," he said in amusement.

I laughed out loud at that, irritation looming. "A break. Right. I need a fucking break like I need a hole in my head."

He put me on my feet once we were outside the gate and held his palms up, sensing the rage threatening to overtake me. "Breathe, Raven."

His words tickled my ear. "Who *are* you?" I asked him while staring down at my warm hands, trying to figure out why I was unable to hurt him.

He sighed and ran his hand through his hair again. "Questions that will be answered when we get to Reales."

I stomped, balling my fists at my sides, and he bit his lip to keep from smiling. "Stop evading me," I demanded.

"I'm not trying to evade you, Raven." He loosened a long sigh and rubbed the back of his neck. "I just need you to trust me for a little longer."

I scoffed, shaking my head furiously. "I don't trust anyone."

His features softened at my words, and his head tilted slightly. "You trust me."

I palmed my eyes again, blowing a bubble in my cheeks. He was right. Despite everything, I still trusted him and didn't know why.

"I like it when you're angry," he told me, his voice low.

I held one of my hands toward him and wagged my finger back and forth. "Don't. Don't flirt with me right now. I hate all of you at the moment."

He chuckled darkly. I could sense him growing closer to me without even needing to open my eyes. "Hate me then."

My heart thundered in my ears at the way his voice scratched. His body lightly pressed against mine, and he pulled my hands away from my eyes. I looked up at him through my lashes. His eyes were dark on mine as his hand reached up to touch my shoulder, lightly gliding over the bruise. "Does it hurt?"

My eyes closed at his touch, and my head fell backward, a soft breath escaping my lips. His touch soothed my every ache.

"Raven," he whispered.

My body felt *awake*. Damn him. Damn this hold he had on me. I wanted him. More than anything, I wanted to let him touch every inch of me. But instead, I raised my head back up and wrapped my fingers around his, removing them from my skin as I shook my head. "I have to find new ways to release other than sex." Even as I said it, my mouth watered for him.

His fingers threaded through mine, and he pulled me flush against him. My tongue licked over my lips as I stared at his full mouth, remembering how it felt on mine. He walked us backward until my spine hit the wall. "This is about more than sex, Raven. I feel like I need to touch you to breathe." His voice was strained, and he leaned into me, pressing his lips lightly against my throat. My pulse beat against his lips, and he groaned into my skin.

I drew in a shaky breath and pulled my fingers away from his, pushing them between our chests. "Do you tell Jeanine that, too?" My voice was cold as I pushed him off of me.

His eyes were like death as he took me in, his forbidden fruit that he was so desperate to taste again. "Don't," he warned.

I ignored his threatening tone and lifted my fingers to my lips, rubbing the pad of my thumb over my bottom one. He tracked my movement and bared his teeth, putting his palms against the wall on either side of me, caging me in. "You have no fucking idea what you're talking about."

"You belong to someone else."

He slammed his palm against the wall at my words, but I didn't move, keeping my nonchalant posture, and shrugged my shoulders. "We have to go to Reales with the understanding that we are nothing."

"Nothing?" he repeated back to me, disbelief in his tone.

"Nothing," I bit out through clenched teeth.

"We are *everything*."

And then his mouth was on mine. Everything I felt for him last night, dancing with him, kissing him, all bubbled up, and I opened my mouth for him. His tongue collided with mine. This was where I belonged. With him.

I threw my arms around his neck and threaded his hair through my fingers. I needed every piece of me touching him.

His hands wrapped around my waist, and his kiss became hungrier, desperate. This was more than a kiss. It was oxygen. It was life. It was strings of a harp, creating a melody just for us. It was beautiful and heartbreaking, and everything. Just everything.

But he was the one who broke from me. He took a step back, putting his fist to his mouth, and shook his head at me. I was breathless, my cheeks reddening from his rejection. I covered my face with my hands, ashamed. Embarrassed.

"Raven," he said.

I pushed off the wall and walked away from him. He groaned and started toward me, but I quickly turned and put my hand out. "No," I cracked out.

He halted.

"Stop. Whatever this is, please just stop. You're killing me," I whispered, hot tears in my eyes. "No more."

He hung his head. I turned to leave again, but right before I entered the gate, I called over my shoulder, "Remind me the colors of Reales crest again? I want to show respect to Mira."

A beat of silence. I didn't think he would answer, but right before I took another step, he did.

"Black and green."

I was back in Cade's room soon after leaving Zeke, pulling dresses out of the wardrobe to put into my large trunk. I added some of my fitted leathers underneath the dresses, just in case I got the chance to explore the kingdom of Reales alone.

Cade stood behind me, watching as I packed. He put his hand on top of mine, and I paused. "You know you can't go out alone at night, right?" He asked me, eyeing the leathers that peeked from underneath my dresses. He really did know me too well.

But I did know, and as frustrating as it was, he was right. I was the queen of another kingdom. It'd be dangerous for me to explore anywhere new on my own. But oddly, I felt like I knew parts of Reales from the fractured pieces of my dreams.

I loosened a sigh but nodded. "I won't go unless you're there. Or Zeke."

Cade's hand released mine at the mention of Zeke's name, and he took a step back from me, his hands resting on his hips. "Do I need to be apprehensive about Zeke?"

It was a fair question. Things between Cade and me were so fucked up, and I could sense his distress at the thought of me spending time with Zeke alone. Should he be worried? Zeke kept telling me we couldn't happen, yet he couldn't keep his hands off me whenever we were together. But he kept leading me on, and then he'd pull away again. I didn't know how to answer that question when I couldn't get an answer of my own.

I dropped the clothes in my hand and let them fall in a heap inside the trunk, and then I turned to face Cade. I looked at him, really looked at him, for the first time since we left the ballroom last night. My Cade was still in there somewhere. The Cade that helped me rule a kingdom for so long. The one who took me swimming so I wouldn't feel suffocated inside the palace walls.

But in between now and then, so much had happened. He'd harmed me physically and mentally, and I wasn't sure how we could recover from that. His jaw was red from Zeke's punch this morning, and even though he had hurt me, I still never wished for any pain for him. I guessed that was because of having an unhealthy attachment to another being. No matter what they may do to you, you still want to soothe all their pain.

And despite all the bad between us right now, I still wanted him on this trip with me.

So, I shook my head at his question, whether I was sure it was true or not. We were all liars, anyway.

His entire body relaxed like he'd been holding tension since we parted this morning.

He took a tentative step toward me, and I didn't move away. He took advantage of my temporary agreement to let him touch me again. He took another small step until there was hardly any space between us. More than anything, I wished to lose myself in him before we left. But I couldn't.

I was truthful with Zeke. I wanted to find a different way to release my anticipation, my tension. But as my hands reached out and wrapped around the hard muscles of his arms, he didn't let me think about it before he leaned into me and caught my mouth in a soft kiss.

The tip of his tongue pressed gently against my lips. I hesitated before opening slightly for him, letting his tongue move in and find mine. He wrapped his hands around my waist, pulling at the fabric of my dress as if he wanted to tear through it so that he could feel my skin.

My head tilted to the side, and he broke our kiss to push his lips against my throat, leaving feathery kisses along my skin. I could feel his hardness right against my sex. How easy it would be just to let him erase all the pain. But then that would mean it was okay that he did what he did, that everything could go back to normal between us. And it couldn't.

As the lust started dissipating and my logical thoughts rushed to the forefront of my mind, I shook my head and took a step back from him. His eyes closed as he exhaled, his hands raised like he was holding me, but they slowly fell to his side. "You were mine yesterday," he said, his voice hitching.

"Do I need to go fuck someone else to get your attention?" His eyes opened, but nothing was soft about how he looked at me. He was suffering, and I was his only antidote.

But his words stung, and I left him standing there to walk out to the balcony, my fingers gripping the edge of the railing.

His boots scuffed the ground as he came up behind me, his forehead resting against my shoulder. "I'm sorry," he whispered, kissing me gently. "I didn't mean that."

"It's worrisome that your first thought when I'm not all over you is to go bury yourself in someone else," I said blandly. But there was a part of me that didn't care anymore.

"That's not what...." He started to say, shaking his head against my spine. "I don't want to. I didn't mean it, Raven. Come here." He put his hands on my arms and slowly turned me to face him. His eyes bored into my hollow ones, taking my hands and resting them against his chest. "We only had weeks, Raven. Weeks together."

I leaned forward and rested my forehead against our woven hands, nodding. There was so much unspoken between us, but I didn't know where or how to begin. I couldn't sort through anything that'd happened over the last few hours, and I certainly couldn't promise him a future right now. Not when I felt so double-crossed by him. "I love you," I whispered against our hands. And I did. I always would, no matter how this ended.

And it was the only thing that made sense right now.

Wetness fell against the top of my head, and I raised just enough to meet his eyes. Tears were falling down his cheeks, and I wiped them away with the pad of my thumb, wishing I could create tears of my own. "Let that be enough for now," I whispered, raising on the tips of my toes to brush my lips across his.

He didn't push for more. He just wrapped his arms around me and held me against him. "Always," he assured me.

But like I said, we were all liars.

Cade left me later to assemble a small troop to accompany us to Reales. I didn't feel threatened — but at this point, I'd rather be safe than sorry. My emotions were spent, and my magic was seemingly lying dormant until I recovered. At least, until Zeke was around me. He seemed to have a knack for knowing how to rile me up.

It would just be me, Zeke, Cade, John, a crew, and a handful of soldiers coming along on this trip. I'd be with Zeke on his ship, and the rest of the men would be on one of Seolia's ships, following close behind us. If I knew Cade, which I did, he'd remain on our tail the entire time, able to see our every move.

He asked me to stay with him again, but I declined. Simply for the fact that I didn't want to be on a ship with at least ten men for a week. After a little more convincing that it was indeed the only reason, he relented and said he understood. But he was still brooding when he left me to finish packing, and I had a feeling it would continue the entire time we were apart.

I followed my trunk being carried out of the castle by two of my servants, stopping to greet Luisa in the courtyard. She encased me in a big hug and promised to keep the kingdom running while we were gone. I didn't plan on being absent for too long, only packing enough clothes for a two-week-long excursion — one of those weeks being on the ship.

I made Luisa promise to check on Isla while I was gone, and she agreed. I was still keeping Isla at a safe distance, desperate to protect her, but when I stepped outside the castle gates, she was there waiting for me.

"Don't be mad," she said, smiling.

I walked right into her arms for one of her big hugs.

"I listened and didn't attend the ball, but I wasn't about to let you leave for two weeks without saying goodbye."

"How did you even know?" I asked through a giggle, shaking my head at my stubborn aunt.

Cade walked up and put his arms around both of us, kissing the top of Isla's head. "I may have had something to do with that."

Isla pulled back from the two of us, only to grab one of our hands and tug at them while she spoke, "You two be safe while you're out exploring the world. Come back to me in one piece, please." Her eyes narrowed at me while she talked.

We both laughed as we embraced once more before Isla began the trek back to her cottage. I watched her for a moment as I leaned my head against Cade's chest. "Promise me you'll always keep her safe."

Cade squeezed my shoulders, kissing the top of my head. "I always promise to keep both of you safe."

I didn't know why this moment made me cup his cheek with my hand and press my lips to his, but I did. He responded hungrily and then started nipping at my nose. I erupted into giggles, and his bright smile could compete with the sun. "There's my girl," he muttered against my mouth.

"Get it all out now."

We both turned our heads to look at Zeke as he passed us, stuck together like glue. Cade's body tensed, and I muttered a curse word and patted his stomach. "We should head to the harbor. We need to leave before it gets dark," I said.

Cade still watched after Zeke, his hand curling into a fist.

"Hey." I threw all my weight behind that word to snap his attention back to me.

"The first fucking time I've felt normal since last night, and again, he ruins it," Cade grumbled, taking my hand in his and pulling me into step beside him.

"Don't let him do that, Cade. Don't let him diminish our moments," I told him.

He squeezed my hand in response.

But when his fingers pressed against the diamond ring still on my finger, he raised it to look at it, his jaw tightening again. "Why do you wear this?"

I bit down on my bottom lip and gave him a slight shrug. "He said there'd be an answer for this in Reales."

"But do you have to wear it now? You're not going to marry him, right?"

I tugged at Cade's hand to stop our walk and shook my head. "No, Cade, I'm not going to marry him. You're too worked up."

He wrapped an arm around my waist, pulling me flush against him. "Do you like it?"

Not particularly, but I threw my arms around his neck and kissed the corner of his mouth in response.

I stared at the diamond ring on my finger that glistened as I wrapped my fingers around Cade's shoulder. I was hypnotized by the way the starry diamonds shined and how it seemed to meld perfectly to my finger. The pear-shaped diamond reminded me of Zeke every time I looked at it.

I felt eyes on me, and I saw him standing a few feet away from us, the corner of his mouth tugged upward in an unholy grin. His gray eyes held me like that for a moment, and then his voice was deep in the recesses of my mind, pulling me to him.

Breathe, Raven.

He broke our locked gazes. And I was left breathless.

I requested that we stroll through the village, as it would be my last time to see it for two weeks. I waved goodbye to the villagers, taking a bouquet from Keaton, our flower shop owner, and complimenting him on how beautiful they were.

He said that he and his husband were trying to grow flowers with brighter colors in anticipation of winter finally ending. The flowers he gave me contained the deepest shades of gold and pink I'd ever seen, and I promised to keep them at my bedside for the journey.

Grace was next, and we shared a long hug. She promised to continue her daily duties of sorting through the books in the libraries, and I promised to bring her back new books from Reales. At that, she burst into tears and pulled me into another tight hug. Cade had to slowly separate us, laughing at how close I had become with the doe-eyed young girl. Grace blushed as Cade gave her a side-hug.

"You're going to break that girl's heart."

He clicked his tongue and shrugged. "I only like blondes."

I smacked his stomach, and he grunted before cackling. "There's that jealousy. Good to see it's still in there somewhere."

I rolled my eyes before yelping as a sudden weight smacked into my legs. I looked down and leaned to pick up the small girl who had attacked me. I shushed Eva's tears, wiping them away with my fingers. "I won't be gone forever, little one," I promised, letting her head fall to my shoulder. I swayed with her back and forth until she quieted.

I smiled at how Cade watched us with longing eyes. He was trying to envision a future for us. I kissed the top of Eva's head before gently setting her back to the ground, kneeling in front of her. "I am going to bring you a super special surprise, okay? So when you see my ship sailing in, you wait for me right here, and I'll come to find you."

Eva nodded, chewing on the fingers of one of her hands. "I love you, butterfly," she whispered, small tears falling down her cheeks again.

I threw my arms around her again, holding her to me until her mother came and gently pulled her away from me, touching my arm in gratitude for loving her daughter. I watched them walk away with a tug on my heart.

Cade's arm wrapped around my shoulders again, giving me a gentle tug. "We have to go, Raven."

———

He led me out of the village and down the grassy knolls into the harbor. When we stepped on the dock that housed the ship Cade would be sailing on, I froze in place as Jeanine made her way up to his ship. "Of course."

I broke away from Cade, crossing my arms over my chest.

Jeanine heard me, stopping her incline. She looked at me before turning her gaze back to the ship. I raised an eyebrow as she turned and descended the ramp. Cade wrapped his arm around my waist. My body was rigid.

"Hello, Queen Raven," Jeanine greeted me with a curtsy.

She really was stunning. Her hair was long, like mine, but a bright blonde. Her skin was so light it was almost translucent. And her deep blue eyes and perfectly pink lips had me envious. She and Cade would be a matching set. "Hello," I muttered. "The ball was beautiful. Thank you for your help."

"It was all Zeke's idea."

I cast my eyes down. She said his name so intimately.

"He wanted it to be special for you." Her voice was low, and she stared at me like she was trying to convey something.

My eyebrows drew in. Cade gripped my dress, and Jeanine's eyes flicked to his hand, but her gaze wasn't one of envy. It was something different. Concern. I cocked my head at her, and she was imploring me with her eyes, but I didn't know what she was trying to tell me. "I hope you have a good trip," was all I said.

She took a small step toward me, and Cade's grip only tightened, the fabric cinching tightly around my waist. She grabbed my hands and gave them a light squeeze. "He was right," she said.

I blinked in curiosity.

"He said you're the most exquisite thing he's ever seen."

My lips parted slightly. Why would he have said that to the woman he was with about me? I was about to say something when Cade said, "We need to go." His tone was clipped as he tried to pull me backward.

I stumbled back a half-step, and Jeanine's grip on my hands anchored me. "I think the queen can walk for herself." Jeanine's voice was steady as she addressed Cade, but she was still looking at me.

Cade responded by wrapping his arm around my shoulders and pulling me to him. Jeanine's eyes cut to his, and I stood there, bewildered by the entire exchange. Jeanine sighed and flashed me a bright smile. "I'll see you in Reales, Queen Raven."

I simply nodded as she released my hands and turned to walk back toward Cade's ship.

"Are you sure you don't want to stay with me? She can go with Zeke."

I was still watching her, trying to read between her lines.

"Raven?"

His voice cut through my daze. "Hmm?" I looked at him, and his jaw was set. "No, I'm okay, really. It'll be fine."

With his arm still around my shoulders, he used it to pull me until we faced one another. "Please come with me." There was something dark behind those blue eyes.

"Cade, no. I really just want a quiet week. Your men are loud."

"I'll tell them to be quiet. We can spend the week in my room. Come on." He tugged me with him.

I shook my head, trying to break free of his grasp. "Cade, no."

He sighed, releasing me. But now he was glaring at me. "I don't understand why you want to spend a week with him."

I shook my head, trying to reach for him, but he shook out of my grasp. "That's not it, Cade. What has gotten into you?"

I tried to grab him again, but he raised his arm to escape my grasp and knocked the tip of my chin. A sharp jolt of pain ripped through my bone. I groaned and grabbed it, massaging it in my fingers. He sighed, running his hand through his hair.

"I'm sorry," he grumbled, grabbing my chin that still stung. "It was an accident."

I heard footsteps behind us, and I shook out of his grasp, seeing Zeke approach us. "We need to go, Raven." His fists balled, and I knew he had witnessed what just happened.

"She'll be there in a second," Cade snapped, gripping the back of my dress again to keep me from moving. His irritation was getting out of control again.

Zeke didn't say anything but took a step toward me.

"I need to go," I muttered to Cade, glancing at him over my shoulder. "I'll see you in a week, okay?"

He stared down at me, contemplating something. Don't do it, I begged him silently. But he pulled me to him and planted a kiss on my mouth, threading his fingers in my hair. I could practically feel the steam coming from Zeke behind me.

Cade tried to deepen the kiss, but I stopped him and pulled my head back. "Let me go."

"I love you," he said aloud.

I knew he wouldn't release me until I said it. My mouth felt dry. "I love you," I muttered back.

He released me with a smug grin as he looked at Zeke. My cheeks heated as I turned, keeping my eyes on the ground as I passed by Zeke and walked to his ship. I climbed the ramp, and I heard him right behind me.

"You know you have the ability to burn people, right?" His tone was heavy with frustration as he pulled the ramp back on his ship.

I let the tears I'd been holding back finally flood my eyes. "He didn't mean to," I sighed.

I expected us to pull away from the dock, but he came to me and peered down at me, gently brushing my chin with his fingers. I couldn't look at him. "Stop letting him have the chance."

A tear escaped down my cheek.

"Raven," he whispered.

All I could do was stare at his chest. I felt ashamed.

He sighed as he released me.

I watched him cast off lines and pull in the fenders as the wind shifted the boat, blowing us away from the dock. I heard Cade shouting at the crew to mirror us as we glided. He stood against the railing of his ship, his arms crossed as he watched us.

"Has he always been like this?" Zeke asked.

I shook my head, staring at Cade, who felt more like a stranger now. "No."

I turned from Cade and wrapped my arms around my waist. I felt sheepish, swinging my foot back and forth against the deck. I glanced up at Zeke. His arms were covered in long sleeves, but I could see the muscles underneath as he steered us forward once we'd safely cleared the docks.

Drool pooled in my mouth at the sight of his arms going to work. I silently cursed, diverting my attention to the water below us.

"That's it? That's all you're going to give me?"

My fingers gripped the boat railing as we swayed, the waters choppy as we started off the harbor. "What else do you want me to say?" I was nauseous, leaning over the railing to try and steady myself.

"When did it start?"

I turned his question over in my head. When did what start? He hadn't touched me until this morning. Though, he had been a little angrier lately. "He's just... it's been a stressful few weeks."

Zeke scoffed, but I couldn't look at him. I was trying to stop myself from upheaving my breakfast.

"She's beautiful. Angelic."

He sighed, knowing who I was referring to. He was quiet as a tear fell down my cheek. I hated how insecure I felt all the time. I used to be more confident. I had fucking magic running through my veins, and I was falling apart all the time at my inability to let people go and realize my worth. But I had one question that I didn't want the answer to. One question that made me sicker than the rocking of the boat.

"Why did you need me when you had her?"

"Raven." My name was a warning on his lips.

I bent over the railing quickly and upheaved the very little I'd eaten in the last two days into the water. I groaned and felt him come up behind me, pulling my hair back as I did it again.

At this point, I wasn't sure if it was from the boat rocking or the emotional repercussions of all my decisions over the last three months.

When I had nothing left in my stomach, I pulled up only to turn and slide down the wall, pulling my knees to my chest and resting my chin on them. All the color had drained from my face, and I closed my eyes.

His fingers brushed my cheek. "You're a mess."

"Understatement of the year," I whispered.

CHAPTER TWENTY-EIGHT

Raven

I was on my back, looking up at the stars from the deck. He'd left me alone to steer us farther into the channel, but he was only a body's length away behind my head. Cade's ship maintained a distance of five hundred yards from where we were. The water had calmed and wasn't choppy anymore, which meant my stomach had settled.

So, I just watched. And thought.

My hair was sprawled around me, and I'd changed into a silky black set of loose pants and a shirt that rustled in the wind, exposing my belly button. I'd left the top two buttons undone to feel the cold wind on my skin, soothing my nausea. My legs were flat against the deck and crossed at the ankles. I'd tucked my arm under my head, tilting my chin toward the sky.

I heard the soft breathing of him behind me. I kept replaying all of his questions in my mind. And he was absolutely right about all of it. What Cade did, touching me like that this morning, was wrong. And maybe because I healed so quickly, I didn't have constant reminders of it on my skin, and I could offer him forgiveness quicker. It was a stupid excuse, and I knew it. I should've been giving him the cold shoulder.

But what Zeke couldn't understand was that Cade had been my best friend for a very long time. It was nearly impossible to just cut someone off after so long. Especially after what we'd become to one another in the last few weeks since Zeke left me. Cade scooped me up and soothed my searing pain from the imprint Zeke had left me on mentally. He promised to love me forever, wanting me to become his wife one day. He wanted a future with me. Zeke walked away from me.

I'll never love anyone as I love you, Zeke had told me last night on the dock, and the words made goose bumps rise on my skin. He struggled to stay away from me, but I didn't understand why he had to. And all he'd tell me was that we couldn't happen. Hearing that repeatedly made it hard to continue latching on to him.

Maybe this week away from Cade would be good. It'd give me a chance to really think about what he'd done to me, the secrets he held. I could never thoroughly think through anything when he was always there, distracting me with his passion for me.

But in all reality, he'd hidden something huge about my life from me. He spent so many nights with me listening to how I wanted an answer about why I was in Seolia and how I arrived there. And the entire time, Cade and August withheld that information from me. And I never would've known had Zeke not told me in the library. "How did you know that Cade knew where I came from?" I asked Zeke quietly.

He didn't look at me, keeping his eyes focused on the water, but his mouth pinched. "John," was all he said.

Right, of course.

My arm shot up as I pointed to the sky. "Shooting star. I'll let you have this one."

He closed his eyes briefly and then opened them again, refocusing on the vast channel in front of us.

"What'd you wish for?"

He remained silent, giving me a slight shake of his head.

"Are you really not going to tell me? I *gave* that to you."

A ghost of a smile played across his mouth. "If I tell you, it won't come true."

"Did you wish for me to stop bugging you?"

"I wish I had now," he replied dryly.

I started to giggle. "I'll try and find another one for you."

More comfortable silence lingered between us. There was so much we hadn't said, but I feared the damage had already been done, and we couldn't turn back. It'd become too tangled. I felt like I was constantly upside down, falling down a dark hole with no light to guide me—just more questions with no answers.

The stars above me flickered, talking back to me, trying to reason away my chaotic thoughts. Unknot them. "If you never left, where did you get this?" I held up my hand, amazed at how the stars along my band seemed to blend into the night sky.

He remained quiet. I tilted my head back to glance at him; he was staring at my ring. I sighed softly, returning my gaze to the ring. "It looks like me." I didn't know how else to say it, but in some unearthly way, it looked like it was meant to be on my finger. "It looks like us."

But how could he have found it so quickly? We rarely had jewelry in the village. "And why are we engaged? I do not understand what that has to do with Mira. I know it's not because you want to marry me."

"There's a lot you don't know, Raven," he replied.

I muttered something inaudible under my breath. There was a lot I didn't know because no one would tell me anything. And he wasn't relenting. I wiggled my ring finger back and forth, and the stars twinkled. I could feel him watching me from above. "I used to feel like you put the stars in my sky," I mumbled, my eyebrows drawing in as my eyes went unfocused, the diamond stars blurring. "But then you burned them out."

I wished I could feel something again instead of this emptiness. I dropped my hand to my stomach, giving up on trying to get anything out of him.

The night was heavy on us, the sky almost black. Swaying on the boat and staring into the sky was the most peaceful I'd felt in a very long time. "Sometimes I think I was a star in another life," I said sleepily, yawning. "Stealing across the sky, granting wishes to those who felt like they had nothing to hope for."

Another yawn; my eyelids were starting to flutter closed. "Burning, burning," my voice was a whisper, "until I had nothing left to give." The glistening of another shooting star was the last thing I saw before my eyes closed. "Make a wish, baby."

I drifted into a deep sleep.

I dreamed of being in the Black Forest. I was chasing after one of my flames, letting it lead me through the winding trees until I stopped in front of the spring.

I took one step closer. Then two, three. I stood in front of it, watching the steam rise from the ripples. I stared at my reflection in the water, my dark green eyes appearing black, matching my hair braided on top of my head. I was wearing my soft velvet red ball gown again.

A strong hand wrapped around mine and pulled me into an embrace. Hands wrapped around my waist, and my arms circled a pair of broad shoulders. Zeke. My eyes rose to meet his. "Just dance with me tonight," he purred.

And then we were spinning. The trees and black sky above us blurred as he twirled me out and back to him, his lips immediately pressing against my forehead.

"The moon has nothing on you, baby."

My eyes snapped open as I gasped for air. I started to cough as I sat up, looked around, and realized that I was still on deck, but the sun was dawning across the horizon.

I whipped my head around to see Zeke sitting next to me, his forearms resting on his knees that were drawn up. I stared at him, my chest rising and falling as I tried to draw deep breaths. "How are you doing that?" I asked him in between breaths.

He just watched me, the pupils of his eyes dilating. And then he stood and walked away. I jumped and followed him, yanking his elbow to tug him back to face me. "How do you keep invading my dreams?"

He just shook his head.

I was tired of his lack of words. I shoved him, and he took a half-step back. And then I did it again and again until he was pushed back against the ship's railing. "Tell me."

"That's complicated," was all he deigned to reply.

"Complicated," I repeated.

He dipped his chin once.

Another moment of silence. I was very frustrated. "Can you be more specific?" I asked him, huffing.

He hesitated, and I shoved him again, ignoring the slight grin that danced across his lips. "I can infiltrate your dreams, your mind. Mentally communicate with you."

His voice in my head.

"Tell me to breathe?"

Another slow nod.

My mouth fell open, and my hands rose to tangle into my hair as I turned away from him, pacing across the deck. "But how," I breathed, my mind dizzy.

"Raven…" he started but stopped, pinching the bridge of his nose. I'd learned that he did that often when he was exasperated.

"You know what?" I held my palms up to him. "I don't want to know." I turned and left him standing there as I pulled up the hatch door that led down to the cabin.

I started down the steep stairs, throwing curse words around. I banged my forehead against the wall as I reached the bottom. It was dark and wasn't on purpose, but it felt good, so I did it again. I needed to restart my brain somehow.

I heard him clomping down the stairs, and I backed away from him, putting my hands on my hips as I glared. He licked his lips, soaking up the anger pooling in my belly. I was tired of doing nothing but feeling sorry for myself for the last three months, wondering about who I was and why I never seemed to be enough for anyone to love without restraint.

Bit by bit, as the seconds ticked by me, I felt my confidence stick to my skin, clawing to get back in. Constantly doubting myself, continuing to trust the one person who'd held secrets from me for fifteen years, who hurt me. I needed to push that side of myself down now. "You want anger? Come here." I beckoned him forward with my finger.

He didn't hesitate and walked to me briskly, closing the space between us. I threaded our hands together and willed my fire to the surface, lighting my skin up as I shifted into Blaze. I felt my fiery red bob cutting at my jawline, my eyes changing. I lit flames in my hands, letting them burn his skin.

"There's my little demon."

His little demon.

His eyes never left mine, and I did it again, my sparks growing. "Don't stop," he snarled.

I released his hands and moved mine under his shirt, lighting against the skin of his stomach. He groaned, but it wasn't from pain. It was pure ecstasy. I panted as Blaze overtook me and coursed through my veins until all I felt was heat. I moaned, rolling my head back as I welcomed my old friend, who I'd kept down for too long.

His eyes roamed over my exposed throat, and he leaned into me, pressing his lips against where my neck met my shoulder. I wrapped a hand around his throat and shoved him off of me. He took one look at me — the way my chest moved up and down rapidly, my flames dancing across my palms, the way my red hair framed my face, the fire that seemed to swim in my irises — and then he was back to me, his mouth crashing into mine, our tongues coming together hungrily.

I extinguished my flames to weave my hands in his hair and pulled hard, making his head break from mine, and licked up the column of his neck. He groaned at the feel of my hot tongue on his skin, and I bit him then, taking his skin between my teeth and tugged. He grasped my chin and pulled me off him, shoving me against the wall and pinning me with his hips.

He cupped my face in his hand, and I leaned into him, peering up at him through my lashes. He leered at me like I was a siren pulling him under. His mouth came to mine again, but he was slower now, the tips of our tongues teasing one another's, moving leisurely. And we stayed like that, making up for our lost weeks. The constant pull to each other, only to be separated again. But then I remembered that he had left me, too.

I shoved at him again. He took a step back, shaking his head. "Don't, Raven," he demanded, desperate.

"You stopped fighting for us," I murmured, tears trickling down my cheeks.

He was back to me, kissing them away, wrapping his arm around my waist, and tilting my chin to look at him. He leaned his forehead against mine. I felt his hot breath on my skin and drew it in, wanting to taste him again on my tongue.

"I am still fighting for us, Raven."

I shook my head and put my hands on his cheeks, lighting my skin again, but he didn't move. "Why doesn't it hurt you?"

"Because Raven…" he started, but then he kissed my lips softly.

I tilted my head back, letting him take more of me, deepening our kiss. His hands pressed into my back like he wanted to meld us together, make me a permanent part of him. The intensity made me thirst for air, and I pulled back again, imploring him with my eyes. "Why can't I stay away from you?"

He sighed softly against my mouth. It made the hairs on the back of my neck stand up. "Because," he began again, staring deep into my eyes like he was touching my soul, "we're mirror souls, Raven."

He kissed me again when my mouth fell open before pulling back just enough to whisper against my lips, "Twin flames."

———

One day. It'd been one day since I left Cade and here I was, already pressed against Zeke, and now I was learning that our very souls may be tied together by force more extraordinary than one could understand.

I stared at him, blinking quickly as I digested—twin flames. Two souls ripped apart, destined to find one another in every universe. Twin flames were a folktale. They hadn't been found in a very long time. "How…" I started, but I wasn't sure what to ask.

He pulled me off the wall and took my hand into his. "I can't think when we're down here together."

I followed him back up the stairs to the deck. Once we were back out in the open, my eyes roamed the open water to look for Cade's ship. I spotted it in the distance, having fallen farther behind us since last night. "I needed to give us some space," he muttered, pulling my hand to follow him to the ship's bow.

I was impressed that he was able to take the lead so quickly. He leaned his forearms against the wooden rail, and I leaned with him, looking at the water beneath us as we glided over it. "Twin flames," I repeated, nodding my head absentmindedly as I shifted back into myself.

He was quiet as he stared at the water. "I knew the night I saw you at the Festival of Dreams. As soon as you stepped into the crowd, you were lit by the flames of the bonfire and my soul connected to yours like a magnet. I recognized myself in you. I had flashes of life before ours. I could feel touches. Hear your name. The next day, when we met in your throne room, you stuttered when you saw me. That's when I was sure that the person I was there to seek out and bring back with me was the very person who held the other half of my soul."

I reached for his hand and gave it a gentle squeeze, urging him to continue.

"That first night, when I took you to the spring, I was honest when I told you that I didn't bring you there for… that," he said with a grin. "But then you kissed me, Raven. And everything I felt from the night before came flooding back. I could feel you in ways I hadn't felt you here in this lifetime."

"But you were so damn angry all the time. I felt a responsibility to help bring that out. Relish it. Help you accept that it's who you are. You always seem to push away everything you're feeling, but it felt like my sole purpose was to help you grow."

His jaw clenched, drawing in a sharp breath before he continued, "I could tell from watching the two of you argue in the throne room that Cade wanted you. So, I fed off that. Even if it killed me to do it, I wedged myself between the two of you just enough for you to finally start fighting back. Admit to yourself that you may want him, let that fury and envy consume you."

Tears slipped down my cheeks, but I remained quiet.

"But, I couldn't stay away from you, Raven. I knew you were conflicted. And I was, too. Because bringing you back to Reales was a mission. And I knew you hadn't realized yet what I had. That we're destined, but I couldn't... I had to walk away from you that night, or I never would've been able to."

I licked my lips, tasting the salt from my tears. "Then why do you keep telling me we can't happen?"

He rubbed his thumb over my fingers as he contemplated my question. "We can't. Not right now. I can't explain all of that yet, but you'll understand soon. It's something I have to let you learn for yourself."

My mind was spinning, and I felt light-headed again.

"But that's why you can't hurt me with your abilities, not physically. I'm the other half of your soul. I can bring out your anger; it feels as good for me as it does for you. But it doesn't harm me."

"And the dreams? Your voice in my head? Is that because of our souls?"

He stared again at the open water. "I'm an empath. I feed off of your emotions, and with enough control, I can communicate with you in your mind, and your dreams. I can pull old memories from the back of your mind so you can see them. Not just you, but with everyone, if I focus enough. It's why..." he trailed off, his jaw ticking. "It's why Mira wanted me on her court."

"You have abilities." My voice was breathy as that hit me. I was not alone. Someone else in the world had magic, and it happened to be the other half of my soul.

"It's a big world out there, Raven. You may be surprised to discover how many there may be like you or me."

"Zeke," I whispered.

He looked at me then, his eyes on mine.

I chewed on the skin of my bottom lip, blinking back tears. "I knew something was different about you. Every time we were together, our heartbeats matched. I could..." I trailed off, trying to find the words. "Feel you. Before you'd even speak or touch me, I knew you were there. It broke me seeing you leave. I waited. I need you to know that I waited."

He hung his head as another tear fell down his cheek, but he gave me a slight nod, inhaling a shaky breath.

"And I need you to know something else." My voice was unsteady. I puffed out my cheeks and blew out a hot breath before I continued, "You were always there, haunting me. I kept trying to push you down, but I couldn't. I would... think about you any time he touched me. It was always you."

He bent to me and pressed his lips to my temple in a soft kiss before resting his head against mine.

We stayed like that for a long time. Just watching the waves. And I didn't let myself feel guilty about any of it.

Because we were woven into the fabric of the universe, destined to find one another here and in every lifetime, and that thought comforted me. After twenty-five years of constantly feeling alone, I had a part of my soul wandering the universe with me, missing me as much as I missed him.

I'd never truly be alone. Not anymore. Not ever again.

CHAPTER TWENTY-NINE

Raven

That evening, we decided to try and sleep. Together. In his bed. We were both on our backs, but I was positive half of him was hanging off. It wasn't a large bed, but he was a large man. We stared at the ceiling, both of us silent. "You can touch me, you know. If you're about to fall off," I told him, holding my breath after I said it.

I could hear his breath and see his hand in his hair from the corner of my eye. He was tortured by us being next to one another but having unspoken rules between us.

"I don't think I can," he grumbled.

I couldn't help but giggle. I turned to my side and reached back, patting his thigh. "Come on. You won't sleep like that."

A full moment passed between us, and he remained still. Finally, and very slowly, he rolled to his side. I felt his chest gently scraping my back, and I leaned farther into him, his arm gingerly resting on my lip. "See. Not so bad," I said.

His breathing quickened, but he wasn't exhaling any of them. I was afraid he might pass out. "Easy for you to say. You don't want sex for release anymore, but I can't be near you without wanting to possess your body."

A smile spread across my face. "I'm not tense with you. I don't need release."

"Is that your nice way of telling me that you don't *want* to fuck me anymore?" His voice was strained.

I snorted and slapped his thigh. "No, you imbecile. I'm trying to say that with you, it was never just to feel better. I just wanted you."

He was quiet as his body relaxed into mine, melding with me. "Wanted," he repeated in a whisper.

I knew what he was trying to ask. "I will always want you. That never changed. It never will. But I have to stop relying on other people to make me feel better and whole."

"Technically, technically..."

My eyes rolled, knowing where he was going.

"You can't be whole without me, anyway."

I turned on my side until we were face to face. I could tell that he was struggling to stay away from me. "Tell me something about yourself. Please. Anything."

His eyes closed as he expelled a long breath. "Raven, the only thing you need to know is that love isn't an adequate word to describe how I feel about you and that I will follow you world to world. Isn't that enough?" He said it so casually, like he wasn't promising to seek me out in every universe from now until the end of time.

I shook my head against the pillow and raised my thumb to press against his bottom lip, pulling it gently between my fingers. "I want to *know* you."

His eyes opened, he kissed my finger's tip, and I released him. "What do you want to know?"

I thought about his question. There was so much I didn't know that I wasn't sure where to start. "Tell me about your brother."

His entire body stiffened. I wondered why it bothered him so much to talk about. "Please," I whispered.

His voice was low, and I had to strain my ears to hear every word. "He's around your age. He's stubborn, but kind. He'd never hurt a soul. The world hasn't broken his spirit yet."

"Does he have abilities like you?"

His head barely shook. It was taking all I had not to take away his pain with my body, my physical way of loving him.

"That's just me. My mother was around when rumors of dark magic flowed abundantly through the kingdoms and kept my abilities hidden for as long as she could. It was John who told Mira about them."

"Is that why you're not close?"

His eyebrow cocked at that.

"I could tell at breakfast. There's tension between the two of you. You don't like when he talks about your mother."

He kissed the tip of my nose. It was intimate, like a habit. And it made me smile. "No, I don't."

"Not a happy marriage?"

"So much I can't tell you yet, Raven. But I want to. Just remain patient a little longer." His expression was sorrowful, and I recognized a darkness behind his eyes.

"I'm so in love with you," I murmured, placing my hand gently on his cheek. "Please let me be."

"You have no idea what I've done." His voice was labored. "What I'm going to do."

"We've all done things we're not proud of, Zeke. Falling in love with you is not one of them." I needed him to know. I needed him to know that I would never regret any of this.

"Raven." His voice cracked on my name.

My heart wanted to wrap around his, beat for him so he wouldn't have to feel any pain ever again. Instead, I gently pressed my lips to his. He remained tense, like he was afraid to relax into me too much, pressing his fingers into the skin of my hip. The heat between our bodies was thick, like sap. When I pulled away, it was with extreme hesitancy. "That's all I can give you right now," I muttered with an apologetic grin.

"That's all I need." He wrapped his arm around my waist and pulled me to him.

My head curled into his neck, one of my legs resting between both of his.

"I love you," he whispered against my head.

My eyes watered. That was the first time he'd said it to me like that. "Tell me again."

He was quiet. I peered up at him, and a tear fell down his cheek. He cleared his throat and looked into my eyes, making me tremble under his gaze. "Raven," he murmured.

My body turned to jelly at his tone.

"I am so deeply, so irrevocably in love with you."

My eyes closed. That was all I ever wanted to hear from him. It washed over me like a gentle wave.

"I love you," he repeated to me, soundly, confidently.

A tear slid down my cheek, and he gently kissed it away. My hands slowly slid up his stomach, brushing against his ribs. He was trying to hold his breath because he wasn't moving. My palms lay flat against his chest. His mouth was still close to my face, his warm breath tickling my skin, making goose bumps rise across every inch.

Without opening my eyes, I turned my head just enough to press my lips against his. He remained still, except for his hand that gently grazed across my thigh between his legs. It moved up slowly, pushing against my lower back, closing the remaining space between us.

I drew out my leg and pushed him until he was lying on his back, moving with him until I was on top of him, my legs straddling his waist. I rolled my hips against him, feeling how hard he was for me right between my legs.

He finally exhaled a breath as his hands found my waist. I rolled my hips again, and he groaned. My mouth collided with his again, and I gently bit down on his lip, sucking it between mine. His hands moved my hips on him again, and I was already so wet for him. "Raven," he whispered, pulling away an inch. "We don't have to do this."

I sat up and ground down against him. His eyes moved down to watch, and I did it again. We really did need to do this.

I crossed my arms and grabbed the bottom of my shirt, slowly raising it over my head. His eyes made a slow trek up my body, and then his hand cupped the back of my head and pulled me down to him again, his mouth hungrily grabbing mine.

I fingered his shirt, and he rose enough for me to push it off him. He chuckled, that raspy sound sending me into a frenzy as I yanked it off him. He knew I was done waiting.

His fingers tore through my thin panties, and mine fumbled for his pants, shoving them before I fully untied them from his waist. I wrapped my hand around his swollen length and met his eyes before slowly lowering myself down on him, my mouth falling slack from the feel of him inside me again.

"Baby," he groaned, gently thrusting up until he was fully sheathed inside.

That name. This feeling.

His fingers pressed into my ass, his gaze on me predatory as I rocked my hips once, twice. I gathered my hair in my hands and raised my arms, my head rolling back as he guided me against him. This was so right. This was everything I'd been missing.

"You are..." he trailed off.

I bit my lip and returned my gaze to his face as I rode him slowly, one of my palms lowering to rest against his chest. His eyes were so dark, so full of lust. "My love," he finished.

I whimpered, leaning down until I could kiss him again. His bucks came faster. I felt so warm and so cold all at once. Everything inside of me was fighting to get to the surface, to be a part of the magic we made together.

He curled an arm around my waist and flipped us, still deep inside of me, as he continued to thrust. My legs wrapped around his waist. "I love you, I love you," he said to me, just like I'd said to him so many times. He was making it up to me.

All his silence. All my doubts.

I put my hands on his throat and warmed them, letting my fire heat us both. He snarled at the bite, and his bucks became greedy, rougher. His head lowered, and he nipped at my shoulder. One of my hands tugged at his hair, wanting more. He bit at me again, dragging my skin between his teeth, and I cried out. "Give me your darkness," I rasped.

He raised his head to look at me, his charcoal eyes staring deep into mine.

"I want it," I breathed.

He started to shake his head.

"I love you, all of you. Every part of you."

His forehead fell against mine, our sweat mixing.

"I can take it."

His thrust somehow seemed to dive deeper. I felt the ache everywhere. He was giving me a taste. "Again," I said, tugging his bottom lip into my teeth again and biting until his flesh broke. He growled and thrust again. I bit until I felt blood, and he did it repeatedly until every muscle in my body was sore.

He grabbed a fistful of my hair and yanked, exposing the column of my neck. His tongue licked the base, and I moaned, pushing my hips against his. My nails scratched down his back while he continued his harsh claiming, his breaths quick and jagged. I wanted this to last forever, but he was too good. He knew my body too well.

I was reaching my peak, and he was climbing there with me. I grabbed his face with my hands and brought it to mine, pushing my tongue into his mouth. He matched my ferocity, our mouths moving sloppily together until he thrust again. I threw my head back, my vision blurring as I came, screaming his name. That sent him over, filling me with so much hot release that I wondered why I doubted him.

He felt for my hand and grabbed it, putting my fingers against the pulse in his throat. He put his hand against my heart, and we laid there, our rapid heartbeats thundering in perfect harmony. I smiled, and he raised his head to mine, kissing me again. And again. Until my lips were raw. He was still buried inside of me, and I wanted to stay like this, forever, on his ship in the middle of the channel. I wanted to burn for him, always.

But I talked too much. After he made love to me again, I decided I needed more answers. "This is a bad time to ask."

"Raven," he groaned, annoyed. He would have been content to spend the week fucking and saying absolutely nothing.

I bit my lip, and he sighed, slowly pulling out of me to roll to his side. I turned on mine and faced him, threading my fingers through his. "Why did you lie to me about Jeanine?"

He kissed the tip of my nose. "I didn't."

My body was suddenly frigid. "Okay, so you are together? Did we just…" I tried to sit away from him, but he pulled me back. "We're not together. We haven't been since I met you."

So he had slept with that angelic creature.

"Raven."

I winced, forgetting he could read my emotions. I had no right to be jealous. Though, I was.

"I didn't know you. The moment, no, the *second* I saw you, I never wanted another woman to touch me again."

I felt guilty. I didn't want another man to touch me, but I wanted to move on from him. And I thought he was touching her. "I can sense your shame, too."

I grated my teeth, annoyed that he'd always be able to tell what I was feeling, which was a lot, and all the time.

"You don't need to be ashamed. It's my fault."

I shook my head. "It's not your fault."

"It is. I pushed you two together."

"I should have waited. I should've… declared celibacy."

He started to laugh. "You can declare it? Just like that?"

"I'm a queen. I can do whatever the fuck I want."

"That mouth of yours."

I smiled, but there was something else eating away at me. "Why are we engaged?"

Shadows clouded over him. I wanted to shoo them away. I'd brought him back to reality. "I can't answer that yet."

"Are we actually getting married? How real is this?"

"That will be up to you."

"Do you want to marry me?"

He was quiet while he studied my face, his arm resting over my waist. He adjusted his head on the pillow, putting his other arm under his head so he could look down at me. "Do you want to marry me?"

"I feel like I already am. Our souls are bound."

"You have free will, Raven. Our souls are bound in every universe. That doesn't mean we'll get married in all of them."

That thought made me frown. "You don't want to marry me in every life?"

He snorted at my question, shaking his head against his arm. "You didn't answer my question. Would you marry me? After you have all your answers. All the information."

"That's hard to say because I don't know the information. And you won't tell me. Am I going to *want* to marry you after we get there?"

His eyes fell from mine. I wanted to press, but he wasn't going to budge.

"In a perfect world, I'd marry you today. Right now. And we'd stay right here and have tiny *little demons* running around."

"You want tiny little demons?"

I hadn't given it much thought before. "With you, I would."

"Let's stay in our perfect world until we get there."

I nodded, leaning up to kiss him softly.

I worried about what our world would look like after we arrived. But for now, I'd live in it with him. My heart may break again, but this was worth it. Time with him was worth it.

I nuzzled my head in his neck.

He pulled me until I was right against him. "Rest, baby."

"Visit me in my dreams."

His raspy chuckle sang me to sleep.

I dreamed of lying in an open clearing with him, surrounded by trees and millions of stars in the sky. Moonlight illuminated our bodies, melded together, holding one another tightly while a sadness hung in the air all around us. "You always love me best in the dark," I said.

"Because you are my light."

We still had five days left in our trip before we reached Reales, and he decided to teach me how to sail. We needed a distraction from how much we wanted each other and time to process, so why not push two stubborn people together to learn a new skill? We'd just started ten minutes ago, and he was already sighing at me, trying to reexplain himself for the third time.

"You have to know which direction the wind is going," he tried telling me again.

The irony of not understanding wind direction was not lost on me. "Can't I just use my own wind?"

He grumbled something. "No, because winds would be going in different directions and counteracting. We'd spin in circles. It's simple science, Raven."

"I don't like science," I muttered, rolling my eyes.

"You *are* science. You're the elements. You can't get any more scientific."

I curled up a ball of fire in my hand and threw it at him. It hit his chest and dissipated. I cursed under my breath, and he snorted. "Okay, can we just skip the wind part and move on?"

He scowled, running his hand through his hair in frustration. "No, you can't *skip* the wind part. It's the most important part!" He was partially shouting in exclamation.

I threw my arms up in the air. "Okay, I don't want to learn how to sail!"

He shook his head and planted his feet. "You are going to learn how to sail."

With a flick of my wrist, I sent a gust of my own wind, clashing against the breeze pushing us north. The stern of the ship started turning east. "Raven," he warned.

I feigned innocence by widening my eyes.

The ship continued to spin slowly off course. He growled at me. "We're never going to get there if you don't stop."

With another flick of my wrist, my wind died out. He stood at the helm, guiding us back on course. "Tired of me already?" I asked, a playful grin on my mouth.

"Remind me never to take you sailing again."

I pouted out my bottom lip. "Remind me never to ask again."

His eyes went to my pout, and they rolled. He was utterly exasperated with me. "You're infuriating."

"People always say that to me, and I never understand why."

"You're not that dense."

My mouth dropped open, and I walked to him, shoving one of his shoulders.

"Trying to steer a ship here," he snapped.

That only made me want to do it again. And again. Until he bent down and wrapped an arm around my waist, hoisting me up and over his shoulder. "I will sail like this for the next five days if I have to."

I hung there idly, swinging my feet back and forth, the tips of my boots hitting his thighs repeatedly. "That's okay. I have a nice view." I pinched the back of his thighs.

He started to laugh, shaking me to try and stop me. I did it again. "Okay, that's it." He let go of the helm and walked to the ship's side, leaning over until we hung off, my lower half dangling over the water.

I squealed and tried to rock back and forth on him to climb down toward the ship's deck. "Okay, I'll behave," I promised him.

He pulled me back over and set me down on my feet. I raced him to the helm and grabbed the wheel. "Teach me how to steer," I demanded, fluttering my eyelashes at him.

After an annoyed breath, he nodded. I turned to face the wheel, and he came up behind me and put his hands over mine, guiding us slowly over the water. He pointed with one finger toward the water. "Do you see the foam?"

I nodded.

"Avoid that. Try and stay on clearer waters." He showed me why as he guided us until we hit the foaming part, the ship rising on small, choppy waves.

My back pressed into his chest as he steered us back to the clear course again, and then his hands released mine, and he took a step back. I immediately missed his warmth but narrowed my eyes, focusing on the water ahead of us.

I took his instructions very seriously and moved the wheel any time foam bubbled up in the distance. I didn't know if I was going in the right direction, but he hadn't said anything to the contrary.

When I turned my head to find him, he was watching me with a lazy smile on his face. I gave him one back, mine a little wider, feeling proud of myself for trying something new.

But then my hair whipped around my face, sticking to my mouth. I tried to blow it out, only for it to whip around again. He laughed as he gathered my wild mane. "What do you want me to do with all of this?" He held my hair up.

"Do you have a band?"

He looked around and dropped my hair.

I closed my eyes as it snapped across my face and into my mouth. "Okay, take your time. I'll just be here choking," I said in between trying to pull it out of my mouth.

He disappeared downstairs and returned a moment later, holding the band out in front of me. I blew my hair out of my face and shrugged. "Trying to steer a ship here."

"What am I supposed to do with it?" he asked, perplexed.

"Braid it. I'll tell you how."

He just stared at me.

"It's a lot easier than steering a ship."

"Yeah, you look like you're really breaking a sweat there," he replied sarcastically.

"I am literally keeping you alive right now. The least you could do is braid my hair."

He snickered but tugged on my hair.

"Okay, first, separate it into three sections."

He ripped apart the tangled strands.

I yelped. "Gently, you monster."

He pulled them apart slower. Almost too slow. I had a lot of hair. "It's going to be night soon," I sighed.

He yanked on my hair, and I giggled, but he eventually separated them between his hands. "Okay, crisscross them."

"Crisscross them *how*?" He asked, grumbling.

"Is there more than one way to crisscross? Start with two strands and then add in the third one. Repeat that to the end.

And then you just wrap the band around the bottom. It's simple science, Zeke."

He bit down on my earlobe. I laughed, tilting my head away. "Be still," he snarled.

I bit down on my lip to keep from laughing. He pulled and tugged at the strands. I could tell he wasn't doing it the right way, but he would get credit for trying. When he finished, I felt down the braid and nodded. "Not bad for your first try," I said as some strands escaped the braid and framed my face.

He came up beside me and tucked the loose strands behind my ears. "Perfect."

My cheeks flushed at his compliment. I was about to respond by kissing him, but we lurched forward. He came behind me and put his hands on mine, steering us through the water as the smaller waves grew more prominent, sloshing against the ship.

I turned my head and followed his eyes up toward the sky. He looked down at me, frowning. "It's going to storm soon."

"How soon?" The sky was clear above us.

"Probably tonight. It gets dangerous during storms. You should stay downstairs when that happens."

"And come up to find that you've been thrown overboard? Nope." I shook my head as we were pushed forward again.

His body pressed mine into the helm. "Raven, I don't want you to get hurt. You fall easily."

I scowled, pushing back against him. "I do *not*."

To prove his point, he shoved at my shoulder from the side, and I stumbled a step. "Okay, well, that's not fair. I wasn't expecting that."

He laughed and did it again. I stumbled again and giggled. He pulled me back, keeping me pinned against him so I wouldn't fall whenever we were tossed forward. "You can stay up here with me, but don't say I didn't warn you."

"Aye-aye, captain." I gave him a small salute.

He stayed against me, helping me navigate the waters until he mentioned food. Then, I realized we hadn't eaten anything since leaving the palace yesterday, and suddenly I was starving. He assured me we'd be fine letting the ship sail along the course on its own so we could fuel up with food.

I sat on the deck and waited for him to gather some things from the hull to bring up. We'd learned we couldn't be downstairs and wide awake together without relenting to our desires.

He brought up the same basket from the night he left me, and a frown formed on my mouth from the memory. He set the basket next to me and kneeled before me, pressing his lips to mine. "It nearly killed me that night," he said.

He pulled back and sat, pulling the basket between us, and flipped open the lid, producing a pear in his hand. I laughed, taking it from him. He grabbed another and took a bite, a satisfied grin on his face as he chewed.

"I still don't understand." I took a small bite of my own.

He was quiet, staring down into the basket. There was so much he couldn't tell me, making our attempt to create a perfect world imperfect. "Why can't you tell me?"

He met my eyes then. "Because I have a job to do, Raven."

"And I'm the job?"

He nodded but looked torn.

"And your job is to get me back to Reales?"

Another nod.

I huffed out a breath of hot air. "We need to work on your communication skills, my love."

"This is a bad time to ask."

I snorted but waved him on with my hand.

"That day in the throne room, I sensed nothing but lust on Cade for you. But it wasn't like that for you."

I lifted a shoulder in a small shrug. That wasn't a question.

"You didn't want him?"

I finished my pear and wiped my fingers off my dress, leaning back on the palms of my hands. "I had a crush on him as a girl," I began.

He had a sour expression on his face, but he asked, so I continued, "He was always around and nice to me. He genuinely wanted to help me. And it was... different, having that kind of attention. For so long, it was just Isla and me."

I tilted my head back, looking at the sky as we drifted. "But I outgrew my crush, and when I turned sixteen, we just became inseparable. It was never anything more than friends. He always had girls around, and I would go out and...." I trailed off and dipped my chin to him again.

He was grimacing.

"How much of this do you want to hear?"

He didn't answer at first, and I knew he was asking himself the same question, but then he sighed. "All of it."

"I would sneak out and cure my loneliness, mostly at the festivals where I could blend. It wasn't often if that made you feel better."

"I am no saint, Raven."

I wrinkled my nose, imagining what that could possibly mean. "It wasn't until right before I met you that I noticed he was staring at me more, wanting me there instead of someone else. I kicked Jeanine out of his room that evening and stayed with him because I was upset about something else. And I wanted you."

He smiled at that.

"The next morning, everything was different. It only got worse when he saw you. He could tell my interest in you wasn't like my other... endeavors."

He sighed, annoyed with me again.

"He knows I'm possessive. I don't like to share what's mine. And he took advantage of that. I think my need to keep him around combined with wanting to heal from my heartbreak led me into his arms." I scooted back to lean against the wall, trying to rationalize everything. "I can't lie to you and say I didn't start falling for him. He was filling a need for me."

The color drained from his face. I stopped talking, but he nodded for me to continue. "But then, once he… had me, something more sinister grew in him. The more he had me, the more he wanted to keep me for himself. Especially after John shot me. He locked me away, and I had to beg to be let out, to be given a chance to breathe on my own. And then I would feel guilty for not wanting him, and the only way I knew how to make it better was to let him have me. He asked me to marry him. Or told me he was going to ask."

"I knew I could have a perfectly content life with him. I told myself I could say yes because I had someone there who wanted a future with me."

His eyes left my face and fell to the floor.

"But the bigger part of me knew I'd always wonder about you, always miss you. I felt like I could never be whole."

He still wouldn't look at me.

"And then you were on my balcony that night, and he was enraged with me. Something snapped in him that night."

He asked quietly, "Did he hurt you?"

"He tried. He wanted to."

The gorgeous man in front of me looked shattered.

"But that's not your fault. You didn't force him to do that."

He swallowed as he shook his head.

"Look at me, please."

He hesitated before he lifted his gaze to me.

"I do not blame you."

"I didn't know, Raven. I never would've…." He trailed off, his fist clenching, "But he did hurt you. He let his rage overcome him, and I'm the one who created that."

I sat up and crawled to him, climbing on his lap. I put my hands on his cheeks and pressed my lips to his. When I pulled back, there was regret in his eyes. "He's angry because I am so in love with you, and he knows I will never be able to give him that. I do love him, and I always will. But you…" I whispered, the pad of my thumb rubbing his cheek, "You are the feeling I get when I see new flowers blooming. You are the sound of the trees in my forest."

A tear slipped down his cheek and pooled against my finger.

"You are the flames in my palms, warming my entire body." I touched the tip of his nose with my own. "You are the taste of rum coating my tongue. You are what awakens my soul when I smell pine."

He trembled against me.

"You *Are*. You surround me."

He curled his arms around me and stood, my legs wrapping around his waist as he started down the ladder into the hull. Thunder rolled in the distance, but his focus was only on me.

"I want to show you something."

He set me down on the floor. The sky darkened above us, leaving little light in the cabin. I lit candles with the tip of my finger while he pulled his shirt over his head and discarded it on the floor. I roved over the muscles of his stomach, my tongue licking across my bottom lip. Thunder cracked outside, but I was frozen in place.

"What is that?" I asked, taking a step closer to him. There was something new on his ribcage, a marking I hadn't seen. It was too dark last night to notice that on the bottom of his ribs, right under his heart, sat an inked drawing of flames flickering under a crescent moon. And with wings outstretched, caressing the moon, was an outline of a raven.

Wetness pooled in my eyes. My heart thundered in my ears. "When?" I breathed, my fingertips brushing over the black ink.

He wasn't breathing as he watched my fingers move across his ribs. "After I left you," he murmured.

I felt so many things. Love. Lust. Fury. Bewilderment. Everything came crashing to me at once, needing an outlet after being tangled inside me for the last three months.

"*You* surround *me*." He worked the buckle of his pants next, unfastening them slowly like he was putting on a show just for me.

My fingers never left his skin, even as he pushed his waistband down, exposing his hip bones. The pace of my breathing increased, my pulse quickening from the deliberate tease of his movements. I felt his eyes burning into me, but I couldn't look away from his ink, his body, drinking all of him in as his pants fell to his feet, revealing his stiff erection.

He'd permanently made me part of him.

Another crack of thunder, and my eyes snapped to his. The boat rocked harder against the waves, but neither of us moved. I dropped my hand from his skin and crossed my arms at my hips, bunching the fabric of my dress in my fingers until it was gathered at my thighs.

His eyes traveled down my legs, my core burning under his gaze. Slowly, so slowly, I raised the dress over my body, exposing my sex to him first. He groaned at sight.

The cool air chill blanketed my stomach and breasts as I dropped my dress down to the floor. The braid in my hair fell apart, my hair curling around my shoulders.

"I love you," I whispered, my insides tingling with euphoria.

He bent down and lifted me by my thighs until I was coiled around him. He set me down on the table, my back arching against it as his mouth gently lowered to mine.

His hands were on my ribs, gliding up my thighs before he cupped my face. Caressing. Exploring. He wanted to touch all of me. And I wanted all of him. Our tongues twisted together hungrily because, *yes*, our bodies fit so well together. And *yes*, something about us felt ethereal. Like Zeus created a constellation where our souls crashed together in the night sky.

His tip pushed into me, and I moaned into his mouth, the walls of my warmth expanding to welcome him back in. He drove into me, filling me, claiming me. I dragged my fingers over the familiar lines of his back. He took me like we'd spent a lifetime apart, pushing kisses against the base of my throat hard enough to feel the sweat around his lips.

He pulled back enough to lock eyes with me. We shared a blissful moment as his tempo slowed, fate sketching this memory in our mind — the way our bodies moved together, the feeling of our souls colliding, finding their home again.

"We need more time," he said, his voice coming out in breathless gasps.

I rose to my elbows, pulling his face to mine again. I kissed his soft lips as that tightening in my stomach only he could provide spread through my entire body. As he was about to push into me again, I whispered against his mouth, "We have lifetimes."

He released into me with a rough cry at my words, pushing me to my peak as I followed him over. We chased our high together, our bodies quivering against one another.

Yes, yes, to all of this. All of him. It wasn't preposterous to fall in love with him so quickly. I was always supposed to. "It was always you," I whispered to him.

The way he looked at me as we came down was a mixture of desire and love, mixed with sorrow for the life we'd lived without one another in this world.

And still not knowing what lay ahead.

He slowly pulled out of me, peppering my face with soft kisses, whispering my name, whispering his love for me.

I sat up just enough to look again at the tattoo he marked himself with just for me. For us. I pushed my lips to it and felt what I'd always known between us — that our hearts beat together in twin rhythms — meant that this devastating man full of gloom and shadows was created for me.

And then we were reminded that we were in the middle of a storm. The wooden boards of the ship groaned against the wind, fighting against the waves that were trying to push it backward and claim it as its own.

He was up the stairs first, leaving me there to finish dressing. What could I wear in a raging thunderstorm, on a ship, where I'd most likely be thrown around like a doll? Either way, I'd be soaked.

I pulled a long-sleeved black shirt out of my trunk and put it on, reaching for a pair of thick, loose-fitting cotton pants that sat right against my hips. I slid on the thick black boots and tied up the laces quickly, throwing my hair up in a messy bun on my head. Not that any of it mattered because it'd be whipping around my face again soon.

I stepped on the deck and immediately raised my arm to my face, trying to ignore the way the drops of water felt like needles on my skin. I tried to find him, but it was so dark outside that I could only make out the outline of his body next to the helm.

I pushed against the wind to walk to him. He gripped the fabric of my shirt and pulled me to him. "I really don't want you out here," he shouted over the howling wind.

"I really don't care," I shouted back. "I'm not losing half of me."

He captured my mouth with his and lingered there a second too long before we were both thrown. My body flew and slammed against one of the walls. *Ow.*

I rubbed my head and pushed myself up to my hands, unsure what side of the ship I was on. I heard him calling my name repeatedly, wanting assurance that I wasn't tossed off. I got on my hands and knees to crawl to him, using his pants to guide me back up until I was standing next to him. He frantically turned the wheel in an attempt to avoid the more giant waves.

I took a step away from him, and he grabbed for me, but I swatted his hand away. He tried again, but I took a small leap out of his grasp. I pushed against the wind that didn't want me here until I was at the ship's bow. I heard him calling for me, but I ignored him and closed my eyes, shifting into Terra.

My golden eyes blinked open, and I held my arms toward the rain droplets falling from the sky. I released gusts of wind to them and dragged my arms down, keeping the rain from falling on the ship. The elements fought hard against me, and my arms shook as I tried to keep my grip. I planted my feet and screamed as I pushed back, the droplets avoiding us.

I was fighting against the very universe that gave me my elements, but he could steer the ship much better without rain constantly pouring down on us.

I howled against the wind's cry, my entire body threatening to crumble, but I fought against it, even as he begged me to stop from behind. He could sense my pain. Drops of blood fell from my nose, but I didn't let up, didn't let go.

My hair whipped wildly across my face and back, having fallen from my lazy bun. I was going to get him through this storm, even if it meant the end for me.

The boat continued to rock under my feet even as I felt it glide onto steadier waves, but the wind howled around me, two elements fighting one another. It wanted to punish me.

I growled as I pushed my arms out as far as they could go, waging war with my breeze, pushing until I felt less resistance. "Let go," I grated out through clenched teeth.

My shaky arms slowly drew in until the last of the universe's elements gave in and relented. My lungs screamed as I tried to draw in air, tasting blood at the back of my throat.

I turned my head slowly back to him as my arms fell to my sides, releasing the hold on my own wind, swaying as blood dripped down my face and neck.

He stared at me, concern hardening across his features.

I heard him shout my name as he took a step toward me. The rain on my skin lessened, and the cold drops felt good against the heat of my skin. I tried to smile as my eyes went in and out of focus. He was okay. He was safe.

And then I collapsed.

CHAPTER THIRTY

Zeke

No, no, no.

I abandoned the wheel and ran to Raven, who was curled up on the ship's deck. "Baby," I said, falling to my knees and pulling her body to me. "Wake up, Raven."

The ship still rocked, but the rain had lightened, and we were still on course. She accomplished what she had set out to do and didn't tell me beforehand because she knew I'd stop her.

I shook her a little, but her head rolled back. I pressed my lips to her face over and over, mumbling for her to wake up, but she wasn't. I stood with her in my arms, cradling her against my chest. I used my foot to pull up the handle on the latch door and carried her down the ladder. She was in so much pain trying to fend off the raging wind. Why didn't she stop?

Because she loves you, my brain yelled at me. I sighed as I gently laid her limp body on the bed, moving her wet hair off her face and slicking it back. She was still shifted, and her ordinarily bright, violet hair looked like a deep purple as it curled.

This infuriating, beautiful creature nearly killed herself trying to save me. I felt for her pulse, though I knew she was still alive. I imagined if she were dying, I would feel like I was, too. I kissed her forehead and removed her soaked clothes. I didn't know how her magic worked. I didn't know if she could warm herself up while she slept.

I dropped the wet clothes in a heap at the foot of the bed and pulled the quilt over her body, rubbing my hands over it to create friction. "Please wake up, my love." I knew I should've begged her to stay down here, but she wouldn't have listened even if I had. All she ever did was give, wanting to use her abilities for the sake of others.

I stood and grabbed a dry cloth, returning to wipe the water off her face, and tried to dry her hair as much as possible. She needed to stay warm. "Little demon," I murmured to her still frame. "If you can hear me in there, can you ignite?"

I rubbed her arms through the quilt again. "You need to stay warm, baby." I pushed into her mind, but it was quiet. Her body was exhausted. I ran my fingers through my hair, tugging at the strands. All I could do was wait for her to wake up, and I'd go fucking crazy while doing so.

I needed to see her smile, hear her laugh. I wanted more of her stories. "I'll let you tell me anything, everything." I kissed her cheeks, her nose, her lips. "Please just wake up." Her stubbornness was getting out of control. "I'll be right back. Don't go anywhere."

I pecked her forehead before I was back up on deck and at the wheel, trying to keep us on course against the water desperately trying to knock us off. I stared at where she'd been standing and recalled the memory in my mind. It was incredible. Terrifying. The amount of power coming out of her fingers. The thirst I could taste on her for control. Seeing her wild mane whipping in the fight of the two breezes.

My eyes moved to the sky. The gray was lightening, the worst of the storm passing by us. I turned and looked at Cade's ship. It was larger than mine and looked fine, but I wondered if I needed to flag them down and let them know about Raven — if Cade would know how to bring her back.

My fingers tightened on the wheel until my knuckles were white. I loathed that he may know more about her than me. That he knew her body as I did. But he'd been around her magic more than I had, and he may have an answer.

I groaned, rubbing my face with my hand. Not yet. I'd give her time to recover before I resorted to that. If he were to find out about the two of us, I worried he'd take it out on her, and I'd hate myself more than I already did.

I'd been selfish with her. I spent too many weeks away from her, and now I couldn't keep my hands off of her. It would've been difficult, but if all she had let me do was stare at her, I would've done it. But we'd starved for one another, and it was like taking the first bite when she kissed me. Now all I wanted to do was eat. I didn't want to share her anymore.

Maybe we could live in our perfect world. We didn't have to return to Reales. We could sail, find somewhere new to go and make tiny little demons. I smiled at the idea. She wanted that with me. A future. A real one, without malice. Without the dirty deeds of court life. She'd be a mother.

My mother. My brightening thoughts were suddenly back to their gloom. I had a reason for bringing her to Reales. My mother and brother didn't deserve torture because I fell in love with my mission. I had no doubt Mira would kill them. They'd be of no use to her, and it would be the best way to enact revenge on me if I were to leave with Raven.

John couldn't do anything against her. Seolia would fall into ruin without Raven. There would be no continuing bloodline, which meant any of the three kingdoms could invade and claim it as its own. No, we couldn't have our future. Not right now. Maybe not ever. And perhaps I was cruel for playing this game with her. But having these last few days together may be it.

There was still a strong possibility she would hate me for what I'd done -- for holding secrets from her. I was no better than Cade in that regard. Except he hid it from her for fifteen years, whereas mine was for three months, and it was to protect her, not keep her under my control.

I was making excuses for myself, and I shouldn't be. What we were doing to her was wrong. There was no way to spin that. But I had a family I needed to protect, too. And Raven understood the need to protect. Maybe I should tell her.

We could come up with our own plan. Stand against Mira. But how could I ask her to turn on her sister before they met? She needed to learn this by herself. She needed the chance to make up her own mind. Raven's soul was dark, but there was a purity about her. A kindness. She was not her sister.

Her kingdom was joyfully thriving. Reales was withering away, overcome with crime and murder. Most of our subjects were trying to escape, only to be caught and have to answer to Mira and me. Mira was all about control. Raven was free will. And maybe, after Raven learned of Mira's plans, her need for family connections would lose some of its value, and she'd remember who she was and what she stood for.

I couldn't tell her. I had to stick with the plan. Otherwise, shoving her to that manipulative asshole on the ship behind us was all for nothing. I could've spent three blissful months with her, making love all over the island. She never would've had to learn of Jeanine, and doubt about my love for her never would've crossed her mind. I needed to continue, but first, I needed her to wake up.

––––––

The night passed, and she stayed asleep. I'd put her in one of my shirts, though her skin still felt clammy. Her mind was still impenetrable. Her subconscious was buried in a deep sleep. I laid beside her on the bed and pulled her body to mine, sharing my warmth. "Wake up, baby," I whispered into her ear. She inhaled deeper. She was in there somewhere. She could hear me.

"Remember how I told you I could see flashes of us in previous lives?" I kissed her temple. "They were glimpses, but you were smiling in so many of them." I pulled strands of her in my fingers. "Always ebony, always as black as our souls. Never purple." I laughed softly, letting her hair fall back to her shoulders. "And your eyes, baby. Always your bright green. So green they're golden in the light."

I felt nothing but despair with her in my arms like this. "Don't burn out, my star." I sank lower into the bed, pulling her back against my chest. "You told me that I put the stars in your sky," I whispered, kissing the back of her head. "But you are my only star. My guiding star."

I closed my eyes, sighing into her. "I will sleep with you, but I need you to wake me up in one of your sweet ways." I kissed her head over and over. "I'm going crazy without you, baby."

———

When my eyes opened, I was disappointed to find her still asleep next to me. I pushed into her mind again, but it was still buried. I had no other choice. It'd been over a day. Cade may be my only option to help her. She was going to think I gave up on her and that these last few days had meant nothing to me.

"I don't know what else to do," I said, squeezing my eyes shut. I sat up and pulled the quilt off us for me to stand, replacing it over her body. I leaned against the wall and watched her for a moment, trying to comb through any other ideas. There was only one I could think of. I could scare her awake.

It meant going way down into the depths of her subconscious, and I didn't like doing it. It could reject me. Or I could get stuck. Anything was better than sending her back to him, though. She was going to murder me when she woke up, but if she woke up with Cade and not with me... I didn't want to imagine where her thoughts would go.

I pulled a chair from the table and moved it next to the bed. Come on, baby. It was time to let me in. I closed my eyes and shoved into her mind. Fear was our last chance. I'd show her one of my memories first. I didn't want to bring any of hers forward if I could avoid it. I clawed through the layers of her mind, casting my own memory.

———

She was in a long, dark hallway brushing her fingertips along the wall as she ran. She was trying to find me but couldn't. A light was beaming from the end of the hall, and she stopped abruptly, hesitant about what she'd find. She could sense it, even in her subconscious. We didn't have much time.

Voices came from the room as she approached, deep tremors mixing with a feminine ones. She crossed the threshold, and eyes snapped to her. She noticed John first, who was giving her a guilty grin. She opened her mouth to speak, but nothing came out. She clasped her throat at the loss of her voice.

Mira approached her next. I wanted to go to her, but I couldn't. Not yet. Mira placed her icy cold palm on Raven's cheeks. "You will join me."

Raven shook her head furiously. I sensed her trying to will her fire forward, but nothing came. She started to panic. I took a small step out from behind the gray throne that seemed to terrify her. She tried to speak to me, but I put my finger to my mouth and shushed her.

Mira, whose hand was still pressed against her cheek, cocked her head slowly as her brown hair started to darken. That wasn't my memory. I took a step toward Raven, but I was being held back by something. I shouted, "Wake up, Raven!"

Mira's brown hair was now black. That wasn't Mira. All I felt was coldness from Raven, and she was getting chillier. I shouted at her to wake up again, but Celestina's head snapped to me, and she scowled. Raven finally met my eyes.

"Wake up, baby."

———

Her eyes snapped open, and she drew in a sharp breath, her hand rising to clasp at her throat. I wrapped my hands around hers, trying to stop her from clawing at her neck. She was awake. My eyes instantly flooded with tears. "Raven," I said, my voice soothing.

"Zeke," she cracked out, letting me remove her hands from her throat.

My name on her tongue sent a wave of relief over me.

"The dream," she rasped, shivering.

I should've given her time to get her bearings, but I pulled her up to me and pressed my lips against hers. Tears fell down my cheeks, and she put her hands against them, returning my feverish consumption. "You were asleep for so long," I said between kisses, wrapping my arms around her waist and lifting her on my lap. "It's been two days."

"I'm sorry," she said.

I tilted her chin to look at me, shaking my head. "Never apologize to me." I leaned my forehead to hers. "I'm just so happy to hear your voice." I kissed her again. And again.

"What happened?" She was breathless from my constant need to touch her.

I moved to release her, but she shook her head and threw her arms around my neck. I buried my face into her neck, smiling through my release of panic. I gave myself a moment to calm down before I met her eyes. "You fought off the storm. You passed out for two days. I couldn't penetrate your mind. You were buried too deep. I had to resort to other measures, and if that hadn't worked, I would call Cade over here."

Her nose wrinkled, and I kissed the tip of it. "Why Cade?"

I gave her a slight shrug. "I thought he may know something about your magic that I don't."

"I don't even understand my magic. All Cade would've done is move me to his ship and turn back to Seolia."

She was right. I hadn't considered that. I pulled on a strand of her purple hair. "You've been this one the entire time."

She giggled. "Terra."

And now I knew they had names. "Show me the others. If you have energy."

She blinked once, and her violet hair turned icy blonde. "Frost." She blinked again, and her blonde turned into that sexy, red bob. "Blaze."

My dick was immediately hard, and my mouth felt dry. A smug grin lifted the corners of her lips. She wiggled against me, and I shook my head. "No. You just woke up from a coma. I'm not touching you like *that* for a while."

She stuck out her bottom lip. I wanted to bite it. "How long is *a while?*"

I shrugged at her question. Determination crossed over her features. I shook my head again. "No, Raven."

She pressed her lips against mine gently, and I let her, but then she increased pressure, and I pulled back. "I'm just as stubborn as you, my love."

She adjusted in my lap until she was straddling me. Fuck, my self-control was already wavering. I rested my hands against her thighs, cocking my eyebrow. I had to seem aloof. But she was quick to call me on my bullshit when she leaned down and tugged my earlobe in her teeth while rolling her hips against mine simultaneously.

I squeezed her thighs, and she smiled against my skin. I tried to shake my head again, but she pushed her mouth against mine, stilling me. Her tongue pressed against my lips, and I opened for her, tangling my tongue with hers. She pushed her hips down again. My erection was painfully straining against my pants. She ground her hips again, and again. The friction between us was scalding, even with the layers between us.

I felt her fingers between us, trying to untie the knot in my waistband. I grabbed her hands gently, and she stared into my eyes. "Are you really telling me no?" Her voice was soft.

When she bit on her bottom lip, all of my resolve dissipated. I released her fingers, and her smile returned as she untied them and pushed them down. I lifted my hips, and she shoved them off as I grabbed the bottom of her shirt and raised it over her head.

My eyes lowered across her body and then back to her face and that red hair. Raven as herself was unlike anyone else, but her as Blaze... it was pure temptation. Staring at her was like taking part in each of the seven deadly sins at once.

I would never tire of looking at this enchanting woman.

She sat up slowly and grabbed the base of my cock, holding it steady as she lowered onto me. Her head rolled back, and I nearly came undone. The fact that *I* could do this to *her*...

My fear of losing her, of never having this again, was still fresh. My fingers were desperate as they pinched into her waist, keeping her close while she rode me.

"Baby," I whispered.

She wrapped her hands around my throat. I felt her heat and groaned, experiencing everything she was in that body of hers. I throbbed inside her, and she was panting, her hips rocking hungrily. "Look at me," I said.

Her chin dipped. Her eyes were red, and my mouth parted at this demon riding me. "What did I do to earn you?"

She answered me with a kiss. I bit her bottom lip, wanting a taste of the raging blood coursing through her. She whimpered in my mouth as I broke her flesh, and her warm blood coated the tip of my tongue. "I could live off you," I said.

She laughed softly, running her tongue over my bite. "Promise me something," she whispered. There was something unreadable in her eyes. Fear, I realized. "Promise me you'll always love me in this lifetime."

My eyebrows drew in. I snaked an arm around her waist to stop her movements against me. My other hand cupped the back of her neck, and I drew her forehead to mine. Her red irises looked like they had flames behind them, and I was stunned by her for a second. "Raven." My voice was low but desperate. "Nothing will ever stop me from loving you in this lifetime or the next."

She nodded against me.

"I promise you."

My words seemed to settle on her because she tried to move against me again, but I kept my arm around her waist and thrust. She moaned softly, and I caught her mouth with mine. Her fingers threaded into my hair, and she used her grip to grind against me over and over until we both started to lose our breath.

Her walls tightened around me and her warmth flooded into my lap. As I came, I breathed out her name, coating her with all of me. And I knew I would keep my promise to her. Nothing in this world would ever keep me from loving her, surrendering to her. I only hoped she could guarantee the same thing.

CHAPTER THIRTY-ONE

Raven

I wasted time in our perfect world, and now we were one day away from Reales. One day left with my mirror soul before things could change between us. I wished more than anything he would tell me. We had a chance of overcoming so much if there could be honesty. I was tired of being surprised all the time.

I spent years feeling like the only one with a secret, but I'd been surrounded by it my entire life and didn't realize that I was definitely not alone.

I leaned over the boat railing, trying to spot life underneath the water as we rushed past. It was windy today, and Zeke practiced again on my hair last night, determined to figure out how to braid it properly. Probably in case I became incapacitated again.

I giggled as I remembered his frustration. He tried to throw my hair at one point, and it smacked me in the face. He had laughed so hard he fell off the bed.

I touched my braided hair and moved it to the front of my shoulder, playing with the end.

"Don't mess up my handiwork," he said behind me.

I smiled. "Why doesn't Jeanine like Cade?" I lowered my arms and leaned farther, trying to reach the water.

His arms wrapped around my waist and brought me back. "Why are you such a child," he grumbled, pulling me to him. He turned me around to face him and nipped at my nose. "Why do you ask?"

I gave him a slight shrug. "Before we left, she seemed protective over me."

"She likes you," he replied bluntly but gently.

I wrinkled my nose.

"I know you can't say the same."

"She's touched you," I mumbled, rising to the tips of my toes to kiss the corner of his mouth. "She's stunning. I don't like thinking about it."

"Her beauty doesn't diminish yours, Raven." He lifted me to wrap around him. "I have never seen anyone more bewitching than you. She even agreed with me." He pressed a kiss to my collarbone. He was distracting me.

"You didn't answer the question."

He sighed.

I flicked his nose. "Why doesn't she like Cade? She tried to fuck him the night of the festival. Is she upset about that?"

"Are you?"

I flicked him again. "Stop. Please just give me an answer. Something. A snippet."

He lowered me until I stood again and cupped his hands around my face, pushing our lips together. I put my palms against his chest and pushed him back. "You're trying to distract me with your body."

He muttered a curse word and ran a hand through his hair. "She doesn't think he's good for you. We both watched you over the last three months." He winced as the words tumbled out of his mouth.

My arms crossed over my chest. "You've been *watching* me?"

"Watching. Stalking. I guess it's all the same."

"You *stalked* me?"

He closed the space between us and grabbed my ass with his hands, bending at his knees until our hips were pressed together. "Of course I *stalked* you. And she helped me. I couldn't stay away from you, Raven. I told you this already."

I bit down on my bottom lip as I tried to remember what I'd done over the last three months. "What did you see?"

At that, he turned his head and looked out over the water. "Some things I wish I hadn't."

I grabbed his chin between my fingers and pulled his gaze back to me, staring deep into his eyes. "I wanted you. Only you. I just didn't know you wanted me, too."

His eyes were clouded with disbelief. I cleared my throat, my cheeks reddening. "Do you, uh, remember when I told you that I would imagine it was you touching me instead of him?"

He nodded once.

"That was in every way. Every time."

"You thought of me while he was fucking you?"

I nodded, averting my eyes from his. When I looked back at him, his smug grin was plastered on his lips. I rolled my eyes and tried to shove off him, but he only gripped me tighter. "You came while thinking of me?"

I covered my eyes with my hand. "It's awful, I know."

He started to laugh, peppering my neck with kisses. "But I told you, you're all I want."

"And you're all I want. I'll *declare celibacy* otherwise."

"You promise?"

He nodded.

I smiled. "I won't, but it's nice that you will."

He growled, pinching at my waist until I laughed. I tried to wrangle free of his grasp, but he kept tickling me until I held up my palms to him. "Okay, okay," I giggled through breaths, "but on one condition." I pulled up at his shirt until his ribcage was exposed. "You take me to get one of these in Reales."

He looked down at his tattoo and then back to me. "You want one of these?"

I nodded, brushing my fingers over his.

"Of what?"

"It'll be a surprise."

He stuck his bottom lip out.

I nipped at it. "You got to surprise me. It's only fair. But I want you permanently sketched on me."

"Baby," he murmured, resting his forehead against mine.

I kissed him softly. "I love you and your shadows."

And I showed him how much right there on the deck.

We pulled all the blankets and pillows off the bed and decided to sleep under the stars on the deck for our last night together. The thought made me frown, and he kept trying to kiss them away. "I really wish you'd tell me," I snapped, my mood worsening as we got closer to Reales and uncovering whatever truth he was hiding from me.

"I want to, Raven." He exhaled a frustrated sigh.

I laid down on our makeshift bed and looked up at him. He stared down at me with his hands on his hips. "I don't want to fight with you. Not tonight."

"How would you feel if this was reversed? I'm scared, Zeke. I have no idea what to expect tomorrow. You're making me feel like I'm going to lose you."

He lowered himself until his knees were on either side of me, his palms by my head. "If you lose me, it'll be your choice. Not mine."

"But you're saying I may want to. That's not any better."

"I wish I could give you what you want, Raven."

I placed my hands on his cheeks. "You're what I want."

"You have me."

I shook my head as a tear fell down my cheek. "I don't. Not really."

He lowered his head and kissed away my tears before laying beside me, pulling at my waist to face him. "You do. Raven, I belong to you. But you will have a choice to make when we get there. I've told you that bringing you back is a mission. You were a job."

I frowned. "That reduces what we have."

"It doesn't. We are meant for one another, but that doesn't mean it's going to be easy. We still have a lot to get through. Please," he begged, holding my chin between his fingers. "Please believe me when I tell you that it's killing me to keep this from you but that I'm doing it for you. It's not my story to tell, Raven. It's not my story at all." There was anguish in his eyes.

I wrapped my fingers around his wrist. "If it's my story, it's yours."

He pressed his forehead against mine, releasing my chin to curl his arm around my waist, and pulled me to him.

"Don't let me go," I whispered.

He shook his head against mine, his arm enveloping me until there were no inches spared between us. I buried my face in his neck, and he kissed the top of my head. "Never, Raven. I will never let you go."

Right before I closed my eyes, a shooting star burned past. I wished we could someday stay in our perfect world with no secrets. I wished for him.

———

I was pulled into a dream full of grief. I shuddered as I walked through a dark castle that had haunted me so often. My subconscious tried to fight back, but a heavy weight pushed me farther down. I walked into a room and saw a small girl peeking out from underneath an iron bed. I kneeled and reached a hand out to her, but the look on her face was nothing but sheer terror. My head tilted to the side.

My mind was trying to grasp onto something. It was tugging at something deep in my depths. Something that'd been buried. I felt a presence next to me, and I stood, my eyes widening as I stared into a woman's face—a woman who looked just like me but malevolent. "Your wings have been pinned too long," she said to me.

My eyebrows drew in before her fingers wrapped around mine, and something thrummed through me. Something dark. Zeke ran into the room as pain shot up my arm. He wrapped his arms around me as I screamed. He yelled at me and told me to let go, but the stranger's fingers only squeezed tighter.

My body crumbled, the blood in my veins feeling infernal. My fingers loosened and Zeke grabbed my hand, yanking it back. The woman tried to reach for me, and then we were thrown.

I shot up, gasping for air. He was right there with me, trying to pull me to him. My arm burned. I held out my hand, but nothing about it was different. "What happened?" My voice was shrill, my chest heaving. "It's searing." I shook my arm.

He grabbed my wrist. "I couldn't find you." He shook his head, his features laced with fear and confusion. "I tried, but I couldn't."

The images of my nightmare scattered. I closed my eyes and tried to bring them back, but all I saw were flames. I felt heavier, darker. "I can't remember anything." Tears were falling from my pain and alarm. "But I feel... immoral." I stared at my wrist, trying to see through my flesh like it'd give me an answer. "There's something new there." I tasted blood on my tongue, and my head rolled back.

He grabbed my face and brought me back to him, searching my eyes. "Come back to me, Raven." He wiped the tears that fell from my eyes.

Something black was wrapping around my heart. "Death," I whispered.

Terror shrouded his eyes.

"I feel like I command death."

As I said it, gray surrounded us. We stood, the blankets falling off, the last remnants of our blissful week together pooling at our feet. "We're here," he said, his voice full of despair.

My mouth fell open at how substantial it was in size compared to Seolia. All of Seolia was contained on a small island that could fit inside the kingdom of Reales. Cliffs surrounded the castle itself, and I counted four high walls that surrounded the castle like layers of a cake, with large homes sitting atop each wall with roofs of black. And on top of the layered cake sat the castle.

It was shorter than mine but wider and had multiple towers ranging from tall to taller. The entire vision took my breath away. I cocked my head to the side as we approached closer. The castle was made of a dark gray stone, so gray that it almost seemed black, which made it appear very intimidating. It wasn't welcoming at all from first sight.

Beneath the lighter gray walls were miles and miles of trees sprouting new leaves with spring on its way, but still appearing bleak and lifeless. Our ship seemed to shrink as it entered the harbor, rough waves suddenly sloshing against the sides, causing me to stumble. He caught me and held me upright by the waist, his hold on me predatory. Something about this place made me uneasy like I was walking into a nightmare.

"Listen to me." His tone was so harsh that it made my head snap to him. "Don't go out alone. Ever. I know you think you can handle it, but I've killed many people in our forest, Raven. More people than you could imagine. And I don't want you near any of them."

I nodded, but he gripped my chin tightly in his fingers. "I mean it, Raven. You wait for me." He turned me to face him and pinned me against the wall. "If someone lays a finger on you, you tell me."

My eyes were wide, frantically searching his.

"The man you fell in love with in Seolia is not who I am here. You're going to hear things about me." His voice was hurried. He was trying to tell me all of this before we docked. "And they're all true. All the evil, all the obscene."

I tried to kiss him, but he didn't let me.

"If someone touches you, I *will* tear them apart. I *want* to hear their bones crack under my hand."

I was losing him somewhere deep in his mind. His fingers gripped my waist. I didn't let him pull away as I cupped my hand around his head and pulled him to me, colliding our mouths together. He didn't soften. "I will kill for you, Raven. And if you decide to disobey, I will make you watch."

He moved to take a step away from me, but I grabbed his collar and yanked him back. "Don't walk away from me without telling me you love me." I didn't understand why or how he became so unrecognizable since we entered the harbor, but everything about his demeanor had hardened, even how he looked at me. "I don't give a fuck who you are here. But with me, you will remain mine. Your shadows are mine."

He stared at me, his jaw tight. "We'll see."

"Say it," I bit out, baring my teeth.

He fisted my hair in his hand and yanked, exposing my throat to him. His lips danced up the column of my throat. "I love you," he snarled against my skin and then released me, walking away.

I was left standing there, panting and staring after him.

———————

He didn't look at me again as he guided the boat against a dock and anchored us. A crew waited below, and he came to me, wrapping his arm around my shoulders and pulling me with him. He kicked the ramp, and it lowered to the dock. With his arm still around me, we descended it.

The crew bowed, but not to me. I tilted my head in curiosity. "Get our things and bring them to my room."

The crew scurried behind us and onto our ship.

I looked at him with so many questions.

"Not yet," he said.

"Shouldn't we wait for Cade—"

He stopped, backed me against a tall, wooden pole, and kissed me, his tongue claiming me quickly. "You're mine here."

I shuddered from the hoarseness of his tone.

He pulled me off and snaked his arm around my shoulders again. Our boots were loud against the dock but not as loud as the thoughts that bounced around in my head. I'd known he had a soul like mine, thirsty to steal lives, but I hadn't expected this. Something snapped in him when we approached these insanely large gray stone walls. Death made his darkness seem welcoming in comparison. And speaking of death, I still felt it settling into my skeleton. It was this place.

Something had awakened in both of us.

He dipped his chin toward a black carriage waiting for us at the bottom of a steep road surrounded by stone walls. "Shift," he said.

I looked at him, bewilderment etching across my face.

"Do it."

I blinked and shifted into Blaze.

He glanced at me and stopped walking. "No."

"Okay, look."

He shook his head. "Every man here is already going to want to fuck you, but when you look like that, they won't try and stop themselves, and I need to make it to the castle without murdering someone."

I blinked and shifted into Terra.

He sighed, shaking his head.

"You're really starting to piss me off," I snapped.

"I haven't even *begun*," he threatened.

My eyes narrowed. "If this is how you think I'll hate you, you may be right."

"Hate me then. Shift into Frost."

I blinked and shifted, but I pulled free of his grasp. "You've *never* wanted to fuck a blonde before, right?" I bit out, sidestepping around him.

He reached for my wrist, but I shook it free from his grasp and walked to the carriage. The coachman came around the side and didn't bow to me but bowed to Zeke. My eyes rolled as I climbed in, sitting on the very edge of the seat next to my window. He climbed in beside me and chuckled darkly, trying to pull me to him. I resisted, looking out my window.

"Get your ass over here, Raven."

"Fuck you."

He growled and wrapped his arm around my waist, pulling me into his lap. I tried to shove his arms off of me, but he was too strong, and I couldn't fucking burn him without turning him on, so I crossed my arms over my chest. He banged the window with one of his fists, and the carriage started to move slowly.

"I will. Right here."

I glanced at the coachman. Zeke settled lower into the seat, moving me with him. "I don't care who sees, Raven. When you're here, you belong to me. I'll have you wherever and whenever I want."

"Except if I choose differently."

The look he gave me could cut through the stone walls surrounding us. "Even if you do, you will not escape me."

"I'm the Queen of Seolia. I belong to no one."

"You're the queen of my soul, and you will always be mine." He brought my face to his and kissed me while his other hand threw a blanket across our bottom halves. His fingers pushed down on the waistband of my pants until they were snug against my thighs and then quickly started rubbing my clit.

I drew a sharp breath through my nostrils and sighed softly into his mouth. My emotions were in a frenzy. This was not the man I'd spent the last three months missing and loving. This one was carnal, possessive, and powerful. And I hated that I loved it.

His raspy chuckle skittered across my skin. I realized he could feel everything I was. "You wanted my shadows," he whispered against my mouth as he fumbled with the buckle of his pants. His fingers pressed deeply into my hips, lifting me just enough to guide my core onto his swollen shaft.

I started to moan, but he wrapped his hand around my throat and pressed his mouth against my ear. "Those noises are only for my ears."

He moved me against him with surprising force and speed. Sweat was already beading on my forehead as I built higher. I didn't want it to end, so I bit hard on my bottom lip to keep from coming yet. But when his mouth found my ear again, I knew he would win this one.

"I love you," he murmured and covered my mouth as I whimpered, coming all over his lap. He came as my name rolled off his lips. Always my name. He slowed my movements on him while we rode our high together and then abruptly shifted until he had pulled out completely.

I pouted as he grabbed the waistband of my pants and pulled them up over me. He started to do the same with his, and I tried to move off of him, but he stopped me. "I can hold you and pull my pants back on."

He pulled me back against his chest, and my head rolled around to rest against his shoulder. I had no idea what to think or feel. He'd be telling me this entire time that I may leave him during this excursion, and now he was fucking me in the carriage ride to the castle. "Have you ever fucked someone in here before?"

"This particular one?"

I really did hate him. I tried to move off him again, but he held me still. "No, Raven. I've never wanted anyone enough to try."

I relaxed a little. "You're being a dick."

He nodded against my head. "I tried to warn you, baby."

"I want to go home," I muttered.

He sighed. "You are home."

CHAPTER THIRTY-TWO

Raven

As we stood in front of the castle, I trembled. I'd dreamed of this castle so many times that I felt like I'd been here before, even though I'd never stepped foot in Reales that I knew of.

I really wished I had waited for Cade. He was at least some semblance to Seolia.

"Stop thinking about Cade," Zeke snapped beside me.

"How could you possibly know that?" I asked him, annoyed.

He grabbed my hand and the large steel doors opened in front us. "You reek of guilt."

I tried to yank my hand away, but he didn't let me. "Are you just trying to get me to break up with you?" I grumbled as he led me through the doors.

"Are we together?" He didn't look at me as he asked.

Tears sprung to my eyes, and I stopped, tugging my hand out of his. He hung his head and rubbed the back of his neck. "I'm sorry."

"Lead me to my room." I shifted back into myself, crossing my arms over my chest.

He took a step toward me, but I shook my head. "I don't give a fuck what you're going through right now. You're being an asshole. I expected some tension from this big secret," — I waved my hands in the air condescendingly — "but I didn't expect you to treat me like this. I'm fucking royalty, Zeke. I can either go back to my ship and wait for *Cade*...."

He glared at me.

"Or you can show me where I'll be staying."

His jaw clenched as he stared down at me. He stepped toward me, and I stepped back, but he caught me with his arms and wrapped them around me, pressing his forehead against mine. My body was rigid. "I'm sorry," he breathed, touching the tip of his nose to mine. "I am. I hate that you're here, Raven."

He tried to kiss me, but I turned my head.

"Baby, I'm fearful, and nothing ever scares me. I am so in love with you, Raven. This place, it's not like Seolia. I've tried to warn you in every way I can without telling you. I'm prepared for you to hate me, but I'm different here, and I have to be." He tipped my chin up to look at him. "Please forgive me. Be patient with me. I wasn't in love when I left here, and now I am madly, and I need to protect your heart. I've broken my own rule with you."

My nose scrunched up. "What rule?"

His lips pressed gently against mine. I hesitated at first, but I was weak for this man. I placed my palm against his cheek, and he grabbed my other hand, taking a step backward and pulling me with him. "I didn't want you to fall so deeply in love with me that you couldn't walk away."

I didn't respond because I didn't know what to say.

Could I walk away from him?

"Stay with me? There's a wing for you if you change your mind."

A slight grin tugged at my mouth as I nodded, causing a rare and wide smile to form across his mouth.

———————

I looked around as he pulled me through dimly lit hallways. The walls were bare, which was the opposite of my castle. Even with how dark it got during winter, we still kept the walls covered in color, whether it be portraits of previous royals or pictures I picked up in the village. I couldn't live with all this gray.

"When will I meet Mira?" I greeted visiting royals as soon as I knew they were in Seolia. It was odd not to be welcomed by their queen.

"At dinner." That was hours away.

"Does that mean I get a tour?"

When he pushed me back against a wall, I realized what he thought I meant. I started to laugh as he kissed my neck. "Not *that* kind of tour."

"That's the tour I received. I want to be a good host."

I giggled as he kissed along my collarbone. I pushed him off, shaking my head. "You *just* had me. At least get me through your door first."

He grumbled, pulling me to him as we continued down the hall. We climbed many stairs and then leveled out into a large corridor with multiple rooms. "Is all of this yours?"

He nodded, leading us to a door at the end of the hallway. He scooped me up and cradled me to his chest. I raised my eyebrow as he opened the door and entered his chambers. "If we don't get married, I can at least say I carried you over the threshold." There was sadness in his voice as he set me down to my feet.

"Baby, I can't live here even if we get married. Even if I wasn't a queen in another kingdom, this place is way too fucking dark."

He laughed, and I followed him through his entry, which seemed like another hall. And then my jaw dropped. His room was huge. It was one ample open space, unlike mine, which split into multiple smaller rooms.

Four large windows spanned across the back of the room and brought in a lot of natural light. All I saw were trees for miles. Tucked in the left corner sat a gorgeous marble bathtub with black finishing. A desk and bookshelves lined the opposite wall. A large circular black table was in the middle of the room with a cart full of liquor beside it.

But his bed... I'd never seen one like it. It rested on the right side of the room and practically took up the entire wall with its four black posts and a sheer gray canopy across the top. The quilts and blankets were made of the most decadent velvet and silk in the deepest greens. "Maybe I could be swayed," I mumbled as I walked to his bed and brushed my fingertips over the quilt.

He wrapped his arms around my waist from behind. My mind raced as I took in this incredibly detailed, extremely gorgeous room. "My chambers aren't even this nice. You're not telling me something."

"All in good time." He kissed along the length of my neck.

My hand cupped the back of his neck. "Show me your village."

He didn't answer and continued to tease, my head tilting slightly. I wanted to stay locked away in this room with him forever, but I'd never seen Reales. If we didn't leave now, we would never. "I need to buy gifts."

"Do it tomorrow," he said, turning my body to face him. He pressed his mouth against mine and nibbled on my bottom lip.

I was already falling into my familiar daze. I pulled back just enough to meet his eyes, and there was hunger behind them. "I'll be all yours tonight. Believe me; sleep is not what I want to do in this bed."

Something in his face changed. He was worried I wouldn't come back with him tonight. I put my hand on his cheek, and his eyes shut as he leaned into my touch. "Maybe it's not as bad as you think."

A sad, small smile crossed his mouth. "It is." He sighed and towered over me again. "You'll need to shift again."

"Why?"

All he did was stare at me.

"I guess that'll be answered tonight, too." I shifted into Blaze. He glared.

I snorted. "Just kidding." I shifted into Frost. "Do I need to prepare myself for you to be a jerk again?"

He smirked, giving me a slight shrug. "Probably. But it's only because I love you too damn much." He grabbed my waist and lifted me to wrap around him.

"Are you going to carry me around here, too?"

He responded by kissing me as he walked us back through his entry, but instead of opening the door, he pressed my back to it. Damn him.

My fingers tangled in his hair, and I tugged at his strands. His head pulled back, a coy grin on his mouth. "Stop." I tried to sound authoritative, but I was smiling.

"I don't want our perfect world to end," he murmured, staring at my mouth.

"I want to know you, and part of that is seeing you outside of this room."

He shook his head, and I nodded. His mesmerizing smile flashed again. The one reserved only for me. "I don't want you to know the 'me' outside this room."

"Give me your shadows," I pleaded with him, kissing the corner of his mouth.

He dipped his forehead to rest against my chest. He was quiet for a moment, but then he slid me down his body, twisting the knob behind me. "Don't leave my sight."

He pulled open the door, and I slipped out, but he grabbed my hand and interlaced our fingers. His jaw was clenched again, and I could see the despair fall on his body like a sheet of black ice.

We didn't pass anyone from my kingdom while we walked through the castle. I wondered if our ship had docked yet. It'd been at least an hour. "They're not staying in the castle," he said.

My head turned to study his profile. He had put on his mask again — the invisible one he wore when we were out of our bubble. "They're staying in a house just outside. It's where all parties of royalty stay when they're here. Kings, queens, and their families are the only ones welcomed in the castle."

"How does this mind thing work? Can you always tell what I'm thinking?"

He shook his head. "I can't read your mind unless you're pulling memories. I've learned what most of your emotions mean. When you think of Cade, there's nothing but shame and fear. When you think of Jeanine, there's envy and frustration."

"And when I think of you?"

His raspy chuckle. "Everything."

"Never shame," I whispered.

"All in good time," he said again.

I frowned, and then I glanced down at my clothes. I was still in my comfortable ones from the ship — a pair of loose black pants that hung off my hips and a black long-sleeved linen laced-up bodice. I looked at him, and he was in a pair of gray pants that clung to the muscles in his legs and a loose, gray shirt with long sleeves that were pushed up to his elbows. My mouth watered as I drank him in. "We can still go back to my room." He gave me a knowing grin.

I rolled my eyes. "Stop *sensing* me."

"It doesn't take an empath to taste the lust from you right now."

"Has anyone ever told you that you're a little full of yourself?"

He snorted, pushing open the large doors that led us back out of the castle. "You could be full of me. Last chance."

I hated that I was contemplating his offer. He laughed, and I shoved at his arm. "I thought you said you'd take me anywhere here. You're exhibiting a lot of self-control."

I regretted my words as he pulled me to him and backed me against the stonewall of the castle. "Do you want to test me?"

I found myself nodding. He caged me in his arms and leaned in to kiss me hungrily. My resolve was weakening, and I started to return his ferocity when I heard someone clear their throat behind us. He growled low and straightened, turning around. Jeanine stood there, smiling at us. My cheeks reddened, and I buried my head against his back.

"Your timing is impeccable," he grumbled.

I couldn't help but laugh.

"I see you two have made up," Jeanine said with amusement in her tone.

I peeked around him to look at her. He reached behind and grabbed me, pulling me next to him, keeping an arm around me. It felt strange to be all over him while staring at someone he had been with. It felt like I needed to stake claim somehow, even though I knew they hadn't been together since he met me.

"But just so you know, Cade is about to lose it if he doesn't find Raven."

"Then he can fucking lose it," Zeke snarled.

I rolled my eyes.

Jeanine held up her palms and shrugged. "I'm just a messenger. But Mira is asking for you."

His body stiffened.

"I'll take Raven to Cade."

"I can find him—"

Their eyes snapped to me.

I clamped my mouth shut. "Or Jeanine can take me."

Jeanine stared at Zeke again and gave him a slight shake of her head. He sighed. I wished I had his ability so I could know what he was feeling. He turned to face me again, rubbing the pad of his thumb across my cheek. When he leaned in and placed a tender kiss against my mouth, I nearly melted.

"I love you," he whispered against my mouth. I was too entranced to say anything back. "Stay with her."

Why were they treating me like I was so fragile? I could literally set people on fire. I willed it forward, keeping it right under the surface of my skin. He grinned. "Keep that anger." Jeanine's arm wrapped around mine, but I didn't want him to leave. And that was the moment the realization dawned on both of us — I wasn't sure I could leave him if what I would learn tonight was as bad as he was making it out to be.

His jaw tightened again, and I wondered how he didn't always have headaches. He didn't say another word as he left us, but I called his name, and he glanced over his shoulder. "I love you."

A small smile, and then he was gone.

I had a sinking feeling that whatever unraveled tonight would break my heart.

"Come on, Queen Raven," Jeanine whispered, gently tugging my arm.

"Just Raven." I glanced over at her with a slight shrug. "I appreciate the respect, but you can call me Raven."

"Does this mean you don't hate me anymore?" she asked lightheartedly.

I laughed softly as she pulled me toward the castle's back. "I'm envious of you."

She stopped and looked at me, bewildered. "You're envious of *me*?" Her brow wrinkled.

And all I did was stare at her like she was crazy.

"Because of him?"

I still stared, my mouth thinning into a straight line.

"We were superficial, Raven. It meant nothing." She tugged me back into a walk.

"Why does he keep having me shift?"

She was quiet, staring straight ahead.

"And why do people bow to him? He said he's on court, but no one bows to Cade, and he's on my court."

Still silent. I looked around as she guided us between two tall towers, straining my neck to see the top. Everything was so gray here, even the sky. It was almost like the sun was fearful of showing itself. I stopped again and faced her. "Please give me something. He won't. He keeps telling me that I'll hate him."

"You will," she responded with sadness in her voice.

I groaned, hot tears pooling in my eyes. One slipped down my cheek, and she sighed, wiping it from my cheek. It was a friendly gesture, and I didn't even flinch, which surprised me. "All I can tell you is this — it's been killing him not to be able to tell you. He wasn't even supposed to let things get this far with you. He wanted to bring you here with you already hating him. That's why he left you and stayed away so long, but he couldn't help himself. He barely slept for three months. I had to make sure he ate. This is big, Raven. And you will feel betrayed. I wish I could tell you something different. If anyone deserves happiness, it's him."

I met her eyes then, and she dropped them. "Why?" I asked with desperation in my voice.

All she did was shake her head. "We're all bound to secrets here, Raven." She tilted her head to the side, urging us to continue.

I looked back to where I saw Zeke disappear. I wanted to find him. I wanted to promise him that I'd always love him. But, I looked back to Jeanine again. She was imploring me with her eyes. I relented, giving her a slight nod.

We passed through the middle of two towers and around the corner of another stone wall. I felt like I was in a maze. I saw a large house and Cade pacing in front of it. It'd only been a week, but he looked older. He looked up as we drew closer and relief washed over his face. He jogged to us. I braced myself.

"Relax," Jeanine whispered.

I nodded once as Cade rushed me, wrapping his arms around my waist and pulling me to him. He tried to kiss me, but I turned my head on instinct. He tensed. "Are you okay? Why are you shifted?"

All I did was shrug because I had no idea. He looked between Jeanine and me with an arched eyebrow. "We've put aside our differences," I said. It was making me uncomfortable how he glared at her.

"I will leave you two now. I have things to do in town." She moved to take a step, but I grabbed her elbow.

"Can I go?"

She shook her head. My shoulders dropped. "He'd kill me."

I knew which 'he' she was referring to, and it wasn't the one standing in front of us.

"But I will see you at dinner."

I nodded and gave her a small smile. She waved before she turned the corner. When I turned to look at Cade, his face made me laugh. "She's not so bad."

He shook his head. "Do you want me to take you into the village?"

Yes. I desperately wanted to know why Zeke had to be the one to escort me in and why they were so guarded. And why I had to be shifted to walk around, but I knew better than trying to find all of that out on my own. "We better not. They're very... odd." It was the only way I could think to describe their behavior about not letting me explore on my own. "We can stay here until dinner."

He looked down at my clothes. "Where are your things?"

I nodded back to the castle. "I stay in there. They do things differently here."

He put his arm around my shoulders and pulled me with him to the house he was staying in. I had the strangest feeling that we were being watched, but when I turned my head to look around, I didn't see anything. "It's creepy here," I muttered.

Cade nodded in agreement. "Eerie. We took wagons up, and their coachmen were heavily armed."

My eyebrow cocked at that, and then I looked around at the stone walls surrounding us. I halted our walk, and he looked at me. "Close your eyes." I waited until he did. "Now listen."

I closed mine, too, and we were quiet as we tried to pick up any sounds around us. The only thing I heard was the rustling of leaves from the trees. "What do you hear?" I felt the faintest brush of his lips against mine, and my eyes fluttered open.

"Just trees."

I nodded, and he leaned in again, but I put my fingers against his lips. "Exactly."

His head tilted.

"In Seolia, you can hear our villagers as soon as we're outside. You can hear the faint shouts of dock loaders, of ships coming into the harbor." I walked to a wall and used my fingertips to guide me along. "There's none of that here." I reached the end of one wall only to face another.

A soft breeze brushed the back of my neck, and I turned my head to see leaves rustling behind me. It was beckoning me. I jogged toward it, and the breeze was heavier now, my hair flying off my shoulders. I ran past the house and reached another wall. I growled, hitting it with my palms. The wall was long, and I couldn't see where it ended. "Why can't we get in?"

Cade came up beside me and tilted his chin up. "I can get you in."

I smiled, and he nodded, bending at his knees and cupping his hands together. I grabbed his shoulder and lifted my leg to step into his hand. Jumping off my other foot, he shoved me up quickly, and my hands grappled for the edge of the wall. He grabbed my other foot and extended his arms, giving me a few more inches so I could grip the edge, grunting as I hoisted myself up. "I can't go over with you, Raven. And I can't get you back over."

I looked into the dark forest and then back to Cade. "I have to say; I'm a little surprised at your eagerness to let me go."

He stepped back from the wall, giving me an exasperated look. "I'd rather help you when there's sunlight than you trying to sneak out on your own at night. You have thirty minutes. I will send all of our soldiers over if you're not back."

"Thirty minutes," I repeated.

"Raven?"

I glanced back down at him, and he tossed me a small dagger. "For my peace of mind."

I sheathed it into the waistband of my pants and nodded.

"Thirty minutes."

I looked to the ground. I was at least thirty feet up. I sat down on edge and gripped it tightly, inhaling a shaky breath before I dropped. I slid down the wall until I landed on my feet. "Ow," I groaned, rolling my ankles.

"You good?" Cade shouted over the wall.

I slapped the wall twice in response.

Unlike our forest, this one had taller trees. And smelled of pine. I groaned as I walked past the trees, cursing at myself. I promised him I wouldn't explore on my own. I blinked and shifted into Blaze, warmth spreading across my body. I could handle myself. I'd killed, too. He wasn't the only one with a past.

I looked around as I explored. There wasn't much here. It was chilly, but I was having trouble understanding why he worried about me being alone. I looked behind me and could no longer see the wall. Another cool breeze enveloped me, and goosebumps prickled on my skin, stopping as a ghost of fear washed over me.

My head snapped toward the sound of twigs breaking and my fingers wrapped around the hilt of my dagger. From every direction, men stepped out behind trees, surrounding me.

I met the eyes of the man in the center. He leered at me. I bared my teeth. Something deep inside my belly was pooling, but I didn't recognize it. I didn't know how to pull it. It was deep. Dark.

The men took a step closer to me, but I remained still, calm. I glanced around and counted five of them. I'd only ever taken down two on my own. "What is a pretty thing like you doing out here?" The center man asked.

I rolled my eyes. It was the same shit I always heard. "You really need some new material," I muttered, keeping my fingers on the dagger.

"Haven't you heard stories, little doe?"

"Not from around here," I answered.

Someone took a step behind me, but my eyes didn't leave the man asking questions. "We keep what we find."

My laugh was dark. "You don't want to keep me."

They were all closing in now, but I remained frozen, my fire itching to be released. The taste of blood made my mouth water, the tip of my tongue brushing against the roof of my mouth. I should be more fearful, but the wind wanted me in here. There had to be a reason.

I glanced around at all the men. They all gawked at me like I was a piece of meat. "You know it's impolite to stare."

They all started to laugh. The talkative man was an arm's length away. I gave him a bright smile. "Do it already."

He drew so close that I could feel his breath on me. I waited, growing a bit bored. He thought this was a game and that I was unwilling to participate, but this was my favorite kind of chase. His arm raised quickly, gripping my chin between his fingers, staring at my mouth. "I can't wait to see you on your knees," he said, grunting like a pig.

I grinned. "I can't wait to see you on yours." I wrapped my fingers around his throat. "Would you like to see a magic trick?"

His eyes widened as I let my fire free, his flesh burning under my fingers. He clawed at my hand as he crumbled. I dropped him once I felt two more sets of hands on me. I crossed my arms and grabbed both necks, starting to burn through their flesh.

"She's a witch!" One of them shouted.

A foot pushed against my back, and I stumbled forward, releasing my grasp on the two men holding me. Hands were in my hair, yanking me back. My neck stretched backward, and I used both hands to wrap around the man's hands, starting to burn. He yelped in pain, and someone pinned one of my hands behind my back. I reached for my dagger with the other and unsheathed it, stabbing through the hand holding me. He stumbled back, and I whipped around, shifting into Terra, and palmed the ground, shaking it underneath the men.

They stumbled as they tried to get back to me, but I growled, breaking the ground apart underneath their feet. They tumbled into my shallow ditches. I waited until they were all down.

And then I ran.

CHAPTER THIRTY-THREE

Raven

I didn't know which way I was running, but all that mattered was that it was away from them. I needed to try and get back to the wall. It'd been over half an hour, and I knew Cade would come looking for me soon. I threw a look back, and all four men were after me. I was semi-impressed that they were so persistent. But, I was a witch, and hatred for dark magic was deep through the kingdoms. I was naive to think that just because my own people accepted me meant everyone else would, too.

I stumbled a step as I felt something sharp pierce the tip of my shoulder, glancing down at the ground to see my blade tumble off my body. That motherfucker pierced me with my own dagger. I shifted into Frost, held out my palms, creating sharp icicles, and threw another glance back as I hurled them toward one man. The first one missed, but the second went straight through his throat. Two down.

I tried to pull at the unfamiliar magic in my belly again, but it didn't move. I was breathless, and my legs were tired. I seemed to be getting deeper into the forest and not closer to Cade.

I heard the water in the distance, which meant I was running out of room to sprint. I stared at my palms. I'd never tried what I was about to, but I didn't have much of a choice.

As the water came into view, I squeezed my eyes shut and cast my palms out, releasing. And then I leaped. I inhaled a deep breath, preparing for water, but instead I felt ice under my feet. I only had a second to rejoice before I heard thuds behind me. I took off in another run, sliding across the thin sheet of ice. It was buckling underneath my feet. I tried to start reinforcing it, but I'd exerted too much energy running and shifting.

The sounds of their feet drew closer, and I threw everything I had left into shifting again into Blaze, throwing fire behind me to melt the ice. I heard splashes as they fell into the water behind me, feeling victorious until fingers wrapped around my ankle and tugged. I slipped and cried out as my chin hit the ice. I tried grabbing for something, anything, but multiple hands were pulling me into the water.

I tried to kick my leg free, but my other leg was caught. I reached for the hands holding me and started to burn, but someone wrapped their hand around my throat and dragged me to dry ground. I wrapped my hand around their wrist and burned until their grip loosened, and they screamed in agony. But then the other two men grabbed my hands and pinned them to my sides.

Well, fuck.

The man I burned crawled over my body, pinning me again by my throat. His legs caged me in as I tried to thrash against him. He cackled, and I spit at him. Anger crossed his features, and my skin stung as he backhanded me across my face. "You're a coward," I bit out.

He slapped me again and blood pooled in my mouth. He leaned close to me, but I didn't look away. I didn't cower. He pushed his lips against my ear, and I turned quickly, clamping down his cheek with my teeth. He wailed in pain and rose, but an arrow pierced through his skull right as he was about to slap me again. His body fell to the side, and the two men holding me looked up. Another arrow pierced into one of them, and one of my arms was free.

The other man was in shock while looking for the source. I used it to my advantage and sat up to grab his throat, burning through his flesh until I felt bone and dropped him. I rolled on my stomach and started coughing, blood dripping from my mouth. I rose to my knees and wiped my mouth with the back of my hand, tilting my head to the sky while trying to catch my breath.

Everything hurt, and I was dizzy, but I refused to pass out. I heard footsteps in front of me and licked my lips as I dipped my chin. I was expecting to see Cade, but instead, I was staring into the eyes of a furious Zeke.

I coughed again and spat out more blood, but he remained still, his chest heaving, his knuckles white from gripping his bow. "Nice shot," I grumbled, standing shakily to my feet.

I glanced back at the water and saw the last of my ice melting, and then I looked at the three bodies. I snapped my fingers, and their corpses became ash. I looked back to Zeke, who was still glaring at me. I threw my arms in the air. "I don't like being told what to do."

That was obviously the wrong thing to say because he turned and started back into the forest. I groaned and begrudgingly followed him — my legs sore, and I was craving a hot bath. I stretched my fingers at my sides. That was the most magic I'd ever used so quickly. I didn't think I could've gotten myself out if Zeke hadn't shown up.

He stayed away from me and strapped his bow across his back. I looked around, wondering how he had found me. I didn't bother asking him because I'd learned that he wouldn't answer my questions unless he wanted to, and right now, he wouldn't even look at me.

We approached the wall, and he pushed it against it, revealing a hidden door. Huh, we both lived life with secret doors and darkness. He walked through it and held it open long enough for me to follow behind him. Jeanine was standing on the other side, grimacing at me. Cade rounded a corner and rushed to me. "Where the fuck were you?" I gritted out, still tasting blood in my mouth. That bastard cracked my lip.

"We were about to go in after you, but then he found us and asked what we were doing trying to scale the wall. When I told him you were in there, he had two of his soldiers stay with us to ensure we wouldn't follow him, and then he was gone."

He reached out to brush my lip, but I yanked my head back, giving it a slight shake. "He got me good. I took two of them down before three caught me."

Zeke stopped and stared at me. I wasn't sure why so I threw my arms up again. His eyes narrowed before he stalked toward me, wrapping his fingers around my elbow and pulling me. I shoved his hand off. "I can walk by myself."

Cade stared between the two of us. Jeanine came up beside me and touched my elbow gently. I glanced at her to see her giving me a subtle shake of her head. I didn't have time to dissect that before Zeke's hand cupped the back of my neck, and he pulled me again. Cade went to grab my arm, but Jeanine stood between us. I threw him one last glance, and his stare on Zeke's hand could kill, but Zeke continued to drag me with him. I tried to pull my head away, but he wouldn't let me.

He pushed through a door in the back of the castle and led me into a dark corridor. "Are you going to say *anything?*" I asked him as we started climbing the stairs. "Of course not," I muttered, and his fingers only squeezed my skin. "You do realize you can't control me, right?"

He remained silent as we leveled out on his floor.

"I thought you were all about free will," I said condescendingly.

His chuckle was dark. Not at all like the raspy one I loved. He opened his door and twisted me until he could shove me backward into the entry. "If this is your idea of foreplay—"

He didn't respond and kept pushing me back until we were in his room. When he tried to make me again, I shoved at his chest. "You're pissed; I get it."

He unstrapped his bow and tossed it on the table. "There is not an adequate word to describe what I am," he growled, baring his teeth.

"I wanted to explore, and you were busy," I snapped, crossing my arms over my chest.

He closed the space between us and fisted my hair in his hand, pulling my head back until my skin stretched. "I told you not to go anywhere without me."

I shoved at him again, but he remained still. "I don't need your permission."

He was seething, and I didn't think he was breathing. He released me and took a step back. "Clean yourself up. Get dressed. We will have dinner soon."

"That's it? You're just going to walk away?"

He didn't say anything but started toward the door. I stood there, my stubbornness not wanting to chase after him, but I did. I grabbed his hand, but he yanked it free and didn't stop. I shoved at his back. "Talk to me."

He didn't, so I shoved at him again. "Do not walk away from me."

He pulled open his door to leave.

"If you walk out that door, I will not stay here."

He hesitated briefly, but then he was gone, slamming the door shut behind him. A hot tear slid down my cheek as I stared at the door. I understood that he didn't want me to go anywhere without him, and I realized I had scared him, but that didn't mean he could just leave me in his room. I couldn't stay here now. I went to my trunk, threw it open, grabbed a dress and diadem, and shut it before I left his room.

I followed the path he took me on earlier and exited the back of the castle. I saw him in the distance talking to Jeanine. She rubbed his arm while he animatedly spoke to her. He left me to find her. Tears stung my eyes at the betrayal.

When he looked at me, I didn't try and hide the hurt on my face. I shook my head as he took a step toward me, instead walking toward Cade. I grabbed his hand and pulled him after me. "I'm staying with you."

He interlocked our fingers and led me to the house.

I felt Jeanine and Zeke stare at us, but I didn't throw them another glance. I was tired of playing these games with him. All the silence. All the brooding. I knew what I did wasn't the best choice, but he didn't allow me to talk to him about it before he left me again.

Cade was quiet as he led me through the house and into his room. There was a mirror, and I walked to it after throwing my dress and diadem on his bed, staring at myself. My face was bloodied and covered in dirt from being dragged. My bright red

hair looked dark from being pulled into the water. Even my
clothes were ripped, the bottom of my shirt shredded.

I sighed and palmed my eyes, pushing until I could see colors.
A sob built in my throat, and tears started to escape. Cade's arms
wrapped around me from behind. I turned into him and let the
day's events finally settle on me. He held me while I cried,
rubbing the back of my head. "You should've been there," I
whispered.

His arms tightened around me. "I know." His voice broke.
"I'm so sorry, Raven." He kissed the top of my head. "Let me
draw you a hot bath. We need to get this blood off of you."

I nodded against his chest, and he kissed my head again
before he released me and disappeared behind another door. I
heard the water running, and I stared at myself again, wrapping
my arms around my waist. We really had left our perfect world.
We were back to silence and misery.

I kicked off my boots and padded into the bathroom, inhaling
the steam from the hot water. My entire body felt heavy. Achy.
He motioned for me to raise my arms, and I did, letting him pull
my shirt over my head. His eyes darkened, but it was out of
concern. I followed his gaze and bit my lip at the bruises covering
my skin. "Raven…" he muttered, touching one.

I winced. "I'll heal. It just was a lot of trauma all at once." I'd
never had to fight anyone off before. My body didn't know how
to process it. I pushed my pants down and stepped out of them.
There was a bruise around my ankle that looked like fingers.

He sighed and shook his head. I grabbed his hand as he helped me into the tub. The hot water wrapped around me like velvet as I sank. He removed his shirt and grabbed a washcloth, kneeling next to me. He dipped the washcloth and gently dabbed at my face, wiping the dried blood off.

"What happened?"

I closed my eyes, trying to relax. "I was walking, and I heard twigs snap. When I turned, five men circled me. I took one down easily, but they all zeroed in on me. I shook the ground and was able to start running, taking another down with an icicle. But the more I ran, the more tired I grew, and when I used the last of my energy to freeze a lake, they caught up to me and dragged me back to land. They pinned me, and one of them kept hitting me. That's when Zeke pierced two with arrows, and I burned the last one."

"We didn't hear you scream."

I laughed softly. "I didn't scream."

He shook his head at me again and brushed the washcloth across my lip.

I groaned. "What's weird, though, is that he asked me if I've heard things, saying they keep what they find."

He leaned back and stared at me.

I gave him a slight shrug. "I think this is a normal occurrence here."

He was about to say something when there was a knock on his door. He kissed my forehead before he stood, disappearing back out of the room. I heard him tell someone that I was in the bath and the click of the door. He came back, and I cocked an eyebrow. "Jeanine. Dinner is soon. We're supposed to meet her outside the house, and she'll show us where to go."

All of this, and I still hadn't met Mira. I slid until I was under the water and shifted into myself, raising my arms out. His hands wrapped around mine, and he pulled me up, wrapped a soft towel around me, and started to dry me off. He shook me a little, and I laughed, and for the first time since we arrived, he smiled at me. He leaned down and brushed his lips against mine. I didn't tense, but it felt wrong. Foreign. "I missed you," he said with a quiet voice.

"I missed you, too."

He smiled again, and shame washed over me. I wasn't sure what was going on between Zeke or me or me and him. It was all confusing and only made me frustrated to think about. But I did know that I yearned for Zeke and only wanted him, which made this all the more complicated.

He led me out of the bathroom, and I continued to wring out my hair. I hadn't requested any new dresses fashioned in the colors of Reales, so I had to pull on one of my heavier velvet ones. I hadn't missed them, but this one was one of my favorites. It was a deep green and clung to my curves but widened as it fell down my legs. I braided my hair and frowned, replaying the memory of Zeke trying to braid it.

How did that seem so long ago already? We'd only been here a day, and I was already exhausted.

I fastened a black diadem on my hair, and Cade came up behind me, kissing my cheek. "Are you ready?"

I knew he meant mentally. I inhaled a deep breath and puffed out my cheeks, shaking my head. My hands were jittery, and I shook them out in front of me. He came around to face me and squished out my cheeks. "You look beautiful. And I'm here. It'll be okay." He kissed my forehead and my lips.

I needed to find a way to make that stop, but I couldn't focus on that right now. He extended his elbow, and I linked my arm through his, letting him guide me to the porch of the house. Jeanine was there waiting for us, and she curtsied to me.

My lips thinned into a straight line. Zeke had left me to go right to her. And we had been making such progress with one another.

———

Jeanine didn't say a word as she led us through the castle's back door, but instead of taking the way toward Zeke's chambers like I was used to, she led us down a different hall. Cade squeezed my arm, and I remembered to breathe. "Relax," he muttered.

I bit down on my lip. I couldn't relax. Jeanine stopped in front of a room, and I peeked in. "This doesn't look like a dining hall."

She gave me a small smile. "It's not. Mira wants to meet you first. I'll take Cade to the dining hall, and she'll bring you in after." She took a step closer and grabbed my hand. "Please remember that you are loved."

I shook my head in confusion at her words. She took a step back, and I looked at Cade. He was waiting for my decision on whether he stayed or went. "I'll see you in a minute," I said.

He nodded and kissed my temple before letting Jeanine lead him away. I took a step into a huge throne room. It was shaped like an octagon and empty except for the throne. My mouth fell open as I tilted my head back to take everything in. It was gray, of course, made of thick stones, but it resembled a cathedral in its shape with windows that reached hundreds of feet up and touched the ceiling.

In the center of the room sat the large steel throne. I wrinkled my nose. That couldn't be comfortable. Mine was plush and golden and much more welcoming.

As I stared at it, memories from my dreams were pushed to the forefront of my mind, and shivers raced down my skin. Everything about this place was just… in your face. I missed the quaint feel of Seolia. And why weren't there chairs or benches? Where would all of Mira's people sit during audience?

"Little bird."

I whirled to the sound of the voice. A woman with long brown hair and green eyes was staring back at me. Familiar. Suddenly everything from my dreams came crashing back to me. The little girl in the mirror. The woman whose ice-cold hand was on my cheek. I gasped, tears falling down my cheeks as I fell to my knees, suddenly very woozy.

"Oh, my dear little bird," the stranger said and fell to her knees before me, taking my hands in her own. "You are home."

I gasped for air, trying to sift through all the shattered pieces as they came together in my head. There was too much happening. My chest was caving as I tried to cry out a sob, and then she was wrapping her arms around my shoulders, trying to quell me as she rubbed my back like we'd known each other our lives.

"You," I stuttered out. "I know you."

The woman leaned back with tears in her eyes and nodded her head quickly, raising a hand to wipe the tears away from my cheek. "We have a lot to talk about."

Her green eyes. They were my green eyes. I felt a memory being tugged from the back of my mind. I could *feel* him in my brain. Zeke. The little girl staring back at me in the mirror. The green eyes. Our matching green eyes. I gasped again, everything in the room seeming to fade as the realization fell on me like a heavy cloak. "You're my sister." I had a sister. I had a family.

She coughed out a laugh through her tears as she nodded again. "Mira."

"Mira," I repeated, but her name felt heavy on my tongue.

Mira reached for my hand and stood, pulling me up with her. She threw her arms around my shoulders in a tight embrace, and I, still in shock, just wrapped my arms around her in return. We stood like that for what felt like years until finally, she pulled back, but only a little. "You're exquisite. Just how I always imagined you."

My mouth fell open, but I had no words. I was absolutely speechless. "You're probably so overwhelmed, my darling. Please, come sit." She curled an arm around my shoulders as she guided me to sit on the throne.

Mira's throne.

"Oh, Mira, I couldn't…."

She shushed me and insisted. "You are our princess, Raven."

I sat on the very edge of the seat as the words hit me. Princess. Princess of Reales. It made me feel itchy. I didn't belong here. This seat didn't want me.

"Show her."

My eyes snapped to Mira's and Zeke as he entered the room. He knew. This entire time, he knew who I was. And he never told me. The betrayal fell heavily on me. Now I knew why he didn't want to tell me. I did hate him. His head dropped as he sensed it on me. But then, his eyes focused on me. I shook my head. Don't do it. Don't invade my mind. But then I felt him clawing through, and my eyes squeezed shut as a blurry picture twisted into a single frame in my mind.

I was on this throne, sitting in the lap of a woman whose face I couldn't quite make out—someone in white sprinkled water on my forehead. Something small glistened as a blurred man approached. The young girl from the mirror returned, and she took me, wrapping me up in her arms. '*Our little baby bird,*' she said in a high-pitched, girly tone.

The glistening circle was placed on my hand. My chubby little fingers pulled it off and shook it around—a tiara.

———————

I gasped as the throne room came back into focus. "Princess," I breathed.

Mira took small steps toward me, like I was a bird that could just fly away. "I am sure you have so many questions."

I nodded. She smiled at me. "Why don't I go ahead and answer all of them for you? Lean back, my darling. You look positively spent."

I looked down at the throne. How could I make myself comfortable on a throne made of steel? But I scooted back a little to appease her and caught Zeke staring at me intently.

"We share the same mother: Queen Celestina. I am Rudolf's daughter and his only heir. You, you belong to King Leonidas."

At that, I felt like the ceiling of this stone dome was falling on top of me.

"Which makes you the rightful heir to Seolia."

Everything was moving too fast. I was burning up.

"She's overwhelmed, Mira," Zeke cut in. I was sure he could taste it on me. Mira looked at me, silently asking if I wanted her to continue. I wasn't sure if I did. Returning home and pretending like this was all a bad dream seemed enticing.

I had a choice to make. Despite the worry etched on Zeke's face, I needed to continue. I deserved to know who I was.

I finally asked, "But... but how?"

Mira sighed and shook her head. "That's where our story is full of sorrow. Our mother was a witch."

That explained the magic.

"And Leonidas knew this. They were lovers, and she became pregnant with you. My father was elated at the news of another daughter, but when Leonidas received word that another heir had been born, he visited our mother again and she confirmed that you are his. And then..." she trailed off, her eyes darkening suddenly, and the room soon became freezing. "He murdered her. And took you."

I gasped, covering my mouth with my hand. My father stole me away and killed my mother.

"He handed you off to one of his men."

August. The night Cade saw me.

"And dropped you in the village like you were merely a peasant. When my father found our mother in a pool of blood, he refused to face the reality that another kingdom had murdered her. The entire kingdom of Reales was told that she had died from childbirth complications and that you had died with her."

I felt like I could faint.

"But Leonidas didn't know that I was there that night, hiding under my mother's bed, and saw everything. I saw him *rip* you away from our mother. My father refused to listen to me for fear of igniting another war. So, for fifteen years, I've waited. And in the meantime, John has been watching over you."

"John," I repeated, unsure how he tied into this.

"John is my uncle. Rudolf's brother. Not yours. There's no relation in case you were worried about this…" — she waved her finger between Zeke and me. "John knew it was Leonidas who murdered our mother, so he broke from Rudolf and pledged his allegiance to Seolia to become one of his closest friends and make sure you were safe. When John learned that you possessed magic like our mother, he realized why Leonidas hadn't murdered you yet."

I felt the need to vomit, but I hadn't eaten anything.

"So, I am the true Queen of Seolia. And he never told me? No one ever told me?" My eyes were on Zeke now, and his were cast down. This couldn't be real. I'd felt out of place my entire life, unsure of why I was given a palace. And I had no idea it had rightfully belonged to me the whole time. "You…" My eyes still on Zeke. "You're a king's nephew, which makes you…."

"Royalty," he finished. "A prince."

Suddenly our engagement made sense. A prince. That was why people bowed to him, why he had his own wing.

"You want to tie our kingdoms together." But why? What purpose would that possibly serve?

"Exactly, my darling. I want two sisters to have their kingdoms united. To always feel like we are one. We deserve that after so long apart. We are family."

I grated my teeth. I had a family in Seolia. Cade, Isla, Eva, Grace, Arthur… There was no air in here. "I need a moment. Or two. I am… overwhelmed." Flustered. Baffled.

Mira rushed to my side, and I leaned back slightly. "Oh, of course, you are, little bird."

I hated that nickname. It made me feel cold all over.

"Ezekiel says you're staying with him. Would you like to return?"

"I need my own room," I replied, staring at the door.

"Of course, little bird. My castle is your castle, as is all the kingdom. You may have whatever you wish. You go rest, take it all in. Please feel free to explore Reales, as it also belongs to you."

I wrinkled my nose. I didn't want this giant piece of stone. I stood, and Mira came to me, wrapping me in another hug. "I have missed you, little bird. I cannot wait to catch up on all our lost years."

I returned the hug, but my body felt stiff.

When she released me, I walked toward the door, but I stopped and glanced at her over my shoulder. "Are there any pictures of our mother?"

"In your room, little bird."

I simply tipped my head in gratitude and let Zeke lead me out into the hallway.

———

I remained stoic as he led me through more dark hallways into a corridor with only one door. When we approached, his fingers lightly wrapped around my elbow. I felt like I was being seared. I pulled my arm from his grasp, but he did it again. "Just let me talk to you, please."

"You fucking knew." I shoved at him. "You knew who I was, and you never said a word." I pushed at him again.

He stumbled back half a step. "Raven..."

He didn't get a chance to finish before I slapped him across the face. "You have broken my heart."

He rubbed his cheek as he stared at me, pain etched across his features at my words. "Raven," his voice broke on my name.

Tears welled up in my eyes. "I thought heartbreak was you leaving me. In Seolia. Today. Seeing you run to Jeanine instead of talking to me."

He opened his mouth, but I continued, "But this. This is betrayal. For my entire life, I have struggled to feel like enough. For anyone. And then you came along, and I finally felt seen, like you wanted me. But all you've done is use me. And keep secrets from me. And leave me, over and over again. You came to my room and asked me questions when you *already knew the answers*."

"Raven," he tried again, but I held up my hands to stop him.

"The fates chose wrong when they split our soul. I can only hope it's rectified in the next life because I want nothing to do with you."

Tears streamed down my cheeks, and when I turned to leave, his fingers wrapped tightly around my arm, and he spun me back, his tears falling slowly down his cheeks. "You don't mean that," he whispered.

More than anything, I wished I didn't. "I used to read books about twin flames. It always seemed like a romantic notion, but as a girl, I romanticized the idea. Thinking how wonderful it would be if I ever found someone my soul connected to on such a deep level…." I trailed off, choking back a sob. "A deep of a level as ours did. But now I've realized that we are not something divine designed by the gods. I could never do to you what you've done to me. And that's how I know that we were a mistake."

He fell to his knees, shaking his head at my words. "Raven," he pleaded, but I felt no remorse for the man at my feet. "You wanted my shadows. Here they are, Raven. We promised to love each other."

"That's the hardest part about this," I whispered. "I will always love you. And that's what makes me hate you."

I turned then, and he cried my name once, twice. I wanted to turn back, but I didn't. I closed my door and fell against it, my sobs so heavy that they were silent. I screamed for my lost love. I screamed for my old life. For my new one. I screamed until my throat burned. I screamed until I had no voice left.

I crawled away from the door because I knew he was still there. I still felt our pull to one another. His black soul wanted to soothe mine, but I needed them split. I didn't want it anymore.

I moved until I was in the center of the room and froze. In front of me, hanging on the wall, was a giant portrait of my mother.

I stood slowly and took small steps toward it. It was painted with the deepest hues of acrylic, but I felt as if I was staring directly at another person. My hands slowly rose as my fingertips brushed across my mother's dress, which resembled one a queen would wear at her coronation. It was a puffy hoop skirt that led into a rich velvet tunic that was embroidered in deep green gems.

Her black hair was piled on top of her head in intricate braids, and a crown made of gold sat on the delicate strands. And her eyes... her eyes were the color of mine, sitting underneath long black eyelashes. Her mouth was full like mine, too, and the shape of our faces both mirrored our sharp jaws and high cheekbones.

"My mother," I breathed as I stared into the eyes of the woman who gave me life. Something in my eye caught my attention, and I walked to the wall next to my bed. Perched upon a bedside table was a much smaller portrait, but still as detailed. My mother was in a simple white gown, her smile wide, her hair curling around her shoulders.

And cradled in her arms was a baby with black hair and green eyes, lips pink as peonies that were puckered in a pout.

Me.

My shoulders hunched forward, my chest caving as I reached to grab the framed portrait, bringing it to my chest. My sobs were quiet, coming from deep inside my chest, pulling at the depths of my sorrow from everything I'd lost.

Everything I'd learned.

I stood like that for a long time, mourning my mother and the relationship I'd never had with her. "She loved me," I whispered, my knuckles white at how tightly I squeezed the frame. For the entirety of my life, I'd felt like I always needed to earn love from others. I was always grasping at it when it was given to me, fearful of losing it—not wanting to let it slip through my fingers like sand.

But once upon a time, it had been freely given by a woman I'd never get to meet, touch, or hear stories from. Only about. The one person who loved me unconditionally, whose arms I had been ripped from because of the very magic that still flowed through my veins.

And now I sat on the very throne of the man who did it; the man who stole my mother away from me. Who made me question my entire being, why I was here, and why I was chosen. But it was my own father who had chosen me and decided to let me live a life of seclusion, away from the palace, in the care of someone he let one of his soldiers choose. He kept my identity a secret until his deathbed when he finally willed me his palace. We could've had ten years together. I could've had some answers to who I was, who I could be, instead of being thrust into it and having to cling to a man to help me through. A man who spent fifteen years lying to me.

I let my new sense of self drift over me until it settled into my very skin. An acidic, bitter taste coated my tongue as a gloom was welcomed into my immortal being. My eyes focused as my heart settled, the fire in my belly pooling as it heated my blood. My heart singed and charred as the flames nipped at my most vital organ. I realized no one could save me from the depths of my mania now. I would numb my pain, my heart.

I would become the Queen of Darkness.

Raven and Zeke's story isn't over yet.

ABOUT THE AUTHOR

Whitney has been an avid fantasy reader since she was seven years old. Never in her wildest dreams did she believe she would ever publish a book, or create an entire new fantasy world from the depths of her brain.

When not writing, she's most likely visiting worlds and lands of imagination, or dreaming up more scenarios to share with all of you.

Follow her on:
whitneydean.com
Instagram (@authorwhitneydean)
Goodreads (Whitney Dean)
Join our Facebook group! (The Witches of Whitney Dean)
Amazon Author

CPSIA information can be obtained
at www.ICGtesting.com
Printed in the USA
LVHW101156200922
728818LV00001BA/4